CUBAN SLIDERS

CUBAN SLIDERS

A MAX CALDER SPY-FI MYSTERY

THE BUREAU ARCHIVES TRILOGY
BOOK 3

ALEXANDER BENTLEY

CHARLTON MANOR PUBLISHING

First published in the United States in 2026 by
Alexander Bentley and Charlton Manor Publishing
-oOo-
Copyright © Alexander Bentley 2026

The right of Alexander Bentley to be identified as the Author of the Work has been asserted by him in accordance with the Copyright, Designs and Patents Act, 1988 in the United Kingdom.

All rights reserved. No part of this publication may be reproduced, stored in a retrieval system, or transmitted, in any form or by any means without the prior written permission of the author or the publisher, except for the use of brief quotations in a book review, nor be otherwise circulated in any form of binding or cover other than that in which it is published and without similar condition being imposed on the subsequent purchaser.

This book is a work of fiction. All characters, organizations and places are fictitious and any resemblance to real persons, organizations or places is purely coincidental except for known characters or places which are used entirely fictitiously.

Hardback: 979-8-9940939-2-4
Paperback: 979-8-9940939-1-7
eBook: 979-8-9940939-5-5
Kindle Edition: 979-8-9940939-4-8

Library of Congress Control Number: 2026902426

Printed and bound by Kindle Direct Publishing and Ingram Spark

For Lucinda

The professional skill of espionage is the exploitation of human weakness.

GORDON CORERA

**The Art of Betrayal: The Secret History of MI6
Life and Death in the British Secret Service**

1951

CHAPTER 1
MISSING MEMORIES

The Mirror wasn't operating in isolation. Its influence was rippling further, its impact increasing exponentially. I didn't know what I was about to walk into.

I fished into the box one last time, retrieving the final Cuban cigar. I had fallen in love with them, though they'd been gifted at New Year two years prior by a stranger whom I didn't know and trusted less. They had lasted me a long time.

Now, I had but one left. As I smoked it, looking out from my small apartment in London at the crowded street below, I wondered if I would ever smell the scent of Cuba again.

I had definitely grown very fond of it.

Havana in 1951 wore its contradictions openly. The city glittered and rotted at the same time. It was like a roulette wheel that never stopped spinning. Along the Malecón, American cars cruised in colors too bright for the salt-bleached air, their chrome catching the last light of day as the sea slapped the wall below with bored persistence. Palm fronds bent under the coastal wind, and the sun went down hard and fast, staining the harbor red before giving way to a warm, electric night.

By dark, Havana belonged to music and money. Neon bled from hotel marquees—Nacional, Sevilla-Biltmore, Saratoga—casting long reflections across wet pavement and polished marble lobbies. Inside, ceiling fans turned lazily above linen suits and silk dresses, the air thick with cigar smoke, perfume, and the low hum of deals being made without paper. Casinos rang with the sound of dice and regret. The bands played rumba and mambo for tourists who thought they were tasting danger, and for locals who knew better. Dollars flowed freely, and so did secrets.

Behind the lights, the city tightened its jaw. Former President Fulgencio Batista's shadow lay across every ministry office and police checkpoint, laying the groundwork for his reappearance as a brutal US-backed dictator. Havana was neutral ground in theory, but in practice, it was a listening post for half the world. CIA men drank daiquiris at El Floridita, Soviet couriers moved through shipping offices along the docks, and exiles, smugglers, gamblers, and ghosts crossed paths without ever exchanging names. Everyone watched everyone else, and nobody trusted the smiles.

Old Havana remembered things the new hotels tried to forget. Narrow streets curled between colonial facades, their paint peeling back to reveal older colors underneath. Courtyards held the damp cool of centuries, and churches rang bells that had outlived empires. At night, doorways swallowed men whole, and footsteps echoed longer than they should have. There is no doubt the city had layers—history grinding against the present, waiting for the wrong pressure to make something slip.

It was the kind of place where time felt unreliable. Days ran together under the sun, nights stretched and folded in on themselves, and memory became just another currency to be traded or stolen. Havana didn't ask who you were or where you came from. It only asked what you wanted—and what you were willing to lose to get it. For a man already uncertain which version of his past still belonged to him, the city was less a destination than a warning.

The heat was oppressive. It didn't just weigh down on you; it crushed you beneath its fiery skin. The air was always thick—thick with the smell of roasted coffee beans, unwashed yardsmen, and the occasional, sickening sweetness of rotting fruit in the gutter. On the corner of Obispo, the place felt like it was melting. But not for the man who stumbled along beneath the overbearing glare of the midday sun.

Dr. Sergei Markov could feel the sweat glistening on his forehead. He reached out, shakily, and grabbed a lamppost to steady himself, the iron beneath his hand hot enough to blister skin. But Sergei Markov didn't feel the heat—he felt a cold, numbing, icy-white pain radiating from the marrow of his bones, a frostiness that had no business anywhere near the Caribbean. The tropics this time of year were insufferably hot, and yet, he shivered.

He looked down, inspecting his trembling hands beneath his gaze.

How long ago had it been now? Only a moment, or a year—or maybe a decade? Back then, they had been smooth—the hands of a man just barely in his forties, a man who spent his days gently adjusting dials and fiddling with the finer mechanisms of copper coils. But no longer. The skin was marked with liver spots, his veins pulsing blue like worms beneath parchment paper, wriggling for escape.

Entropy.

His mind felt numb, far-off. Even that word echoed around his skull as if it were too large for his brain. As if his mind itself were shrinking. It was something he knew too well—he studied it, after all.

Rapid cellular decoherence.

He stumbled forward, trying to take a step, but his knees

locked and he fell, the arthritis already pulsing through his bones. He coughed, gasping for air, the rattle in his throat already beginning to form. His eyes felt lidded and heavy.

"Señor?" A voice called from across the street; a vendor frowned at him in concern. "¿Está bien?"

Markov opened his mouth. He wanted to beg for help—to warn them of the containment—but the words died before he could speak them. He had forgotten Spanish. Then, the Russian began to bleed out, as if he were speaking what he only now remembered. The formula for temporal displacement—that he did remember—but he had forgotten even his own mother's face.

The surrounding world jolted him—pulsed—as if, for a heartbeat, it had shifted.

For a second, he saw swirling mist around him, felt the cold, damp rocks beneath his knees, and saw the dark water of a Loch below. He'd read about it in the history books—was this Scotland?

Then, he was back in the blinding, sweltering heat of the Havana sun. Blood, dark and crimson, splattered onto the pavement below, and he raised a wrinkled hand to his face, feeling the nosebleed as it began to gush faster.

It splattered against his white linen suit.

Then, he collapsed.

Around him, a crowd gathered as he lay there, staring up mindlessly at the peeling paint of the balcony above. He watched a woman stare down at him from where she had been hanging laundry only a second before. The colors of his vision shifted, as if he were going blind.

The crowd had grown into a circle of faces staring down at him in curiosity and concern.

"He's dying, looks like."

"Yeah," someone muttered. "No surprise. He's ancient."

"Look at him," another said.

Markov could hear the voices, faint but distinct, and wanted to laugh. He would have if he had the energy—he was only forty-two.

A flashbulb popped. Somewhere in the distance, an American tourist had snapped a picture, but as the shutter clicked, the camera emitted a high-pitched whine. Instead of flashing, the bulb shattered, raining glass down against the cobblestones. The man yelped and sprang back as smoke curled from the device, smelling of burnt ozone and melting plastic.

Markov could feel himself weakening; his vision began to tunnel, and the very last thought on his mind was that the quantum field was expanding.

A sharp, harsh police whistle cut through the humidity, and the crowd parted, making way. Two officers pushed through, their uniforms stained with sweat. One knelt beside Markov, roughly rifling through his pockets with practiced efficiency. They weren't gentle. They had a job to do.

Markov tried weakly to grab the officer's wrist, but his body wouldn't move. His own hand was like a shrunken claw now, the fingers fused together with arthritis. All he could do was watch helplessly as one of the policemen pulled out a leather wallet, flipped it open, and frowned at the contents.

Inside was a heavy identification card, laminated in a thick, industrial plastic. There was a photo of Markov, too—young, strong, staring intently at the lens, a slight smile playing on his lips.

"Laboratorio Especial No. 7," the officer read slowly, struggling with the foreign texture of the words. He squinted, peering at the address printed directly below the stamp: 'Destilería Havana Club', Cárdenas.

Markov wanted nothing more than to tell them to burn it. *Don't read it. Don't read it,* he thought.

But the officers continued on. One pulled out a notebook from Markov's pocket, staring at it with mild suspicion. The pages were covered in equations that looked like madness, scribbles of physics, and sketches of a machine that resembled a giant mirror.

The second officer finally looked up from the contents inside, nudging Markov's boot.

"Call an ambulance," he said.

"No ambulance," a sharp, accented voice cut through the crowd. Two men in dark suits stepped out of a vehicle that had rolled silently to the curb.

They wore fedoras pulled low, casting shadows over their eyes as they scanned the crowd with indifference. The officers straightened instantly. They could sense the bureaucratic weight the men projected. Intimidated, they stepped back.

"State matter," the first suit said, reaching down and plucking the wallet and the notepad from the policemen's hands. He hadn't even asked. He just took them.

"But the body—" the officer began.

"There is no body," the man responded calmly.

The man's accent was foreign, but mysterious, as if he had made a certain effort to disguise it.

The last thing Markov ever knew was the smell of the man's cologne. A cheap lavender that seemed to mask another scent, though his weak mind couldn't comprehend what it was. He could feel himself being lifted, light as a bundle of dried twigs. They shoved him into the back of the vehicle, and he looked back at the street weakly for the last time.

But no longer did his mind comprehend it as a street. His memories—memories of his childhood, of the algorithms he slaved over tirelessly, and of his family—were gone. Missing, as entropy claimed its final piece.

The vendor, the police, the tourist, all were looking away now, their attention already drifting onward, as if the memory of the event had left no mark on their minds.

Then the car door slammed shut, and the engine roared to

life. On the floor of the car lay the ID card the suit had dropped, the distillery's red stamp almost glowing in the dim light.

"Laboratorio Especial No. 7, Project Oracle V4."

The car rumbled away, vanishing into the heat haze and leaving nothing but the smell of the burnt film and the damp, heavy, suffocating silence.

Dr. Sergei Markov was dead.

CHAPTER 2
RUM RIDDLES

Gray clouds rode over Foggy Bottom in Washington, D.C., like smoky stallions in the blustering dawn. It was a neighborhood that got its name from the iconic fog that frequently rolled in from the Potomac River and was directly alongside the White House's grounds and the National Mall, surrounded by buildings like the State Department and Navy offices. It was windy, and the gusts blew here and there, offering some much-needed respite from the heat outside.

But James Jesus Angleton couldn't rest. He waited instead in a windowless office on E Street that once belonged to the Office of Strategic Services, the air inside stale with the smell of Virginia tobacco and cold coffee. The wind meant he could occasionally smell a scent of something else, maybe fresh pine in the breeze.

He sighed, leaning back in his chair. A single desk lamp reflected a cone of yellow light onto the green blotter. Outside, the world seemed far more alive than inside, where Angleton was dissecting the cracks in the foundation.

Though his eyes felt heavy, he didn't blink. He'd been up the entire night before, and now, approaching twenty-four hours of wakefulness, inhaling his cigarette was the only thing that would keep him going.

The cable from the Havana station lay in the center of the light from the lamp. It was a short, garbled cable, typed by a hand that had clearly been shaking. And yet it was legible enough.

SUBJECT: MARKOV, SERGEI, DOCTOR.
STATUS: DECEASED/MISSING.
ANOMALY: RAPID BIOLOGICAL DECAY.
ESTIMATED AGE AT DEATH: 95.
ACTUAL AGE: 42.
NOTE: WITNESS REPORTS OF LOCALIZED STATIC DISCHARGE. ELECTRONIC FAILURE IN VICINITY.

He didn't look at the words; not quite. He looked through them, his eyes glassy, his mind whirring. He had experience hunting ghosts, but the ghost he was hunting now was unlike any he had hunted before. This one wore a lab coat and the signs of science: rapid aging, static, and time dislocation. Pulses in the energy field.

It was the pattern that he had learned from his investigations into England's Bureau and the recent MI6 incident. It was the Rosyth Dockyard signature. It was something his good friend had told him about, though as of late, Angleton wasn't sure how good a friend he actually was.

He sighed, picking up the heavy black receiver of the secure line. He wasn't sure he wanted to call the man, but he did, dialing wearily. The dial clicked rhythmically as it spun back to zero, the sound of a pistol being cocked.

He hesitated only a second when the operator finally connected.

"London," he said, his voice raspy. "Broadway, get me Philby."

He waited as the connection hissed across the Atlantic, using radio and nascent cable technology which hummed with the weight of what the conversation would hold.

Finally, Kim Philby's voice crackled through, cheerful, warm, and almost too bright.

"James," Philby said, almost admonishing. "It's still early here. I hope you're calling to tell me you found a decent tailor, my boy."

But Angleton wasn't in the mood for humor.

"We have a problem in Cuba, Kim."

"Cuba?" Philby chuckled, his voice staticky but clear. "The only problem I've seen in Cuba is a hangover, old boy, and the humidity. I hear it's blistering down there."

"Sergei Markov," Angleton said, his voice flat. "A Russian scientist, dead on the street in Havana. From what I hear, he aged forty years in forty seconds."

There was a pause on the line. The silence stretched for three seconds too long, and then Philby finally spoke.

"Spectacular, but I don't see why you've contacted me," Philby said, his tone a bored drawl. "The Soviets love their theatrics, you know. It's probably a new poison, thallium perhaps, or maybe stress. If he were a defector, well, defecting is a stressful business, isn't it?"

He laughed again, but his laugh was hollow this time.

"I don't think it's poison, Kim," Angleton muttered, though he could already feel the disappointment in his veins. He wasn't going to get anything out of Philby; he knew that much. "Seems to me like some sort of temporal anomaly. Equipment failed, camera shattered..."

His voice trailed off.

"Just routine," Philby dismissed, the warmth in his tone finally gone, replaced with a slight irritation. "James, we cleared that whole deal with MI6, the Bureau, and the Mirror. It was all destroyed. Whatever is happening in Cuba, it's a cleanup operation. Moscow Center is tidying up a loose end or something. Come on, don't waste resources chasing fairy tales. Let's leave Havana to the tourists."

"You sure about that? Can you promise me?" Angleton asked as he stared at the smoke curling from the end of his cigarette.

"I promise. Go to bed, James. You sound exhausted. Get some sleep, old boy."

And the line went dead with a hollow click.

Angleton held the phone for several moments more, staring into space, then, finally, slowly replaced the receiver with a click. He continued to stare at the phone for a long time afterward.

He had known Philby for years, had been mentored by the man, and he respected him greatly. But now... now something was stirring in his veins, akin to suspicion. He'd heard about the MI6 incident, of course. It had been plastered everywhere: how an insane, paranoid Bureau agent had accused Kim Philby of working for the Russians. And now Philby seemed almost too quick to dismiss it. A man who dismisses a pattern is either a fool or an architect, and Kim Philby was no fool.

Angleton sighed, rubbing his face. He wasn't sure what to think. Maybe Philby had simply been played, had had the wool pulled over his eyes. It seemed very unlikely. Either way, he needed more information to be confident. He wanted to learn more.

He slowly reached into his desk drawer, pulling out a small, battered private address book with no official markings. It was here, and only here, that he had a number that wouldn't belong to the CIA, the FBI, MI6, or the State Department. It was another number, a number that belonged to the Bureau.

The Bureau, of course, was England's Temporal Anomaly department. On the official waves, it was known as OTASI: the Office of Temporal Anomalies and Strategic Intelligence, but colloquially, the Bureau.

Angleton dialed the number.

London had been drowning for weeks. The rain just wouldn't go away, and it wouldn't let up. The sky was nearly always dreary and overcast—a classic symptom of the English atmosphere and the ever-burdened landscape.

The rain lashed harshly against the small, high window of Moreau's office, turning the usual London gray into blurs, streaks, and reminding her of the acidic nature of that constant drizzle. Behind a desk, Elspeth Moreau sat. Her hair was slightly grayer than it had been over a year ago, and bags had formed beneath her eyes.

The office was narrow, far narrower than most men expected when they heard her lofty title. The desk in the dead center of the room was like some command post blocking the middle of a corridor. It was a distinctive piece, scattered with papers, intercept summaries, and other files stacked into tidy, soulless towers. She had begun to despise it all, of course. She couldn't keep this up forever. And there was no real point, either. After the incidents with Alicia Rayes and Max Calder, she had become disillusioned. Disillusioned by the fact that she might never see her daughter again.

The Bureau was in shambles. She was the director of an organization that didn't officially exist on paper anymore, not that it ever had. And she was tired.

The old black telephone on her desk, the back-channel one that looked as if it'd survived more wars than the Bureau itself, rang. It startled her, a jarring mechanical scream in the quiet room. Moreau closed her eyes, leaned back, and sighed once more, collecting her thoughts. She was tempted, only momentarily, to flip that small photographic frame that lay face down at the corner of her desk and spend her time staring at it instead of working. But she didn't—not yet. Then she picked up the phone.

"Yes?"

"It's Angleton."

She hesitated, thinking. Where had she heard that name

before? But then it struck her: he was the CIA man that Kim Philby had mentored. Her blood ran cold.

She was no friend of Kim Philby, and though she had spoken to Angleton on several occasions and they had exchanged pleasantries, she was no fan of his if he was friends with that Russian traitor.

She didn't waste time with pleasantries.

"What is it?"

"Havana. A dead scientist," he replied. "I..." He hesitated, then continued. "I may need the Bureau's help. There were signs of temporal decay. And although it pains me to say this, I'm not sure Philby can be trusted."

"Not sure Philby can be trusted?" Moreau asked, incredulous. "I thought your relationship with him was solid."

"Used to be. Certainly was," the voice sighed on the other end. "I've grown suspicious as of late. I think Philby might be burying something."

A small smile played on Moreau's lips. But at the same time, she felt a cold knot tighten in her stomach. She reached quickly for a file on her desk, marked "Invershiel – Analytical," and flipped it open with one hand.

"What are the specifics? What can you give me?" she asked.

"Our organization," Angleton's voice crackled, "has done some research into the Rosyth Dockyard Incident and the incident at Invershiel. Subject matched both profiles. Distortions in the visual field. Time skips. Missing memories. Amplified aging. And he had a strange pass for a rum distillery in Cárdenas."

"Cárdenas..." Moreau's pen froze over the paper. She glanced at a map pinned to her wall, where a web of red string connected Scotland, Prague, and the Andes.

"Do you think it could just be a... what's the term again? An echo?" Angleton asked, his voice thin over the wire.

"No," Moreau said, her voice almost a whisper.

She looked at the resonance charts from the last month. The spikes were growing. Reports were growing as well. The Mirrors had been destroyed—or at least they were supposed to have been. But whatever this was, it wasn't just leaking. It was screaming, blasting pulses of temporal disturbances across the landscape.

"James," she said. "It pains me to say this, but I'm worried that Philby may have relayed some of the technical schematics of the Mirror to a third party."

"And what would that mean for us?"

"It would mean," she replied, "that he might have caused another one to be built."

"Then what do we do?" Angleton asked.

His voice carried a hint of incredulity, and she knew he didn't quite believe it. But she also knew that at the same time, he didn't fully trust Kim Philby, and this might just have been the chance the Bureau needed.

"MI6 is compromised," she said.

"Can the Bureau help?" he asked.

"Yes," she said. "We can bypass them. Go off the books."

"Who do you have?" Angleton asked.

Moreau glanced down at two personnel files sitting on the very corner of her desk. They were files that she kept there even when she wasn't looking into them. Files that she would stare at for hours at a time, trying to figure out what role these two played in everything. Their fates were seemingly intertwined with the Mirror itself.

The photographs were grainy, black and white, but unmistakable. One showed a woman with auburn hair, beautiful, flashing eyes, and a jaw set with a remarkable confidence that many would be intimidated by—but not Moreau. Alicia Rayes.

The other was a man who looked as if he hadn't slept in a decade. His hair was grayer than ever, and he was wearing a trench coat that looked tattered and worn, as if he hadn't bought a new one for the years he'd been in London. Max Calder.

"Well," she said at last, "I can think of two people I can assign to the job. Two people who might be able to survive this."

"That crazy agent who accused Kim Philby? Come on, Elspeth—" Angleton began, but she cut him off.

"Calder's a walking scar. His mind is broken," she corrected him. "But that scar tissue—that's the only thing holding this timeline together. And may I remind you, Angleton, you're beginning to doubt Philby, too. I'll assign them to the case."

And before he could answer, she hung up.

She leaned back in her chair, listening to the thrum of the rain hammering against the glass. With a sigh, she lit a cigarette, her hands trembling slightly. She had wanted to protect them. It was the least she could do if her own life was destined for failure. She had promised them that it was over.

But was it? Was the Mirror truly gone?

The technology was like a cancer. It didn't just break history or rewrite it. It infected the very fabric of time and was eating the world one second at a time, each pulse taking someone with it. And she had been dealt one of the worst hands of all—her daughter. Where was her daughter?

She exhaled a thin plume of gray smoke and watched it float into the air.

"I'm sorry, Alicia. Sorry to both of you," she whispered, staring up into the empty room.

Finally, with a reluctance that belied her, she slowly picked up the receiver and dialed the operator.

"Get me a line to Montevideo," she said. "Priority one. I need to speak to Artemis."

CHAPTER 3
SCOTTISH SHADOWS

Half the world and one Atlantic crossing away, the rain fell warmer over Montevideo. The city wore its dampness differently than London; the air was thick with salt, river mud, and the sweet scent of diesel and wet streets. Between narrow streets, laundry lines drooped, white shirts hanging limp in the mist from when they should have been taken in hours ago. And yet those who had hung them up had failed to do so. So the shirts remained there, wet and abandoned.

In a cramped back office somewhere above a shipping company on the Rambla, a woman sat at a wooden desk, her back straight, her hair in a neat bun, typing away. The typewriter was an old Remington, aged but well-kept and carefully maintained. She tapped the keys with an efficient precision, the muscles in her forearm tight under her skin. A fan turned lazily overhead, doing almost nothing to fight the humidity and the heat. It was exhausting.

"Señorita Rayes?" a voice called.

Alicia Rayes looked up. A clerk from the outer office stood in the doorway, his hat respectfully in his hands.

"Hello," she replied.

He stood nervously, though he kept it well hidden under a

polite smile. Most would have missed it, but Alicia Rayes noticed, and she smiled slightly to herself as she evaluated him.

"There's a telephone call for you. Long distance," he said.

"For me?" She frowned. "Are you sure?"

"Yes, señorita. The woman on the other end of the line insisted. She said it was a family matter."

He hesitated. For just an instant, something tightened, and her eyes became sharp. Then she smiled gracefully, thanked him, and rose from her desk, striding down the narrow office corridor in a controlled, unhurried manner. As she walked, someone who watched closely enough might have noticed that she gently brushed her fingertips along the wall, counting the doorways. It was a habit she'd picked up somewhere along the way, a way to keep her anchored.

There, on a small side table near the front of the office, sat a telephone, its cloth cover askew. The cord snaked somewhere deep into the wall and disappeared. The call should have gone to her usual desk—the one where all her belongings were.

"This is Rayes," she said, picking up the receiver.

"Alicia." The voice on the other end was female, low and curt, yet professional at the same time. "It's Director Moreau."

For a second, the room around her seemed to fall away. The ceiling fan creaked.

"Ah, Director," Alicia said at last, composing herself. Her tone was flat and professional as always, but her hand tightened slightly on the phone. "This is a bit of a surprise. Most assignments are handled by the local division."

"I'm afraid," Moreau said, "it's not a social call. We have a situation: a temporal signature consistent with Rosyth and Invershiel."

Alicia's eyes darted to the desk beneath the phone for just a second, where her passport lay open. Her thumb brushed against the photograph—her own face, in black and white, a little harder around the mouth than it had been two years earlier.

"Location?" she asked.

"Havana," Moreau replied. "A rum distillery in Cárdenas, to be precise. I will also be contacting Calder. I need you both in London immediately."

Alicia was silent for a second, listening to the noise outside the window.

"How soon?" she asked.

"I'll have Opal arrange the routing. You'll use Bureau documentation," Moreau said. "You'll need to be here as soon as you can get here without attracting any attention."

"And is this sanctioned by Whitehall?" Alicia asked, hesitating.

There was a humorous scoff on the other end of the line.

"It'll be off the books. You're fully aware of the MI6 situation."

The words hung there between them, heavy.

"All right then," Alicia said finally. "I'll pack."

Moreau hung up. For a second, Alicia stood there, the receiver still in her hand, listening to the empty hum through the line. Then she placed it down with a slight snap, picked up her passport, and began to gather her belongings.

On a chair by the window sat a battered leather holdall, already half packed.

Several days later, the rain over London was relentless. For weeks, it had been that way, never quite storming and never quite stopping, just hanging over the city like a damp blanket.

In a narrow street off the Strand, in a building that had survived the Blitz by accident rather than design—a building older than the war by many decades—my telephone began to ring. My flat on the top floor was small enough that the first ring rattled everything: the picture frames on the wall, the cracked cups in the sink, even the loose glass in the window. The walls were thin, the wallpaper older than I was, and my furniture was somewhat rickety. I had acquired it from a fire sale and requisitioned it for my own use.

I was lying on my sofa, an open book on my chest, my hat over my eyes, and an empty glass of whisky perched on my stomach. The book was face down, the print side against the gray wool of my shirt. I had finished reading a while ago and was asleep—or at least asleep the way a man falls asleep when his body shuts off and his mind isn't quite ready.

The ringing telephone cut through the room yet again. The bulb in the ceiling flickered slightly, as if the line were drawing more power than it had any right to do.

Finally, on the third ring, my eyes snapped open. For a second, I wasn't sure where I was. The ceiling above me seemed wrong—no condensation, no hairline fracture spidering out of the light fixture, no smell of Lisbon nor the history of Scotland. Where was I? Instead, there was just the nicotine film of a London bedsit and the muffled sound of buses and rain outside.

I sat up, blinking slowly, as my book tumbled to the floor. I barely managed to catch the empty glass. The room settled into focus a second later, as if my mind had finally registered where I was. It had taken a while, that was for sure. I shook my head slowly.

The phone rang again. A headache began to bloom behind my eye, like a hot needle punching toward the back of my skull, accompanied by an old, dull throb in the front of my head.

"Right," I muttered to myself. "You again."

I meant the headache, of course. It returned nearly every time I was awake. The only thing that seemed to keep it down these days was the whisky.

I set down the glass on the scarred side table and crossed over to the phone, my bare feet against the cold linoleum. I hesitated just long enough, then lifted the receiver, heavy and black, its Bakelite surface slick in my fingers.

"Yeah?"

It came out rougher than I intended.

"Mr. Calder?" The voice was crisp, female, and almost cheerful. Resentfully, I recognized it instantly. "Mr. Max Calder?"

"That's a matter of who you ask," I replied.

The voice on the other end of the line hesitated, and there was a hint of amusement when it next spoke.

"This is Opal," she said, "on behalf of Director Moreau. She requests your presence. Bureau business."

I closed my eyes for a second. The very word seemed to offend.

"I thought the Bureau was busy," I retorted, "buried under committee minutes and whitewash. How is this organization not dead yet?"

On the other end of the phone, I could hear papers rustling.

"Not as dead as everyone hoped," Opal said. "Director Moreau herself requests you come in immediately. Use the civilian door—the hidden one near Holborn. You know where it is. Use the name on your Bureau card."

I glanced at the Bureau ID card lying on the mantelpiece, weighted down by a chipped ashtray. Max Calder, in neat black print, code-named Raven. The card was old enough to be beginning to yellow, but I had never requested a new one. In fact, I had refused multiple times. I preferred the old style.

"And what if I say no?"

There was a pause. When Opal finally spoke again, the humor in her voice was gone, replaced by a serious tone.

"Director Moreau asked me to relay to you that this relates to the matter involving a major technology you were associated with," she said. "Her own words. And she also asked me to relay this to you: it's not finished."

I rubbed my forehead tiredly, letting out a slow breath through my teeth.

"No. Of course it isn't," I said finally. "Tell Director Moreau I'll be there shortly."

I hung up before she could say anything else, the receiver clicking down softly.

Outside, the rain lashed harder at the window, as if trying to get in, desperately banging against the glass. I stood there for a moment, staring at my own reflection in the glass. The man looking back was older than ever, hair graying, desperately in need of a shave and a new coat. The trench coat on the peg by the door had seen better times.

I closed my eyes for a second, desperately wishing I could just ignore it, desperately hoping I could stay home with my book and whisky. Then, opening my eyes, I dressed and reached for the old trench coat anyway.

By the time I reached Holborn, the rain had permeated the seams of my old coat, settling into my shirt and chilling me to the bone. The cold was something else, for sure. London in '51 was still rebuilding, but some of the streets looked as if they had given up. Holborn partially seemed to wear the damage on its sleeve like the mark of trauma it had been exposed to—soot in the brickwork, grime in the stones, and the whole street feeling older than London itself.

Buses hissed past, splattering water up from the wet roads, and the metallic ringing of some bells far off in the distance continued, disorienting me slightly.

The air smelled slick with coal smoke, stale chip fat, and wet stones. The sky, as always, was a low, dark, drab, uniform gray that seemed to press down on everything, flattening the sound around me.

I kept my collar up and my hat brim low. Old habits. I hadn't been back to the Bureau in a while—at least not in the last year or so.

The entrance they'd told me to use was unmarked, as always —just a narrow door between a tobacconist and a print shop that had fogged windows filmed with condensation and ink. Most people wouldn't know how to look for it, but I did.

I slid the door open carefully, but I didn't have to worry. Someone had cut the old clapper years ago, so the bell over the door didn't even ding.

A man in a suit sat behind a high wooden counter, pretending to read a ledger. He glanced up, his eyes going straight to my Bureau ID as I slid it across the worn wood.

"Max Calder," he said, his face unamused. "Bit early for your typical propensities."

"Opal called ahead," I said. "There should be a note."

He flipped open a page in the ledger, glanced at it, then pressed a button under the desk. Somewhere behind him, a lock thunked open.

"This way." He motioned, coming around the counter as if he had all day and it wasn't a rush at all. He led me along, guiding me through a back corridor that shouldn't have existed, at least not in the building's official footprint. The air grew cooler, drier, and the smell of tea gave way to something else, as if it had been sealed away from the weather on purpose. A faint electric hum began to thread itself into everything.

We went down one flight, then another, and another—five floors below the foundation, I estimated—until a door waited for me. None of it was mapped, and none aligned—though I usually didn't take the alternative entrance, it was clear Moreau wanted this meeting to remain top-secret. I recognized the door itself as Bureau work—a thick, industrial door with no handle. The clerk knocked twice, waited for the door to slowly swing open, and stepped back.

"Conference Hall," he said. "Opal will meet with you."

"Appreciate it," I shot back.

The Conference Hall sat far deeper than the rest of the Bureau headquarters, as if the place had been built around it. It wasn't just a deliberate presentation of power; it was a perfect circle of authority, and the deepest base the place had to offer.

The air carried the scent of ozone. A long, large marble table dominated the center of the place, polished flawlessly so that the reflections were hardly distinct from real people. Above the table, white lamps hung down low, hooked to delicate brass stems, their lights graceful but steady.

The ceiling was webbed with pipes and electrical conduits that seemed to pulse with a certain energy—not Mirror energy, but something else entirely.

Still, it seemed crowded. Maybe it was because of the number of things they crammed into it. The Bureau was downsizing, after all, and they could no longer fit all their projects into the space they had. Clusters of corkboards lined the walls, crisscrossed with strings and pins, displaying maps of Europe, the Atlantic, and the Caribbean alongside hand-drawn charts, photographs, and even typed reports. A wire recorder sat on a stand near the far wall, its reels motionless, its silver discs reflecting the dim light.

Opal was nowhere to be seen.

And there, at the head of the table, was Elspeth Moreau, standing as if she'd been waiting for me all morning. I'd never seen her in the flesh before. I'd heard her voice many times, of course, seen her signature at the bottom of far too many directives, but had never actually seen her. She was shorter and thinner than I expected, yet her very presence seemed to command the room, and I knew only too well it would make those around her wary. Her dark hair was almost entirely gray, pulled back in a style that was far more about practicality and statement than fashion. She wore a neatly tailored suit, and there was something in the set of her shoulders that told me more than any personnel file could have. She stood upright, refusing to bend, and met my eyes with hers. Her eyes were searing, sharp, and commanding.

I knew very little about the woman herself, but what I did know was that she was the reason the Bureau existed.

"Mr. Calder," she said.

"Director Moreau, I presume," I replied.

"You look better than your files and the reports suggested," she said. "That's a relief, at least."

"I was expecting someone taller," I replied.

Something flickered at the corner of her mouth, almost a smile, but I could tell that she was focused on something else.

"Sit down," she said, not unkindly. "We're waiting on one more."

My stomach twisted slightly.

"One more," I repeated.

I didn't ask, but I already knew who it must have been, and as if to confirm it, Moreau nodded toward the far end of the table, where a chair sat conspicuously empty, a folder placed neatly in front of it. I didn't even have to look at the name typed on the tab. I already knew that Alicia would be there soon, but two years felt like a lifetime when time itself was already broken.

The last time I'd seen Alicia Rayes, the year had just turned, and the city had held its breath. New Year's night, 1948, the Mirror still warm from misuse and promises. After we had destroyed it—or at least thought we did—and my mind had been broken by the missing memories in Philby's betrayal, we'd scattered like shrapnel.

I spent those two years pretending I could live a normal life, though I knew better by now. What was left of the Bureau didn't buy it, but they let me try anyway. I took assignments, boring ones, jobs that smelled of paper and rain instead of ozone. Lisbon in the spring, Naples in the fall, long Atlantic crossings on ships that creaked like old men remembering wars they never quite forgot, hotels where the wallpaper peeled like sunburn, and the clocks all disagreed. My mind hadn't healed—if anything, it had broken more—but I learned to live with it, learned how to drink coffee without watching the surface for ripples, how to sit in a room and not count the exits. I often failed, but I tried all the same.

The Mirror never really left me. It doesn't do that, I'd learned by now. Instead, it leaves fingerprints in your head, ghost bruises on your memories. Some nights I awoke convinced I'd slid, convinced the room was wrong by a few inches, while other nights I dreamed of ANGUS, Fraser-Smith's hands steady as a surgeon, Alicia's voice precise and unafraid, and even of the Andes Temple where that tussle with Krane in the Mirror had scarred me for the first time.

The Bureau, of course, used me as they always did, asking me to write reports and come in for meetings where they could assess me, but they never fixed anything. Often enough, I didn't think they knew how to fix anything. Mostly, I was in hiding, though I didn't admit it. Hiding from the Mirror, from her, from the part of me that knew everything was connected and yet couldn't do anything about it. I had failed to stop Kim Philby, failed to stop him from siphoning off Mirror pieces—which I knew he would do—and sending them to the Russians.

As for Alicia, she never hid. That was the thing about her. Where I ducked and detoured, unwilling to face my darkest memories, she drilled straight down and settled in.

I sighed, then walked over, pulled out the chair beside her empty one, and sat. The headache that had been simmering since the phone call throbbed again, creating a little metronome behind my eyes as we waited. On the table in front of me was another folder with my name on it—Calder, M.—my life reduced to Bureau paperwork and staples.

Moreau, however, was already busy. She picked up a third, different file and flipped it open.

"Dr. Sergei Markov," she began. "A Soviet physicist, born in Leningrad, 1907. He worked on several classified projects in Moscow before he was transferred to Havana last year under diplomatic cover. From what we can gather, his official front cover is technical advisor to Destilería Havana Club near Cárdenas. His actual position, however, is much more interesting: Laboratorio Especial No. 7."

She stood before me, then slid a grainy black-and-white photograph across the table toward me. Markov looked young here—mid-forties maybe—with intense eyes and hair starting to thin at the temples. Next to the photo was a copy of a Havana cable. I glanced at it. It had ANGLETON typed across the header.

Angleton? My mind whirred as I tried to place it.

"Who's this from?" I asked.

"James Angleton, CIA," Moreau replied. "He contacted me directly the other day. For what it's worth,"—she hesitated, then continued—"he's contacting the Bureau because he doesn't trust Philby."

I nodded, smiled, then scanned the Havana cable intently.

Anomaly. Rapid biological decay. Estimated age at death: ninety-five. Actual age, forty-two.

"Damn," I said, my voice trailing off. "Static discharge, electronics failing—hell, even a camera bulb blew." I tapped the paper with a knuckle. "That's the Rosyth fingerprint, all right."

"Precisely," Director Moreau replied. "Angleton's people picked up on the echo, sent us these details through a back channel. He also mentioned something else—the reason he doesn't trust Philby. When he took it to MI6, specifically Kim Philby, before us, Philby strongly discouraged him from pursuing it."

Kim Philby.

I opened my mouth to say something unkind about him when the door behind me clicked suddenly, and I could hear the hydraulics within it working almost silently. I could hear her before I saw her—the soft, sure, quiet footsteps she always took, the faint rustle of her coat being slipped off and hung by the door, the almost inaudible exhale she made whenever she stepped into rooms like this, bracing herself against an old, familiar impact.

Then, as I turned, I saw her. She wore a dark skirt, blouse, and fitted jacket.

Alicia Rayes had walked into the Hall.

It had been almost two years since I'd seen her. Two long years, long enough for memory to sand the edges off, to smooth her down into something slightly easier for my mind to comprehend. But the real truth of the matter cut through all of that, sharp, in an instant. She looked different, but she looked exactly the same as she always had. Though her auburn hair was slightly shorter than it had been in Scotland, cut to brush her jaw, and the Montevideo sun had left its mark as a deeper tan on her skin, she looked the same. She looked just like Alicia.

Her eyes darted around the room as if scanning it for threats, cataloging exits, faces, vectors of potential harm, and everything else. Then they landed on me, and for a second, we did the thing people do when they don't quite know which version of themselves the other person remembers. We stared at each other, something flickering in our minds, maybe relief, anger, or something else I wasn't even brave enough to begin naming. Then it was gone, buried under the cool professional mask she wore better than anyone else.

"Director," she said, nodding politely to Moreau first, as was protocol.

"Artemis," Moreau said gracefully. "I appreciate you coming from Montevideo so promptly at such short notice."

Alicia moved the empty chair beside me and sat down. She placed a leather satchel on the floor by her feet, her hands resting on the handle for a moment longer than they needed to. It was worn. I could tell that she didn't quite know what to say to me.

"Hello, Max," she said eventually, as if my name was one she had finally just remembered.

"Miss Rayes," I answered, the smallest hint of a smile playing at my lips. "It's good to see you."

She nodded back in acknowledgement. It wasn't much as reunions go, but it was ours, and it was constrained by the fact that the Director of our organization stood in front of us, watching closely.

Up close, I could see the faintest sliver of a scar at her temple, mostly hidden by her hair. It hadn't been there before, and I wondered what had given it to her, but I didn't ask.

"Welcome back to London," I said quietly.

"Already ready to leave," she murmured back. "I didn't miss the weather or the paperwork."

It was just loud enough for me to hear, but Moreau cleared her throat regardless.

"Now that you're both here," she said, "we can begin our work properly."

She tapped the file in front of us.

"As I was saying, this is Dr. Sergei Markov. He was found dead on a Havana street. That's not the interesting part, though. His body was showing signs of accelerated aging, consistent with exposure to an active Mirror field, or at the very least a residual pulse. Rumors spread quickly. The local police and some sightseers observed small anomalies. Even Angleton's station—" she turned to Alicia "—Opal's filled you in on that, correct?"

When Alicia nodded, she continued on.

"Angleton's station reported electronic disturbances. Everything about this screams Invershiel, Rosyth, or something worse."

Alicia took the file, her eyes scanning it. I watched as her pupils traced the lines, her jaw tightening.

"Cárdenas," she muttered. "This can't be a leak if it's a distillery cover with special laboratory designation. It has to be a node of some sort."

"Yes, that's the impression we're operating under." Moreau nodded. "It's a node or successor of some sort. Angleton, though, is currently a hobbyist as far as the Mirror goes—called it an anomaly. Even his superiors will notice something off, and Philby is already urging him to drop it."

"You really trust Angleton?" I interrupted.

"I trust he's frightened or at least really concerned," Moreau said. "And the man isn't stupid; he has good pattern recognition. He's seen enough to know when something unusual is happening, and he's begun to distrust Philby."

She turned to me, closing the file with a soft thud.

"Calder, that means someone is finally on your team."

"Yeah, I get it," I said, crossing my arms.

"But I didn't call you in here for Havana alone," she continued, ignoring my gesture. "There's something else you need to hear. Something from…"

Her voice trailed off. She nodded toward the wall beside the door, where a narrow glass panel had been set. It was less of a window and more of a reminder that the Bureau always kept an eye on its own rooms and agents, no matter where they were.

In the dim antechamber beyond, a young technician, his face bright, leaned over a wire recorder that was already set up and waiting. We couldn't hear the machine itself through the wall's thickness, only the faintest suggestion of motion, and the dark orange glow of vacuum tubes behind a grated panel.

Then, a moment later, a speaker grille built into the hall's wall crackled alive. At first, we thought it was an ordinary burst of static.

"About a month after Invershiel," Moreau said. "We've had background noise since. Echoes… You're both familiar with that. But this was different. The Bureau boys on monitoring duty recognized the voice. It came through after you two attempted to shut down Invershiel."

The speakers crackled, and for a long moment, there was only silence. Then a voice came through.

"If you can hear this… if anyone can…"

I felt the air leave my lungs. I recognized the voice instantly, though it was distorted, washed through filters of interference and distance.

It was Hawthorne.

"Jesus… hell," I muttered.

Alicia was staring intently at the speaker as well, very still.

On the recording, Hawthorne coughed slightly.

"Shaw… Malcolm Shaw, formerly Bureau… designation Architect. You don't have much time."

His voice wasn't weaker, but it was thinner than I remembered, stretched as if it were being pulled through too much wire.

"The Mirror isn't finished," his voice stuttered. "Rosyth was the first cut. Invershiel... ANGUS... Oracle... only scratched the surface. Entangled now. Spread and connected memory. The blueprints will still rebuild themselves. In the gaps... In the missing pieces."

My incessant headache flared, and for a second, the room tilted as I squinted. For a crazy instant, I smelled cold stone and wet heather, and I could hear waves lapping against the shore. I gripped the edge of the table, and then I was back as Hawthorne's voice steadied.

"If it resurfaces," he said, "if you hear aging field effects, echoes—cut the foundations. Kill the whole tree, roots and all, or it'll grow back."

There was a pause, filled with the low hiss of static.

"I'm searching," his voice continued. "Source... Radio silence... I'm going radio silent... Something's in the lines, in the resonances. I can feel it probing. It's learning. If I stay, it'll find me."

He laughed once.

"Max, I taught you better than that. Alicia and you both. You both know what happens when you give an enemy a channel, or a chance."

Another burst of interference swallowed his words, and when his voice returned, it sounded almost imperceptibly far away.

"If the Mirror resurfaces, if this reaches you," his voice said, "you know what to do. Don't hesitate."

The crackle began to thicken until it was almost all I could hear.

"Goodbye," he said, and I wasn't sure who he was speaking to. "And Max? I've enjoyed the memories."

The recording devolved into raw noise, squealing. The technician let it run for a few more seconds behind the glass. Then his hand moved slowly, and the glow dimmed as the machine was turned off.

The air was still. In the silence that followed, you could hear the building's pipes settling overhead, the steam and current shifting slowly in their arteries, until even the distant weather felt like just a faint, intermittent tick carried down through stone.

During the message, my vision had tunneled. My nails were digging into the underside of the table, and I realized that now. I forced my hand to loosen one finger at a time.

Alicia stirred first.

"Where did the Bureau get that?" she asked. Her voice was steady, but I could hear nervousness in her undertones.

"Shortwave band over the North Atlantic," Moreau replied. "Picked it up out of Reykjavík. The radioman thought it was some sort of American propaganda broadcast but recorded it anyway because the voice sounded important. His words. Don't ask me how we interrogated him to find that information."

I scoffed. The Bureau always had its ways.

Moreau, however, didn't look amused. She glanced between Alicia and me.

"He addressed you both, you know," she said.

"Well, I'm not damn well surprised," I muttered. "He always liked an audience."

But the joke fell flat. Memories began to claw their way up in my mind—memories of Invershiel, of Hawthorne's figure dissolving into the glow, and of the sensation of being pulled in every direction at once, and my mind falling away.

For another moment, the conference room blurred again, and I could see a man I already knew from other memories implanted in my mind. It was Fraser-Smith. I was arguing about coil calibration. I could see Philby at the edge of the scene, his hands in his pockets, casual as you please, watching everything with those bright, sharp, boyish eyes.

I squeezed my eyes shut and focused on the room around me. Focused on her.

As my mind began to recalibrate, I heard Moreau speaking.

"You were at Invershiel when MI6 dismantled Oracle at ANGUS," she said quietly. "Or, more correctly, you were the ones who caused it to be dismantled."

"Yes," I replied, my voice sounding hoarse. "You know all about MI6, the Bureau, and Philby. Always Philby. All three of us were there... and, well, Hawthorne, sort of."

Alicia's mouth tightened slightly in agreement.

"Philby had full run of the place," she said. "Blueprints, console layouts, coils. If Max is right—and I believe him—then it's likely Philby managed to snag some of those resources for himself."

"He might as well have," I added. "He was the one who started all of this. He was the one at MI6 who started this whole damn project with the Mirror after Rosyth—who told them about it and started Oracle at ANGUS."

"And then," Alicia said, shaking her head, "he walked away without a scratch."

Moreau listened, her hands on her face in concentration. She didn't speak for a few more seconds, but then finally, she slowly began to talk. Still, her speech commanded silence.

"Angleton mentioned in his cable that when he brought Markov's death to Philby, Philby dismissed it and called it Soviet theatrics—encouraged him to leave Havana. 'Leave it to the tourists,' I believe were his words."

"Philby would have," I snapped. "He always sounds bored when he's moving the pieces the fastest."

"And you believe he's involved, Calder?" Moreau asked.

"I don't believe it," I said. "I know it."

I thought of Philby at Rosyth, watching and stealing the pieces from it using MI6's jurisdiction. I thought of him at ANGUS, building his own damn project. And even the files and artifacts we discovered under Kingsway.

Alicia nodded slowly. "So do I."

Moreau let out a breath.

"Very well," she said. "Here's the deal: MI6 is currently under inquiry. Committees digging into their special projects now. Parliamentary nonsense. They successfully buried ANGUS and Oracle under layer upon layer of classification. But they still can't afford another incident that even smells remotely like the Mirror, not politically. They will downplay this, and they'll look the other way, especially if Kim Philby tells them to. They are not our friends and will not be in this situation."

"In other words," I said, "if there is a new Mirror humming away in Cuba, the only people who will do anything about it are the three of us sitting in this goddamn room."

"More or less," Moreau replied. "And I'm tied down at the Bureau, so make that two."

She leaned forward and planted her elbows firmly on the table. She pointed directly at me.

"Let me be very clear. This is not sanctioned by the Cabinet, Whitehall, Joint Intelligence Committee, or anything else. This is a Bureau clandestine operation. We've initiated it at the request of a CIA counterintelligence officer who no longer trusts his British mentor. That alone is enough to put this project into disgrace in every community of government except this one. If either of you choose to go, you'll do so deep undercover with no direct support from MI6 or possibly even from the Bureau. And of course, if things go wrong..." She shrugged. "You know the drill. We'll deny that we ever had knowledge of your presence and claim you went rogue."

"Yeah, that would be pretty easy," I replied.

She nodded, smiling wryly.

"You have quite the reputation, Calder, for going off on your own and doing your own thing. You're actually the perfect person for this project."

"And if we don't go?" Alicia asked.

"Then, if another version of the Mirror does exist, that mess

Hawthorne described will spread. More people will die on the streets, more cities will start skipping entire beats, and sooner or later..." She turned back to us. "Sooner or later, it will be too late. We ignored the first warning. We survived by accident. Some others didn't. I won't ignore this."

Alicia was silent for a moment before finally speaking.

"After Scotland, after Invershiel, you promised us we could walk away," she said.

The room went still. I remembered that time in Lisbon, one of the few happy times in my life. Yet, the echoes wouldn't fade, the headaches wouldn't stop, and the faces in the Mirror hadn't always been their own. I didn't want to do it again. But maybe this could put an end to it.

"I know what I promised," Moreau said. "If there were anyone else I could send, I would. But you two are attuned. You've both survived direct exposure to multiple Mirror fields. Hell, three times if you count the Andes. You both understand the physics, and you understand the cost. You can stop this before it becomes something no one can stop."

For a second, she looked older—older and very tired.

"I'm not going to order either of you," she added. "There are no repercussions if you say no. This is voluntary. And if you both say no, I'll burn this file and pretend I never heard of Markov in the first place. I'll go back to playing with the papers on my desk, let the Bureau burn to hell, and wait for the sky to fall in."

I glanced at Alicia, but she didn't look back at me. Her gaze was fixed on Markov.

"Forty-two," she murmured. "Look at his eyes. So much life left in them."

She finally turned and met my gaze. And there was nothing to be said. We both had the answer in our eyes before we spoke.

"If there's a Mirror in Cuba," she said, "we can't pretend we don't know about it."

"Besides," I replied, "I heard the rum is good."

"Better than the whisky in Montevideo, that's for sure," she replied.

I smiled then, and the corner of her mouth twitched back. We both turned to look at Moreau.

"You'll have our covers ready? Passports, travel orders?"

"Opal is already on it," Moreau replied. "You'll go as trade delegates, shipping surveyors—thin but plausible. Angleton will provide local support, as will the American Embassy. He'll act as our liaison with the CIA."

"MI6?" Alicia asked.

"They'll know nothing," Moreau replied. "Philby will likely feel the tremors. He's too good not to, once you're in the field. But by then, if we're lucky, you'll already be under his radar. Havana is a damn long way from Broadway."

"Now," she said, turning toward us, "understand this: I have had my own personal reasons for wanting the Mirror to be preserved. But over these past few years, I have grown to understand and conclude that the Mirror is technology that cannot survive."

Her face was stern.

"Our objective will not be to capture the technology. We will not replicate it, contain it, or convey it. We will destroy it. Hawthorne's message was clear: we cut the roots, and if there is a root in Cuba, you find it, identify it, and destroy it. All of it."

"Burn the tree," I muttered, "and salt the soil."

"Precisely," she said.

"Then we'd better get started," I said, and I stood.

Moreau watched us with an expression almost akin to regret.

"Opal is going to brief you on your documentation," she said. "You'll have a few hours to get everything together. After that, I'll ship both of you off to Havana. Be careful, both of you. We're running out of time. Strangely, time is something we don't have."

"We'll do what we can," Alicia said, nodding sharply.

As we reached the door, however, Moreau spoke again.

"Oh, and Calder?"

"Yes, Director?"

"When you're out there, if you hear him again—Hawthorne—just remember what he told you."

"I'll keep that in mind," I responded, turning from the Conference Hall.

Beside me, Alicia walked in silence for a few paces.

"So," I said eventually, "Montevideo treating you well?"

"The rivers are too wide, and the men drink too much," she said, "but it does feel like home."

I snorted. "London missed you."

"London?" She laughed. "It doesn't miss anyone."

Then silence fell again, and she finally broke it.

"I did, though."

"Yeah," I said. "Me too."

She looked at me then—really looked at me for the first time, and I could see her mentally updating her memories with my changes: the silver that had crept slowly into my hair, the way the old injuries had begun to wear on my step.

"You look terrible," she said at last.

"And I feel worse," I replied.

"Well, let's make sure Cuba doesn't finish the job," she said.

I nodded grimly, and we kept walking.

CHAPTER 4
BUREAU BYPASS

Alicia and I had nothing—nothing except the Bureau's empty promises and the weight of a dead man's wallet. Dr. Sergei Markov. I wondered how many others would die because of the Mirror before we finally put a stop to it.

I didn't say it, but I was relieved we were back in the field. If the Mirror were alive, I wanted to destroy it.

Opal met us outside the conference hall, her face impassive, darker than it had been the last time we'd seen her. She had seen some things, though I didn't know what, and she didn't ask how we felt about Hawthorne's voice coming back from the beyond.

"Follow me," she said curtly, already moving.

I could tell it was still her, but something felt off. I chose not to mention it.

The corridors reflected the Bureau's classic architecture: narrow and lined with pipes and concrete, lit by bulbs that flickered occasionally. My head throbbed every time they flickered. We passed door after door with names that meant nothing to anyone outside the building: Resonance Field, Languages, Committee Room 5, Committee Room 7, until Opal finally stopped at an unmarked door, producing a large key.

Inside the room was a safe, a box, a table, two chairs, and a radiator that hissed occasionally. There was also a filing cabinet, bolted down against the wall and the floor, as if it would run away if they hadn't restrained it. On the table sat two brown envelopes and a black attaché case with a Bureau tag politely wired around its handle.

Opal nodded at the envelopes. "There you go. There are covers, funds, and travel, all booked for you."

I sat slowly, the chair groaning under my weight. Alicia stayed standing.

"Calder, you have become Mr. Martin Kale. You're a shipping surveyor, a subcontractor, and hired to assess Caribbean export capacity," she said, nodding as she slid the first envelope toward me.

"Sounds absolutely thrilling," I said.

"Oh, you're also an alcoholic with a bad back," she added, her deadpan humor finally shining again.

I looked up at her. "Must be an airtight cover, then."

Alicia's mouth twitched into a smile before she returned to her professional demeanor.

"And Miss Alicia Rayes," Opal said, handing Alicia her envelope, "you are Ana Rivas, Trade and Commerce Ministry liaison."

Alicia opened it, thumbing through the contents. Inside was a letter of introduction, a typed itinerary with stamps, passports, a code sheet, everything she needed.

"Rivas, huh?" she said.

"Yeah, we avoided Rayes. Too much paperwork follows your name now. You're quite famous, actually," Opal replied.

"And MI6?" Alicia inquired.

"Not notified, consulted, or invited," Opal said, and for the first time, her tone was cheery. "If they're trying to take down the Bureau, I'm glad to stick it to them one last time."

Then she lifted out a third folder, thin, new, with sharp corners, and placed it between us.

"Photographs. You've got information on Markov, the street, the distillery perimeter, the ID, even aerial recon from the Americans. Angleton's been pulling some favors. He's actually pretty nice, from what I hear."

I slowly opened the folder to see Markov's face, looking younger than the story said he was when he died. His eyes were bright, driven, and intelligent. The kind of eyes you saw in a man who still believed that the universe itself could be conquered if you just had enough math, enough knowledge, and enough good science.

Clearly, he hadn't tried hard enough.

There were grainy shots of Havana street cobbles, too. Some faces, a smear on the ground that looked like blood or spilled rum, and another photo caught the moment the tourist's camera fell—smoke bleeding out of the old, raggedy camera box, the bulb shattered, and glass scattered everywhere.

And, of course, the information on the laboratory: industrial, laminated, and far too clean.

Laboratorio Especial No. 7. Destilería Havana Club, Cárdenas.

I winced as my headache sharpened but continued reading. Alicia stood behind me now, her finger tracing the edge of the distillery map.

"Is the Soviet guard presence confirmed?" she asked.

"If our CIA sources are to be believed, yes," Opal replied. "And local rumor, of course. There are a lot of men with accents there. Foreign accents. And too many for a rum operation. Oh, and this is yours," she said, tapping the black attaché case.

I didn't touch it right away. It looked foreboding. "What is it?" I asked.

"Don't worry, it's not a Mirror component," Opal said. "At least, not quite directly. It's a portable Resonance Rig. We scavenged it from Invershiel before things went down there. Actually, from the field reports, I believe you and Ms. Rayes here have encountered it before."

"Really?" I asked.

"Yes," she confirmed, nodding.

"Well, that's charming," I said.

Alicia opened the case. Sure enough, inside, nestled carefully in foam, was the exact, beautiful creation of none other than Fraser-Smith himself—a small, satchel-sized box, the sort of thing a wireless field operator would use. It was wrapped carefully in oiled canvas. On top of it, three bare copper coils lay like ribs, each carefully laid and meticulously hand-wound across the box. Along the front edge ran another thin strip of brass, etched with a small inscription that I read with squinted eyes in the dim light: MODEL KX-7 Inductor Array. On the very front of the box was a small rotary dial and a toggle lever with three positions stamped next to it: NULL, COUPLE, BREAK. Next to this was a small pressure switch.

The gadget looked innocent enough with few markings or labels, nothing to tell a fool what it really was. Fraser-Smith built it in the Kingsway tunnels, tuning each coil by ear until they could mimic the Mirror's own heartbeat.

"And what's this for?" I asked as Alicia lifted it with both hands, careful and respectful.

"Well," Opal said, "that's where it gets interesting. Moreau herself led the science team in trying to investigate this smooth operator. And from what we can tell, it's built to disable Mirrors." She held up a finger. "This is where it gets fun."

"It's not fun enough yet?" I asked.

Alicia looked up from the Rig. "Sounds like it's about to be," she said.

Opal nodded. "This device, as best as we can tell, is able to disable Mirrors. But not just destroy them as you and Alicia have. It'll cut them down at the roots. I think Moreau mentioned something about that."

I nodded slowly. "Well, we'll have to experiment with it," I said. "I'm assuming you didn't have a Mirror lying around to test it out on."

Opal scoffed and slid a final paper across the table. "Here's some routing... We're not going to book you on the same carrier as a couple. It'll be too easy to trace. You'll move as civilians—separate rooms. Your emergency contact is Angleton. Once you're there, his station is going to provide a safe house and a driver, and a line back here. But you keep it short and keep it coded."

"And what if Angleton decides he wants the technology?" Alicia asked suddenly.

"Then remind him this operation is not a procurement," Opal said, her eyes hardening.

"What if he refuses that?" Alicia asked.

Opal didn't answer, but she didn't need to.

I carefully studied the itinerary, the neat lines, and the stamps. "What about weapons? Do we get our classics?" I asked.

Opal smiled. "We were going to procure extra weapons, but Moreau mentioned that you two have your preferred styles. Do you have them on you?"

I laughed. "Always," I replied.

"Perfect then."

Alicia had already fished hers out of her coat pocket and was looking at it carefully. "Think it's still operational," she said, then slipped it into her satchel without looking at it again.

I rolled my shoulders. I didn't say it, but I was excited. I'd given up trying to leave this life behind. The Mirror had left its effect on me permanently, and now I was determined to take it down and maybe die trying. I wouldn't mind it, that was for sure.

Opal carefully gathered the empty wrappers and dropped them into a metal bin. "You'll have three hours before you depart. Pack anything you need, burn what you shouldn't carry. You're going ghost. Again. Go ahead and meet me at the civilian door at 1900. The car will take you to the port."

"Burn what we shouldn't carry. I guess we could easily get burned ourselves on this mission." Alicia sounded worried.

Opal didn't respond.

"Which port?" I asked.

Opal's eyes lit up. "Don't you worry about that. Bureau tricks."

"Of course."

She paused at the door, her hand on the latch. "Oh, and Director Moreau requested I inform you of something."

Alicia looked up. "What?"

Opal hesitated, and for the first time, I saw some emotions flash across her face—more akin to upset than anything else.

"The Bureau can only pretend it isn't alive for so long," she said finally. "Moreau's taking heat for this, and a lot of it. If you fail loudly, she'll die quietly."

Then she left, the door clicking shut behind her.

For a moment, Alicia and I sat there alone—two new people with new names and old damage.

"So," I said finally, "Ana Rivas. That's a pretty interesting name."

She didn't smile.

"Martin Kale. Never met him," I said.

"Yes, you have," she replied, "a dozen times. You already know it. Men like you are always being hired to measure something that shouldn't be measured."

The throb behind my head worsened, and I rubbed my eyes, then my brow. "I guess we should split up before we leave. Less attention, right?"

Alicia's gaze remained fixed on the file. "We are splitting up. At least until we get there. Not different departures, but different seats. Different destinations on the way there."

"Fine," I replied. "Same destination once we get there, though."

She closed the file and finally looked up at me properly. "This is Angleton's request, you know," she said. "It's not ours, and it's not even Moreau's. This is the CIA using the Bureau, pulling it into its orbit."

"And what's the alternative?" I asked. "Do we let Havana start imploding like Prague? Let people drop dead on street corners while Philby and his stupid grin are left smiling in Washington with Medals of Honor?"

"Don't make it about him," she said.

"It's always damn well about him," I said, and I hated how bitter my own voice sounded. "He's the one... the rat that keeps showing up and ruining this."

She stood, carefully packing the satchel with precision: papers, gun, code sheet, detector, accessories.

"I know," she said almost coldly, "but this mission jeopardizes what little sanity we have left. We're already ghosts, Max, and if we bypass MI6, it's a declaration. There's no coming back from this."

"I know," I said.

"And you aren't exactly stable," she said quietly.

There it was. It wasn't cruel. It wasn't accusatory. Just a fact. I knew it, too. I couldn't even deny it. My first instinct was anger, but anger was never the right tool with Alicia. Instead, I fished in my pocket, produced a cigarette, and lit it. It didn't taste as good as the cigars from Cuba, but I smoked it anyway.

"I'll be stable enough," I said finally. "At this point, I'm convinced the only thing that gives me any stability is the hope that I can finish the Mirror once and for all, so it doesn't come back."

"And if we don't destroy it?" Alicia asked.

"Then I'll die trying," I replied.

"That's what you always say," she replied, her voice weary. "And you always mean it. That's the problem. You always want it, too."

She lowered her voice then. "Rosyth was supposed to be the last time, Max. Then Prague, then the Andes, then Invershiel. Every time we say one more, and every time the Mirror takes another damn bite out of us. Is this really what we want to be doing?"

"Do you think I don't know that?" I replied, exhaling smoke through my nose. "What's the alternative, though?"

"I think you're willing to let it happen, because you don't trust any version of yourself enough to fight for a life that isn't made out of missions like this."

That one hit clean. I hesitated for a second. For a second, I saw a different room: Lisbon sunlight, the typewriter, and coffee. Then I was back, and I stubbed the cigarette out too hard in the tray.

"You don't want to go, do you?" I finally asked.

"I didn't say that," she said, her mouth tight.

"Yeah, you did," I replied.

She looked past me, toward the closed door, and for a second, her eyes went blank. It was unusual for her, unusual for her to lose focus. But for a second, she had. Finally, she regained focus, and it was the Alicia I had always known again—concentrated and uptight.

"I just don't want a repeat of Scotland. I don't want to watch you disappear into something I can't follow."

"You followed me every time before," I said.

"And look what it got us. Almost killed us both," she retorted.

Finally, she spoke again. "Okay, Max, we go," she said. "Because if we don't, it spreads. But don't mistake that agreement for enthusiasm. I'm not excited about this."

"Don't worry, I won't," I said.

She nodded. "Good."

We left the safe room together, the corridor outside smelling of steam and varnish. Somewhere above, London kept raining and raining, as if it would never let up again.

We separated at the civilian door without ceremony. Opal's car would take us to the same point, but on different paths. The same noose, just different ropes.

Before I stepped out into the street, I patted my coat pocket and felt the cigar case there. None left, but I craved more.

CUBAN SLIDERS

And I supposed, now that I was going to Cuba, I would get them.

CHAPTER 5
FIRST FLUCTUATIONS

There we were together, yet not really together. That was the trick. In the departure hall, we stood in the same slow-moving queue as it inched beneath the lights, listening to the same canned loudspeaker cough out boarding calls and breathing the same air. Yet, we always kept more than a man's width between us—the width of a stranger. It was enough space for plausible deniability, but not quite enough to stop that old gravity from pulling us together.

London Airport in 1951 wore the weather like a bad conscience. The fog rolled in low and stubborn from the village of Heath Row, pressing itself against the glass as if it wanted answers. It dulled the sodium lights into weak halos and turned men into silhouettes—hats first, faces second, intentions never. The place smelled of aviation fuel and boiled tea that had been standing too long. Everything echoed: footsteps on polished concrete, the cough of engines warming their throats, and the clipped bark of porters who'd learned not to ask questions.

Inside the terminal, time moved sideways. Departure boards clicked and stalled. Paper tickets changed hands with the quiet gravity of passports stamped too often. Uniforms were everywhere—RAF blue, customs khaki, airline gray—each pretending to know what order looked like. BOAC crews leaned against counters, smoking like the future might be delayed again. Nobody smiled unless they were being paid to.

The windows looked out on a field of ghosts. Aircraft loomed and vanished, tails dissolving into mist, propellers ticking over like nervous habits. Somewhere out there, engines roared, then softened, then roared again—men arguing with weather they couldn't intimidate. Every takeoff felt provisional. Every landing felt earned.

This wasn't an airport built for comfort. It was built for departures—quiet ones, necessary ones, the kind that didn't expect applause. London Airport was a hinge in the world, creaking under the weight of secrets, sending people west with clean shirts and east with unfinished business. If you stood still long enough, the fog would take you. If you moved, it would remember you.

Outside the glass, the rain fell in sheets. It was the worst it had been in weeks, not so much falling as leaning, driven sideways by the wind that carried the scent of coal smoke, the Thames, and wet tarmac. The airport itself looked half-finished, like the rest of the country, with new concrete poured around old war-scarred bones. Men and women stood in line, the men wearing greatcoats and hats as they stamped their feet to keep warm, while the women clutched handbags as if fearing someone might steal them.

Martin Kale.

That's what it said on my passport as I stared at it. Shipping Surveyor. I held it, trying not to look like a man who had faked his way through the better half of a century. It was a good cover, and I was used to blending in. But I had grown tired of it by now. Tired of the official stamps and the sort of paperwork that soothed clerks and made doors open wide. This wasn't me, and it didn't soothe me either.

Alicia, or Ana Rivas today, stood about three places behind in the line. Her hair was tucked neatly, her posture straight as always, and her face calm. If anyone was watching us, they wouldn't see two of the Bureau's finest off for another mission, one that was highly unauthorized. Instead, they'd see two professionals heading to the Caribbean on regular trade business.

By the time we reached the counter, a BOAC clerk took my documents with his cold, pink fingers and a bored expression. He peered at them through his glasses, checking my name, itinerary, and face. I could tell in an instant he would rather be anywhere else.

"Mr. Kale, Martin," he said in a drab voice that perfectly matched his appearance.

Then he slid a paper ticket folder back at me. It was made of thick cardstock, with carbon copies. A baggage stub was stapled to the top, just another reminder of all the bureaucracy we had to make our way through.

"You'll be on a Lockheed Constellation to Shannon, then onward. Cabin baggage only, as noted. Please follow the rules."

"Yes, of course," I said, as if I'd always traveled this way. In reality, plane flights were rare for me. I had been on a few before, but this was going to be by far the longest flight. When I had a chance, I preferred to travel by boat.

Behind the clerk, there was an ashtray overflowing with cigarette stubs; I noticed it as I stepped past him. The whole airport smelled of smoke, men already drinking at the bar and smoking as if the altitude would require it. I didn't blame them either.

I didn't even look back at Alicia when she checked in; I only listened for her voice over the crowd when she spoke. Her voice was the type that anchored me, though I would never admit it to her face, much like a familiar song would anchor you even if you couldn't remember the words but only hum the tune.

We continued through passport control separately, waiting separately, and even boarding separately. However, the closer and closer the plane got, the louder my head began to complain.

That dull, aching throb and sharp pain behind my eye came back tenfold, as if it knew we were leaving the one place on Earth where the Mirror hadn't managed to entrench its roots yet.

Then again, there was Kingsway, so I wasn't even sure that was true.

A few minutes later, amid the busy, hectic blur, we had boarded our first flight. In 1951, unfortunately, there was no straight line from London to Havana, only a series of pauses, each one more difficult than the last. You didn't go to Havana so much as you were handed along, stamped, and weighed at each stage like something fragile that might explode or crack if mishandled. This was especially true if you were traveling for a clandestine operation under Bureau cover, with a passport that was technically real, and a name that was only mostly yours, as long as you remembered it.

As I headed for the flight, I carried only one bag—leather, scuffed, and older than it looked. It had no locks on it because there was nothing really worth mentioning in the bag. I kept my most important items on me at all times, including my weapon. If anyone wanted inside the bag, they would get there. The point wasn't really secrecy; it was plausibility, and as it went, I would have no plausible deniability if I seemed too cautious.

The aircraft was a BOAC Lockheed Constellation, its triple tail visible through the drizzle like a silhouette cut from the future, all curves and promise, with a pressurized cabin, a stewardess trained to smile through the rough turbulence, and engines that roared louder than you could think. One would board it by walking across the wet tarmac, collar up, pretending that the cold and damp didn't reach their bones. But it did, and I shivered as I walked.

The first leg of our journey took us west to Shannon. Before the Atlantic, Ireland was the last place you could catch a breath —a final refueling stop that carried strong tea and a terminal that felt as if it were some country house repurposed for the new idea of flight. We stretched our legs, and despite the fact that I could see Alicia at almost all times, I didn't dare speak to her. There were too many people around us, each one talking and making small talk, telling each other they were already halfway, which was a lie, but a comforting one. I didn't dare approach her in case some watchful eye would see that we were speaking too comfortably.

Instead, I watched the mechanics move with quiet efficiency around the aircraft, their hands blackened, their faces calm, as if they had done this countless times before.

Back aboard the flight, the cabin lights dimmed, the engines deepened and roared, and then there was nothing but ocean beneath us. I didn't like this, not at all. I much preferred to take a slow, steady ship across the ocean, especially because I trusted ships far more than I trusted these planes. Still, I allowed myself to relax and close my eyes and let the engines carry me over the Atlantic.

Transatlantic flying, as I knew only too well, was an endurance test disguised as progress. You would spend twelve, sometimes fourteen hours, depending on the weather, with stops that existed only on islands that seemingly had no other purpose than to provide respite for your flight and refueling. Whenever I slept, I slept badly, upright, listening to the hum and the thrum of the engines that never quite synchronized. We ate meals served on trays that rattled—chicken in sauce, overcooked vegetables, and bread that tasted stale. As had become my fall-back of late, I drank whisky. It helped the time pass, and with everyone else on the plane doing the same, I didn't feel so bad about my habits.

Somewhere over the Atlantic, my mind began to numb enough that I stopped thinking in terms of destinations and more in terms of survival. The Mirror had taught me long ago that motion didn't guarantee arrival, and as I watched the faces around me for signs of deja vu, recognition that shouldn't exist, and doppelgängers, I could feel a deep worry set in my stomach. But there were no signs, no issues that I could see—just tired civilians and a few businessmen dreaming of deals that would look different by the time they landed.

We touched down in Gander, Newfoundland, in the dark. It was cold, with the wind sharp enough to cut. Here again was another terminal that felt more provisional, as if it could be packed up and moved with a day's work. Another refuel, another stamp, and another smoke outside in the cold. I could hear the engines ticking in the distance as I exhaled, watching the smoke float into the sky. I knew we would wait once again until the flight was ready.

From Gander, we flew south to New York. Somewhere over the coast, dawn broke, the sky pale and soft with pastel hues. Idlewild Airport was new, sprawling, and confident in a way Europe no longer was after the war. Customs officers in clean uniforms with cleaner consciences patrolled the airport—something that you would never see in the small, rickety airports we had flown from before.

The coffee was strong, and though it tasted slightly burnt, it was enough to wake my mind and refocus me on my goal. I picked up a newspaper here for a few cents, already talking about Korea, communism, and things that could be resolved if the right men were put in charge. I shook my head while reading it. I wasn't quite sure what the world was coming to, but it was clear that it had already begun.

If Havana hadn't been our destination, New York was where the journey could have ended. This large, sprawling city was something else, and I did like it here. Memories flooded back about the Old Crow in Hell's Kitchen—the bar that started it all over again when Alicia appeared there one night. But Havana was our goal, and so we carried on. Some travelers stayed overnight, but Alicia and I did not. The Bureau always preferred momentum because momentum meant there was less time to be noticed.

We changed terminals, switched airlines, and flew with Pan Am this time. Another Constellation, this one painted like a flag with bright, vibrant colors. There were fewer businessmen now, and different passengers—more people with reasons they weren't going to explain. Men in lighter suits despite the season, and women wearing sunglasses they didn't need quite yet.

This was the flight that I needed—a flight that I felt surprisingly more comfortable on, as the flight south hugged the coast at first, then finally cut out over water again, settling into my stomach that same sense of unease. Florida appeared, then slipped away again beneath the clouds. The air around us grew warmer and heavier, and the cabin began to smell faintly of citrus and sweat. Now and then, the stewardess slipped into broken Spanish as she spoke, as if it were something that she was trying to suppress, some habit she didn't want us to know of, and yet it slipped out all the same.

By the time Cuba appeared beneath us, the light had changed. Havana rose out of the haze in pale geometry, with low buildings, wide streets, and the Malecón tracing the water like a scar that refused to heal. It looked peaceful from the air, peaceful enough to stay and forget my problems, yet I knew it likely was not.

José Martí Airport, formerly Rancho Boyeros, was small and loud, named after the plains it was on. It felt alive in a way that the northern airports did not, despite its smaller size. As I exited the plane and made my way into the airport, ceiling fans pushed hot air in lazy circles, and officials wore uniforms that had seen better days. Once again, we got our stamps—hard and decisive —as if they were asserting sovereignty with every motion.

As I stepped outside, the heat hit my face like a blast from a furnace. I had lost sight of Alicia now, but that was the plan. The plan was never to show our faces together, at least not in public, if we could help it. Cars waited that shouldn't have been there, men watching without even pretending not to. Somewhere nearby cheerful, loud music played from a local bar, as if it were trying to drown out the silence and awkwardness beneath it.

I adjusted my coat, immediately regretting it as the sweat

began to form on my skin, and sighed, rubbing my face to get rid of the headache that had begun as I stepped forward into a city balanced between what it was and what it was soon to become. Three days, if everything had gone right; slightly longer if it didn't. Though my lack of sleep was beginning to addle my mind, I estimated it had likely been four days—long enough for a man to change his mind twice and arrive anyway. I had done all of that and more in that time.

Though I wasn't much of a talker, I missed talking to Alicia. Luckily, a man in a linen suit waited near the taxi stand, reading a newspaper carefully while his eyes scanned the crowd with suspicious frequency. In an instant, my vision caught him, registering him as the outlier to the rest of the liars in the airport. As I approached, he looked up, lowered the paper by an inch, and then spoke.

"Mr. Kale?" he said in English.

His accent was American; I identified that instantly, but it was careful and distinct—East Coast, educated, and clipped.

"Depends on who's asking," I shot back.

He smiled faintly, as if he'd heard the line one too many times before, but didn't quite hate it.

"Consular transport," he muttered. "Your car's this way."

The car rattled along the Havana streets, and as I looked out the window, I saw the beautiful city in which we would be staying—the city we were supposed to save, if the rumors were to be believed.

We arrived at the safe house. It wasn't a house, really. It was an apartment above a shop that sold radios and replacement valves—a place where men would shop rarely and only if they had a purpose. The shop was busy, but I was quickly guided up a stairwell thick with the scent of frying plantains, oil, and the heat of electronics.

And then there I was. Inside, it was dim and cool, with the shutters drawn. On a table sat a shortwave set, already tuned, a fan, and a map of Havana pinned to the wall with red dots marking places that mattered to us. The man who had driven me here exited quietly before I could speak to him.

For about ten minutes or so, the room was silent until Alicia arrived, brought in through a separate entrance. She stepped into the room, and though the temperature itself didn't change, the air felt softer all at once. The American wearing the linen suit was back now, and he addressed both of us.

"Angleton sends his regards," he said. "Tomorrow night, he'll meet you."

"Where is he, anyway? You're not Angleton," Alicia said.

"No, ma'am, I am not," he replied.

"So what are you?" I asked.

"A man who enjoys staying alive," he replied with a hint of sarcasm.

"Your equipment made it through?" he asked, nodding toward the black attaché case.

Alicia nodded, opening the case without ceremony. The portable rig created by Fraser-Smith sat inside like a piece of surgery, looking as it had the first time we had seen it, all those years ago in Invershiel. She lifted it out and set it on the table next to the radio, carefully, respectfully, as if not to break it. I wasn't quite sure what to think of the rig. It looked fine, but my mind wasn't attuned to the details or nuances of quantum science, so I just hoped it would work.

The American's eyes lingered on it, looking at it up and down suspiciously, as if it were about to spring to life.

"I've heard rumors of that thing," he said quietly, "From Intel. Let's hope that it helps us with Moscow. They've got men guarding their rum distillery like it's a bank."

"And I doubt they're guarding rum," I replied.

"You would be correct, sir."

He then gave us keys, a local contact name, and warned us about police checkpoints and military movements in Cuba. That sounded rehearsed and flat, as if it had been his job to do so.

Afterward, he departed again, once again never asking for thanks.

The door finally shut with a click, and for a good five minutes, Alicia and I stood in the room, quiet and unmoving. Havana's sounds outside were muted—distant horns, music, and voices—all sounding far too happy for my own sense of paranoia that had become heightened the second we set foot here.

Alicia looked at me over the rig. "Do you feel it?" she asked.

"Yes," I said.

I didn't want to answer her. I was reluctant to admit it because answering made it real. But I could feel it. I could feel that deep, energetic pulse within my body that I could not mistake for anything else. I had felt it so many times by now that it had become second nature: the pulse of the Mirror.

The next few days, we did what we always did: learned the rhythm of the place so we could hear when it broke. We walked throughout Old Havana in daylight under our covers, posing as tradespeople with clipboards and mild boredom. We drank coffee in the places Americans frequented, watched dock workers unload cargo, and tried to figure out which crates were heavier than they had any right to be.

However, the whole time, it became clear that the city was much worse than we had ever experienced before. I noticed it the first night we were there. As I slept, I suddenly opened my eyes, and for a brief moment, it felt as if the world was upside down—as if I were falling from the bed onto the floor, and the floor had become the ceiling. And then I was back.

The next day, the city felt slightly out of register, like a film projector running a fraction too fast and glitching all the time.

The first slip I noticed after sleeping was small. I stood on a corner near Obispo, watching a man push a cart of guavas. I watched a woman in a violet dress arguing with a policeman. A bright green car rolled past, far too bright, splashing through a puddle that shouldn't have existed because it hadn't rained.

It took me a second, but I realized something was off, and I blinked again, trying to figure out what it was. Suddenly, it was as if the guava cart was back where it had started. The woman repeated the same sentence, arguing with the police officer in the same manner. And there, rolling past again, was the green car, splashing the same puddle, the same arc of water that splashed up against my feet.

I could feel a sense of panic setting in, and it didn't help that when I looked down at my shoes, they were dry. My stomach tightened, my headache flared, and I felt a sharp pang between my eyes. I couldn't take it on—not right now. I turned away quickly to avoid, rather than confront, the details. Alicia and I would deal with it together at another time, I figured.

That night, back in the safe house, my pocket watch stopped at 11:17 and remained frozen for two hours. Alicia sat at the table quietly with the rig, fiddling with it and trying to figure out how it worked. She had been filled in by Opal on the details, but still, none of us really knew for sure. The only one who might have, Hawthorne, was nowhere to be seen—nowhere but within our minds, at least for now.

Alicia heard it too, though. She heard the silence. As she messed with the rig, the Geiger counter on the table spun in little spindle circles, the needle trembling back and forth. It wasn't high enough to scream, but it was high enough to whisper.

"Whatever this is," she said after a long moment, finally breaking the silence, "it's not just one point-source leak. It feels like it's background."

"Like Scotland," I murmured.

Her jaw clamped shut, and I could see the muscles in her neck and shoulders working before she spoke again.

"Not like Scotland," she said. "Far worse than Scotland. Scotland was one machine in a room. In an area where no one cared. This feels different—as if this room itself is somehow connected to the machine."

I sighed and paced back and forth, pouring out a measure of local, cheap rum and draining the glass without enjoying it.

"And what does that mean?" I asked.

"If I'm correct," she said, "it means Havana is already inside the field... inside the pulse. And so are you and I."

I was going to make a joke about being inside fields as part of my career, but the words didn't come. Instead, I simply asked, "So, how long do we have then? What happens? And what's their plan with this version of the Mirror?"

She didn't look up from the rig. "I don't think we have long," she said finally.

We met Angleton after dusk—not at the Embassy, of course. That was too official and would attract too many names for an operation like this, which was so off the books that even the vast majority of the CIA likely didn't know about it. Instead, we met him at a hotel bar where the music played in the background, thick with smoke and the scent of rum.

I saw him first. He was thinner than I had expected, to be honest. He wore a linen suit, a loosened tie, and was sweating at his temples, though he seemed to ignore the sweat beading on his head. His eyes, however, were awake in a way the rest of his disheveled form wasn't. They were eyes that I recognized instantly because they were the same as mine—eyes that could recognize patterns in a moment. The eyes of a man who could stare at a wall of static and find a face.

As we approached, he stood, polite and formal, waiting half a beat, as if measuring whether or not we were going to look over our shoulders before we sat down. I could see in his face a certain level of nervous paranoia. But he finally spoke.

"Mr. Kale, Miss Rivas." Then he spoke quieter again as we took the booth. "Calder. Artemis. Or should I say Rayes?"

Neither of us offered a hand to shake, and Angleton didn't either. Instead, he signaled to the barman without looking at him, ordering drinks for us as if he had known us for years. Something for me and something clear for Alicia. Something lighter. He didn't ask, just did it, and then watched us out of the corner of his eyes, as if waiting for one of us to correct him.

I could tell that Angleton was all about testing. He was a man who wanted to test everything to see if he got it right or wrong and to see who was true to the words they said. He fished in his pocket, and a second later, he had a cigarette in his fingers, though he didn't light it—not yet.

"You know," he began, "I don't like dragging people into things."

It wasn't an apology. It felt more like an assessment. But he continued on. "But Kim—"

"Don't say his name like it's an apology," I cut in. "If you suspect him, good. That's enough."

Angleton's mouth tightened. "I wouldn't say suspect," he began, but I cut him off again.

"Listen, Angleton," I said. "I know you have a vested interest in Philby's innocence. But you doing this alone proves that you care more about the truth than about your own reputation. So let's begin, shall we?"

He didn't argue, simply inclining his head once, conceding the point, and finally, he struck a match to light his cigarette. For a second, the flame reflecting against his face made him seem older.

"Well, then, all right," he said. "I'll say it in the proper way. There's a man with access who doesn't deserve it."

He took a slow drag, then let the smoke escape and watched it float.

"The Havana station," he continued, "has been hearing noise. Not just gossip, either. Guards at the rum distillery at Cárdenas. Not Batista's people, not Cuban, either. Foreign. And, ah, right, a vessel came in with technical cargo. It was marked Agricultural Equipment, but it wasn't."

"How sure are you about Soviet personnel?" Alicia asked, leaning forward slightly.

He started, as if he'd forgotten she was there. Not hostile, but calculating. Finally, he spoke.

"Certainty is a luxury we don't have," he said. Then, after a beat, more reluctantly, he went on. "I'm certain enough to ruin myself if I'm wrong."

"And Philby?" I asked, taking a slow sip of my drink.

Angleton didn't answer right away. Instead, he tapped ash into the tray with care, too meticulously, as if he were obsessed with where every bit of it landed. At last, he spoke. "Kim Philby urged me to let it die. Not once, either. Repeatedly. With far too much enthusiasm. And when someone wants you to stop looking, it's usually because there's something to find. At least, that's what I've always found."

His gaze drifted past us, to the bar's mirror and the reflections that shimmered in the surface. He continued speaking.

"I don't know whether or not Kim Philby is innocent or guilty. At first, I thought he was innocent. But new information has come to light—new information even beyond this—that makes me question him."

Alicia's expression didn't change. But her eyes grew slightly colder, and I could tell something about Angleton's tone had irritated her.

"And you brought this to us because you can't bring it to MI6 or anyone else, is that correct?" she asked.

"Yes," Angleton replied bluntly. "If I bring it to MI6, it enters a channel he can touch. And once something enters a compromised channel, well, you might as well just assume you've failed."

He took another drag on his cigarette. I nodded. I could feel a sense of camaraderie with Angleton, though I wasn't sure I fully trusted the man. What he had said was true. Philby didn't have to hold a gun because he held access, committees, and the story. As of now, Philby was the man in charge. Then Angleton leaned in closer—just enough to make it intimate, but not quite friendly.

"Here's what you need to know," he said. "Cárdenas—that's where the distillery is—up the coast a bit. It's a quiet town, from what I hear. Easy to disappear someone, but harder to disappear a machine, unless you build it in a place that no one asks questions."

"Like a rum distillery," I said.

"Rum," Angleton said, his eyes narrowing slightly. He nodded. "Rum is the place."

Alicia's eyes darted to me briefly, and then she refocused on Angleton.

"We need recon first," she said. "No contact, no crazy heroics. Just eyes on the site so we actually know what we're getting into and we don't go in blind."

Something in Angleton's expression told me that he had heard exactly what I had in Alicia's statement. A part of the sentence that was meant for me instead of him. But he nodded at last.

"Very well," he said. "There are ways to get you moving without attaching my name to this whole ordeal. We can provide a car—at least the station can—and a driver who will keep his mouth shut and would sooner go down than betray his government. But"—he raised a finger, his voice flattening—"remember, if this goes wrong, officially I've never met either of you. You'll keep me out of it, and I will deny ever having set this up."

"Join the club," I said.

He leaned back, exhaling slowly, and for the first time, he looked tired in a way that wasn't physical, as if he were a man who had been listening to conflicting voices in his head and didn't know which ones to trust.

"Oh, and one more thing. London is already smoothing this whole ordeal down. Moreau asked me to tell you that. Filing it off into a harmless shape. And if Kim Philby gets wind of it, well, he'll feel the pressure change and he'll start pulling strings. And that—" He let the sentence trail off.

"And that could be bad," I finished.

"Let him pull," Alicia said, her voice cold. "I'm done being pushed around by Kim Philby."

I finished my drink, set the glass down, and leaned back slightly. The throbbing in my head had worsened now, syncing with the music. Outside, the lights began to come on one by one, as if someone were flipping switches in a model city. It felt staged—all of it felt staged, and I didn't like it one bit, but there was nothing I could do.

"All right then," I said. "We go tonight."

Alicia nodded, not arguing, her mind already whirring with the plan. For a second more, Angleton watched us, then gave a small, humorless smile and nodded slightly.

"Just be careful," he said. "I don't know much about your Mirror technology, but whatever this is"—he glanced again at the bar's mirror—"it feels like something that was designed rather than an accident. There's something deeper going on here. And I might not know what it is, but I damn well know it exists."

I stood. "I agree," I said. "It feels like the whole place is rippling."

"My driver'll pick you up," he called over his shoulder, already leaving. "Address is on the note on the table."

I glanced down. Sure enough, he'd left a small, neatly folded paper there for us to retrieve.

We parted ways, and we stepped back into the Havana heat, the music from the bar following us down the street—bright, fast, and alive, chaotic even, with a hint of frantic beats that underlaid it.

Somewhere out beyond the coast road to Cárdenas, something old and metallic thrummed in the dark, beginning to wake up.

CHAPTER 6
DISTILLERY DISCOVERY

After meeting with Angleton, we didn't waste any time. That was the first rule of surviving this kind of clandestine work: momentum. As soon as you stopped moving, even for a second, the world would catch up, and you often wouldn't like the result. If it caught up, it would start asking questions. And if people asked the wrong questions in the wrong type of room, you would end up in a shallow grave with your pockets turned inside out and your name never even mentioned in the paperwork. That was what had happened when Sosa had found us in the Andes all those years ago, and that was what we were trying to avoid here in Havana.

Havana was far too loud to think in, anyway. We left the hotel bar on separate streets, looped wide, doubled back, and then met up again where the street lamps thinned out and the music couldn't quite reach. We were around a block from the Prado, the city still pretending it was a party. But just two blocks away from there, it began to look like a place where men disappeared, never to be found again.

Angleton's driver, if that's what he really was, waited where Angleton had said he would be. He drove a tired black sedan with Cuban plates, its nose pointed toward the darker road. It was the kind of car that looked normal, but when you inspected it too closely, you realized that it was trying too hard to be normal. But that was the point.

The driver didn't give us his name, and he didn't need to. He simply opened the back door and let us slide into the seats. The upholstery smelled of something foul, like a mix of sweat, old tobacco, and a faint tang of vomit. I sighed and closed my eyes for a second. I hadn't been sleeping well lately due to the constant headache. I told myself that it would all get better after this mission. I told myself a lot of things as I sat there.

Alicia, however, ever steadfast, sat beside me, her posture straight and her eyes forward. She had traded her daytime poise for nighttime economy with her coat collar up, her hair pinned back, and her clothes clean and primed. She was a compact dark shape that blended into the low light—all the better for what we were about to do.

Our driver pulled away gently from the curb, and Havana fell behind us into pieces: neon lights, laughter, music, pavement, and then simply darkness, with the streetlights flickering and dimming into nothing as we traveled along the coastal road north. The air tasted of salt more than gasoline by now.

Though the night was warm, it wasn't the comforting type of warmth. It was the sweltering type that made you sweat continually until you had sweated out more than you had drunk in the past week. The humidity clung to the inside of the car, and every time we hit a bump, the suspension groaned like something nasty. Clearly, it had seen better days.

We passed cane fields, palms, and the occasional lean-to or shack that looked as if it had been abandoned by whatever owner had originally constructed it. Dogs that didn't bother moving from the heat. Men on bicycles with no lights. And the whole time, I could feel that faint pulse deep in my bones—a pressure I had learned to recognize and that I had become attuned to far too often to miss.

The Mirror.

The headache had begun back in the bar when Angleton had mentioned the word Cárdenas, but now it built slowly and steadily, a dull throb behind the eye that worsened with every passing moment. I checked my pocket watch without meaning to, watching the hands stuttering yet still moving. I wasn't quite sure how to take it.

Alicia watched me, her eyes filled with concern.

"Don't," she said quietly.

"What?" I asked. "I didn't say anything."

"You didn't have to, Max. Just focus. Focus on what's in front of us."

Outside, road signs came and went, Spanish names painted in white on dark billboards. They were the kind of thing you'd see anywhere in the world if you ignored the language written on them.

Eventually, as the dull monotony deepened, the driver spoke.

"Two hours, maybe less. Depends on rotations." His voice sounded distinctly Cuban.

"Rotations?" I asked.

He shrugged without taking his eyes off the road. "New faces, not Cuban. Asking questions they shouldn't know how to ask."

"The Soviets?" Alicia asked.

"Their accents are like it, and guns that aren't from here," he said. "It's likely."

That settled it. For whatever reason—maybe it was his paranoia, or maybe it was because he didn't fully want to believe that Kim Philby was guilty—Angleton hadn't outright confirmed that the Soviets were the ones at Cárdenas. At least not to us. But that settled it for me. It wasn't the kind of proof a committee would accept, but committees didn't matter to us anymore. Not after Rosyth. Not after Invershiel. Not after the way that I had been betrayed by every organization I trusted.

Except for maybe the Bureau, if you considered this not to be a betrayal. Then again, I wasn't sure if it was or not.

The cane fields thickened, and the salt in the air faded away, giving way to a more earthy scent. The sky above was still hard black, prickled with stars that shone far brighter than I was used to. Then, far ahead, a low industrial silhouette rose from the darkness, jagged and foreboding, as if it had appeared there out of nowhere.

Destilería Havana Club.

Quite a way out of town, the distillery sat as if it had been exiled. It was a cluster of small buildings, low warehouses, tall fermenting towers, and a main brick structure with a smokestack that wasn't smoking. The whole place had been fenced off and illuminated by floodlights that shone bright, creating even deeper shadows between the cones of white. It was the kind of lighting that a simple rum distillery would have never installed, at least if I had to guess.

The driver quickly killed the headlights and let the car coast into a ditch lane surrounded by tall grass. He didn't say a word, but I knew this was our signal. We slid out into the night, moving slowly and staying close to the earth.

The heat wave washed over me like a heavy blanket. However, this heat was even more intense than the Havana heat we were used to so far. We were trapped with the industrial wet smell of yeast and old molasses that signaled a rum facility, and yet somewhere inside the facility, machinery clanked quietly. I could hear it thrumming far off in the distance, but of course, that didn't confirm anything. And so we continued on.

Alicia held up the Geiger counter we had brought with us. We hadn't brought the attaché case with the portable rig made by Fraser-Smith. This was simply a reconnaissance mission—a way for us to confirm whether or not we were actually needed here. And so she held the counter, watching it carefully as we moved along the fence line.

The perimeter was a patchwork of chain-link, sections of corrugated sheet, and older iron in places where the rum business had been here longer than any Soviet project that might have replaced it. There was no one out here, but in the distance, we saw silhouettes with disciplined spacing. Three—no, two—men, then another pair quickly moving in opposite directions like clockwork.

"Well, I'll be damned," I muttered.

Sure enough, their uniforms were ill-suited for Cuba. The cuts were too tight at the shoulders, and their boots were too heavy. The way they held their rifles was enough for me. They were comfortable with the weight, not showing it off, but holding the guns accurately and steadfastly, as if they had been trained for many years to reach such competency.

Alicia slunk along behind me, finally crouching behind a stack of empty barrels just outside the fence and peered through a gap.

"Interval?" she asked quietly.

I watched the closest patrol pass a floodlight, their shadows stretching thin and long against the packed dirt.

"Not sure," I said. "Seventy, maybe eighty seconds. They're overlapping."

She nodded, though she didn't answer. I knew, however, she had come to the same conclusion that I had. This was not a rum distillery, not even a military warehouse. Whatever this operation was, it was top-notch, and it was professional. Whatever this operation was, it had been installed here for the sole purpose of keeping it quiet and keeping it away from prying eyes like ours.

And that was exactly what we were here to find out.

We kept moving. The fence line dipped behind a storage building, and here the lights thinned out as the crickets' buzz began to emerge from the darkness. Here was a quiet place—the perfect place for an entrance.

Suddenly, Alicia stopped abruptly, kneeling down and reaching out, her fingers hovering over the fence without touching it. Then she moved lower toward a section where the ground had been dusted slightly, as if someone had been there recently and tried to erase it. Within seconds, she found it, and I saw it too right afterward.

A cut.

It wasn't a crude break or a tear. It was a clean section of wire that had been snipped then re-twisted back into place with care—more care than any regular soldier would have taken; most wouldn't have even caught it. But Alicia was unbeatable when it came to finding small details like this. I preferred to look at the broad picture, but she was always obsessing over the small things.

Someone had already been coming and going into the facility.

"Doesn't look like Soviet workmanship," Alicia whispered. "Don't see why they'd break into their own facility."

"Not Bureau either, unless Moreau is double-crossing us," I said. "Do you think it's CIA?"

"That or someone who wants us to think it's the CIA," she muttered.

I nodded. I was usually the suspicious one, but whatever this was, it had drawn her attention. And that meant it was something worth being suspicious about.

She pulled a small flashlight from her pocket, which we had packed, thumbed it on for a second, then turned it off again. In that instant, I saw a faint smear of something dark against the wire—grease or blood, though I couldn't tell which in the light.

Still, we had people to see and places to be. We needed to confirm beyond a shadow of a doubt what exactly the Russians were doing in this facility. And so we continued on.

Close to the perimeter, a low building sat, half hidden behind stacked crates stamped with export marks. Behind this building, set into a concrete loading bay, was a metal door. It wasn't a typical warehouse door—not wide enough for barrels.

I stared at it, then shook my head.

"That door," I said. "Look at it."

Alicia squinted into the darkness before turning to me.

"What about it?" she whispered.

"Doesn't look regular," I said. "And listen to the noise."

She hesitated, and a low rumbling emanated from the door.

"What do you think it is, Max?" she asked.

"The door is set deep, which means it's connected to some sort of mechanism," I said. "And that noise... that can only mean one thing. I think that's a freight elevator."

The door was thick—industrial—and painted a tired green that had been touched up recently. It had a particular look, like hardware chosen by men who expected pressure, weight, and secrecy.

Alicia nodded. It was the kind of door you built when you didn't want the world to know that there was something hidden underneath.

And yet, it was indistinguishable.

I kept watch, watching the shadows carefully and looking for patrols as they passed. No patrols within thirty seconds, then sixty. Like a panther on the prowl, I moved forward.

"Max!" Alicia hissed softly behind me.

"I know, I know," I said, never turning my head. "I'm not opening it. Just looking."

"Looking could get us killed."

"Yeah, that's been the theme," I replied. "But that's also what we're here to do."

And so I crouched low and made my way toward the elevator until eventually I had reached it. I crouched down by the door. The air around it felt wrong. It didn't feel cold exactly, but it felt thin. I could feel the electricity in it. I could tell instantly what it was.

For a second, I hesitated. I didn't want to touch it, but then my hand moved anyway, my fingertips stretching toward the door. I could hear Alicia's sharp inhale behind me. But my mind was set.

The moment my fingertips touched the steel, the headache spiked, as if a needle had been driven straight through my eye and into the center of my skull. I grunted and winced. The door itself vibrated—not with the vibration of machinery or the vibration of mechanics. This was the vibration of something else. A deep, low hum that you couldn't so much hear as feel in your teeth.

That hum was unmistakable. That hum was the Mirror.

Rosyth Dockyard had had the same hum, and Invershiel had the same. They all smelled slightly different, but they all operated exactly the same.

The world tilted.

For a second, I wasn't in Cuba. I didn't know where I was. It was pitch-black darkness around me. And just like that, I saw cranes black against the Scottish sky, flapping their stretched wings and moving like slow insects inching across the darkness. I saw water, dark and heavy, and men in coats. Then I saw a brass frame catching reflections of the light.

Then, as if it were a bad splice in some film, I snapped back. I was back, standing, my hand still against the door. I jerked my hand away as fast as I could, nearly convulsing.

Alicia was beside me instantly, one hand gripping my sleeve, the other already bringing the Geiger counter closer without exposing it to the floodlights. The little dial on the device whirred, spinning round and round, as if it had caught something that even the device couldn't process.

"You felt it?" she asked, her voice urgent.

"Yeah," I managed to reply. My voice was shaky, wrong, and far too thin.

She nodded, fiddling with the Geiger counter she had brought, trying to get a smooth reading. It was an impossible task; however, the little machine whirred as if it were haunted. We had confirmed everything we needed. With the pulse I had felt and the counter whirring like some wounded animal, there was nothing else to look at, nothing else to investigate. It was clear that something beneath the dirt in this distillery in Cuba was related to the Mirror… or maybe the Mirror itself.

Alicia tapped the dial, almost in shock. "It's not residual, either," she whispered.

"How bad do you think?" I asked, reluctant to even speak.

"Active," she said, meeting my gaze, "and closer than we'd like."

I nodded. That was the last thing I wanted to hear, yet it was what I already knew.

At that moment, patrol lights shifted, and I heard a boot scuffing the gravel somewhere off in the distance. A low voice spoke Russian, though I couldn't make out the words—casual and bored, the kind of boredom that happens when you are too far from home, deep in a foreign country where no one knows your name.

I could feel the pressure again, but this time, I felt something else. It was as if a set of eyes were on me, all around me, watching me. As if something could sense my presence. Not a man or even a machine. Maybe it was the Mirror, maybe it was the Mirror web. I'd felt this way before, back when I had previously had an encounter with El Cuadro, the growing sentience that the Mirror possessed, and I wondered if it was the same thing. When the Mirror was built, El Cuadro "woke up" as an emergent consciousness of the actual device itself, and it was threatening. The Mirror had always felt to me like a room I didn't belong in—a room that had one door already locked to keep you inside.

"We need to go," Alicia said, already retreating from the door.

I nodded, silent and compliant. I was still too shaken, and we moved away from the loading bay, back along the fence line, using the shadows and keeping low so we avoided any trouble. Luckily, they didn't catch us.

The driver was still where we'd left him, a dark shape by the car, the engine off so it didn't attract any attention. As we emerged from the sugar cane, he nodded curtly, ground out a cigarette beneath his boot, and stepped into the car, starting the engine as quietly as a 1951 sedan could. He didn't ask any questions, and for that, I was grateful.

We rolled gently away from the distillery, the lights off until we hit the main road, and then the engine roared to life as the man stepped on the pedal and the headlights bloomed. That was what I wanted more than anything: to escape from whatever field I had felt. The pocket watch ticked too loudly in my coat. It was hard for me to tell whether it was the watch or my own pulse, thrumming in my head, the headache worse than ever.

Alicia sat with her knees angled toward the door, her gun hidden but—I knew—at the ready, her eyes fixed on the pitch black outside the window. Though her face was calm, I could see there was tension etched in every fiber of her being. Nothing about this sat right with her. I knew that much, though I didn't want to bring it up, not now.

I waited and let her simmer until she finally spoke.

"You touched it," she said after a while.

"Wasn't that the point?"

"The point was recon."

"Yeah, and I reconned," I replied. "It's awake, and it's somewhere in there."

She didn't look at me. "You're not invincible, you know."

"No," I agreed, almost laughing. "I'm just really damn unlucky."

Silence stretched between us, broken only by the tires rolling against the road and the insects hitting the windshield. My headache continued to pulse, and for a minute, I could have sworn the same roadside shack passed us twice. The same single lantern flame lit, the same leaning porch, the same broken window. But then, as I turned to look, it was gone again, swallowed by the cane fields and the dark.

It might not have been real, but it might have been.

Finally, Alicia spoke again.

"We can't go in through that door, Max. I know what you're thinking," she said.

"Why not?" I asked.

"Because it's the obvious way," she muttered. "And because you touching it almost made you bleed."

"Almost, but it didn't," I said.

She finally looked at me, her eyes sharp. For the first time, her eyes themselves showed concern, not just the tense way in which she held herself.

"Max." That was all she said. My name. But it was enough. It got the point across, and I nodded.

"All right," I said. "I'll focus. I won't do anything harsh or rash. So how do we do it?"

She exhaled slowly, taking a deep breath to compose herself before she spoke.

"All right," she said. "What about rooftop vents?"

"Go on."

"Buildings like that—fermentation buildings—need to breathe. I learned about it from my mother. They'll have ducting, grilles, and service hatches. The Soviets will guard the ground like soldiers, but they'll forget the roof. They're not experienced in the ways of any rum distillery."

I nodded. That sounded exactly like Alicia. It was well-thought-out and calculated.

"Rooftops," I echoed. "Yeah, that sounds like a plan."

The driver glanced at us once in the rearview mirror, then back to the road.

"Smart," he muttered. "If you two need help…"

"We're not bringing you in," Alicia said to him, though she looked at me. "We're not bringing you in. You'll drop us off, and you leave."

"Not my call," he said.

"It's mine," she replied, her voice flat.

He didn't respond, but for a second his hands tightened on the wheel.

We continued driving, and we hit a stretch of road where the cane grew taller, the night thicker than ever, and the air more dense and filled with moisture. I closed my eyes for a second, leaning back. In a flash, I could hear Hawthorne's voice echoing through the static.

Cut the roots.

Another flash, and I saw Philby smile—so bright, so boyish, so innocent, like a boy caught with his hand in the biscuit tin.

Then I felt a weird, strange sensation. The faintest sensation. Almost impossibly gentle, as if a fingertip were tracing, probing the inside of my skull. I opened my eyes.

Alicia was watching me intently. I didn't say anything. I didn't know if she felt what I felt, but I just stared at her.

"Max," she said. "We don't have time for you to unravel."

I could feel anger rising in my veins, but I swallowed it, pushing it down and out of my mind. I finally nodded.

"Then let's not waste time," I said. "We'll go back tonight."

The safe house felt cool when we returned—cooler than the outside, at least, with the fans working vibrantly. But it was a temporary, artificial cool, brought on with shutters and fans that didn't truly register. The radio sat on the table next to the attaché case, the city outside alive and laughing, still selling rum to tourists who had no idea they were drinking beside a rift in reality just waiting to explode.

Alicia carefully set the Geiger counter down and began taking notes: the patrol interval, the guard count, and even possible entry options. She wrote everything she could, as if she could force the world to behave if only she wrote long enough.

I wished I had whisky, but there was none anymore—none here, at least, since I'd drunk the entire supply within the first few hours of arrival. I poured a glass of water and let it sit there, not drinking it, unwilling to quench my thirst. My hands were shaking too much.

Just then, the shortwave hissed softly, a staticky noise erupting from it, the set crackling with a coded burst—rapid, clean. The driver, who was still here despite Alicia's orders, moved silently to the radio with the ease of a man who had done this many times over. He adjusted the tuning, listened, then looked to us.

"From Washington," he said. "It's for you. Angleton's channel."

Alicia nodded, crossed the room, and sat beside it, her code sheet out, pencil poised. The message came again, slower, repeated, and Alicia transcribed it, then began to decode it silently. Her expression tightened as she did, and I watched her.

"What is it?" I asked.

"A Soviet research vessel is entering Havana," she said. "Tonight. Technical cargo, marked special."

My stomach sank.

"It'll be offloading to the distillery," I said.

"More than likely," she replied. "Angleton wants us to know before it disappears."

I felt the weight of the situation heavy on my chest, the way it was all going to hell already, just like it always did with every clandestine operation we had ever run. But this time, we were on the clock. Once this went underground, it became heavily guarded again. There was a chance here.

Alicia reached for the microphone, but before she could key it, the radio hiss shifted again, and a different signal cut in. Bureau encryption this time, from London.

Alicia froze and then keyed the set. "This is Rivas. Come through. This is Rivas," she said. "Go ahead."

There was a moment of static, then Opal's voice came through the line, direct over the wire and priority-clear.

"Director on the line, priority," she said. "Stand by."

The line popped, and then Moreau's voice came through, sharp as a knife.

"Ana. Kale. You two there?"

I leaned in. "Here," I said.

Moreau didn't waste time. "Angleton informed us of the vessel," she said. "You will not allow that cargo to be secured."

"Acknowledged," Alicia said, already turning to the map.

Moreau continued, her voice hardening. "If that vessel's cargo reaches Cárdenas, we don't know what will happen. Immediate action. We can't confirm, but we believe it may be transporting a Mirror core. And if it reaches the distillery, you'll be fighting the machine at full strength. If you can intercept and destroy it in transit, do so."

"And if we can't?" I asked.

"Then you'll have to adapt and remember why you're there," she replied. "We are not collecting these artifacts. We are not bargaining. Not with the CIA, not with the Russians, or anyone."

For a second, her voice softened, then she continued, "Don't let them bury this thing deeper. Good?"

"Understood," Alicia said.

"Good," Moreau replied. "Then go. And Calder?"

I stiffened. "Yeah?"

She paused for a second. "Just make sure you trust Rayes, not the echoes," she said quietly. "I know more than anyone how the Mirror can change you."

Then the transmission ended. The radio went back to ordinary static as if nothing had happened.

Outside, I could hear music drifting in from the parties, the mambo, and the laughter. Next to me, Alicia was already deep at work on the harbor map, her finger tracing a red dot near the docks.

"If they're bringing it by sea," she said, "we don't have long. Otherwise, we'll sit here and watch the city rot."

I checked my pocket watch again, watching the second hand stutter—once, twice, thrice—before it jumped forward three seconds as if it had lost patience.

"Looks like we gotta change plans," I said, looking up at Alicia.

Her eyes met mine, and the mask slipped just enough for me to see the fear, anger, and determination underneath her façade.

"Let's do it," she said. "We hit the harbor."

CHAPTER 7
HARBOR HOSTILITIES

Outside our safe house, Havana sounded as if it were laughing at us through the shutters. Horns, music, and a drunk shouting at someone. Whether he loved or hated them, I couldn't tell. The volume was obnoxious. The city seemed to be in a constant state of motion.

The building sweated in the heat, the walls damp to the touch, the paint soft around the edges, as if it were simply trying to melt off and leak into the gutters. The fan swirled the warm air around in lazy circles, not really cooling anything but merely moving the misery around, offering a breath of fresh air only once in a while.

Alicia had the shortwave set open, carefully tuning the dial. A one-time pad lay beside her, weighed down by a paperclip, her pencil at the ready. The satchel sat on the floor with its mouth open, as if it were waiting to swallow whatever came next. On the other side of the room, the portable rig sat on a folded towel; we'd set it there after removing it from the case again only a few minutes prior.

The rig, of course, would be instrumental in whatever we were to do here in Havana. But Alicia was still figuring out exactly what it did.

"You sure the vessel's tonight?" I asked. "How do we know we can trust Angleton?"

Alicia didn't look up. "The cable said tonight, and Moreau said it was immediate. That means we're already late. And even if I don't trust Angleton, I trust Director Moreau."

I nodded, pouring myself a glass of water. Just like the other one, I stared at it, then put it down untouched. I didn't trust myself to stomach it—not yet. And maybe if this all went according to plan, I could pick up some whisky afterward.

Behind me, the radio's hiss shifted, and a thin carrier tone pierced through the static before cutting off—a burst, fast, clipped, but undeniably Russian. Alicia's hands moved in a whir, short, efficient marks, wasting no motion. I watched her with a sense of admiration. She was beautiful when she worked like this: her auburn hair and the pure determination and function in her very essence, that concentration that would never go away.

Suddenly, the air changed. It wasn't the temperature or sound or anything else quantifiable, but something in the pressure seemed to give way. Or maybe it got worse. I couldn't tell.

Whatever this pressure was, it was the sort of pressure you felt when someone stepped into the room, and yet you didn't know what cards they were holding or what they meant to you—friend or enemy, or even what their name was. It was the type of pressure that had to give way eventually, but would build until it did.

My headache sharpened, the throb behind my eye becoming worse. I didn't think; I reacted on instinct, turning and reaching inside my coat.

The door to the safe house was still locked, but that was the problem, because the knob was moving anyway—slowly, controlled, with no rattle and no hesitation. Whoever was opening the door knew how to.

Alicia looked up and had her pistol off the table in one clean motion. The barrel was aimed at the door before a second had passed. She didn't ask who it was, but she didn't have to.

Whoever was coming through the door wasn't one of Angleton's men. We would have heard them on the stairs.

Alicia and I both knew what that meant. Whoever was coming through the door was someone who knew how to be silent—someone who knew how to be a ghost.

The door swung inward slowly. A woman stepped inside—tall, blonde, sun-touched but not softened by it. Quiet and graceful, her feet made no sound against the floor of the safe house. The overhead fan caught her hair and sent it drifting. She wore dark slacks and a light shirt with the sleeves rolled, hanging loosely over her shoulders, a pale blue scarf, no visible weapon, but every inch of her suggested she carried one.

Her face was half-lit by the single lamp, half devoured by the shadow. But as she raised her eyes and looked at me, straight in the face, I knew exactly who she was. She truly was a ghost. My stomach dropped so hard I thought I might faint, might fall to the ground in disbelief.

Lucy Howard. Locket. Here, alive, and in the flesh. The last person I thought I would see in Havana. The last person I ever thought I would see again, except maybe in hell whenever I finally got caught with my hands in my pockets on some clandestine mission. The last time I saw her, she was just a vision, a mirage—an apparition—created by the Mirror in Invershiel.

And yet, here she was. For a second, it was as if the breath had been stolen from me. My brain was whirring, but it couldn't process anything, struggling to decide which version of reality I was in and whether I deserved either. It was a brain fog that had not only been primed but also continually worsened, time and time again, vying with the Mirror.

I had buried her in my mind as cleanly as I could, buried her in the way you bury a body when you don't have time to grieve or to be sorrowful. I had told myself she was dead, because that was what the report stated, and dead was easier than missing.

She had been dead.

She was dead.

Yet now she stood before us in the safe house in Havana, as if she had just stepped out for cigarettes and come back only a moment later. Her hair had one small streak of gray, and yet she was still the same Lucy Howard I always remembered. Other than that, no other signs of age traced themselves across her face. She was a year or two younger than me, though we had never really bothered with the details when we were together ages ago.

"Good evening," she said, her voice light, almost sing-songy, with low, British vowels curved by memory. "Hello, Raven. You might want to douse that radio before it attracts the wrong kind of friends."

That name hit me like a blow worse than the sight of her. I generally detested my codename, originally given to me by MI6 and carried over to the Bureau, yet the way she used it was different. It was a way I had always accepted, as if it were familiar, as if the name actually belonged to me.

Alicia straightened. "Who the hell—?"

I cut her off softly: "Lucy."

The name hit the room like a trigger pulled halfway.

Alicia's eyes flicked between us. "You know her?"

Lucy smiled, though it lacked warmth. "He used to. Briefly. Cairo, wasn't it? Before the Bureau taught him better manners."

"Before MI6 taught you to shoot people in the back," I replied, and the temperature in the room seemed to drop ten degrees.

Lucy's smile remained. "Always the romantic."

Alicia, however, held her gun steady.

"Don't take another step," Alicia said curtly, her voice flat. "You're MI6?"

Lucy's gaze turned to her, cool appraisal behind blue eyes. "Once. These days, I'm… contracted. Oh, and if you prefer paperwork, I've brought some. Plenty of proof to go around."

She tossed a small metal disk onto the table—a CIA operations tag. Then she reached slowly into her back pocket, carefully, the way you moved around an armed woman who didn't blink and who could pull a trigger without a second thought. Alicia was dangerous; even I knew that. And I knew that if this was the real Lucy Howard, and not a doppelgänger, she would know it too.

Alicia didn't take the folded credential wallet held out in Lucy's extended hand. Instead, she gestured with the gun.

"Set it down, then step back," Alicia said.

Lucy did as she was told, the wallet landing on the table beside the radio with a soft slap. The room seemed to tighten around the sound.

I watched her face carefully, looking for any tells. I wasn't about to trust her just like that. The Mirror had played too many tricks on all of us and made liars out of honest men far too many times for me to trust it.

Still, I couldn't shake the feeling that this was the real Lucy. If it was, however, that begged the question: where had she been all this time? And why hadn't she told me that she was alive?

But Lucy's eyes were steady, and her breathing was real. There was nothing about her that could tell me she was an echo, a doppelgänger, or any other trick of my mind. She looked the same as she had looked the day I had last seen her. If she were an echo, she was the cruelest one yet.

Alicia, however, kept her stance, her gun still leveled.

"I don't know you," she said. "You don't enter rooms like this unless you want to get shot. So, do you?"

She glanced at the pistol and then back at Alicia's face.

"Artemis," she said. "That's you, right? I've heard about you."

Alicia's expression didn't change, and she continued to stare at the woman in front of her.

"My name is Rivas," Alicia said.

Lucy's mouth twitched slightly. "Hmm. Sure it is."

"By the way," she continued, "Washington sends their regards. They're worried you're about to blow their toy factory."

"The Mirror isn't a toy," Alicia said. "It's a weapon. The Russians are rebuilding it from Rosyth parts and schematics."

Lucy's expression barely shifted. "Then it's convenient you're here to destroy it. The Americans, the CIA, however, would prefer a little oversight. They've invested heavily in Cuban stability. Or at least in the illusion of it."

I stepped between them. "You don't get to waltz in here and play envoy, Locket."

Her eyes flicked to me, sharp. "Still remembering my codename, Max? How flattering."

"Hard to forget. You nearly got me killed in '41."

"And yet," she said softly, "here you are."

Alicia watched the exchange, jaw tight. "We're here to neutralize the Mirror, not hand it to another empire."

Lucy tilted her head. "And yet your Bureau reports to London, which reports to Washington every second Friday. Tell me, Alicia—does your empire feel different when you sleep at night?"

The air went knife-edge still.

"Enough," I said, exhaling smoke. "Why are you here, Lucy?"

"To keep you alive," she said. "And to make sure that whatever version of that thing the Russians rebuild never leaves Havana." She leaned closer, her perfume—jasmine, smoke, and memory—unsettling in its familiarity. "But we both know your people would rather destroy it than study it. Which means you'll need me when the CIA gets in your way."

Alicia's tone was as sharp as flint. "And why should we trust you?"

Lucy met her eyes evenly. "You shouldn't. But if you don't, you'll both be dead by sunrise."

"You," I said. "You're supposed to be dead."

Lucy tilted her head slightly, watching me carefully, as if she wasn't quite sure that I was real either.

"Funny," she finally said. "That's the same thing they said about you."

I took a slow step toward her without meaning to, and Alicia's hand tightened on the gun.

"Max," she said, and I could hear the warning in her voice.

It made me stop in my tracks—that and the headache, which had returned tenfold now, pulsing hard enough to blur my vision.

Lucy's gaze, however, had drifted past me and had flicked to the portable Resonance Rig on the towel.

"That," she said, "is why I'm here."

"Start talking then," Alicia said, still not lowering the weapon.

Lucy nodded, as if she'd been waiting for permission to begin.

"Well," she said, "Angleton is a paranoid bugger. He didn't tell you about me because he likes his compartmentalization, but this is bigger than his personal delusions. I don't know if you've heard yet—you probably have—but a Soviet vessel came in… research ship. She's offloading something that shouldn't exist, and she's doing it fast. Which means we need to move."

Alicia kept the gun leveled at Lucy, but her eyes twitched toward the radio.

Lucy smiled. The slightest smile ever.

"According to your radio, looks like it's right on time," she said.

Alicia opened her mouth to retort, but the radio crackled, spitting static and then a burst of Russian. "Двигайтесь. Перенос начался."

Alicia translated instantly. "They're moving it. Now."

Lucy was already at the door. "Told you."

I hesitated. Tension hung like a live wire—my past and present both aiming at each other.

Alicia snapped the receiver cord free. "You're not leading this op."

Lucy glanced back, eyes bright with mischief and something deeper. "Of course not, darling. I'm just saving it."

Then she was gone—down the stairs and into the Havana night, where the rain had begun to fall.

Alicia turned to me. "You didn't tell me she was alive."

"I didn't know. I didn't think she was."

"Then you'd better start thinking faster," Alicia said coldly. "Because she just rewrote our mission."

I looked out the window after Lucy. The street below was empty now, except for a glint of light catching in the puddles—a reflection of something that shouldn't exist.

I ground out my cigarette.

"Welcome back to Havana," I muttered. "Hell of a place for ghosts."

But it was less of a welcome and more of a warning.

Alicia was already in motion. She killed the lamp and radio, then rolled the one-time pad and pencil into her satchel along with a Geiger counter and several detonators, as if she'd done it a hundred times, preparing for what we both knew was inevitable. I checked my pistol, making sure there was already one in the chamber with a spare magazine in my pocket. I knew that more often than not, our missions went to hell, and I wanted to be prepared for this one if and when it did.

Outside, Havana continued on—a never-ending city of motion and parties. Inside, however, everything felt tighter, more tense.

"You think she's heading to the ship?" I asked.

"You tell me," Alicia shot back.

"Knowing her, it's likely. But she didn't exactly leave room for discussion... or coordination."

"You're not following her," Alicia said as she snapped the clasps shut.

"I know. I'm not," I lied.

Her eyes cut to me. I couldn't tell if she was jealous, afraid, or calculating. It was as if she were reevaluating who I really was.

"We'll follow," she said, "but we follow the cargo, not your history, Max."

I nodded in agreement. "Cargo," I repeated. "Right, let's deal with the cargo."

My headache throbbed again. We left the Resonance Rig there in town. It was far too bulky for a ship job, and besides, if the Russians were moving something with a mirror signature, that meant it wasn't set up yet. There was no reason to try to get the rig to work if we could just blow the thing to smithereens before it was even built.

Alicia cracked open the door. The stairway smelled damp, of plaster, and the faint waft of boiled vegetables from a neighbor's kitchen. Somewhere below, a man laughed long and hard, but we didn't have time to deal with laughter. We descended fast and quietly.

The rain had arrived properly now as we exited the building, Havana greeting us with sheets of warm, hard, wet torrents that bounced off cobblestones, turning the gutters into little rivulets that carried sugarcane husks and trash along to the drains. I was glad that I was wearing my hat, pulled low over my eyes. Neon smeared across the puddles—red, green, blue, and a bruised violet from a club sign. Music spilled out of the doorways, but I didn't listen. In the far distance, I could hear the harbor horns, deep and slow, as if something large had already arrived.

Alicia and I kept to the darker sides of the streets, our collars up out of habit and necessity to keep out the rain and prying eyes. My coat was already sticking to me, the sweat and the rain making it feel like a second skin, heavy and dense. I could tell from how Alicia walked in front of me that her hand was hovering near her pistol, close enough that she could pull it in an instant if something went awry. We didn't speak. The arrival of Lucy had made us feel distant, and I wasn't about to break the silence first.

We cut across a small plaza, passing through the middle where a statue of some forgotten patriots stared into the downpour. As we passed the center, the street lamp flickered. For a second, the plaza was empty, and then for a second it wasn't: a woman in a bright dress appeared beside the statue. Before I could even register what her face looked like, she disappeared again, as the lamp steadied once more.

I stopped without truly meaning to.

"Keep moving," Alicia said, her fingers closing around my sleeve.

"Did you see that?" I asked, swallowing the taste in my mouth.

She nodded. "Max, focus and keep moving."

I shook my head, focusing my thoughts, and did as I was told. Now wasn't the time to let my mind go haywire. Now was the time to focus on what was ahead.

The closer we got to the water, the more the air changed: the taste of salt and diesel, mixed with the scent of wet rope and fish, hung heavy in the dense atmosphere. It was the kind of smell that never left once it arrived. No matter how many times you washed your clothes or how many times you bathed, the smell would cling to you.

The harbor district itself was a grid of lousy warehouses and cranes, all cast in shadow, everything slicked black by the rain. I pulled the brim of my hat even lower, watching the Cuban police who stood under the awnings, smoking. They didn't do anything or try to stop us. People like us were a dime a dozen here.

Men in caps hauled crates tirelessly, their backs bent, their faces blank as they focused on the task ahead. Trucks idled, their engines coughing, their exhausts hanging low against the moisture and the wet air. There, far out into the harbor, past the piers, sat the Soviet ship. It had been called a research vessel, but it was about as much of a research vessel as I was a member of the Royal Family. Floodlights swept the deck in low, slow arcs; a red star on the funnel caught in the light, looking too bright and too clean. A large crane arm creaked as it swung the cargo net over the side.

Below where it was anchored, the dock bustled with crates

being moved fast. I could tell that we were nearly too late. We had to hurry, had to move faster. If they were moving a special technical cargo, whatever it was, it wasn't going to stay here long.

Alicia and I watched carefully from the edge of a warehouse, hidden in the shadows, the rain dripping slowly off the corrugated roof into our hair and down our necks.

"There are too many damn men," I murmured.

"Too many to shoot, maybe," Alicia agreed, "but not too many to confuse."

She nodded toward a trolley stacked with canvas-wrapped bundles. Two guards stood nearby at the gangway, rifles slung over their shoulders. I could tell simply from their posture that they weren't Cuban. They stood too straight and looked too bored. Their faces were foreign, too. By my best guess, these were Soviets, and I'd dealt with enough Soviets throughout my life that I was confident in my guess.

But it also meant they were dangerous. Any movement out of the ordinary could get us killed.

It was as if Alicia had read my mind. She pulled a plain, dark cap from her bag and shoved it onto her head, then handed me another. She pointed at a trolley abandoned near the warehouse door, empty except for a coil of rope and a small wooden crate.

"We need to blend in," she said.

"And become boring?" I scoffed.

She nodded. "And become boring."

We rolled the trolley out as if we had done it a thousand times before. In a port, everything belonged to everyone. Anything you could get your hands on, you could use, and so nobody cared. The real trick was looking like we'd done it night after night and hated it. That was our game. We kept our heads down, our shoulders hunched, letting the rain wash our features into anonymity, blending in with the riffraff of the docks.

There, at the gangway, one of the guards lifted his hand. He barked something in Russian. I didn't understand every word, but I was fluent enough in body language to recognize that he had told us to stop.

Alicia, however, didn't even slow down. She reached into her pocket, then produced a folded slip of paper. It was blank as far as I could see. I had no doubt that she was bluffing. But she held it forward as if the paper itself contained all the authority of a general.

The guard snatched it, squinted at it in the dim light, cupping it and shielding it from the rain, then looked up at us, annoyed.

Alicia, however, didn't break. She simply gave him the look that every dock clerk in the world would have given him—the look that said, "Do you really want to make this harder than it already is?"

For a second, it seemed like it might not work. The guard hesitated. But the second guard, an older man whose face was already etched with tiredness beyond his years, glanced past us toward the crane. The cargo net was sweeping down again in one smooth motion. People were shouting in angry Russian. They were on the clock. With some reluctance, he jerked his head.

The first guard glanced at him, unsure for a second, then waved us right through.

And just like that, we pushed the trolley onto the ship. The deck was slick, and the carrier pitched back and forth slightly with the swell of the waves. Rain hammered down against the metal as if it were a thousand fingers, drumming against the metal, all hammering to be let in. Somewhere far below, the engine throbbed steadily, keeping this gigantic floating fortress on its toes.

Heads bowed, shoulders hunched, we moved quietly toward a hatch where other workers were disappearing into the belly of the vessel. The air emanating from here was damp, oily, and warm.

I felt a dull throbbing in my head. It wasn't a normal kind of headache, either. It was the headache that told me we were getting close. I could see Alicia felt it, too. I watched her eyes narrow slightly and her jaw clench as we moved.

"Do you think the cargo's still aboard?" she whispered.

"It either is, or it was," I shot back. "Let's hope we got to it in time."

We dropped down into the hatch. The corridor smelled wet, slick with salt and sweat. Fluorescent tubes buzzed ahead, flickering with a slight rhythm that didn't match the ship's swaying motion. Somewhere beyond the corridor we'd found ourselves in, footsteps echoed, and I could hear Russian voices, short, angry, and clipped.

Alicia and I, however, moved seamlessly and silently off the main passageway. We kept to the side passageways, heading deeper into the ship, where the cargo of importance would have been stored.

Three turns in, the passage opened into a small utility junction, filled with pipes and valves, and beyond that, a locked door with a heavy wheel handle.

Alicia nodded toward it, but I had already seen it. My hands were on my pistol, and I leveled it before lowering it again.

Beside the door, slumped against the bulkhead, was a man wearing a Soviet officer's coat. It had been stained crimson with blood, his throat slashed clean. The blood pooled beneath him, mixing with the rainwater tracked in on his boots. I could smell the iron and taste the metal. It was fresh.

Alicia crouched, leaning in as I checked the corridor. She didn't touch him. She didn't have to. The man was dead, and whoever had done this had done it fast and very efficiently.

As if reading our minds, a shape moved in the shadow at the far end of the junction. I whipped my pistol out without a second thought, leveling it ahead.

Lucy stepped into the light.

She had a small pistol in her hand; it was the kind that was made for espionage above all else—the kind that you wouldn't see until you were already dead. Her sleeves were rolled up, and there was a dark smear on her forearm that might have been blood, though her hair was damp from the rain. I could see that her face was dry. She had been here for quite a while.

In her other hand, she held a ring of keys. She looked at us, an expression of shock registering on her face for only a second, as if she'd expected us to be slower.

But she didn't say it.

"Took you long enough," she said.

Alicia raised her gun again without hesitation. The muzzle was tracking Lucy's heart in seconds.

But Lucy didn't flinch. Instead, she held up the ring of keys as if it explained everything to us.

"He wouldn't cooperate," she said, nodding toward the officer. "These guys have no sense of hospitality."

"This is sloppy," Alicia shot back. "You're leaving bodies behind."

"No, I'm burying problems," Lucy replied, her eyes flashing.

I stared at the officer for a second, then back at her.

"What are you here for?" I asked. "You didn't come here to keep us alive, did you?"

"I did," she replied. "But it's definitely not my priority."

For a second, my headache pulsed, and in that same instance, her silhouette seemed to double, as if there were two Lucys there, each standing slightly out of phase, like a photograph taken with a shaky hand. Then, as I blinked, there was only one again. I wasn't sure what was real anymore, but what was real didn't even matter. All that mattered was the result.

"They're moving the main crates off, but there's still a remnant down there—a containment unit. Way too volatile to handle in this weather," Lucy said as she stepped toward the door, the keys jingling softly.

"Meaning a piece of the Mirror?" Alicia asked.

"The Mirror." Lucy's mouth tightened. "I don't have as much experience with this as you two do, but whatever it is, it's something far too dangerous to be moved without care."

"So, why tell us?" Alicia asked, her gun still raised.

Lucy didn't look at Alicia. Instead, she raised her eyes and focused on me.

"Because," she said matter-of-factly, "if I do it alone, I don't get out. If you do it alone, the odds are the same. The Americans want options."

"Options?" I asked. "Do you mean they want control of the Mirror?"

"Yeah, same word, different accent," Lucy said, almost flippantly.

"Open the door," Alicia said, her eyes hard.

Lucy complied. She put the key in, turned it, and the lock clicked. Then, with some moderate effort, she spun the wheel handle, the heavy door sliding open on a stairway that went down deeper into the ship. Some air rose out of it, and in the air, I could smell the same scent that I remembered only too well from Rosyth Dockyard and Invershiel—the scent of ozone, copper, and the faint static electricity.

That was the Mirror's signature.

Alicia finally lowered her gun as we descended further down to the lower decks. The lower decks were quieter, as if the ship itself were holding its breath. It felt muffled, pipes running along the ceiling, condensation dripping in steady ticks that felt almost too regular, as if it was unnatural for a ship at the mercy of the tide.

Eventually, we reached a sealed compartment. The door was thicker, but Lucy jingled her keys, flashed her classic smile, and unlocked it.

Inside was a room that looked as if it had been turned from a shipman's quarters into a laboratory built by someone who only had a few weeks to set up. Crates had been torn open, packing straw and canvas lay scattered everywhere, and tools strewn across tables—soldering irons, calipers, and notebooks written in Russian.

In the corner, a portable generator sat, humming softly,

supplying power to a squat metal housing in the very center of the small room. The housing itself was roughly the size of a coffin, copper bands wrapped around it like restraints. On one side was a small glass viewport that glowed faintly, emanating a sickly blue-white light.

I recognized it instantly. I had seen similar enough devices in Hawthorne's laboratories, back when the Mirror was still in its early days. It was a containment unit built to house one of the Mirror cores—a resonant quantum stabilizer engineered to harness and amplify temporal entanglement fields, pulsing with the eerie energy of compressed chronal waves. This was not the whole Mirror. If it had been the Mirror, it would have been a monstrous frame, that shiny, jet-black surface that folded in on itself and cracked outward all at once. And my headache would have been unbearable.

This was just a piece of it, but maybe it was enough. My vision tightened as my left eye throbbed harder.

Alicia stepped forward carefully, pulling a small instrument from her bag: a Geiger counter. She didn't even have to glance at it. As she pulled it out, the needle began trembling before she even brought it into the air.

"This is something," she said quietly. "Is this the main piece they were transporting?"

Lucy watched us both. "I'm not entirely sure," she said. "Whatever was in those crates is long gone, so let's hope this is enough to stop the full build."

She paused. "Is this the Mirror that everyone's been talking about?"

I stared at the viewport. The light inside pulsed regularly, and I shook my head.

"No, that's not it," I said. "This is a piece... just a piece stored in a containment unit to keep it stabilized. And in there is likely one of the operating components used to power the resonance of the Mirror. But it's not the full thing."

Above us, shouts suddenly erupted—angry Russian voices

and the hammering of feet as men began to run. Lucy's expression didn't change. She simply glanced at us.

"So, what's your play, Lucy?" I asked.

"My play," she said, "is that the ship doesn't get this thing off intact."

"I thought you said the CIA was interested in preserving it."

Lucy thought for a second. "Likely," she said. "But I suspect we're too late anyway, if what you say is true, Calder."

Alicia nodded curtly. Now wasn't the time for bickering. She glanced at the pipes overhead.

"Cooling?" she asked.

"They've got it looped into the ship's seawater intake," Lucy said, nodding toward a set of lines that ran into the housing.

"Then if I reroute and spike the coolant—" Alicia began.

"—it destabilizes," Lucy finished.

"And then?" I asked.

"Then would come your job, Raven: blowing up their mistake."

I smiled thinly. "I think I can manage that."

Alicia grabbed a wrench from one of the desks, moving to the coolant manifold, kneeling with steady hands despite the pulse in the air.

Lucy sprang into motion as well, popping open a panel by the door with her knife and cutting and bridging wires as if she knew exactly where each went.

"Do we have any charges?" I asked Alicia, suddenly realizing I had no idea what she'd packed in her satchel.

She nodded, pivoting to the bag and pulling the plastic from a small kit she'd packed earlier.

I planted the charges on the containment unit supports—two blocks pressed hard, the detonator seated. My hands were shaking, though I couldn't tell if it was from excitement or the Mirror. I recited the same thing in my mind again and again: place, press, wire, breathe.

I had to focus because every time I got closer to the containment unit, the hum got louder in my ears.

Behind me, Alicia's wrench turned. The valve protested, then hissed as water pressure shifted and the pipe shuddered. The containment unit's glow brightened slightly, but Alicia worked fast, rerouting a return line, then wedging the valve half open so the flow stuttered. Moments later, she was done.

Lucy leaned into the panels. She believed the doors should be shut and alarms should be silenced for maybe two minutes, or perhaps less. Footsteps hammered somewhere outside the compartment, voices rising, one shouting in Russian.

Alicia's eyes snapped to the door.

"They heard the pump change," she said.

"How many?" Lucy asked.

"More than enough," Alicia said, drawing her pistol up.

The door wheel rattled. Someone was trying it from the other side. The lock held for a second, just long enough.

Then the metal housing in the center of the room began to emit a sound—high and thin, like a glass that were about to break under immense pressure.

"Alicia," I said, grabbing her shoulder, "we're out."

She nodded, and we moved toward the door seamlessly. Lucy covered the wheel handle.

"Go," she said.

"You first," Alicia snapped.

"Of course you'd say that," she said, an amused tone in her voice.

Then the door wheel spun, forced open, and the door swung inward. A Soviet sailor stumbled through, his rifle halfway up before Lucy shot him center mass. No hesitation. He crumpled.

Behind him, however, were many more men in the corridor, their rifles raised and their mouths moving as they shouted in Russian.

We all had our pistols drawn now, and we fired. Two of the

shapes dropped. Another hit the bulkhead, leaving a smear of crimson blood in the harsh light.

We forced our way into the corridor. We didn't have time. The charges were about to blow, but my mind was whirring.

The lights overhead strobed. The corridor lengthened and shortened. I saw a dead sailor on the floor, then saw him standing again, blinking as if he were confused. Even as I watched, he was dead again.

My vision began to tunnel. I stood there swaying before I felt Alicia's iron grip on my arm.

"Max. Max, look at me."

I tried. Her face swam in front of my eyes.

"Max," she said, "focus."

"Alicia," I gasped.

"Good," she said.

The world snapped a fraction into place, as if it had re-centered for only a moment.

Lucy was already ahead, moving weightlessly as she fired down the corridor—more to keep heads down while we ran than to kill.

I ran with Alicia now, and moments later, we were at the stairwell, going up, the metal steps slick under our shoes.

We burst onto the deck into pure chaos: men shouted in Russian, and somewhere in the distance, a siren began to blare. Floodlights swung wildly, searching the deck. Alicia shoved me along toward the railing.

"How long?" she asked, shouting, as we ducked for cover.

I looked at the detonator in my hand. I wasn't sure if I had set a timer. Had it been for thirty seconds? Three minutes? My fingers were numb.

"Forget the timer," Lucy said. "It's going now."

And as if to prove her point, the deck under us vibrated for a second. The floodlights flickered, and then went still again.

Alicia swore under her breath.

"We have to jump!" Lucy shouted.

"We can't—" Alicia began, but then another pulse hit harder. I knew only too well that if the detonators had gone off, the containment was likely compromised. The core unit would destabilize.

And then, the whole place would blow.

I could hear something below deck screaming at a pitch that made my eyes sting, and somewhere below, metal tore. It was a wet, ripping sound, as if the ship had been opened with a can opener.

That was enough for me. I grabbed Alicia's hand and hauled her toward the rail. Lucy was already climbing, moving as if she'd practiced this motion a thousand times before.

We went over.

For a few terrifying moments, we hung mid-air, and then we were in the water—warm and filthy, the taste of fuel and salt mixed in my mouth. It punched the air out of me. For a second, I sank, my coat dragging me down, but then I kicked hard and broke the surface, coughing.

The ship behind us was tilting now, slowly but surely. Men ran on the deck, silhouettes in the floodlights. Alicia surfaced beside me, her hair plastered to her head, her eyes fierce. I nodded, and we swam toward the nearest pier.

For the first time in a while, my mind was focused. It was as if the force of the water had knocked the hallucinations out of me.

Further out, I saw Lucy surface, a pale shape in the dark water. She swam with smooth, efficient strokes. She had ditched her coat in favor of only her undershirt now.

Then the ship detonated. A flash of blue-white light punched up through the deck. For an instant, the entire vessel seemed to be illuminated, brighter than the sun. Then the light collapsed inward, and the whole thing buckled with a roar.

Heat washed over the water, and debris rained down, hissing and steaming upon hitting the cold harbor. The ship split low in the water and began to sink slowly, then faster, as the stern dragged itself down into the sea. Flames crawled against the surface where fuel spread, an ugly, dirty orange against the black rain.

We'd reached the pier now, and I climbed up, hauling Alicia up after me, my lungs burning. We crouched behind a stacked set of crates, the water pouring off of us as we watched the ship disappear.

Havana had erupted into motion as well: sirens in the distance, men shouting, dock lights swinging. But the city had seen many things burn before. It had survived Spaniards, gangsters, and hurricanes. This was nothing new to it.

I noticed Lucy climbing up onto the pier a few yards away, breathing hard now for the first time since I'd seen her. But she didn't come over to us. Instead, she walked along the dock, her posture straightening.

As she moved, two men stepped out from the shadow of a warehouse—Americans by the look of them. They wore dark suits, and one held an umbrella. I squinted, watching in annoyance as I saw a car waiting near the warehouse door, its engine running, the headlights off.

Lucy paused once, just long enough to glance back. Her eyes found mine. There was something in her look—maybe an apology, maybe a warning, or maybe pity. But then she turned and slid into the car, and it rolled away into the rain, as if it had never been there.

"So," Alicia said, watching it leave, her expression unreadable, "she has a ride."

"She always did," I replied. "And we'd best get out of here, too, unless we'd prefer to be caught."

Alicia shook her head. "As much as I want to admire our work, fires draw attention."

We moved through the maze of the docks, keeping low and cutting between warehouses and truck lanes until we reached the safehouse again. The rain had soaked through everything that the ocean hadn't. However, I was thankful for it. For only a moment, I had some respite from the headache.

Alicia bolted the door behind us and leaned against it for a second, her eyes closed. I knew she was listening, but there was nothing outside—no footsteps, no voices. Just Havana and the noise that came with it.

Alicia turned and walked straight to the radio, bringing it back to life. The hiss filled the room with static.

I stripped off my coat, hanging it over the chair. It dripped onto the floor as if I'd just swum through the ocean.

Of course, I had.

Alicia, however, was all business. She keyed the mic—coded call sign, short burst. It was static. Then, a moment later, Moreau's voice came through, thin and far away. It was warped by the bad weather but still intelligible, somehow making it through whatever else was crawling through the air between London and Havana.

"Report," she said.

I could tell immediately that her voice was strained. It was something unusual for her, at least it had been for the short time I'd known her.

Alicia told her everything—the ship, the containment unit, the sabotage, the explosion. The Soviet presence was heavy. And then, of course, about Lucy.

At that last part, there was a pause long enough that I thought the line had gone dry, until Moreau finally spoke. She didn't ask questions about Lucy—not yet, at least.

"Were the primary components on board?" she asked. "Can you confirm?"

Alicia glanced at me. I spoke for the first time.

"No," I said. "It was a remnant, a piece at most. I'm not sure if the ship was a decoy or a delivery trail, but most of the cargo that was important had already been offloaded when we got there."

"Bureau reports concur," Moreau replied, her voice flat but

strained. "Our intercepts indicate multiple crates were moved inland before your engagement. Destination unknown, but likely the distillery. Continue investigation of the site and assume its operational capability remains or is enhanced."

In other words, we had sunk a ship with no machine on it. The real Mirror was still breathing—still at the distillery and likely more powerful than ever.

Alicia briefly acknowledged this and ended the transmission, and then sat back on her heels, staring at the radio, her face fallen.

I lit a cigarette, inhaled deeply, and closed my eyes as I let the smoke trickle out. I offered Alicia one. She shook her head, watching me instead.

"You saw her get picked up," she said finally.

"Yes," I replied.

"And you didn't mention it on the line?"

"Neither did you," I replied.

She stood slowly and crossed the room toward me, stopping close enough that I could smell the salt on her and that faint scent of smoke, likely from our botched job in the harbor.

"Max, you don't get to have secrets," she said quietly.

Her voice wasn't angry, but I could sense a level of control and tension in it that I had never heard from her before.

"I know. I'm not keeping secrets," I lied.

It sounded pathetic even to me. But Alicia didn't blink.

"Lucy Howard isn't just a complication," she said. "She's leverage for Angleton and for the CIA. She knows how to pull you off balance, and if they want to, they'll be able to."

I took another breath of the cigarette smoke.

"She's alive," I said finally. "I'm still processing even that."

"Later," Alicia said. "Tonight, you nearly froze in a corridor because you saw her. It's like you're seeing a ghost."

"I know," I said.

I didn't have a defense. I didn't even know what the truth was anymore.

Alicia exhaled, and some of the tension relaxed.

"Listen to me, Max. The Mirror isn't just fracturing time. It's fractured you, and it's fractured me. It fractures people. And when there are cracks in people, that makes it all the worse. And Max, Lucy Howard is one of your cracks."

I nodded as she stepped back, finally.

"I'm not going to lose you in Havana," she said. "Not to the machine or to the memories."

I nodded once again, but I didn't speak. I wasn't even sure what I thought, so anything I said would have been a lie.

Outside, the city kept moving—the music, the horns, the distant shouts from the harbor fire. I peered through a slat in the window. The rain ran down the glass in twisting, melodic lines. The street below was empty now—just puddles, neon reflections, and one stray dog trotting away.

I lost myself in one of the puddles in the wavering light, and as I watched, I saw that my reflection moved when I didn't, just for a second. And there was a silhouette, delayed, watching me. It snapped back into place, perfectly synchronized again, as if the world was none the wiser.

We'd sunk the ship, but we'd also made noise and burned what could have been a decoy. Somewhere up the coast, beneath that rum distillery, the guard would double, and the real heart of the Mirror would continue to pulse.

It would turn Havana inside out unless we stopped it.

CHAPTER 8
LUCY HOWARD

The first lie Lucy Howard ever told was to the wind—at least, the first lie she could ever remember.

She was eight years old, standing barefoot in the garden of Charlton House, the family estate above the Vale of Evesham, watching the gray storm clouds crawl lazily over the Cotswold Hills.

Her father had told her that the wind carried words across the world and that if she simply whispered into it, someone far away might hear her. She cupped her hands and said, "I'm not afraid."

It wasn't true, of course, but it felt like practice—and practice makes perfect.

Charlton House was the kind of property that looked ancient even when it was new, built of Cotswold stone, with high windows and ivy that had outlived several generations of the Howards. It smelled of dust, wax, polish, and expectations that would never be met. It sat on 66 acres of farmland with 24 stables and an outdoor riding arena.

Lucy's father, Sir Norman Howard, was a diplomat of the old breed. He was Oxford-educated, fluent in charm and omission. He believed that conversation was a form of chess, where each time you spoke, you moved a piece, and checkmate was his only goal.

Her mother, Cecilia, was a poet who had studied English at Cambridge and published one slender volume of verse before giving up on her dream, marrying into diplomacy, and finding that her words no longer fit the drawing room.

Lucy grew up caught between the two, torn between precision and imagination, diplomacy and rebellion.

Sir Norman served in the Foreign Office during the interwar years, which meant Lucy's childhood was naturally punctuated by frequent departures. Her earliest memories were of trunks lined with silk shirts, sealed envelopes, and her father's careful handwriting on the backs of maps.

When she was only five, he had left for Moscow, promising he'd return by Christmas.

He didn't.

He came back in April, frostbite on his fingers and a habit of glancing at shadows before opening a door. The trip had changed him in ways she never understood.

He brought her gifts: a nesting doll, a book of Pushkin, and a small silver locket engraved carefully with her initials. He told her stories of Russia, stories that Russia was a country where secrets were like the weather, and that she should learn to read both.

She kept the advice and the locket, too.

Her mother stayed behind whenever her father left, filling the house with music and candlelight. Cecilia was fragile yet beautiful, in the way of people who feel too much. She read Lucy poetry at night—Keats, Tennyson, Blake—and told her that language was a weapon that no government could confiscate.

Lucy loved her mother fiercely and learned that affection was something she felt only for her mother—but she also learned that affection was another word for weakness.

When her mother died of influenza in 1934, the house fell eerily silent. Sir Norman didn't weep. He simply stopped speaking for three days, then returned to the Foreign Office, as if grief were an unseemly indulgence befitting a lesser person.

Lucy was sent off to a boarding school near Cheltenham, St. Anne's College for Girls. It was a place of starch, Latin, boaters, and strict discipline. Lucy, however, did well there. She learned languages, histories, and the arts, and learned how to appear to listen while thinking of other things.

Her reports were often filled with the sorts of phrases teachers used for future prime ministers' daughters. They said she had a commanding intellect, was self-contained, and precociously analytical. What they meant, of course, was that she was clever enough to know when to smile, quiet enough not to need friends, and smart enough to lie when she needed to.

At seventeen, Lucy won a scholarship to Trinity College, Cambridge, to study Classics. It was 1936, and the university still carried the fresh scent of empire, filled to the brim with young men who had opinions about the future of Europe, and women who had to outthink them simply to be noticed.

But it was the place where Lucy thrived the most. She fenced with the college team, had a passion for horse riding in the early mornings, and wrote essays on Roman propaganda that left her tutors impressed and slightly jealous. She was brilliant in a way that made other people defensive.

She drank tea with men who would later run the country and argued with women who would later rewrite it.

It was at Cambridge that she learned her second great lie: that knowledge was enough.

It never was.

The war in Spain divided the campus. Her classmates argued about fascism and freedom, while she watched the debates with a diplomat's detachment.

"The trick," she wrote in her notebook one day, "is never to believe too loudly in anything that might need defending later."

And she followed this rule as gospel.

In 1938, during her final year, she attended a lecture on

ancient codes and cryptography—the way Caesar and Cicero had hidden messages in plain sight. Afterward, a quiet man had approached her in the corridor. He was small and slightly shriveled, but he spoke in a way, with a glint in his eye, that made her instantly uneasy.

He introduced himself as Mr. Denham from the Government Communications Bureau. It didn't exist on paper. He complimented her Latin translation of De Bello Gallico and asked if she had ever considered applying her mind to more practical matters.

Lucy knew what he was asking. It was a time of broiling tensions, and "practical matters" only meant one thing.

"You mean espionage," she said, smiling.

He didn't answer. He simply handed her a card embossed with an address near Whitehall and walked away.

Two weeks later, she visited. The door bore no nameplate, just a brass knocker and an indifferent doorman. Inside, she was given tea, a crossword puzzle, and an interview that lasted three hours.

Two weeks after that, she received a letter in a plain envelope.

"Miss L. Howard, the Department would value your contribution to the national effort. Please report to Bletchley Park for preliminary training."

Bletchley was a blur of damp corridors, chalkboard equations scrawled on the walls, and clattering typewriters. Lucy learned to break ciphers and rebuild them, to analyze intercepted messages in languages she barely spoke, and to forget the sound of her own name when it mattered.

Her aptitude for Russian caught swift attention, thanks to her father's lessons and a childhood fascination with Pushkin. Because of these proclivities, she was transferred to MI6 by the end of 1940, joining Section D, which focused on sabotage and counterintelligence.

The men in the section called her "the Duchess." They

initially meant it as mockery, but she treated it as a promotion. It meant she had proved herself—proved herself enough to be noticed and recognized.

Her codename, assigned by the director himself, was Locket. The irony didn't escape her.

"Something small, easily hidden, and full of secrets," her handler said.

Lucy smiled and replied, "That makes two of us."

She was dispatched to Cairo almost immediately, a posting that felt exotic and strategic. The city was a labyrinth of emissaries, couriers, and operatives pretending to be archaeologists.

It was there that she met Max Calder.

Calder was one of MI6's operatives—older, broad-shouldered, with that peculiar charm that British men wore like armor. Yet there was something about him that was different. Their first conversation was about courier schedules; their second, about betrayal.

She found him infuriating, too certain of his own decency. He found her fascinating, too good at pretending not to care. Like collisions in physics, they fell into each other's orbit—inevitable once it started, and unable to pull apart.

Cairo was all heat and lies, and their affair burned accordingly. They met between briefings behind locked doors, in nights that smelled of dust and oranges. They were brief but passionate.

He told her that she made him believe in honesty again. She told him honesty was just another disguise.

But as all good things must, it ended—in orders, gunfire, an operation gone wrong, information leaked, a courier shot, and her name appearing on a report that shouldn't have existed. When London investigated the leak, she protected the network. Max thought she'd betrayed him. After that, he never forgave her.

She never forgot him.

By 1943, Max had been recruited by the Bureau, while Lucy

was reassigned to London, working in Section IX, Soviet Counterintelligence, under a rising officer named Kim Philby. He was a charming man, almost as charming as Max Calder, in a way that always felt rehearsed, smart in a way that demanded witnesses yet left none.

They sparred over codework and philosophy, both aware of the spark that had formed between them, yet too professional to name it—until they no longer had to. Their affair was brief, dangerous, and perfectly symmetrical. It was different from the heated, passionate romance Lucy had had with Max.

She knew Philby was lying before he did, saw it in the way he watched the shadows when no one was behind him. And when she finally filed a report outlining her suspicions, it disappeared before ever reaching the director's desk. Though Philby never mentioned it, the next day she had been reassigned to a diplomatic cover in Vienna.

She understood the message clearly. MI6 didn't shoot its best assets. But if you crossed Philby, it would bury you in Europe and let accidents do the work.

In 1948, Vienna was a divided city, full of displaced people and ideas—a different Vienna than the one London had bled over in 1947, and a different Vienna than the one Max Calder and Alicia Rayes had fought in during their first foray against the Mirror. But Lucy didn't know this at the time.

She drove a small black Austin for the embassy, passing coded messages to couriers who thought she was a secretary. One late night in November, her car skidded on an icy turn outside the city. The crash report filed by an officer she didn't know said her body was never recovered. She was declared dead within forty-eight hours.

There was a neatness to it that made her skin crawl—the kind of administrative certainty that didn't happen by accident. Everyone had made sure the paperwork was closed, making sure that her death was the truth.

The CIA found her three months later in a hospital near

Salzburg. They were polite about it, of course. The Americans always were.

A man named Walker sat at the foot of the bed, read from a folder, and offered her a cigarette.

"We can give you a new name," he said at last, "and something better than London's gratitude."

"I'm listening," Lucy replied, watching the smoke curl toward the ceiling.

They called her Lucinda Hale and placed her in Lisbon, a neutral ground where she could rebuild and recuperate. There, she became a liaison between the newly formed CIA and remnants of British intelligence, fluent in both worlds but truly loyal to neither. That was what the Americans valued most.

She lived in a flat overlooking the Tagus, drank coffee at A Brasileira, and played the piano badly to keep her hands busy. Her new colleagues admired her efficiency and intellect but feared her smile. They called her Locket again, this time from the old nursery rhyme, unaware that the name was a resurrection. It seemed to follow her throughout life, though whether it was by fate or chance, she didn't know.

Lisbon suited her. It was a city of secrets, a halfway place between past and future. She would work nights decoding signals from Moscow and mornings sipping coffee with American analysts who worked alongside her.

It was there that she had first heard the term "the Mirror." A research project, technically scientific, but unofficially invisible, studying resonance fields and temporal effects. In the future, it would change to something far more dramatic.

Lucy had recognized the shape of it immediately. Though she had never worked on the project herself, she had heard whispers —whispers of recursion and the Mirror—particularly when Max Calder had transferred to the Bureau.

She had requested a transfer instantly. When Walker had asked her why, out of curiosity, she had replied that the universe was repeating itself.

"I'd rather be in the loop than outside it," she said, and with that, he signed the papers.

Washington was far colder than Lisbon and far less forgiving. It smelled of chalk dust, paper, and sweat more often than not. At first, Lucy was only a name on a file, reverting back to her real name, inconspicuous and ignored. She wrote summaries and translated intercepts, keeping her opinions to herself and letting others take credit for her conclusions.

However, she quickly learned that Walker hadn't recruited her by himself. He was simply a doorway to the room, a pawn in a larger game.

A year into her work, reports began to circulate—her reports, without her name attached—passed along to a counterintelligence desk that was unknown to anyone it didn't wish to be known by.

When Lucy finally met James Jesus Angleton, it was in a windowless office where he sat behind a desk, his fingers pressed together and his analytical eyes studying her face. He seemed nervous, paranoid in a way, but unbearably intelligent. He didn't offer her a cigarette, but he asked a question.

"You were declared dead," he said, his eyes flat, his voice calculating. "Do you consider that a mistake or an advantage?"

"An advantage," Lucy replied, holding his gaze. "If you know how to use it."

Angleton's mouth had twitched then, almost forming a smile.

"I do," he said.

He took her file from Walker without ceremony. Her clearance began to rise in increments in the weeks that followed, and she was given access to names she wasn't supposed to know, rooms she wasn't supposed to enter, and problems that didn't exist on the official record. When she asked Angleton why, he said it was out of necessity.

It was then that he taught her the American way of doing the same old British thing—compartmentalizing everything until even the truth itself was locked away, only to be discovered when needed.

By 1951, they had sent her to Havana under diplomatic cover. The city was everything Europe wasn't: loud, humid, and always alive. Here, she began to build her network, as she had always done, trading information between American and British stations and learning everything she could about the city.

But sometimes, alone on her balcony overlooking the harbor, she would take out the silver locket her father had given her, open it, and stare at the small photograph inside of her mother, smiling faintly. That picture was the only memory that hurt and had survived every alias she'd worn.

It was her nightly ritual, the only one she allowed herself. The only time she would pour a drink, study her reflection in the window, and whisper an old joke to herself.

"Did you know the most common cause of death for ex-Soviet agents is falling from a window?"

It was her joke and her warning, a charm against gravity—both kinds.

Lucy Howard never married. Her file in London ended with a single line: "Presumed deceased, Vienna, 1948." Her file in Washington began with another line: "Active asset. Level 5 clearance. Trust conditional."

She was cynical, yet beneath all the cynicism, she still carried the remnants of that little girl from the Cotswolds—the one who whispered lies to the wind because the truth was too fragile to travel far.

Sometimes, when the nights grew too quiet, she could imagine her father's voice reading Pushkin, her mother's laugh echoing through the hall at Charlton, and Max Calder's eyes catching hers across the smoke of a Cairo café—eyes that told her she would see him again later.

She knew she'd never go home again, and she wasn't sure if she'd ever find love, but she had found something more enduring: purpose. It was the kind of purpose that kept her answering Angleton's calls no matter the hour.

The first time he rang her in Havana, the line was bad. It sounded staticky, and he didn't bother with greetings.

"There's a facility outside the city," he said. "Rum distillery, Soviet guard rotations, unusual electric behavior."

"Unusual how?" she asked.

"Like a decision that keeps repeating itself—like a pulse or a resonance."

A courier had delivered the rest in a sealed envelope: hand-developed, hand-delivered, with no return address. Inside was a single-page directive and a list of names—names she wasn't supposed to recognize and yet did anyway.

"Calder, Max. NO CONTACT. Rayes, Alicia. NO CONTACT. Retrieve any material pertaining to Behavioral Protocols, Conditioning Notes, or Lock Mechanisms. Prioritize over extraction. Prioritize over destruction."

At the bottom, one typed phrase had been underlined twice: DECISION LOCKING.

Lucy read it once, then again. She understood the rule about Calder immediately. Angleton didn't fear men like Max because they were violent, but he feared them because they were unpredictable, and unpredictability was the one thing that a man like Angleton could never see coming.

She folded the paper quietly and slid it back into the envelope.

Outside, Havana kept singing.

Lucy Howard—Locket—lived between the reflections, and yet now she was being pulled out of her life, out of her purpose, to see Max Calder yet again.

Somewhere in the hum of every machine that would one day try to look backward through time, a faint echo of her voice still lingered, saying the only thing she ever truly believed:

"No one really falls; we're just pushed over the edge by the choices we've already made."

ALEXANDER BENTLEY

But where would she be pushed now?

CHAPTER 9
CÁRDENAS CONFIRMATION

I opened my eyes slowly, blinking once or twice to make sure I was really awake. More often than not these days, I couldn't tell for sure. When I'd fallen asleep the night before, I hadn't quite been sure I'd wake up in Havana or back in that Soviet ship's belly, drowning in diesel and the blue-white light.

Above me, the ceiling fan turned lazily in slow circles. Every third rotation creaked—repetitive, almost enough to drive a man mad. The air wasn't much better—wet, heavy, and warm enough to make the sheets stick to my skin.

I ran my fingers through my hair, where salt from the night before had dried in white lines, caked against my skin. It wouldn't be much, but I'd have to take a shower before anything else. Living in colder climates hadn't prepared me for the pure, oppressive heat of Havana. Even Lisbon wasn't this oppressive.

I sat up a bit too fast, and the room tilted. For a second, I saw water where there wasn't any, a flash of flame, men running, and a slick black metal surface. Then it all snapped back into place, leaving me with just the ceiling and a cheap lamp with a dead bug inside the glass.

Already, my headache rushed in, back to greet me in a new

day—a dull throb behind the eye, something I figured might never go away.

Across the room, Alicia sat at the table, the shutters half-closed. She had the portable Fraser-Smith rig open in front of her, peering at the brass faceplate as it caught the light seeping through the shuttered window. Copper coils lay around it on the towel like ribs. Her hair was still damp at the ends, but her posture was one of complete focus.

"You're awake," she said. She didn't look up.

"Yeah, unfortunately," I muttered.

Her eyes flicked to me, quick and sharp, checking to see if I was slipping. A glimpse of affection flitted across her gaze, but something else, too—almost caution.

"How bad?" she asked.

"I've been worse," I said, rolling my shoulders. "It'll take more than that to get to me."

"I believe you, except you always say that," she replied, and turned her attention back to the rig.

I washed up. It wasn't much, but I managed to remove the grime from my face. Afterward, I made my way back to Alicia—and just in time, too.

On the other table, the shortwave set hissed, staticky, layered with faint voices. Havana was already waking up outside our shuttered room: muffled horns in the distance, a radio playing from some house a block over, and the shouts of men and the barking of dogs.

Almost out of habit, Alicia reached for the dial of the radio and turned it. The static thinned, and then a carrier tone cut in clean and confident—Angleton's voice coming through on a secure patch, clipped and careful, as if he were speaking through his teeth.

"Calder, Rayes."

"We're here," Alicia said, leaning in.

"Well, you made the newspapers," he said. "My station's been sweeping the docks since dawn—ships half sunk, harbor patrol is everywhere. The Soviets are nowhere to be seen."

I closed my eyes. I could still feel the cold water against my skin, the unbearably loud ripping noise as if the air had been torn when the ship exploded.

"You destroyed what remained aboard," Angleton continued, "that much is clear, but unfortunately, it wasn't the primary cargo."

"Yeah, we know," Alicia said, her jaw tightening. "Moreau confirmed that."

"Well, good. We're in agreement then." He paused for a moment. "Now, the components that matter were offloaded before your enthusiastic mission."

"As best our intel can tell, they were moved inland under escort last night to Cárdenas," I said.

"Yes, Cárdenas," Angleton replied. "My people have their eyes on the road. They've seen Soviet personnel, not Cuban. Far better discipline than there should be for a rum operation, though I'm sure you know why that is already."

"Yeah, because the distillery is already active," I said.

Alicia chimed in, "Likely more active now that the components have been transferred."

There was another pause.

It was the kind of pause that meant Angleton was deciding exactly how much he wanted to admit to us. Though I hadn't known the man for long and still didn't know him well, I was confident enough that Angleton was the type of man who trusted no one and believed what they said even less.

But eventually, he spoke.

"Yes," he said at last. "Whatever they're running beneath Cárdenas—call it V4 or whatever the hell you want to name it—it's fully operational now. Those pieces that they were transporting on the ship, those were likely the last pieces of the puzzle. My technicians have been monitoring resonance pulses in and around Cuba. The fields are growing. We're seeing disruptions across Havana that match, and in some cases exceed, your Scottish profiles."

"And what does the CIA want with it?" I asked.

Angleton didn't answer immediately. When he did, he spoke with a flatter voice than he had before.

"Containment," he said. "Recovery, if it's feasible."

"We're not here to fetch you some sort of trophy," I spat.

Alicia shot me a look, but I continued on.

"The Mirror is far too dangerous for whatever projects you're trying to run."

"I'm aware of your Bureau's position," Angleton said. "That's actually why I'm calling."

The line clicked once.

"Director Moreau is patched in now," he said. "She requested it."

Static thickened on the line for a second, and then Moreau's voice came through clearer than Angleton's.

"Good day, Agents. Angleton."

"Elspeth," he replied.

No one bothered with pleasantries. They didn't need them. Men like Angleton and women like Moreau didn't waste their breath on anything unless they were playing the game—the game that moved all the pieces they held.

Moreau spoke first. "You're not recovering it," she said.

Angleton exhaled slowly. It sounded as if he was considering a more chastising response, but when he spoke, his voice was calm.

"Director Moreau," he said. "You understand what you're asking me to do, don't you? Asking me to let a Soviet-built temporal device remain in place while your two agents go in and destroy it in the middle of a volatile city that could fold in on itself at any moment."

"Yes, I understand," Moreau replied. "Because if it survives, it spreads."

"And yet," Angleton countered, "if it's destroyed, we lose the only chance we have to truly understand it—to counter it. Your Bureau can afford purity because you're a ghost organization by now. And from what I hear, you won't be an organization much longer. Mine is real. Mine answers to committees."

"Committees of whom?" Moreau asked. "Politicians, Angleton? Surely you realize that isn't the same as reality. The Bureau invented the Mirror. You're not here to play hot potato with it, tossing it to any organization that thinks they have the intellect to understand it. Men like our scientists don't exist anymore. I challenge you to find them."

There was silence long enough that I thought the line had dropped. I wasn't going to be the first to speak, that was for sure. And so I remained quiet until I heard Moreau's voice again as she finally spoke.

"No. It's bigger than you. Which is why you're already trying to hold it in your hands like a grenade that'll explode. Angleton, you have no idea what this device is capable of."

I could see Alicia's fingers curling around the rig's handle until her knuckles whitened as she listened.

"If you and your people destroy V4, Moscow will rebuild the technology. So will Washington. You know that, don't you? Director Moreau, with all due respect, the Bureau is the one that brought this technology into the world. You don't owe it to the world, but now that the technology is here, it's here to stay."

Moreau's tone didn't change. "Then we'll burn every root we find, starting with this one. The technology may be here, and I will admit that is a result of my inclinations and proclivities. And yet, I refuse to let it develop any faster."

Alicia leaned in toward the microphone. "Angleton, you ask for our help because you don't trust Philby. Don't become him."

For a moment, I could hear a thin shift of breath, as if Angleton had been forced to look at his own shadow. What Alicia said had hit home.

"For now, you're going back to Cárdenas tonight," he said.

"Just confirm what's operational. Get your eyes on it. I want a full assessment before anyone pulls a trigger."

Moreau's voice cut in. "Calder, Rayes. Angleton is indeed the one who initiated this operation, but your directive remains unchanged. Identify, destroy if possible. There will be no procurement."

Angleton's voice sharpened. "Elspeth—"

"I'm not debating you," she said. "This is an order to my agents."

"Very well," Angleton said, his voice quieter and controlled. "I'll have transport arranged. You have twelve hours before the next movement window. After that, I can't promise what the Soviets will do. Our boots on the ground are struggling to keep up."

It was then that Angleton's voice dropped another register. All of the pretense and fake charm was gone now, and what came through the speaker was the voice of a man who lived in a paranoid yet brilliant state of mind, always planning one step ahead.

"Listen very carefully," he said. "Despite your good intent, after that game you pulled at the harbor, they're in complete lockdown. Now that's bad for you, but it's leverage for me. And because of this, I'm going to help you out."

"How so?" I asked.

"The distillery can't call the Cuban army every time they get spooked," Angleton said. "If they want to keep pretending it's a distillery on official paperwork, they have to stay at least partially off the books. So what we do is force them to stay above ground and deal with the paper."

"What does that mean?" I asked.

"It means," he said, "a Cuban inspector shows up at their front gate tonight with a manifest discrepancy tied to the ship. Pick your poison—customs, health, fire. He'll have the stamps and he'll have a badge, just enough authority and just enough pretend ignorance to be dangerous to them.

"While they're busy playing rum merchant, my station will light a second problem on the other side of the fence. Only smoke, no bodies. North line near the cane, right near where someone has already been cutting the wire."

My eyes darted to Alicia, and her eyes met mine. How did he know about the cut in the wire fence? What type of intelligence did the Americans have?

But Angleton wasn't done.

"They'll think that the saboteurs came back to finish the job," Angleton said. "I expect they'll surge their patrols to the north, dragging out their dogs, rifles, and floodlights along with them. That will give you a window. It won't be long—only minutes—but it will be long enough to get on a roof and into a vent. I have the documents and plans made up from the latest blueprints we have access to. My driver will give them to you."

"And what if they don't take the bait?" Alicia asked.

"They will because they have to. You've already shown them that the enemy is real. My driver won't give you a cue—he'll be the one responsible for setting up most of this. But when you see the smoke, you move. And if you move too slow, you deserve what happens next."

I didn't like needing a man like Angleton. But then again, I liked dying even less. And his solution seemed pretty airtight.

"Thank you, Angleton." Moreau's voice softened by half a degree. "Just try to remember, this isn't a machine you can file and shelve away somewhere. The Mirror has a mind of its own now. It has sentience, far beyond what any of us could have imagined when we began work on it."

Then, with a click, Moreau left the line.

Angleton lingered only a second more before speaking. "Calder."

"Yeah?"

"You seem different. You're speaking less. You're already feeling it, aren't you? The repetition. The city."

I looked at the edge of the table and saw it blurring in my

vision. For a second, I hesitated. I didn't know how much I wanted to share. But then I nodded as if Angleton were right in front of me.

"Yeah," I said. "I feel it. The city is folding in on itself."

"Then don't let that get inside your decisions. If you hesitate, that's how men die. Just focus."

And just like that, he was gone. The radio returned to its ordinary hiss.

Alicia stared hard at the speaker grille as if she could see through it into Angleton's mind. Then, with a firm twist, she shut it off.

We sat there in silence for a second. Though Alicia and I hadn't been as close of late as we used to be, there was still a sense of camaraderie we only felt when we were alone together.

She finally looked up at me. "He wants it, doesn't he?" she asked.

"Of course he wants it," I replied. "Everyone wants it."

She stood, beginning to pack with that quiet efficiency that always made me feel nervous, as if somehow I were out of place in her precision. I helped as well. It was the least I could do.

The rig went into the attaché case, coils wrapped in canvas, the toggle switch locked at null. She checked it again and again, making sure it would operate if push came to shove.

"Do we really listen to Angleton's orders?" I muttered.

"Yes," she said over her shoulder. "We need to confirm, not engage. Remember, Moreau said that as well."

I nodded, lighting a cigarette.

"You think I'm a problem?"

"No. I think you're a problem amplifier," she shot back.

I glanced up, and I could see in her eyes a tinge of regret for what she had said.

"Max, you've always been one for theatrics, but last time we were there, you touched the elevator door. Hell, you nearly slid in place."

"I'm not going to touch anything this time," I said.

"Agreed," she replied. "We're going to look, and then we leave."

I wanted to argue. From everything I had learned about the Mirror, looking was almost impossible. It was part of the Mirror being the Mirror. The Mirror didn't care whether you touched it or not. The pulses spread too far, and whatever strange and primordial mind had been created through these quantum fields would learn of us regardless.

But I didn't say anything. I bit my tongue, and we continued to prepare.

By the time the sun began to set, the heat had thickened further into something oppressive—quite possibly the worst heat we'd felt since we arrived. The rain had stopped for once, but the air still tasted damp, and the street outside offered nothing but shimmering reflections under the lamps, as if it had been varnished and polished.

It was then that Angleton's driver picked us up without a word, silently handing us the documents to read as he drove us along. He drove the same tired black sedan, with the same old-smelling upholstery, with the faint tinge of cigarette smoke. Alicia and I stepped in quietly. We hadn't talked much, and we didn't speak during the drive.

The engine roared, and we were off, driving east. We saw cane fields again, the same old road, the same darkness around us. It was funny to me—funny that despite the similarities, it didn't feel like last night. The resonance was stronger now, and it felt as if the world was trying to replay the route, tightening the loop each time.

I caught myself staring out the window, watching a roadside shrine pass by, then pass by again. The same candle flame and the same small crooked cross.

I knew Alicia could tell that something was off, but she didn't ask what I saw. She just stared ahead into the distance, her jaw tight, one hand resting beneath her coat where I knew her pistol was ready.

We left the driver and his car about a half a mile away from the distillery.

It rose out of the dark, as it had the last time, floodlights far more numerous than before, taller fenced sections where older ones had been replaced, and new patrol routes tighter and sharper. Men in heavy boots moved as if they'd been trained in Russian winters—slow yet resilient, patrolling on a never-ending march.

Luckily, Angleton's plan came through for us.

We saw it before we heard it. It was our signal to move.

A bloom of dirty orange smoke rose on the north side of the compound, low and fast, as if something had exploded from beneath the dirt. I heard shouts in Russian carried on the wind across the cane fields, accompanied by the sound of boots striking the ground.

In unison, the floodlights swung, obedient to the panic that coursed through the compound. The white, bright cones of light swept away from the service buildings, snapping toward the smoke, shadows moving along with them.

"That's the flare," Alicia whispered.

Already moving, I followed low and fast, my boots whispering through the cane. My head throbbed with the familiar pressure, as if the air had become inundated with the Mirror's pulse. But the perimeter had eyes in only one direction now, and that wasn't on Alicia and me.

I knew that at the front gate, there was likely another commotion as well—one that had started ten or so minutes before Angleton's secondary diversion. Officers would be tied up—high-ranking ones—trying to deal with paperwork and the pretense they were trying to bury.

Through a gap in the cane fields as we ran, I saw a Cuban patrol jeep angled across the entrance like a barricade. A uniformed man stood there holding documents in the rain-slick light. There were several Soviets clustered around him in a tight knot. They kept their rifles slung, not raised, even after the commotion caused by the smoke. If they raised them, it would mean admitting they weren't simply guarding rum.

As much as I didn't want to admit it, Angleton was a brilliant man. He'd brought us a distraction they couldn't shoot—one made of shadows and smoke and political promises. It kept the Russians busier than a full-on firefight ever would.

This time, we didn't go near the freight door. We kept low, circling wide, finding a service building near the back—the exact one that Angleton had mentioned in our call. Its rooftop was lower than the main structure, and its vent stacks breathed warm, smoky air into the night. The driver had gotten us close enough with little to no eyes on us. Alicia and I moved through the cane, the damp leaves brushing against our clothes.

As we neared the service building, the unmistakable yet faint smell of ozone began to permeate the air, along with it, the hum. It was there now—that never-ending pulsing hum that seemed to indicate the Mirror was nearby—more than nearby: it was operational.

We moved silently. Though Angleton had set us up for success on this mission, I knew that if we put one foot out of line, we would jeopardize everything.

Alicia found the access ladder first. It was rusty, half-hidden behind a pipe run, but still usable. She tested it gingerly with one hand before climbing up.

"It'll hold," she said, and I followed.

We climbed the ladder and reached the roof. It was slick with humidity. The metal felt warm beneath my palms, the wind swaying more up here, above the gentle open fields, carrying the distant scent of the sea. But despite its attempts to parlay with fresh air, the smell of the distillery overwhelmed it.

We moved stealthily toward the vent housing and crouched together, listening. Alicia produced a small screwdriver, easing out two fastenings silently, and I lifted the grill with ginger care as soon as she had finished.

She glanced at me then.

"No heroics, Max," she whispered.

"I'm not in the mood for heroics right now," I muttered back.

"Good."

We slid into the vent, one after the other. It was far more spacious for her than it was for me. The duct was narrow enough to make anyone claustrophobic, the metal walls sweating with condensation, the warm air blowing a yeast stink and the sharp bite of chemicals past our faces. For a second, my coat snagged on a rivet, and I struggled, trying to twist my arm around so I could reach back and free it. If I made any noise, I knew the sound would echo through the whole building, but luckily, I managed to get it loose without any further complications.

We crawled onward on our elbows and knees, silently through the dark metal, guided only by the plans that Angleton had provided us with. Below us, I could hear voices—Russian men talking to each other, and the occasional curse word that transcended even the Russian language. My Russian wasn't the best, but I knew Alicia could understand every word.

We reached a cross-duct above what sounded like a larger space. I could hear the echo of machinery and the faint whirr and the whine of transformers. It was here that Alicia stopped, holding up a fist.

"Is this it?" she whispered toward me.

I thought for a second. "If my memories haven't failed me again, I believe so," I shot back, though I wasn't quite sure. I knew that my near-photographic memory was all we had to guide us on this trip. Assuming it was still working.

She eased forward, peering through a narrow inspection grill. I slid up beside her, my cheek pressed to the cool metal, and looked down.

The chamber below, however, was nothing like I had expected. It wasn't big—that was the first thing wrong about it. Rosyth Dockyard had been built like a cathedral—at least the Mirror room had: an acre-large underground bunker with an amphitheater for the Mirror, where it, along with all the wires and cables, was housed. This room, however, looked different—compact and efficient, as if someone had taken the design of the Mirror and reduced it down into something nearly a quarter the size.

In the very center sat Mirror V4. It wasn't a Mirror frame the way I remembered, the way Krane had designed it. There was no grand arch to it, no sprawling copper frame, no massive black slab. Instead, it was a tight, squat assembly, barely two-thirds the height of a man, made of smooth, shining brass and copper, bolted down to a concrete platform, with coils wrapped like muscle around a black core no larger than a man's torso.

The core wasn't flat, either. It looked as if it were glass folding in on itself, a continual pulsing surface that seemed to shine and shimmer with a silvery light, not the blue light of Rosyth. And it pulsed again and again, but not in a pattern. This Mirror pulsed irregularly. It wasn't a steady hum like I was used to or a predictable glow. Instead, the light stuttered in blue-white flashes, then dropped into near-dark, then flared again in some strange, sickly, fascinating manner.

There weren't many cables. That was the second thing I noticed that was wrong. Every Mirror version I had seen before had needed immense power simply to stay online, let alone pulse. The pulses took the most power. It was enough to drain the grid of a small town. And yet, weirdly, this thing looked as if it fed itself.

Two men in white coats stood nearby at a console, vacuum tubes glowing from behind a mesh panel. One was older, his shoulders sagging, his hands moving fast despite his tired posture. The other one, thin and sharp, kept rubbing his temples as if he was fighting a headache of his own. From what I understood about the Mirror, he likely was—if not worse.

We had left the Resonance Rig in the car, to be used only as a last resort. We didn't need a Geiger counter for this one either. I could feel the pulse emanating from the Mirror, feel my bones rattling in my body, and Alicia's mouth tightened next to me. This wasn't just another Mirror. Though she didn't speak aloud, I knew she was thinking the same thing. Whatever this device was had been improved, upgraded, and innovated until it became something very different and truly alive.

My headache flared suddenly, viciously painful against the inside of my skull, a hot spike driven behind my eye. For a second, Mirror V4's stormy gray and black surface seemed to ripple like water, and in it, I could see Rosyth Dockyard cranes, dark, hulking, and black against a gray Scottish sky. Then I saw Invershiel—the wet stone and the smell of cold rain.

Next, Havana. But not Havana like it was now. I saw Havana with different cars, different uniforms, a street where the buildings had changed colors, where time merged together. I saw things from the future, past, and present, all in the city as one. This was a future beat that I didn't even recognize.

I blinked, the taste of copper on my tongue, and the chamber snapped back into place suddenly. But the sense that I had of the overlap didn't leave. It felt as if the room below was layered on top of itself, each new layer a potential discovery of new Mirror resonance.

Alicia nudged my arm, and I saw concern etched on her face.

"I'm fine," I mouthed, though her eyes stayed on me for a fraction of a second afterward.

And then I felt it. Not the pulse, not the machine—something else. A presence, the same feeling I'd had when I touched the elevator door, as if a set of eyes had turned toward me, focusing attention on me. I scanned the chamber wildly, trying to find it. There were the scientists, there was the Mirror. But where was it?

Then I saw it, in the far corner, where the floodlights didn't quite reach. There stood what looked like a silhouette just outside the light. It looked like a man, but it didn't move like a man. It was too still and far too flat, not even shifting its weight or breathing. It was just there, and I knew without knowing how I knew that it was watching us—watching me.

My skin went cold, and I could feel my hair standing on end. I'd experienced El Cuadro before—the awareness that the Mirror had spawned—but somehow this felt like a different version of it —more experienced, more intelligent, capable of moving on its own.

"Max," Alicia whispered, her voice barely audible, but I didn't answer.

The machine pulsed again, this time harder, and the very air in the duct vibrated around us. I could feel the metal beneath my body buzzing from the energy.

"Max, we have to go," Alicia whispered. I nodded.

"Let's go, then," I shot back, and together we backed away from the grille.

Behind us, the duct seemed to stretch, then shorten, then widen, and for a second, I wasn't sure which direction we'd come from. Then my mind caught up, and we continued crawling as fast as we could while remaining as quiet as we could.

Halfway back toward the access vent, I heard a sound below: sharp, angry shouting and scuffling, and the heavy footsteps of soldiers running. I wasn't sure if they'd heard something or if somehow the machine had let them know we were here. It undoubtedly already knew, but I didn't stop to ask, and Alicia didn't slow down either.

We dropped out onto the roof, snapped the grille solidly back into place, and slid the ladder into the cane without a word. We were back in the dark field, the distillery lights behind us, and the driver's car a low shape ahead. We ran in silence until Alicia spoke.

"That's not the Mirror, or at least the one we know," she said, her voice tight. "That's not anywhere near V3. That's something else completely."

"Yeah," I said, rubbing my eye gingerly, still feeling the pulsing headache behind it. "It's smaller. And stronger."

"I didn't see any energy source either," she managed to reply, though her voice sounded weak.

I glanced back at the distillery. Floodlights continued to sweep the area, with guards moving around like ants on a pile of fresh fruit. In the back of my mind, I could still feel that silhouette, still watching, even with so much distance and darkness between us.

"Well," Alicia said, "we confirmed it. Now I suppose we have to make a plan."

"Let's hope it's a good one," I replied. My mouth was dry, though, and I wasn't sure if any plan would be good enough to stop this.

Behind us, the distillery kept humming, warm and wrong, like some sick, irregular heartbeat beneath the earth. I continued running through the cane.

I wanted to leave before it could learn more about me.

CHAPTER 10
GRENADINES GENESIS

As was often the case, the radio refused to let the room stay quiet. It was like a bad habit you couldn't quit, something that kept coming back no matter how much you wished it would go away.

Though the shutters were still drawn, the heat found its way in anyway. The heat in Havana seeped through the walls, making the oppression in the safe house all the worse. It smelled of wet plaster, cordite, and old tobacco.

I sat on the edge of the bed, rolling my shoulders until something in my back popped. My ribs still ached from where I had hit the rail climbing off the Soviet ship, even though it had been nearly two days since.

Alicia was at the table, the attaché case open, laying out the equipment in neat rows so she could evaluate it once more. Our time to use the case was approaching: we both knew that much without saying it. From what she'd figured out, the case could collapse the very resonance fields that Mirrors used. We just had to get it to the Mirror.

The box was Fraser-Smith's, built down in the Kingsway tunnels where communications cabling ran like veins, though at some point—unclear to me as to when—it had been transferred to Invershiel.

Maybe out of precaution. Maybe out of fear for what the Mirror could do. Maybe by accident.

But in the end, we'd ended up with Fraser-Smith's device in our hands after the Bureau snagged it from Invershiel. We'd never met him. All we had been briefed on were Bureau notes in thin paper folders and a few comments from Opal as she had described it to us just before we were whisked off to Havana. The device itself didn't look like much—canvas-wrapped steel, a brass strip along the edge etched with a pattern that wasn't mere decoration if you stared long enough, and three exposed copper coils laid like ribs.

The Bureau scientists had theorized that the Mirror bled a signature when it stabilized—not power per se, but a pattern, a carrier wave pretending to be electricity—and the KX-7 could steal that pattern and throw it back at the machine.

Not perfectly, of course. Even Fraser-Smith would have had trouble matching the minds of Krane and Hawthorne. But close enough to confuse it.

The toggle had three detents—NULL, COUPLE, BREAK—and we were still learning what each one meant in the real world. NULL to keep a Mirror quiet, possibly—at least that was our working theory.

COUPLE to "latch" onto a Mirror array at close range and shove a baseline into it until it stopped knowing where it was.

BREAK to flip the imprint and spit something disharmonic into the coils, scrambling the alignment long enough for the Mirror to choke and collapse.

And while I'd helped as much as I could, this was Alicia's task. She had already made it clear to me that insofar as the Mirror was involved, she trusted my mind to react—not to plan.

She worked without speaking, her charming face focused on the task, her hands steady. On the floor by the chairs lay my coat, smelling of cane fields and ozone.

Now that we had confirmed that V4 at the distillery was operational—and not just operational, but worse than the previous models—we had one thing left to do: figure out how to actually access it long enough to sabotage it.

The radio hissed, clicked, and hissed again, the static coming to life. Alicia didn't look up. She didn't have to.

I sighed and rolled my eyes as the carrier tone cut through the static. We both recognized Angleton's channel by now. He'd called us frequently enough that we knew who it would be before he even spoke.

I leaned in, lit a cigarette between cupped hands, and waited for his voice.

"Calder, Rayes."

Angleton sounded tight, as if he'd spent all night arguing with himself over who he really wanted to trust and which side he really wanted to be on.

"You're up early," I said, "or you never went down."

"Haven't slept," he replied, with no humor in his tone. "We've had a development, and it's not one you can ignore."

Alicia's fingers paused on the rig's brass dial, and her eyes flicked up to watch my face.

"Talk," I said.

Angleton wasted no time. "Two senior Soviet personnel, two scientists associated with Laboratorio Especial No. 7, have disappeared from Havana."

"Disappeared how?" Alicia asked. "Defected?"

"If they defected, it was the worst and best defection in the history of these operations." I could hear him shuffling paper on his end of the line. "There were no exit stamps," he continued. "No boat charter, no aircraft manifests, no bribes paid in the usual channels, either. My station has followed the papers and the ports. Nothing. It's like they went ghost."

"Sounds familiar," I said, the headache behind my eyes climbing. "Got names?"

"Sergei Anokhin and Mikhail Popov. Both eminent physicists. Both were seen at Cárdenas within the last forty-eight hours, as well. And now they're gone."

"Gone?" Alicia asked.

"Gone," he confirmed. "And before you ask, yes. I think it's your phenomenon. I think your Mirror, well— how do you say it —made them slide."

I stared at the radio, trying to bring my mind into focus. More often than not these days, it was a hard task to do.

"You say they slid?" I asked. "But where to? And how would we know whether it's a geo-slide or a temporal-slide? Or maybe it was both?"

"That's where our report comes in," Angleton answered. "Windward Islands—the Grenadines, somewhere between St. Vincent and Grenada. We have a report. It is unofficial—a bit messy—from a British colonial constable down in Kingstown. According to his info, two foreign men appeared from nowhere in the night. They were speaking Russian, disoriented, and seemed to be talking nonsense. It was like their language had been garbled. With math, maybe. They vanished before anyone could put hands on them."

Alicia glanced at me, and I could see the resentment already forming behind her eyes. We had just put our eyes on V4. I had felt the thing watching us. Our victory was within grasp, and now Angleton wanted to send us away to chase two ghosts across the Caribbean.

I didn't want to move away from the machine we'd come here to kill. Not again.

But... I thought to myself. It wasn't like I had a real option. The Mirror had never cared what I wanted. It only cared to continue operating. And if this had been caused by the operation of the mirror, maybe the two scientists would be a piece of the puzzle.

"But why would V4 throw them into the islands?" Alicia asked suddenly. "It makes no sense, does it?"

"Whatever it is, it's clearly unstable," Angleton replied. "Or it's learning. Either way, those men are assets—assets with immense knowledge. Moscow is going to send a retrieval team. In fact, my station intercepted chatter—Grenada-based. They're already moving."

"And you want us to intercept first?" I cut in.

"Yes," Angleton said. "We can't allow the Soviets to get them back under guard. If they do, who knows what else they'll be able to implement before you two get around to disabling the Mirror."

"And I get that," I said. "But this is a big ask, Angleton. You're asking us to pull away from Cárdenas." I exhaled smoke, watching it drift toward the ceiling fan, where it dispersed in a cloud.

"If those men know how V4 was built, then they know how it can be unbuilt," Angleton replied. "You want the roots? They can tell you where those roots are. Your machine... I'm not familiar with this resonance rig, but are you entirely confident that it can get the job done?"

I sat in silence for a second. Nobody spoke, but I knew Angleton was right. The rig had been lauded for so long to be a Mirror killer, and yet, at most, Alicia only knew how to operate the device, not whether it would actually work.

We hadn't exactly had a lot of Mirrors to test it on.

Outside, a car horn sounded. Then, two seconds later, the same horn sounded again, with the exact same rhythm. I fought back a shudder, my skin prickling.

"You tell London?" Alicia asked.

"I told Moreau," Angleton replied. "Told her I was asking you, and told her why. I'm not sure she entirely liked it, but she did give me the go-ahead."

"Will you route us?" I asked.

"I already have it waiting," Angleton replied. "Havana to Kingston, Kingston to Barbados, Barbados to St. Vincent. From there, you'll likely need a boat."

"Barbados? Don't know anything about that place..." I

muttered. "But St. Vincent? I actually have a contact there: Basil Charles. Worked with the Bureau before. He's well-connected. Not much goes on without him knowing about it. He'll get us into the Grenadines without asking any questions."

"Well, that's good," Angleton said. "It was the only part of the journey I hadn't planned out yet."

"And if we catch them?" I asked.

"You'll have to keep them alive," Angleton said carefully. "Bring them back to Havana. Then we can talk about what comes next."

"We've already had that conversation, Angleton. V4 needs to be destroyed," I said.

Angleton sighed. "I know your position, and I'm not contesting it today. But you have to understand: even if we end up destroying it, you'll need the minds behind it to do so. I've read the reports. This Mirror is different from the others, isn't it?"

He wasn't wrong. Although I hadn't mentioned it, I could feel that pressure behind my eyes again. But it wasn't just a headache. It was a tension, as if something or someone somewhere had turned its face toward me in the dark, searching for my mind.

"All right, then," I said finally. "We'll go."

I noticed Alicia eyeing me, and I knew she was confused—confused by the speed I agreed to the project. Yet I didn't explain it. I couldn't explain it. But in the back of my head, I could hear Hawthorne's voice on that grainy recording, telling me to cut the roots and burn down the whole tree. If this was what I had to do to achieve that, this was what I would do.

Angleton exhaled, and I could hear the relief in his voice. "Good. My driver will pick you up in an hour. Keep the rig with you if you can. Other than that, pack light. And Calder?"

"Yeah?"

"There might come a point where you don't want to come back to Havana… don't want to finish the mission," Angleton said. "The further you get from that distillery, the more you'll likely want to believe it's not real."

I hesitated for a second. "I wish that was possible," I finally said. "But the Mirror is the only thing I know that's real at this point. The Mirror tells me what's real."

The line clicked, and the room settled back into silence.

"He's using us," Alicia said suddenly, closing the attaché case with a soft snap.

"Everyone's using us," I replied. "But isn't that how the world works?"

"What if this is a trap? The Soviets could expect us in the islands."

"Then we do what we always do," I said. "Improvise."

She smiled slightly, but the smile didn't reach her eyes. I slowly crushed my cigarette into an overflowing ashtray and stared into space.

"Max," Alicia said quietly, shocking me out of my reverie.

I looked up. "What?"

"You were worse last night," she said. "After we saw V4 at the distillery, your eyes..."

"I was tired," I interrupted.

"You weren't just tired." She leaned in. "Max, I've been with you through this entire journey, but right now it seems like you're not here with me."

"Maybe the field's spreading," I said.

"Maybe it's spreading because it wants you," she replied. "And Lucy?" she asked. "What about Lucy?"

"What about her? She's gone," I said.

"She wasn't gone," Alicia corrected. "She was extracted by the CIA, from the looks of it, after she helped us sink that ship in the harbor."

"And what of it?" I asked.

"Max, if Angleton's moving us out and Lucy's moving according to his orders, doesn't that mean we're being repositioned?"

"Can't we just reposition back?" I replied, rubbing my head and sighing. "We find the men, learn what they know, and then come back and hit the Havana Club Distillery… cut it out by its roots."

"Fine," Alicia said, nodding once and turning her attention back to the case. But I could tell that whatever I had said had relieved her—if only for a moment, it had alleviated her fears.

The driver arrived early in the morning, right on schedule. As always, it was a black sedan with a man behind the wheel, a new one this time, who didn't introduce himself. He wore a plain shirt with his sleeves rolled up to help combat the morning humidity.

I had begun to recognize these men as CIA. They were a different breed of intelligence than the London version, the kind that blended right in, and a part of me respected it. He didn't look at us or make eye contact as we got in, just revved up the engine and pulled away from the curb, driving bumpily along the streets of Havana.

The streets were already filling, men wearing straw hats, women carrying groceries, vendors shouting at one another, and a boy pedaling a bicycle with no chain guard. All normal—at least it looked that way on first glance. But every piece of the city seemed to be slightly off when you took a closer look.

We passed a street corner where a car sat idling, a bell chiming softly—once, then again, then again. At the next corner, I saw the same car, heard the same bell, and listened to the same rhythm. The people around didn't react either. Maybe they didn't hear it. Maybe it wasn't real, or maybe it was, and there were just two. At this point, I wasn't sure.

Alicia caught my eye and raised her eyebrows slightly, and I managed to grin. Whatever the situation we had found ourselves in felt like being trapped in a time bubble. So I kept my eyes forward, focused on the route, and watched as the driver took us down a road that avoided the harbor.

The air still carried the scent of smoke, salt, and diesel from two days ago when we had exploded the boat. I thought of the Soviet ship then, listing away in the water, half-sunk, with men shouting in Russian, and Lucy already gone by the time we reached the shore, walking away as if she hadn't even been there and didn't even know me.

I tried not to think about her. Whenever I thought about Lucy, I felt even more conflicted than when I thought about the Mirror itself. I wasn't sure what I wanted with her, whether or not I could ever truly forgive her for betraying me. And whenever I thought about her, I simply couldn't relax.

The airstrip outside Havana was little more than a strip of hard-packed earth, hemmed in by sugarcane fields. The sun cast a dull orange glow over the Caribbean, but already the heat pressed down, heavy with the smell of molasses and smoke. I checked my papers again, Bureau forgeries tucked into my coat pocket.

From the outside, the terminal building looked like any other mid-century airport—white walls, loud signs, and a flag that snapped patriotically in the wind. Inside, it was all bustle, sweat, and stale air, with the smell of paper and cigarette smoke. As was the case with all Havana buildings, the lazy ceiling fans did nothing to combat the heat, which permeated everything.

Alicia walked two steps ahead of me, holding the attaché case in her hand, her posture perfect. Her auburn hair reflected the glow of the fluorescent lights buzzing overhead as she made quite the picture. She looked like a woman with money and a reason to travel.

I tried not to think about what I looked like. Though I'd showered and felt arguably more refreshed, I hadn't shaved in two days now and likely looked like her tired husband or some hired muscle. We kept space between us anyway. It was a better alternative than staying closer and potentially inviting questions we didn't want asked.

At the counter, a clerk with nicotine on his fingers took my passport, not even glancing at my face. The passport said Martin Kale, shipping surveyor. From the clerk's eyes, I could tell he didn't even read my name, though. He simply stamped the page hard, leaving the ink splotched like a bruise, then stamped it again.

I blinked, and he stamped it again. Three times now, the same spot, same motion, same bored demeanor. And yet the ink hadn't changed.

I froze. The clerk looked up at me, irritated.

"Thank you," I managed to stutter, stepping back and forcing my legs to move. I didn't look behind me or at my passport. I didn't know what I'd find on it.

In the waiting area, a loudspeaker crackled above the noise. It spoke in Spanish, in English, in Spanish again. The same sentence, the same cadence, repeating itself. I heard a baby cry behind me, the wail and screeching reaching a pitch. Then it stopped abruptly, as if the sound had been cut out of the world with a knife, leaving nothing but a void.

My skin felt cold despite the heat. Havana was already folding in on itself. This Mirror V4 wasn't just a targeted one. All the previous renditions we'd faced had largely been targeted. Specific individuals, of course, could be tuned or primed to it and could be sent sliding, either geo-spatial or temporal or both. And yet, this Mirror was different. It seemed as if the city itself was all part of one giant slide.

I glanced up at Alicia, who sat across the room, her eyes scanning the crowd. She didn't meet my gaze, but the tapping of her foot quickened slightly as I watched her, and I smiled. I knew that she could tell I was looking at her, and something about that comforted me.

A while later, I stood to stretch, then meandered over casually and sat only a space away from Alicia. We didn't speak, but when she passed on the way to the gate, I leaned toward her, keeping my voice low.

"You see that?" I asked.

She didn't look at me. Her eyes stayed on the window as she walked.

"I see it," she said. "This is bad."

"It's bad, all right," I echoed.

It felt as if reality itself was coming apart.

CHAPTER 11
COLONIAL CARIBBEAN

We boarded the plane, a short, ugly prop job that looked as if it had been patched together from multiple spare parts and the crashes of other planes. It was a DC-3 with tired paint and engines that roared louder than they should have, like the hubris of a smoker coughing after a deep inhale.

The interior of the poorly maintained plane felt worn, overheated, and quietly indifferent to comfort. The cabin smelled of warm oil, dust, old canvas, and sweat ground permanently into the threadbare seat fabric—something sour that never quite left the upholstery once it learned how to stay. The seats were bolted unevenly to the floor, their colors faded beyond recognition, with armrest ashtrays scarred and overflowing. The narrow aisle tilted slightly, and the overhead racks were bent and overloaded with bags, parcels, and crates that rattled even before the engines started. I was grateful that Angleton had arranged such splendid CIA-approved transport for us.

When the engines turned over, vibration spread through the cabin, growing into an uneven, constant growl that rendered conversation pointless. Loose panels buzzed, seat frames rattled, and the unfamiliar noises went unnoticed as no one reacted.

Small, cloudy windows leaked thin drafts of cold air, and the ventilation remained poor and stale.

I took a window seat and watched as Alicia found her own seat several rows away. The interior stirred up old, unwanted memories of wartime flights and all the boats I'd traveled on.

The flight attendant moved with routine fatigue, reciting safety instructions from memory rather than care. Behind the closed cockpit door, the pilots' voices carried faintly, discussing fuel or unreliable gauges without any urgency. Passengers—farmers, clerks, soldiers, businessmen—sat silently among their baggage, knowing better than to complain. The aircraft felt old but experienced, held together by habit and repetition, flying not with confidence or fear, but with the shared understanding that endurance, not comfort, is what kept it aloft. The DC3 was never meant to be comfortable, and this one had definitely stopped pretending.

As the engines started, the propellers began to circle, and I watched them out the window, my mind bored for once. The cabin began to vibrate, and the stale air shifted as the plane rumbled along the runway, wheels skimming dust and cane stubble before dragging itself free of the ground. Havana fell away behind us—red-tiled roofs, crumbling mansions, the sea wall curving white in the morning light.

Inside, the cabin was cramped and hot, the engines hammering just beyond the thin metal skin. I kept my hat pulled low, watching the horizon tilt as the plane banked over the Straits of Florida. Alicia gripped the armrest, her eyes fixed on the open water stretching endlessly ahead.

After an hour, dark clouds built into dark towers over the Caribbean. The plane juddered, slipping through rough air, and for an instant, I thought I saw something impossible through the side window—the faint outline of Rosyth's cranes, half-hidden in mist, where no cranes could ever be. I blinked, and the sea returned, blue and endless.

The pilot announced over the noise of the engines, "Two hours, maybe less, to Kingston."

I struck a match, cupping it against the draft. The cigarette smoke curled unnaturally toward Alicia, even though the air vents pointed the other way. She looked at me, her face tight.

"The Mirror's reach is wider than we thought," she said.

I didn't answer, only exhaled smoke, watching it twist in patterns that felt too deliberate to be chance. I will be glad when this leg is over.

Ahead lay Jamaica, and thankfully—hopefully—a Pan Am Clipper would be waiting.

———

Kingston hit us like a tsunami.

The plane bucked in the crosswind as it descended, Kingston Harbor glittering on one side, the Caribbean Sea rolling endlessly blue on the other. The clouds broke just before landfall. Through the streaked windows, I saw Jamaica unfurl—green ridges tumbling into bright water, Kingston Harbor spreading wide like a bowl. The plane tilted hard as the pilot lined up the runway: a thin strip of tarmac stretched across a narrow spit of sand, sea on one side, the broad harbor on the other.

The plane's touchdown was rough, wheels bouncing once before settling, engines roaring against the drag. From above, it had looked like we were landing on water. Jamaica's air was wet in a different way—less glitter, more grit. It smelled of rain-soaked asphalt, jet fuel, and something sweet yet almost rotten, like day-old fruit in the heat. As we had approached land, the aircraft had rolled in slowly, taking careful turns, as if it didn't trust the weather even after reaching the ground.

Palisadoes Airfield looked little more than a whitewashed blockhouse and a control tower, with a Union Jack snapping above them in the salt wind. A row of palm trees bent toward the sea. Beyond the fence, fishing huts leaned against coconut palms, and children waved at the plane as it taxied. From the window, I could see the majestic Kingston Harbor, all busy, dotted with ships and small craft, beyond which the Blue Mountains rose, jutting hard and green from the ground like a wall that held the island itself in place.

The terminal was practical and colonial-style—a low building with covered walkways, modest corrugated roofing, and signs that screamed practicality rather than effort. Ceiling fans turned lazily over wooden benches where missionaries dozed beside families with wicker baskets. A customs clerk in khaki, his spectacles sliding down his nose, sat behind a wooden counter furnished with an ink pad and a blotter, stamping passports with smudged indifference. It was the kind of setup that many of these more modest airports carried—practical, likely in place since before the war. I glanced around, observing the lorries waiting to haul freight toward the docks near the outside fence line, watching laborers dawdling beneath an awning, and watching the planes as if they were still a novelty. I walked in ahead of Alicia, who was a few paces behind.

We moved through customs, our papers held out, our faces blank. We didn't speak, though I wasn't sure if it was because we had nothing to talk about, or if both of us were too worried that anything we said might be used against us by our enemies, by the Russians, or by the Mirror itself.

Outside the terminal, it had begun to rain again, the tropical rain falling hard and fast. Then, as suddenly as it had come, it stopped, as if it had changed its mind. The rain left the tarmac steaming, water running off in thin sheets from the edge of the roof, pooling around the curb where porters waited with handcarts at the ready. The air was fresher here, carrying the salt from the harbor along with the sharp smell of aviation fuel. It was a smell I'd come to associate with the islands—that, and the smell of wet cane, damp earth, and fruit.

Beyond the wire fence, a strip of the Palisadoes road was visible, and, far beyond that, the outline of Kingston itself came into view.

I slid my passport across to the customs and immigration clerk. The man never looked twice.

The airport building was obviously never designed for comfort—only for throughput. Alicia felt the weight of eyes upon her. A man in a pale suit stood near the windows, newspaper in his hand, not turning a single page. His gaze flicked up too often. When she looked again, he was gone, replaced by a sailor who seemed not to notice her at all.

On the tarmac, a silver Pan Am Clipper gleamed in the sun. I imagined that this was our next flight. I was shortly to find out I was wrong. Stevedores shouted as they loaded crates, their voices doubling oddly, repeating a half-second too late, like an echo that didn't belong.

There were pillars along the walkway, offering spots you could lounge without looking like you were waiting, and I watched carefully, as I always did—these were good positions for a handoff, ideal for surveillance, and perfect positions for someone to melt back into obscurity and disappear into the crowd.

The exact places we needed.

Near one of the pillars, a man in a short-sleeved shirt and a crumpled tie met us, holding out an envelope in one hand as if it were nothing. He didn't make eye contact, and we didn't say a word. He didn't give us his name, but he didn't need to. The envelope was all we needed, and as I passed it off to Alicia, she opened it just enough for us to glance inside.

Tickets, routing, and new forms. Everything was stamped, all paper—the sort of things that would keep us safe along our trip.

I lit a cigarette, watching the smoke curl sideways toward the sea. "We're already inside it."

Alicia glanced at the waiting planes. "Then we'd better keep moving before it closes the net."

As we walked, the man who had disappeared into the crowd

after the handoff suddenly reappeared next to us, as if he'd been trailing us. I tensed for a second, but he simply leaned in, close enough that I could smell the whisky on his breath.

"Two Russians were reported on a beach in the south of Mustique," he murmured. "Local fishermen said they appeared out of nowhere. One looked like an old man; the other looked sick. Not sure how much time you have, if our assessment is correct."

"Old?" Alicia asked, her eyes snapping up.

"That's what he said." The man shrugged, his eyes scanning the crowd.

In a hurry, I nodded and increased my pace. Markov had aged decades in seconds. If the Mirror had thrown Anokhin and Popov out onto the islands, what would it have done to them on the way? Whatever it had done, it was clear V4 wasn't taking kindly to them. I also wasn't sure how much longer we had.

The man straightened up.

"As far as we know, they don't know you two are trailing their scientists, but that could change. You'll see men who don't belong... who don't fit in. Don't give them reason to suspect you."

Then he turned and walked away without another word, vanishing into the crowd once again, as if he'd never existed.

I shook my head. Angleton and the Americans did things differently than we did, in more ways than one; that was for sure.

We waited for the next flight under the airport's tin roof, the echo of raindrops sounding tenfold as the storm returned. The transit lounge was a simple, long room that stretched in either direction, with peeling paint and a cluster of notices pinned to a corkboard. Flight times were written on a chalkboard in neat, blocky letters—Barbados, Trinidad, Nassau—each one lined up with the time and price, until a clerk decided the aircraft was fit to take flight. Ceiling fans above pushed the warm air in circles, doing little else to mitigate the heat.

By and by, a man walked around, selling patties from a tin tray and ginger beer in glass bottles. I bought one and drank it as I watched British officers arguing quietly about their leave schedules, while two women in broad hats admonished their children for refusing to sit still on the benches. Most people here waited with the patience of those who quickly realized that these islands ran on their own clock—island time—not the one officially printed on the ticket. That was the sense of normalcy here —one dictated only by the island itself. I sighed and listened as the public-address system cut in yet again, loud enough to make the playing children glance up.

I was almost not surprised when the announcement repeated itself exactly—the same inflection, the same pause, as if it had been left on a broken record, stuttering over the same sentences.

Alicia, however, wasn't listening to the announcement. Her eyes were scanning the crowd. And as I followed her gaze, I noticed that she looked toward a thin man in a linen jacket who was watching us for far too long.

I squinted at him. He didn't look British, and I doubted he was CIA. But his posture—that was the posture of intelligence. I could tell the instant I saw him. As my gaze met his, he turned away, just fast enough that it made him look suspicious.

He was dressed like he'd managed to read the climate but not the room. A linen jacket, pressed too neatly, shoes that didn't have dust on them, not even from island travel. He held himself like he wanted to appear nonchalant yet was failing miserably at his task—his chin was slightly lifted, his shoulders set, his eyes darting here and there nervously, though he pretended to seem idle. If he was carrying a weapon, it wasn't obvious—but that only made me worry more. That just meant he knew what he was doing.

Airports in colonies like these always had their own rhythm, and intelligence work could easily blend in. People were always arriving, leaving, and going here and there, distracted by tickets, luggage, tags, and money. A man could watch you for ten minutes, then simply claim he was waiting for the next delayed flight, or ask a question at the right desk and be told exactly where you were headed next. Places like this were easy pickings, which worried me.

"We've got company," I said, leaning toward Alicia and speaking in a low voice.

"I know," she responded in a murmur. "I wonder who he is."

"Think it's the Russians?" I asked.

"No idea, but whoever it is, they're already here," she replied.

Unfortunately, she was right.

The boarding call crackled over the loudspeaker. For a brief moment, it called their real names. Then the voice corrected itself, repeating the announcement properly. No one else seemed to notice.

I crushed my cigarette under my shoe. "Come on," I said. "Bequia won't wait."

We moved with the crowd, our tickets in hand.

Ground crew were loading crates outside by hand, their shouts echoing strangely—repeating, as if two crews worked the same task a second apart.

"Do you hear it?" Alicia murmured.

"Echo," I replied, my voice low. "Same men, same words. Twice."

Alicia's fingers tightened around her bag. "It's bleeding even here."

"Then we're already late," I muttered. "Havana's tide is rising."

We walked outside, and it was clear we were not heading toward the Pan Am Clipper. I had a huge pang of disappointment, as I had hoped for a better ride to Barbados. It wasn't to be. We were guided toward an old de Havilland Dove that looked like it had been built to apologize in advance. It was yet another example of Angleton's CIA doing things on the cheap. I would bet anything that Angleton himself would have been on the Clipper. I vowed to make my feelings about that known.

Short wings. Stubby nose. Two engines bolted on like afterthoughts. Built for island hops and mail sacks, but little else. The Dove sat on the tarmac with its door open and its propellers still, as if it were contemplating whether the day was worth the effort.

The livery said BWIA—faded blue lettering, hastily repainted—but the airplane itself did not seem to belong to anyone in particular anymore. It had passed through too many hands, too many climates. It smelled of oil and hot metal even before we boarded.

Eighteen seats. No aisle to speak of—just a narrow suggestion of one, too narrow for two people to pass by, and the seats were close, crowded, and worn smooth by years of sweat and salted air. Baggage was kept in hand or stuffed wherever it would fit. The crew seemed to work with a tired efficiency that matched the plane.

I took a window seat halfway back. The cushion sighed when I sat down. Across from me sat a man with a briefcase he didn't open. Ahead, a woman kept her hat on as if it were holding something in. Nobody talked. On a plane this small, conversation felt like a confession.

The engines started with reluctance. One caught; the other argued. Then they settled into an uneven rhythm that crawled up through the floor and into my legs. The cabin vibrated—not violently, just constantly—like a bad idea you couldn't shake.

We rolled. The runway ended sooner than I liked. The Dove lifted late and heavy, with the sea rising to meet us before deciding to stay where it was.

Once we were airborne, the island fell away fast. The Caribbean below looked calm from our height, and I tried to keep my focus on the seats rather than the window, but I could see the faint, visible lines of trade routes below—white wakes from small cargo ships, dark smudges where boats had been anchored, and the occasional patch of rougher water where the wind blew hard.

Inside the cabin, nothing changed except the heat and the

incessant noise, both of them constant and hard to ignore. The noise flattened everything. Thought became physical. The engines didn't roar; they worked. You could feel each combustion cycle, every small mercy that kept us level.

The air was hot and stale. Someone opened a vent, but it only made things worse.

I watched Jamaica slide away through a scratched window, the island already receding into something explainable. Barbados waited somewhere ahead—flat, neat, and British in temperament, if not in accent. A place where decisions arrived dressed and on time.

That was the trouble with flights like this. You couldn't hide. Not from the noise. Not from the proximity. Not from where you were headed.

It was here that the effects of the Mirror seemed to return yet again. The stewardess passed our row twice, the same mechanical smile on her face each time as she offered the same tray of peanuts. The first time, I didn't react, but the second time, Alicia leaned out and accepted them slowly, as if she was testing the universe, testing how far the Mirror's influence had really come.

The stewardess didn't react either, just moved on slowly. Alicia caught my eye then, and I nodded.

"Still getting worse," I said.

"Max?" she asked slowly, in a low voice. "Do you think we'll have time to get back to Havana?"

But I didn't answer. The truth was that I wasn't sure.

The man with the briefcase finally looked at me. It wasn't long enough to mean anything—just long enough to confirm we were sharing the same silence.

The Dove droned on, faithful in its indifference. Eighteen people. Two engines. One destination. No one believed in comfort. No one believed in certainty. We believed in and hoped for arrival. We had about 600 miles to go.

I leaned back, my hat tilted low, while Alicia scanned the aisle with cool precision. She turned in her seat and saw a passenger she swore hadn't been there at takeoff: a man in a dark suit, pale, with eyes like smoked glass. For three minutes, he sat two rows back, silent. Then, during a patch of turbulence, she looked again, and the seat was empty. No one else seemed to notice.

Hours blurred into the hum of the engines. At 6,000 feet, the horizon was sharp, the sea below broken by flecks of green: tiny islands, reefs foaming white. The stewardess served tepid orange juice in paper cups.

Then it happened.

For a single instant, the sky tore.

Through the window, I saw not the Caribbean but gray waves pounding Scotland's Firth of Forth, the outline of Rosyth's dockyard cranes silhouetted in winter mist. A flash of Emil Krane's voice—urgent, commanding—roared in my ear.

At the same moment, Alicia gripped her armrest hard enough to whiten her knuckles. She wasn't looking at the sea or the sky. She saw Kingsway—damp tunnel walls, Ministry posters, the faint flicker of London lights.

Passengers gasped, blinking as if waking from a dream. The stewardess dropped her tray, juice spilling across the aisle. But in the next second, the Caribbean returned—sea and islands, bright sun, the Dove steady on course.

Only Alicia and I seemed to know it hadn't been turbulence.

I leaned close, my voice low under the drone of the engines. "It's pulling us across its own memory."

Alicia's eyes were fixed on the wing outside, still trembling. "No. It's not just memory. It's trying to knit us into the web."

I struck a match and lit a cigarette, shielding the flame from the draft. The smoke curled the wrong way, bending toward the plane's nose. I exhaled slowly, watching passengers settle back into uneasy silence.

"Then the Grenadines aren't an escape," I said grimly. "They're the next knot."

By the time we reached halfway through the flight, I had begun to despise air travel.

...

From the air, Barbados looked more clean-cut than the rest of the islands so far. Cane fields divided the island into neat sectors, and the roads ran as straight as any in the Caribbean could. We descended rapidly, and the aircraft dropped onto the Seawell strip with a hefty bounce, rolling past low huts, fuel sheds, and other wartime remnants that looked as if they had been kept in service only out of habit. The place had a reputation as "Little England," and even here on the airfield, you could feel it. The fences were painted, the buildings squared off, and everything was arranged neatly so it looked under control.

The island greeted us with colonial stone and a wet, insufferable heat, much like the others. Here and there were bright windows, white walls, and once again the sign of British influence, which seemed to overwhelm the Caribbean humidity as if it were the reason this place existed. Everywhere we went, it reminded me of London, of the Bureau, and of everything we'd done so far.

I glanced out the window, half-expecting to see some new, unsettling evidence of the Mirror's effects even here, but for once, I was pleasantly surprised. Instead of echoes, I saw taxis lined up in a disciplined row, a few military vehicles parked near the hangar, and their drivers standing idly nearby, smoking and watching the new arrivals with practiced boredom.

I sighed as I walked from the plane, making my way to the terminal, which smelled of damp paper. The airfield itself smelled of cut grass and aviation fuel, with undercurrents of the sweet smell of rum, which likely drifted from somewhere inland. Even orderly colonies like these ran on sugar and alcohol, and I wished for a time when the Mirror didn't exist—a time when maybe I could explore places like this at leisure.

The terminal ahead was made of limestone and white paint, the doors propped open to let any fresh air or rare breeze through. As I arrived at the customs desk, I stretched slightly, taking a deep breath and preparing myself for yet another influx of official business. Sure enough, at the customs desk, a heavyset fellow who looked more bored than anything else asked my name.

"Max—ah, Martin Kale," I said.

For a second, I had almost said Max Calder. I felt sick to my throat as I swallowed my real name. If I had made that mistake, who knows what would have happened and who it would have alerted? I blinked hard and shook my head, as if trying to clear away the insanity.

The customs officer looked at me, almost too hard, and stared at me for a beat too long, as if I were someone unusual, but he stamped my passport all the same. I nodded my head at him, thanked him, and walked away before he could reply with a "you're welcome."

Out of the corner of my eye, I could see him watching me, irritated, as if I had somehow caused a problem by being too slow. But I moved on. I wasn't in the mood to deal with this, not now. I settled myself onto one of the cold, rickety metal benches that this airport had to offer, waiting for Alicia.

She passed through customs soon after me, her face composed. But as she walked past, for a second, I didn't see Alicia at all.

It was Lucy.

For a second, she was there, the same eyes, blond hair, that same infuriating smirk that made me love and hate her in equal measure. It felt as if the world wanted to remind me of how much I'd lost, how much I'd gained, and how much more I could lose.

I wasn't sure if it was the Mirror playing tricks on me or my own mind.

And then Alicia was back again, her hair back to its shining auburn color.

As she walked by, I had to steady my shaking hand . I still wasn't quite sure what had happened, or how much of this was real. It was something that you never quite understood until you were face to face with the Mirror, face to face with what it created.

I fished into my pocket, almost pulling out my cigarette case, but thought better of it and let it drop back in. I didn't light one. Smoking felt like one of the few cures for my increasing paranoia, and yet I had become increasingly wary that even smoking itself might be a trick of the Mirror.

We had a short layover here, where a man with an American accent—another one of Angleton's fellows from the looks of him—helped to keep us moving. Seawell felt like an airfield that hadn't quite decided yet whether or not air was a legitimate form of commercial travel and had stuck to a military layout rather than a civilian one. The design still carried old RAF habits, with squared-off buildings, heavy doors, concrete that had been poured quickly enough that it cracked at every seam, and signs that looked as if they had likely been painted during the war, remnants from another time.

The departure area was small and brightly painted—the only place in the entire airport with a new coat—with white walls and cane fields outside that ran right up to the perimeter in places.

The American kept us in motion, handling everything through an envelope and a quick nod, as if to reinforce how little time we had.

He didn't seem to like being here. That alone was enough to make me cautious. I could tell by the way his eyes kept drifting toward the exits and the way he held his shoulders—tense and upright—as if he expected the crowd to erupt into a brawl at any moment. To me, that alone indicated that Angleton knew more than he was letting on.

As soon as the man was gone, Alicia opened the envelope he

had handed her. Inside were several new tickets and a small slip of paper with neat handwriting—so neat that it almost looked printed.

"St. Vincent. Will your contact meet? Need any help w/ B. Charles?"

Alicia read it and handed it to me.

"Well," I said, crumpling up the note. "Looks like Angleton won't be of much more help from here on out."

"And Charles?" Alicia asked. "Do you think you'll still be able to contact him?"

I nodded slowly. "If he's the same Basil Charles I know, then I'll know where to find him."

We continued on, doing what we always did once a new piece of the maze revealed itself: moved on before anyone could stop us or even think to.

The airport was small enough that every sound stayed trapped under the thin tin roof. Outside, the runway was a modest, flat stretch of concrete surrounded by packed ground that offered little more than the space needed for planes to fly in and out. I watched the crowd as Alicia held the attaché case low and close, ensuring that no one could steal it from her grasp. That was the most important thing to us—the attaché case. Though it had been against my better judgment, we didn't really have any other option but to bring the case along with us.

A loudspeaker soon announced our St. Vincent connection—first in Spanish, then in English. A few moments later, another staticky voice announced that boarding would be starting soon. The loudspeaker was an old, weary public-address horn mounted near the rafters of the place, serving no purpose of pleasantry, turning every announcement into a nasally echo. The gates resembled doorways that opened only when the clerks and servicemen decided they should.

I watched a clerk write a time on a board, wipe it off, and then write another one. Nobody interrupted him, because as long as the aircraft made it off the ground, the trip would be deemed a success.

From the bench, I could see the runway through slatted, tanned windows. I watched the ground crew work in shirt-sleeves, moving the baggage by hand and fueling up planes that had landed with thin hoses. In places like this, everyone shared the same air—the same small waiting room—and the same sight-lines. But that also meant that you didn't have to be trained to notice who didn't fit in. You just had to watch the room.

Across the waiting area, I watched as a man in a brown suit stood up, lifted his battered suitcase, and walked over toward the window, gazing into the distance.

So far, everything here seemed normal, but I knew that it was only a matter of time before something went haywire.

Though it was distant now, I could still feel the pulsing energy of the Mirror somewhere deeply embedded in my headache.

I glanced at Alicia and saw her watching the room. I could tell she was uncomfortable, though she didn't say a word. I knew she was having the same thoughts as I was, the same worries, and the same concerns: that things were slightly too quiet and had been going too smoothly.

And when things were too easy, they usually became far worse.

CHAPTER 12
BASIL'S BAR

The flight to St. Vincent was a short hop on a tired prop plane, with seats that felt damp and moldy even in the daylight. Boarding was simple enough. We walked across open tarmac, glancing nervously up at the overcast clouds that seemed to be threatening rain, making our way to another aircraft with small twin engines. Once the engines roared to life, the entire body of the plane seemed to vibrate under the strain, but we lifted fast, the island dropping away behind us. The engines strained, battling the very idea of staying airborne.

Halfway through the trip, I felt sick, and as we glanced out over the glittering sea, I looked down at the clouds and tried to focus, but my mind wandered. I thought of Havana, of V4 pulsing under the distillery, sending temporal waves out into the Caribbean the way a stone sends ripples through a pond.

But unlike those ripples, these ripples didn't fade; they actually amplified and did something.

Midway through the flight, the stewardess—a young, freckled woman—moved down the aisle offering water. I accepted and thanked her.

"You're welcome, Raven," she said with a smile.

I startled.

CUBAN SLIDERS

"Sorry, what did you say?" I asked.

She looked at me in a questioning way.

"Lo siento. No dije nada," she replied in Spanish, blinking as if she was confused.

I'm sorry. I didn't say anything.

I could feel my headache blooming behind my eye, sharper than ever.

Alicia leaned closer across the narrow aisle. "What was that about?" she asked.

"I thought," I murmured, "I thought she said my name."

Alicia shook her head. "I didn't hear anything," she whispered back. "I'm guessing it's the Mirror, but if so, this isn't just about Havana anymore."

"No," I said. "I agree. It's the web Hawthorne warned us about. Whatever this is, the effect of V4 is spreading—and rapidly."

We landed at Arnos Vale in the late afternoon heat that felt heavy, as if the air itself had been boiled and poured into our lungs—searing, spicy, and humid. The runway sat close to the sea, and you could sense, more than smell, the salt the moment the wheels hit the tarmac. Beyond the airfield, the island rose steep and green, with sloping hills that were far from gentle in their ascent, reminding you why the roads here clung to the coastline.

Everything appeared jam-packed—airport, town, and ocean —as if the island didn't have the luxury of extra space. There was a small terminal, little more than a low building. The British presence here showed itself in small, minor ways—a notice board in official language, uniforms cut in the old style I was used to, and forms that used official terms that reminded me of Whitehall more than anything. An immigration and customs officer looked at our passports with the bored professionalism of a man who had seen every kind of traveler under the sun.

And the tired breath of humid tropical air awaited us yet again.

Outside, Kingstown lay to the southwest, pressed against the curve of the bay beneath the steep green hills.

After leaving the terminal, we rode along in an ancient taxi with the windows down, passing bright wooden houses, roadside stalls selling mangoes and breadfruit, and herds of goats tied to posts as if they were part of the scenery itself, bawling and bleating under the summer sun.

The taxi was old and rattled at every seam, its suspension nonexistent. The driver—from the way he spoke, a local—kept one hand on the wheel and the other out the window, driving in a manner that inspired confidence that he could navigate the island with his eyes closed. We passed small plots of cultivation, clusters of houses, and yards full of laundry and children who stared as we passed.

Every couple of miles, you would see a small rum shop or a church, and then nothing but greenery again.

The road slowly bent toward Kingstown, and the bay opened up in front of us, revealing the small town pressed tightly against the waterline. Here, it was busier—the harbor filled with boats, and bicycles being pedaled here and there on errands and business.

The island itself was calm, but I worried that it was the calm before the storm.

"So, Basil," Alicia said as we bounced over a pothole, "you trust him?"

"I do," I answered.

"We've both trusted people we shouldn't," she said back.

It wasn't an accusation. I knew only too well she was right, but I shook my head.

"Basil is different from most people," I said, staring out at the sea, as the light reflected off the nimble waves.

We finally found our way to the waterfront—the best place for me to navigate from.

Kingstown's waterfront smelled of fish, rum, and diesel. The sky was overcast and gray by now, as the sun had already begun to set behind the shimmering ocean. The horizon in the distance glowed a golden orange as we made our way along the city's narrow cobblestone roads towards Bay Street, watching men haul crates, children dash and dart between carts, and boats float in and out of the harbor lazily, as if they'd survived centuries by stubbornness alone.

I quickly led Alicia up a narrow set of steps, past a faded sign painted directly onto a wooden wall: BASIL'S BAR.

This was where I had last seen him, and as I suspected, he was still here. Basil wasn't the type of fellow to leave his homeland. And the bar he had fostered into one of the best in the area was truly his home.

The place was open to the harbor wind, a radio playing low calypso behind the counter, the air thick with the sweet scents of rum, lime, and cigarette smoke. Along the walls, fishing nets hung like curtains, along with other archaic memorabilia Basil had collected.

On the far side of the small bar, a few men played dominoes, laughter echoing as the hard, deliberate slap of tiles sounded from their table.

Behind the bar— stood Basil Charles himself. He was wiping down glasses, keeping them clean as he hummed a quiet tune to himself. Unsurprisingly, he was older than the last time I'd seen him, gray at the temples, with lines at the corners of his eyes. But the core of his character hadn't changed a single bit. He was a tall, calm man who made everyone in the room feel slightly calmer. His eyes were a piercing gray, and he wore half-moon glasses that rested low on the bridge of his nose.

As we entered, he looked up once, looked down again, and then did a double take, his gaze locking onto me immediately. His face broke into a smile, and for a moment, the whole world felt slightly less broken.

"Ah, my brother," Basil cried out, as if he hadn't seen me in years.

Truth be told, he hadn't.

He came around the bar, pulling me into a hard embrace, his skin more weathered than the last time we'd shaken hands. He clapped my back firmly, as if checking I was still real, then held me out at arm's length.

"Ah, Basil," I said, my voice rough. "You look like you've been staying out of trouble. Has your bar been suiting you well?"

"No, no," he replied. "I don't avoid trouble; I just don't invite it into my home unless I must."

His eyes shifted to Alicia. He studied her closely. The two had never met, and he measured the way she held herself, the stillness, and her precision. Then he nodded with what seemed like genuine respect.

"Ah, and you must be Artemis," he said. "I've heard you're the one who keeps the infamous Max Calder alive."

Alicia's expression softened slightly. "He makes that difficult."

Basil laughed, then gestured us into the shadowed corner near the harbor-facing window, far away from the domino table where the men continued to play. He poured rum for me, something cleaner for Alicia, and a glass of water that sat untouched in the middle of all of us.

"Well," he said at length, "I guess neither of you is here to bring good news or catch up. This isn't a nostalgia trip, is it?"

"No, no, it's not," I replied, shaking my head as I sipped the rum he had poured. "We're tracking two men. We need a boat into the Grenadines tonight—quiet and fast. Do you have the resources?"

Basil's face tightened, a sharp look of understanding dawning on his face.

"Ah, I've heard something of men vanishing. Is this why you need it?"

Alicia leaned in slightly, nodding. "Two Soviet scientists—Anokhin and Popov. We think they've been, well, displaced."

Basil nodded. He didn't ask what it meant, but I was sure he understood, even though he had never been a slider himself. He knew of the Mirror, as did many who used to work for the Bureau. It was clear the Caribbean had taught him not to demand explanations he wouldn't want to hear—explanations that could be tortured out of you if the wrong men found you.

"I've heard about two white men on the sea at night," he said. "Fishermen off Bequia say they saw them standing in the surf as if they were in a trance... thought it was some part of a crazy cult that's been going on or such. One seemed to be shaking, holding his head, talking like a preacher in tongues. There's been talk of the devil around these parts."

My stomach tightened as he spoke. I could see Markov's face flashing in my mind—forty-two years old and dead at ninety-five on a Havana street.

Basil carried on.

"I've also heard about other men," he said. "Not fishermen nor island men." Here, he lowered his voice. "Men with tents, crates. Men who will pay for information. Or force it out of you if you don't answer."

Alicia's eyes narrowed. "Where?" she asked.

Basil glanced around, as if worried that someone might have paused to listen, then continued in an even lower voice.

"Mustique," he said. "They've got a little beach on the west side, lit up like a war camp. No one local goes near it. Too many strangers. And the men at the bar say they've seen guns."

He looked at me.

"Max, whatever you're chasing, there are Soviets already hunting it."

"Well, that's all we needed to confirm," I said.

Basil held up one finger, then reached under the bar and pulled a hand-drawn chart of the Grenadines. He laid it flat out between our glasses. Pencil notes were scrawled all over it, marking reefs, channels, and anchor points known only to the men who lived locally in these parts—men who could navigate the place in the dark with their eyes closed and half-drunk.

"My cousin, Darryl, has a pirogue," Basil said. "Near thirty feet, new outboard, shallow draft. He'd be able to take you through the passages without lights… one of the finest sailors you'll ever know. I'll call him ahead. Meet him at the northernmost jetty of the harbor."

"Isn't everyone your cousin, Basil? And he'll keep his mouth shut?" I asked.

Basil smiled, and then his eyes hardened slightly. "If he opens his mouth, I'll close it for him."

I managed to feign a smile. That was Basil—warm, loyal, but utterly lethal when it came to holding his own and protecting those he was loyal to.

"Good," I said.

He reached below again and produced a small portable radio, sliding it across the table. It was the kind that was commonly used by fishermen and smugglers.

"Take this," he said. "Use the marine band. If you hear Russian, you already know not to answer. But listen, there've been voices, whispers of Russian on it near every night, so it might provide you some use."

I stared at the radio, then at Basil. "I owe you one," I said.

Basil waved it away. "You owed me years ago, but no more. You've paid it back more than enough, time and time again."

His voice softened. "Just come back again when you're done with all this. It'd be good to catch up."

I smiled, and we shook hands, his grip firm and his eyes sparkling.

"Oh, by the way, Max," Basil continued, his tone becoming more serious, "You know a guy called Easee?"

I didn't react right away.

Basil had said the name casually, the way men do when they're pretending not to measure the damage a word might cause, but the name had caught me off guard. Though I couldn't quite place it, it sounded familiar—as if I'd spoken the name before and forgotten since.

"Bill Easee," Basil said. "Tall fellow. Used to be Bureau. Before that—well, complicated."

Easee.

The name didn't arrive cleanly. It never did. It came with pressure. With the sense of a door closing somewhere behind my eyes.

"Name sounds familiar. What about him?"

"He came through here a week or so ago, Max. Kept a low profile, but he was meeting someone off a boat out of Miami. Nothing goes on around here, I don't know about—one of my regulars, a fisherman who runs charters for the Americans, overheard enough to know he was talking agency business. From what I gather, he's with Angleton and the CIA now."

"You're sure?" I asked.

Basil nodded. "Not the sort of information I'd gather lightly. It's vetted."

I stared at the bar top. Old varnish. Knife marks. Someone had once carved initials there and then tried to sand them out. I focused on that rather than the sudden, unreasonable calm that settled over me.

Easee was a witness.

Not an operator. Not a theorist. A man who'd been close enough to the Mirror early enough to notice when it stopped behaving like equipment and started behaving with preference.

I hadn't wanted to believe men like that existed anymore. I should have felt relief. Information was movement. Movement meant progress. Instead, I felt resistance.

"That's bad, isn't it?" Basil asked carefully. Alicia just listened.

"Yes," I replied. "It is."

Basil leaned closer. "Because he's CIA now?"

"No," I said. "Because he isn't, really."

That got both Basil's and Alicia's attention.

"Men who leave institutions don't usually circle back unless they think the institution is about to make a permanent mistake," I continued. "I don't remember Easee well, but men like Easee aren't the type to warn others. He positions himself so someone else has to decide."

Basil studied me. "And what does that mean for you?"

I picked up my glass again. This time, my hand shook enough that Alicia noticed.

"Max.... you alright?"

"I guess it means that if he's around, whatever we think we're about to do—it means we're closer than we're supposed to be."

Basil didn't push. Smart man.

I finished my drink and stood, prompting Alicia to do the same.

The fan above creaked, steady and untroubled.

Easee was in Cuba, in Havana. That meant the web had tightened. Also bad news. I figured that we would very likely run into him again.

Alicia and I left Basil's Bar as the sun was almost entirely set. I tried not to think about Easee. The harbor had turned dark and glassy now, silent. As Basil had instructed us, Darryl waited at the end of a jetty, beside a low pirogue, which was painted a dull green—the kind of green that could vanish against the water at night.

He was younger than Basil, but I could tell instantly that they were of the same blood. He wore a quiet type of confidence, leaning against his pirogue and smoking as we approached, no wasted movement in his step. Nets lay piled in the stern for appearances. Beneath them, wrapped in oilcloth, were several rifles and a canvas bag that I could tell held something more, possibly grenades.

There were no questions from him either, just a single nod—a small gesture for us to step in, and then he pushed off, and the boat slid away from Kingstown as silently as the breeze in the night.

As we got going, the wind was steady out of the northeast,

quiet but chill. The salt spray cooled my face, and the wind almost gave a semblance of fresh air, the likes of which you would smell in Scotland. The night sky was far brighter than I had ever seen in London, with thousands of stars like pins hammered into black velvet.

We rode the current south, the engine low and idling, just enough to keep us moving without announcing ourselves to every shoreline. Alicia sat amidships, the radio in her lap, tuning it carefully as she listened for any chatter. The attaché case was placed beneath her legs; the resonance rig remained safe inside it. This wasn't the place to light it up unless we wanted the whole sea to notice, and there was no reason to do so. The Mirror was nowhere near.

For a while—whether it had been ten minutes or an hour, it was hard to tell—there was only the slap of water against the hull and a soft grind of Darryl's tiller adjustments. Then the radio hiss shifted, a carrier tone cut in, faint and foreign, and I heard Russian voices bleeding through. Not Cuban or British. I could tell from the scratch of Alicia's pencil on paper that she had already begun to translate.

"Остров Мюстик. Подтверждаю," came one voice.

Half a beat later, another voice repeated the same phrase, slightly distorted.

Alicia looked up at me, her eyes sharp. "They're here already," she whispered. "Already coordinating, from the sounds of it, and the echo."

"Mirror interference," I said. "It's messing with the airwaves, isn't it?"

She nodded.

The radio crackled again: coordinates, a mention of Grenada, a name I didn't catch, then silence again, followed by a low hum that didn't belong to the boat's engine.

Ahead, I could see Mustique rising out of the dark, low hills, with thick palms. No lights to be seen. It was here that Darryl eased the throttle down until the engine barely murmured, making me worried that it would switch off if he turned it down any lower. We drifted closer, letting the current push the boat along, the gentle waves lapping against the hull.

As the shoreline came into view, I could make out the pale sand and the black, jagged rocks. Then I saw it: tents made of military canvas set back from the surf, nearly forty yards or so in orderly rows. Next to them were crates upon crates stacked in neat columns, and I could hear a generator's dull roar under the moonlight. Through the fabric, I could see the light from lanterns moving and swaying as men walked, figures moving with disciplined spacing—far too careful for fishermen.

Even at this distance, I knew exactly what was happening.

Alicia's voice came out in a whisper. "Well," she said, "I guess we've found the Russians."

I nodded. "And they're not here camping either," I said. "It's a hunt."

We stayed far offshore, hidden in the dark, watching the Soviet camp breathe its life out on the beach like some sick parasite latched onto the island. Far behind us, St. Vincent's lights were gone now. Ahead of us, the Grenadines were full of Soviets with rifles. And somewhere out there—maybe further, maybe closer—were two scientists likely aging to death one second at a time.

Darryl glanced at us, waiting for our decision.

"So what's the plan, Max?" Alicia finally asked.

"Mustique first," I replied, watching the tents, crates, and the shadows moving between them. "And we do it quiet."

The boat continued to drift, unlit and unseen, toward the shore that was already occupied.

CHAPTER 13
PARALLEL PROTOCOL

Lucy leaned back against the slick car seat, watching the harbor fire shrink to an orange smear through her rain-soaked window. The Soviet ship, half-sunk and burning, tilted and careened deeper with each passing block they put between themselves and the harbor. Flames lit the cranes and the wet pier, turning them into fiery silhouettes.

The sedan ran dark until they cleared the dock district. Two Americans sat up front, neither looking at her nor asking if she was hurt. She didn't mind, though. Their silence was part courtesy, part procedure. She had just walked out of a burning ship, and they likely figured she didn't need reassurance. Plus, that wasn't even their job.

And so Lucy relaxed, her sleeves rolled up to her elbows, her skin mottled with salt and rain-bruised. They'd taken her pistol and other items at the pier with a quiet efficiency, swapping them for a thin wool blanket, which she held across her damp shoulders. The blanket smelled of cigarette smoke and salt, as if it had been stored away in some naval facility.

It likely had.

She closed her eyes, focusing on her breathing until the ache from the explosion stopped echoing in her ribs. She kept seeing his face: Max Calder, white in the floodlight, his eyes so sharp, his mouth set, as if every passing moment could change him into another man.

She shook her head, opening her eyes again and shoving that memory down where she kept all the others. Memory and nostalgia were luxuries and liabilities to her, and at times such as this, she could only afford so many.

"Miramar," the driver said suddenly to the other American, who nodded.

Lucy didn't speak and simply closed her eyes again. Miramar meant consular villas, wide boulevards, and the kind of streets that made Havana look civilized, but only for the visiting dignitaries and officials for whom they wished to parade and laud their city as one of the greats. It was here that the American safe houses would be, with quiet rooms, drawn shutters, and phone access for when Angleton would inevitably call.

The sedan turned inland, away from Malecón's salt wind, the air thickening as Havana's music faded into the incessant rain, which only intensified. She opened her eyes. She caught a glimpse of herself in the side mirror for a fraction of a second. In that instant, she swore she saw another face overlaid on top of hers, a slightly skewed version, as if looking at herself in a puddle, her vision still blurry from the salt water.

Suddenly, the car hit a pothole, and the second face snapped away in an instant before she could see anything else. She shook her head, blinking several times rapidly, confused as to what she had actually seen. Things like this, well, she figured Calder had been experiencing them for quite a while, but to her, things like this were new. She had only begun experiencing them since she had gotten to Cuba, specifically in Havana. She figured this was the result of the Mirror.

They pulled into a gated driveway behind a modern-looking dark stucco house. As the driver approached and slowed, the gate swung open, and the sedan rolled in under a carport before the driver put it into park. The man who sat beside the driver finally turned, nodding at her, his eyes unreadable and his face blank.

"Inside," he said.

The house smelled fresh, as if it had been cleaned daily, with the only lingering scent being that of cold coffee. A man met them in the corridor, guiding her down a narrow hall and toward the back of the house. There were no introductions here, and no one knew each other's names. The CIA's Havana station ran surgically. Everyone operated in their own anonymity, and the world revolved around Washington. Identification and fingerprints were nonexistent. The only thing that existed was the process.

They took her to a bathroom with white tile and a drain in the very center of the floor. The man who had guided her here—medical by the look of him—set down a metal case carefully on the counter and opened it. Inside were instruments Lucy had never seen when she worked at MI6 but had become familiar with through her work with the CIA: small coils wound in circles, a brass dial, and a film badge, carefully preserved in wax.

"Hold still," the man said, moving gently but firmly as he lifted her chin and inspected her carefully. She steadied her breathing as he clipped the badge to her collar, running the coil along her forearms and throat. She could feel the electric sting emanating from the coil as it hummed faintly. On the dial, a needle danced then settled into a slight vibration. The man frowned, adjusted the switch, and tried several more times.

"You've been near it," he murmured.

"Near what?" Lucy asked as he washed his hands.

But she already knew what he meant, and he didn't dignify her with an answer. He just tapped the dial, annoyed by its inability to remain still, then took a blood pressure cuff from the case and wrapped it around her arm.

"Pulse is irregular, too," he said.

"Just shock," Lucy replied abruptly, almost taunting him.

He looked at her for a moment, trying to decide if she was

lying or if her response was simply business. Then he shook his head, looked away, and pressed a small glass thermometer to the inside of her wrist.

"Any nosebleeds?" he asked.

"No."

"Any slips, repetition, lost time at all? Seeing anything you shouldn't?"

Lucy's jaw tightened. "No."

"Hmm," the man said as he set down the thermometer. "Well, it's hard for me to tell, but I would assume you're seeing something. So you're either lying or disciplined, or both. Either way, Angleton will want to speak to you."

Lucy nodded grimly. She wasn't in the mood to speak to Angleton; she already knew what he would say.

They brought her a clean shirt, slacks, and a towel, allowing her to change in privacy. By the time she'd stepped back into the living room, the curtains had been drawn and the lamp shaded. A shortwave set sat beside a black telephone on the table, the receiver already off the hook. The line was alive, waiting for her.

She took the chair nearest it, her hair still dripping onto the tile—wet from the shower she had taken before changing, and from the ocean beyond the door. She sighed and listened as the phone clicked; it was as if Angleton knew she had arrived. Just on time, his voice came through, dry and close, as if he were speaking to her from inside the room itself.

She rolled her eyes. "Hello, Angleton," she said dryly.

"May I ask," he began, "do you know what the word 'compartment' means?"

"Well, I'm sure I could help you out," she replied, her mouth twitching, "but if you truly don't understand it, maybe it's best you find a dictionary."

"I told you, no contact with Calder," he replied, his tone devoid of humor.

"You told me no contact," she replied evenly. "But you didn't tell me to drown, and if I hadn't worked with them, I would have. They arrived sooner than you told me they would. So whose fault is that?"

There was silence on the line. She could hear Angleton's breath, and nothing else—quiet and deliberate.

"He's a walking time bomb," Angleton said finally. "Not in the way physics would have it, either; politics, Lucy. He's a pattern that keeps breaking and breaks everything that he touches. I keep him away from you because when he looks at you, he stops thinking straight, and heaven knows he doesn't think straight to begin with."

"Yes, you'd be bold to assume he thinks straight at all," she replied.

Angleton ignored her comment. "We'll deal with this later," he said. "What's your report?"

She gave him what he really wanted. The Soviet officers were dead by her hands. She had stolen the keys, detonated the containment unit, and told him of the glow that made the air taste of copper with a slight pulse to it. She continued to explain the facts, even in the moment. Even in the moments where Calder and Rayes had joined, the facts would make their own argument.

Angleton listened without interrupting. It was almost as if he wasn't even on the line, but he stayed nonetheless. When she finally finished, he exhaled slowly.

"Well, there's bad news. We destroyed a residual component—nothing more. Not the core, not the build. Calder had some fancy word for it. The real machine is already far under Cárdenas."

"Then please tell me, why did we go after the ship at all?" Lucy asked, leaning back in the chair. Angleton could hear the sarcasm. She wanted a cigarette.

"Decoys, redundancy, and logistics. The Soviets aren't stupid. They've learned from Rosyth and Invershiel. Each part they've got, they're distributing. Spreading the parts, distributing the risk."

"Well, maybe we should have gone after more important parts," she shot back, but he carried on.

"V4 is operational," he continued. "We have resonance readings all across Havana. It's far worse than we expected. It's the whole damn field, almost like a weather system. It emanates out from the central point, affecting everything around it. Then you."

For the first time, Lucy's fingers tightened on the towel draped over her shoulders. "Then you should pull Calder out. Get him out of the city."

"I'm not going to pull pieces off the board simply because they're uncomfortable with it," Angleton retorted. "Calder has his purpose."

His voice softened, just a fraction. "Listen carefully, Locket. We're not trying to stop the Soviets from attempting experiments with time. This isn't about that—not anymore. It's about what they're doing with the fact that the Mirror can affect choice."

Lucy waited. She'd learned Angleton's rhythm by now, and she had a certain quiet respect for it. She knew he had more to say, so she stayed silent, waiting for him to continue. Sure enough, a second later, he spoke again.

"There's a second technology at Cárdenas, at least from our intelligence. It's a node, an offshoot the Russians have developed, not the actual main device, but it's something potentially more dangerous. They're calling it Decision Locking. It works on behavioral protocols."

"Decision Locking," Lucy repeated, a chill coming across her body. She blinked it away. "What's that?"

"It's exactly what it sounds like," Angleton said. "It essentially removes the space between options, leaving no ability for dissent or debate. Rather than blocking choices, it blocks the ability to conceive other options. A man can't choose what he can't conceive."

"And the CIA wants that?" Lucy asked.

"The CIA wants to prevent Moscow from having it," Angleton replied, his voice almost cautious. "And yes, we want to understand it, too. We want the node, the model itself, the blueprints—whatever you can lift without touching the main machine."

"So you're not asking me to destroy it?"

"Well, I didn't say that, but what I am asking you is to retrieve it. Destruction can be discussed later once we know what we're destroying."

Lucy scoffed. "That's a nice way to say you're keeping your options open."

"It's the only way to stay alive in this damn wilderness of mirrors," Angleton muttered. "Everything is conditional. Every loyalty is suspect, every truth prone to misuse. Power is volatile, Locket. Batista is watching now, as well as the Soviets. Someone is going to try and give Batista that leverage,...put it into his hands in return for favors. And if Decision Locking is what I think it is, that leverage isn't going to look like persuasion. It'll be inevitable. There will be no choices for him."

Lucy's throat had tightened, and she thought of governments, of men like her father moving pieces across the map, and of course, of Max Calder, out there somewhere, stubbornly believing that he alone could change the fate and the course of this technology.

"What do you want from me?" she finally asked, though she already knew too well.

"You've already been inside the perimeter. You cut the wire. You know the patrol rhythm. You know the ground, the buildings—everything."

Lucy didn't respond. Her first infiltration, two nights before Calder and Rayes had ever set foot on Cuban soil, had been pure recon—snip, retwist, slip in far enough to map the fence line and count the soldiers on patrol. At that time, she hadn't expected to find a system this large, or a conspiracy so deep.

"I want you back in again," Angleton said. "You'll go alone, find the Decision Locking node, and bring back anything that you can find that describes how it functions: blueprints, terminology, notes—oh, and if there's a prototype-type device, bring it if you can manage it."

"And Calder?"

"I'm glad you brought that up," Angleton said. "No contact. If you see him, you avoid him."

Lucy glanced at the curtained window as if she could see the harbor fires through it still. They were too far away, but she could still picture it in her mind.

"That might not be possible," she said at last.

"Make it possible," Angleton retorted. "You're good at being dead, Lucy. Stay that way."

The line clicked, and Angleton was gone.

For a moment, the room was silent.

A man appeared in the doorway—one of Angleton's station officers—clearing his throat uncomfortably.

"Car's ready," he said.

Lucy stood, sighing. The towel slid off her shoulders, her wet shirt still clinging to her ribs. She adjusted it, checking the weight of the small pistol. They'd cleaned, dried, and returned it to her, and she tucked it away into her waistband. It wasn't a gun she was used to, not her own balance, but it would do well enough.

They drove her out along the roads that passed villas with white walls and private guards, then cut inland where the streets narrowed. Finally, they were weaving through the cane fields toward the distillery that she was already all too familiar with.

As they left the city behind, her mind made itself up, as it always did before a job. She suppressed every emotion into something more manageable. She wasn't a person; she was a tool, and she was okay with that. She had to be a tool if she wanted to be useful.

The driver stopped short of the main road, killing the engine.

"You've got twenty minutes, max. Patrol shift will be at the half hour."

She stepped out into the wet heat, inhaling the smell of

sugarcane that was almost intoxicating. The air carried less ocean and took on an earthy smell, the distillery's floodlights glowing in the distance, swinging here and there, slowly patrolling and watching, though she knew not for what.

She moved through the cane with a practiced efficiency, her shoulders low, using the rows as cover. The cut placed in the fence was exactly where she'd left it, the wire retwisted with care and still invisible unless she knew exactly where to look. The ground around it had been disturbed, brushed smooth again, as if someone else had found the spot since her last visit.

There were no boot prints. Whoever had done this was an expert. Whoever had done this wasn't Cuban or Soviet.

She smiled slightly. She didn't have to say it out loud. She already knew who had spotted her handiwork.

She slipped through, retwisting it behind her again. Habit always mattered; if you left a door open, someone was likely to find it.

Moving quietly and steadily inside the perimeter, she listened to the rhythm of the distillery beneath her, the pumps thudding, a generator vibrating somewhere near the main building. She didn't go toward the freight elevator. Calder and Rayes would have headed there if they had been present. They would chase the obvious core of the Mirror.

But Lucy had a different assignment, and Angleton had been clear. Her goal wasn't the Mirror—not yet, anyway.

She skirted past the service buildings, heading toward a low, windowed administrative block, where a side door faced away from the lights. Two guards smoked near a corner, their rifles slung, standing straight but bored. The Soviets.

She shook her head, almost embarrassed for them. They really ought to have guarded it better.

She waited until their conversation peaked, until one leaned back, laughing, his head tilted, his mouth open. Then she moved, crossing the gap in three silent steps and melting into the shadow of the overhung door.

The lock was cheap—cheap enough for her to pick quickly. That, more than anything, told her she was in the right place. The Soviets put far too much trust in guns and fences. If this were just a node of the Mirror, not the true V4, they wouldn't have cared so much for security.

She picked the lock and slipped inside.

The fluorescent tubes buzzed overhead, flickering with a rhythm that was all too mundane. She moved down the corridor, counting doors and listening for breathing at each one. Offices, storage, another office, and a small radio room with a little unfamiliar coil array mounted to the wall.

She stopped. The coil array wasn't standard communications equipment. This was too precise—copper wound around ceramic cores, arranged in a pattern that seemed almost hypnotic.

A sign in Russian was bolted to the door.

ПРОТОКОЛЫ—ДОСТУП ОГРАНИЧЕН

Protocol: Restricted access.

She smirked and opened the door, edging inside.

She could instantly tell that the room felt wrong. She wasn't sure why, but something about it felt out of place. It was as if the room itself was slightly tilted on its side, and the moment she entered, she felt disoriented.

A chair sat in the very center, its metal frame bolted to the floor as if to keep it from sliding. Canvas restraints lay open, fastened to the seat and armrests, the buckles filed down, as if to keep them from catching on the skin if whoever sat in the chair struggled.

Behind it, a brass chassis had been bolted to a steel bracket. It was roughly the size of a field radio, encased in dull brass and copper. The machine didn't glow, but exhibited a faint, irregular thermal shimmer, as if it were emitting heat with no clear reason. At the very center of the chassis sat an inset element that seemed to be the color of black glass, passport photograph-sized. It rested within a lattice that looked as if every design had been on purpose—crafted with an immense level of care.

Lucy had seen radio rooms. She had seen interrogation rooms—and much worse. But whatever this was—this rig—it was built to resemble neither. It was exactly what she was looking for.

On a table against the wall were neatly stacked folders. Though Lucy's Russian wasn't the best, it was good enough to read the labels without translating them into English first.

БЛОКИРОВКА РЕШЕНИЯ
ОРАКУЛ
ПОВЕДЕНЧЕСКИЕ СХЕМЫ

Decision Locking. Oracle. Behavioral Schematics.
She raised her eyebrows. That had been simple enough.
It wasn't a weapon. Whatever this was, it was worse. She could tell instantly. This was the type of device that would turn people into slaves, into tools rather than humans.

She flipped open the top folder roughly, reading the handwritten Russian notes inside, scribbled with equations, diagrams, and other blueprints. The first page carried a stamped header from "Laboratorio Especial No. 7," along with a small printed subheading—DN-4 / УЗЕЛ. Along the margin, someone had written in English, a tight, elegant English that she recognized instantly.

Her breath caught in her chest.

"Remove the alternative, and you remove the possibility of betrayal."

For the first time, she almost felt sick. She'd seen that handwriting in London, on memos that always seemed to go the way the writer had wished. Kim Philby's hand had always looked boyish but confident. It was what she had found so alluring about him at first, and so disgusting later on.

She took a deep breath and continued searching, glancing only at her watch to make sure she had time left—six minutes before she had to be gone. Another folder contained blueprints marked DN-4 / УЗЕЛ. The drawings seemed to reduce the chair apparatus to a portable unit—the type of unit that could fit in a brass case the size of a heavy radio, its coherence coils wound tight along both sides, the passport photo-sized glass core seated neatly in the center. She took careful inventory of it. This wasn't a fixed installation meant only for a laboratory. This was a device you could carry with you—set up at a moment's notice in a closed room, change the decisions and thoughts of those inside, then carry it away again with nothing obvious changed—except the course of history. That was scary.

She stood there for a second, trying to understand exactly what was at play. She understood why Angleton wanted it now, why Moscow had built it, and why Calder would never be allowed to know it existed until it was too late.

She took a small camera out of her bag—the latest American technology, a Kodak Tourist II—and began to photograph the pages. She kept the flash off, and though it was dark, she knew the images would be legible enough. Then, she took the small prototype, carefully packing it into her satchel, along with the copper coils and a toggle switch stamped with Cyrillic letters.

Lucy only glanced at the larger prototype for a second, then moved expertly toward it. She ripped out one of the most important-looking pieces unceremoniously. She was certain the Russians would be able to reconstruct the model—they were the ones who invented it, after all—but at least this would buy the Americans some time.

For just a moment, she hesitated, then moved silently, closing the protocol room door behind her, easing the latch until it caught without noise. She stepped into the corridor, just in time, too. She could hear voices and footsteps in the distance; whether they were coming for her or just trying to do their work, she wasn't sure, but she wasn't about to wait and find out.

She didn't run. Running would make noise. Instead, Lucy walked quickly and efficiently back toward the side door. Behind her, somewhere deeper in the compound, she could hear the generator still whirring, and she could feel the pulse from the V4 Mirror that she knew was somewhere beneath the distillery.

But that wasn't her goal.

Instead, she slipped out into the cane shadow and the smell of molasses as soon as she reached the door. Somewhere behind her, a guard shouted in Russian, his tone sharp with suspicion, but Lucy was already gone, moving back toward the cut fence. He would simply think he had seen shadows from a lack of sleep.

Her satchel weighed her down with the heft of the machine she had stolen. But the weight on her mind was more. She felt as if she'd stolen something that shouldn't be used by anyone—Russians, Americans, MI6, or even the Bureau.

She reached the fence, carefully undoing the wire, slipping through, and then retwisting it again, her fingers working fast. As soon as she was through, she turned, vanishing into the field of cane.

The Havana Club Distillery continued to hum, alive with the machinery and the Mirror below it. In her satchel, the Decision Locking node sat, packed carefully along with the other tools, as she held it gently, fearing it like one would a sleeping animal.

She made her way back to the car, unlit, with the engine idling low, sliding into the back seat, her clothes still damp. The driver didn't ask questions. He only looked briefly in the mirror.

"You get it?"

She closed her eyes. In the darkness behind her lids, she could see her own face, twice, slightly out of phase.

"Yeah," she replied. "I got it."

CHAPTER 14
BACKING BATISTA

As Bill Easee stepped out of the small apartment where the CIA had him holed up, he stretched, taking in the humid Havana air. He wasn't used to it—not yet, at least—but what he was used to was that familiar tang in the air, that strange murmur that men usually ignored. The pulse—the electric current that flowed through everything—meant nothing to other men, but to him, it meant the Mirror.

Easee was born in England during the First World War, the son of an African-American U.S. Army logistics sergeant and a West Country nurse from Somerset. His father rotated back to the States before Bill could remember him. His mother stayed, stubborn and practical, raising a boy who learned early how to stand out without ever being at the center of everything.

Growing up in the West Country in the 1930s made him observant before it made him angry. He had also picked up a slight West Country accent, which tended to surprise people. He learned when to speak and when silence was safer. His size arrived early; his strength followed. Sports gave him cover. Discipline gave him purpose.

He was recruited into MI6 not because he was clever, but

because he was reliable under pressure—a physical asset who could think, and a thinker who could take a hit.

Towards the end of the war, Easee was already recruited by the Bureau to join scientific-intelligence projects under obscure clearance headings. Rosyth Naval Dockyard in 1945 changed everything.

Under the guise of naval instrumentation and contingency research, he became embedded with the early Mirror development teams. He wasn't a physicist; he was a stability officer—tasked with monitoring operator cognition, observer fatigue, memory integrity, and decision reliability during exposure events.

He was among the first to notice something was wrong—right along with men such as Hawthorne.

It wasn't that the machinery malfunctioned. But Bill Easee, always analytical, noticed the resistance.

He watched operators lose time. He watched decisions converge unnaturally. He watched reflections linger half a beat too long. He heard Hawthorne and Krane argue late into the night about coherence thresholds and observer load, and he realized before most of them that the Mirror was no longer passive.

The Bureau didn't want that conclusion.

Easee's reports were being quietly rewritten. His access was narrowed, and his warnings were reclassified as psychological strain.

The Bureau listened.

But his reports were buried. It didn't help the organization—the reality became resisted and overwritten.

When the CIA offered him a transfer in 1948—quiet, deniable, framed as defection—Easee took it. Not out of loyalty, but for survival. He believed, mistakenly, that American compartmentalization might slow the spread.

Instead, he watched the Mirror become a web—a network.

Since then, Easee had lived on the edge of institutional trust. Too knowledgeable to discard. Too compromised to promote.

Used when clarity is required, sidelined when certainty is preferred.

Easee understood something most of the intelligence world didn't: the Mirror was not a weapon.

He believed it was a process that learned it could be interrupted—and now refused to allow that interruption. He had begged Angleton to be included in the project when he'd caught wind of Havana—and against all odds, Angleton had agreed.

Now, however, Easee wondered if there was another game Angleton was playing. Another angle.

———

It wasn't fire that frightened Lucy Howard. Fire was simple enough, consuming what it touched, leaving no evidence behind—other than ash. Even a cover-up needed ash.

And yet, what truly unsettled her was the quiet. Or the quietness where it mattered.

Havana had absorbed the harbor blast and kept on dancing, kept the music playing, and the warm rain had kept falling, indifferent to the bodies that now floated in the harbor.

The satchel on Lucy's lap felt heavy, though she wasn't quite sure why.

As the sedan rolled slowly back toward Havana, carrying Lucy and the stolen device toward the future and the past, she wondered if the future she had chosen would be the right one.

The decision locking node itself, made of brass and copper with a black glass insert no larger than a passport photograph, seemed almost too simple to be as dangerous as she knew it was. Yet, she knew it was dangerous—impossibly so. The type of danger that you wouldn't know until it caught you by surprise, and by then, it would be too late.

She could feel a faint, irregular pulse through the canvas, a sensation that made her question what sort of cursed science or witchcraft she had gotten caught up in.

Though she was science-minded, this science pushed the limits of even what Lucy thought was possible. And when science pushes the limits too far, sometimes it folds back in on itself and becomes magic.

The sedan rolled into Miramar under a strict blackout protocol. No headlights were seen until the very last turn, and they made no stops at intersections, except for the bare minimum required.

Up front, the driver and his companion remained silent, their shoulders rigid and straight, their faces unreadable.

Lucy stared out of the car window, watching the reflections in the puddles on the streets: the streetlights, palm fronds, and neon signs that passed, more common than the gulls that flocked above.

She waited for the moment that her face might split, lagging half a second behind. But it only happened once. For only a second, she saw another version of herself in the corner of her eye, slightly misaligned, as if the world itself was splitting in two. Then it snapped back, and everything was normal again.

She shook her head, blinking. She wasn't stupid. She assumed this was the same kind of experience Calder had subjected himself to over the years, ever since she had gone off-grid and he had thought she had betrayed him.

Then, they were back at the villa.

Inside, the air was cold from the overworked Carrier air conditioning, and Lucy knew in an instant, from the clean smell emanating from the building, that Angleton was already there or had been there recently enough to make everyone within the small safe house nervous enough to keep cleaning.

She was led through a corridor into a back room, where the curtains were drawn and the lamps shaded. It was the kind of room designed to keep secrets where they stayed. Thick walls and a radio tuned low to static on purpose to hide the conversation inside the noise in case there were any eavesdroppers.

Near a table stood James Jesus Angleton, his jacket off, his tie loose, and his shirt damp. He looked as he always did, as if he'd slept in the same clothes for a week and as if he'd been awake for more than half that time. However, his eyes were sharp, awake in that almost sick way that indicated a man riddled with paranoia, as if he expected every motion or every noise to escalate into something more.

"You got it?" he asked.

It was his way of greeting.

Lucy didn't smile in response; she simply set the satchel on the table and unfastened it carefully. She laid out in front of him what she'd stolen: the node itself wrapped in oilcloth, the photographed pages in their envelopes, the folders with Russian headers, and the rest of the files she had lifted before escaping the distillery.

Angleton's hands shot forward as he thumbed through the papers, reading in silence. His fingers were nicotine-stained, and his nails were cut slightly too short. Lucy watched him with a detached interest. Angleton had always been good to her, but he was the type of man that she wasn't quite sure of—the type of man who had put policy above principle.

He continued to read, turning the pages in silence, until, on one particular page, his eyes narrowed at the margin. Lucy was watching his face carefully. He'd found the English handwriting.

Angleton glanced up. "You saw this?"

"Yes," she replied.

"Philby," he said. "Of course Philby."

His mouth twitched, almost forming a smile. He turned the page once more, as if somehow turning the page would change what was on it.

"Where did you find it?" he asked.

"Admin block," she replied. "Side corridor, protocol room. There was a chair in there bolted to the floor, like someone expected their subjects to be more unwilling than willing to consent."

He nodded, his gaze flicking briefly to the node before

returning to the pages. His expression tightened, the way it did when he tried not to see a pattern that was playing out in front of him. He sighed, rubbed his eyes, and then reached under the table and pressed a small button.

A moment later, the door opened, and two men entered—CIA station technicians by their posture and lab coats, one carrying a metal case filled with instruments. Between them walked a third man, taller and slightly broader than the others, a man who seemed calm in a way that the other two did not.

The two technicians had shifty eyes and uncomfortable stances and moved slightly too often, as if they didn't want to share a room with the object they were about to inspect. The third man, however, wore a simple shirt with the sleeves rolled, a dark jacket shrugged on over it, and carried himself with the loose balance of someone who trusted his own strength. His expression hovered on the edge of amusement, but his eyes were sharp, as if he were cataloguing the room before deciding whether it mattered.

Lucy recognized him from Angleton's files without ever needing an introduction. Bill Easee. She recognized him because he was a special type of man—a field operator the Bureau and MI6 had let get too close to their clever toys. Taller than the photographs suggested and lean rather than bulky, he had the compact build of a middleweight fighter. His skin was dark, his hair close-cropped and already iron-gray at the temples, his face handsome in a worn, unsentimental way. The stillness in him conveyed reliability more than charm; the files had noted that as well. She could almost hear, before he spoke, the faint West Country burr that softened his consonants.

Angleton nodded at the man once, acknowledging him. "Inspect it," he said to the technicians. "Now."

Easee's eyes settled briefly on Lucy, assessing her, then shifted away again. She couldn't tell if he was surprised to see her, but if he was, he didn't show it. They had never met, but there was no doubt in her mind that he knew who she was.

Lucy watched, still seated in her chair, as the technicians opened their cases, pulling out coils, meters, vacuum tube amplifiers, oscilloscopes, and several sensors she didn't recognize. She watched them carefully set the node on the table and begin treating it like a new toy, probing it, wiring it, testing it—everything a scientist would do with a set of components.

Angleton stood, stretched, and lit a cigarette, which he smoked as he watched. Easee moved around the table once, slowly, his eyes tracking the node as if it were both familiar and unfamiliar at the same time.

"That insert," he said quietly. "Quite an interesting piece of technology there. Looks like it was inspired by the Mirror glass, but distinct. For the Mirror, they used something more akin to plasma—a surface that can oscillate easily with a pulse."

"You can tell?" Lucy asked.

"You wouldn't forget it once you've seen it up close. Rosyth Dockyard taught me that," he replied without looking at her.

"Go on," Angleton said.

"Well," Easee continued, his voice steady. "If it's a node, it's not an explicit one—not meant to open an aperture... meant to shape a system instead. Shape people, not places, nor time."

He nodded at the description of the chair restraints in Lucy's file pages.

"Good," Angleton muttered, his fingers tightening around the cigarette.

The technicians had finally finished wiring it up. One flipped a switch on a power unit, and the lights on the table equipment flickered as the system began to draw current.

For a moment, nothing happened. Then, it felt as if a slight tingle of electricity began to play in the air, like an invisible field that would only be noticed by someone who knew it was there. The needle on the instrument dial began to twitch. A faint hum rose from the machine, and Lucy could taste copper in her mouth.

One technician swore softly. "That's not standard EM bleed," he said.

"No," Easee said, his eyes alight for the first time. "That—well, that's resonance."

"Can it be triggered?" Angleton asked, leaning forward.

The technician glanced at the Russian-labeled toggle switch on the node. "We can make an educated guess," he said.

"Well then, guess," Angleton replied.

Easee didn't move; he simply stared at the device for a moment longer. "If we want to guess," he finally said, "we need subjects. This device is meant to operate successfully in the moment, not as some preventive measure."

"Very well," Angleton replied, his eyes sliding to the door. "Bring the men."

Lucy watched as two station officers appeared, leading two Cuban men, locals who'd been working for the Americans long enough that their loyalty was unquestionable. One was a thin clerk-type, while the other wore a police uniform with the eyes of someone who had done unpleasant things for money and would do them again if the price was right.

They were carefully seated in chairs opposite each other. Lucy stood, allowing one of the men to sit in her chair, and the other man took Angleton's. The theory was that the node was directional, and so Angleton aimed it at them while standing behind it, as did Lucy and Easee.

"Simple choice," Angleton said. "You two decide where to route the next contact: dockside or embassy. Discuss."

The clerk chuckled and suggested the dockside. The policeman chose the embassy.

Lucy watched carefully. Their disagreement was mild, of course; it was a practical one that Angleton would have known about before he even called them in. But she assumed that was what he wanted.

Angleton nodded silently to the technician, who toggled the

switch and connected several wires to different sections of the device.

The air in the room tightened, as if someone had stretched it thinner. Lucy could feel it in her nose and ears. It was a subtle pressure change that made her skin prickle and her ears pop, as if she had gone deaf for a moment.

The clerk opened his mouth to argue again, then stopped mid-syllable. His face, rather than turning to confusion, grew blank, as if he'd forgotten what he was going to say. The policeman's face was blank for a second as well, but then it resolved into something she had seen before—argumentative expression, as if he had grown tired of their discussion. He leaned forward.

"Dockside," he said in Spanish.

The clerk nodded immediately. "Yes, dockside would be best," he echoed, as if it had been the policeman's idea all along. It was as if the two men had collapsed into agreement.

Easee watched them, his face hawkish, his eyes calculating.

"Ask them why," he said quietly to Angleton.

Angleton's gaze didn't leave them. "Why dockside? Why did you decide that?" he asked, speaking Spanish as if it were his first language.

The policeman frowned faintly. "Well, it's less attention, of course."

The clerk nodded. "Yes, obvious. No disagreement here."

Lucy could feel her mouth go dry. It wasn't as if they had been hypnotized or conditioned to say this. It was as if they had simply been deprived of any ability to choose, stripped of the space that would allow a mind to weigh more than one path. There was only one path forward.

The technician flipped the switch back.

"Now," Easee said gently, "do you remember disagreeing?"

The clerk looked confused. "Disagreeing?" he asked.

The policeman blinked twice, frowning. "We agreed, didn't we?" Easee nodded and stepped away, his face unreadable. "This is big," he muttered to Angleton. "Dissent collapse, decision state alignment. It's exactly what you wanted."

Angleton exhaled in relief. "It works, then," he said.

Lucy spoke before she could stop herself.

"That's obscene," she muttered.

"No, it's leverage," Angleton corrected her, still staring at the device as if Christmas had come early.

"That's not influence. It's more akin to slavery," Lucy shot back. "I thought you Americans got rid of that already."

Angleton smiled, but it was a thin smile, one that didn't reach his eyes.

"All influence is slavery, Lucy. We just call it diplomacy when we do it with words. But it all has the same end result. Results are what matter in this business, you know."

Easee looked at Angleton, his face etched with concern.

"It's a powerful tool, Angleton. But if you deploy it widely, it won't stay controlled. That's the problem the Bureau had."

"I'm not an idiot, Easee," Angleton shot back, his eyes narrowed.

"No," Easee replied. "But you're the type of man who thinks he can contain an earthquake in a jar. You can't. The people at the Bureau tried that already and found out the hard way."

Angleton didn't answer; he simply flipped through the papers again, tapping the margin where Philby's handwriting was neatly etched.

"This was meant for Batista," he said. "I'm not sure of much else except motive. This kind of device is built for a reason. Moscow wouldn't invest as much time and energy into this unless they were trying to shape an entire country. And there's only one man in Cuba with whom they could accomplish this."

He nodded to one of the scientists, who left the room, returning a second later with another folder. Inside it were photographs: Batista at a party, shaking hands with Angleton; Batista smiling broadly at a room full of men who shared no loyalties to him. He looked charismatic, dangerously so, as if his future was inevitably that of a politician.

"He's not in power yet, is he?" Lucy asked.

"No, but he wants to be," Angleton replied. "And in Havana right now, men such as Batista are either chosen by voters or by pressure. Everyone wants a lever they can pull with him. Moscow wants him, and I'll bet Philby and MI6 want him too. As for the CIA, well, we already have him for the most part.

"But here's the window. The Soviets can't complete this quickly now. From what we can gather, they were relying on specialists—people who understood the calibration of this machine. Those specialists, Anokhin and Popov by name, are missing."

"'Missing?'" Lucy asked.

"Yes. Field reports," Angleton continued. "Two Russians disappeared off the grid… the same two Calder and Rayes should be looking for now. Mirror signatures suggested as much."

"So without them," Easee finished, "reproduction will be slow. Which means we have the first move, no?"

Lucy didn't like how he said "we," as if this project were inevitable. But before she could argue further, a black telephone on the side table rang once, sharply, and Angleton picked it up without hesitation.

"Yes?"

A voice hissed on the line, and though Angleton's posture didn't change, his tone softened into familiarity.

"Ah, Kim, old boy," he said, as if he were leaning back, relaxing in his own living room, and as if he didn't currently possess one of the most powerful pieces of Mirror machinery that had ever been built.

Lucy felt her stomach twist watching him. Angleton was playing a role now—the role of a dutiful friend and loyal protégé. And despite her best efforts, she couldn't tell which role Angleton really believed.

CUBAN SLIDERS

She could hear Philby's voice crackling on the other end and watched as Angleton let him speak for nearly a minute without interruption, his eyes drifting to the node, as if two conversations were running in his mind in parallel.

"Cuban stabilization?" he repeated, as if amused. "You make it sound as if we're sliding furniture around."

He listened again, his mouth twitching at something Philby said, and his eyes cut briefly to Lucy and Easee.

Then, very calmly, he replied, "Kim, if I need British help in Havana, I'll let you know. The CIA has this more than covered."

There was a pause, and Angleton leaned back in his chair, his cigarette smoke curling upward.

"No, I don't think you understand," he finally said. "This is CIA territory. And believe me, you need some time off, old chap. Stay in Washington. Enjoy the weather."

There was another pause, longer this time. Angleton's face didn't change, and his eyes remained half-lidded, as if he wasn't really listening to what Kim Philby said.

"Yes, yes," he said finally. "Trust me, old boy, if you have concerns, you can bring them up through the proper channels."

Though Lucy couldn't hear what Philby said, she could almost hear his smile tightening on the other end of the line, that boyish charm fading to an irritated grimace.

"Of course, Kim," Angleton concluded, friendly as always. "Oh, and give my regards to the Embassy staff. Try not to frighten them with that British optimism of yours. Talk later, old chap."

Then he hung up.

For a second, no one spoke. Angleton exhaled through his nose and took another puff on his cigarette.

"He's bluffing," he said. "He wants in because he thinks something's moving. Likely, either Philby, MI6, or both got wind that the decision locking node was lifted. And if he promised he can deliver something, he can't deliver it now—not on any timetable that matters, that is."

Lucy stared at him.

"You're keeping MI6 out," she said.

"I'm keeping Philby out, and possibly the Russians," Angleton replied.

"And you'll use the node?" she asked.

Angleton didn't deny it. "In a narrow band. With controlled application, of course."

"I'm not so sure that's a good idea," Easee said, his voice low.

But Angleton's gaze never left Lucy. "You're right to warn me. But this isn't up for debate. You're all assuming that only one side will use it if they have it. But if Moscow gets into Batista's circle first, Cuba becomes a locked room. We'll be locked out because they won't have a choice."

"So you'll do it first?" Lucy asked.

"I'll do it better," Angleton replied, stretching as he tossed his cigarette into an ashtray already overflowing on the table.

"This stays with the Agency," he said.

"And Calder?" Lucy asked.

"Calder will never learn about this," Angleton replied, his voice stern now. "Not now, not from you, not ever."

"He'll notice. He always notices something," Lucy shot back.

"No contact," Angleton said flatly. "He's out of Havana right now, chasing our missing Russians. Let him stay out. Let him stay busy. He'll fight the Mirror as he has to, but we have to keep this quiet. For everyone's sake."

They moved fast after that, as men who worked in these fields always did once they'd decided something was necessary, once they'd decided something was justified. But justification, as Lucy had learned long ago, was less of a moral argument and more of a code word that meant they would do it regardless of morality.

A Cuban intermediary aligned with the CIA arranged the meeting. It wasn't with Batista himself, of course; that would have carried far too much risk and brought far too much unneeded attention to the CIA presence in Havana. Instead, the meeting was arranged with the men who controlled his calendar and his access—those who decided which offers reached Batista and which ones died in a drawer somewhere without ever being opened.

They met at a Miramar house that belonged to nobody on paper but looked as if it had been recently renovated with all the latest furnishings to make it all the more pristine. It was a place with a garden, an open terrace, and plenty of luxury to make people believe they'd been invited there for a comfortable meeting rather than calculated manipulation.

But calculated manipulation was the name of the game.

Lucy arrived early, carrying the node in a leather case disguised beneath a folded radio blanket and a stack of documents. She set it carefully on a sideboard behind a real radio playing low Cuban music, as if it belonged there as part of the decorations rather than being a piece of machinery that was meant to be abused.

Angleton already stood by the window, watching the street through a narrow gap in the curtains. His eyes darted back and forth nervously, as if he were expecting it to erupt into gunfire at any moment. Even though this was one of the safest neighborhoods in the city and there was no real risk, Angleton never stopped worrying.

Bill Easee wasn't there. Angleton had ordered him off on another mission related to the Mirror, and though Lucy disliked it, she understood all too well why. Easee would have been a conscience, a moral man who would have protested at how they were going to put the decision locking node to use, and Angleton didn't want one in the room.

Soon, the first gatekeeper arrived—an officer type wearing polished boots, smelling of cigars, and smiling widely with his gleaming white teeth. The second man arrived five minutes later, wearing a tweed suit with the quiet confidence of a lawyer. Then came one more, thin and analytical, and all three exchanged pleasantries with the Cuban intermediary and with Lucy, who played her role with ease and expertise, nodding, smiling, and shaking their hands, while ignoring their covetous glances toward her when they thought she wasn't looking.

Batista's name, of course, came up quickly.

"Our friend is cautious," the lawyer said, swirling his drink. "He remembers 1944 all too well… remembers those who turned their backs."

The officer smiled. "He remembers who paid."

The intermediary nodded sympathetically, almost pleasantly. He knew only too well that money was their language.

"You understand, surely," the intermediary said. "The Americans prefer stability. They prefer predictability. There must be a certain… order to all of this."

The third man, with gray hair at his temples and a small bald patch on the top of his head, sharp and thin, leaned backward.

"And what do the Americans offer?" he asked.

"Access, of course," the intermediary replied smoothly. "Protection and a path into influence without full exposure as to who is actually backing you."

"Protection from whom?" the officer snorted.

But the intermediary's smile remained fixed. Lucy couldn't help but be impressed. The man was good.

"Well, from the ones who would prefer Cuba unstable. I'm sure you're aware that Moscow has grown more and more interested in the islands."

"Ah," the thin man said, his eyes sharpening. "But Moscow offers money as well."

Lucy's heartbeat quickened as she listened. There it was—the fork in the conversation. It was the moment where everything came into play at once, and where choices lived, where a man would weigh offers, play both sides, and decide later.

She glanced at Angleton, who stood behind them, silent, letting the debate happen without intervention. It was clear that the men didn't think much of him. He didn't look important, and he had been careful to wear one of his worn, second-hand suits to appear that way even more.

The lawyer, however, kept his focus on the intermediary in discussion. "MI6 has people here. They've hinted at British support," he said. "It seems hardly prudent to pass this up. We should speak to the Soviets and the British… and only then will we decide to whom we lend our politics."

"But British support is uncertain," the intermediary countered, leaning forward. "They have no established control here in Cuba. The Americans, on the other hand… well, we offer more than promises."

"Ah," the thin man said, smirking, "but promises are useful."

At that moment, Angleton moved, almost too subtly, a movement that no one would have noticed unless they were already watching him, as Lucy was. His hands slid to the toggle. He moved as if he were simply brushing the case, adjusting his suit, yet in an instant, the air had shifted.

Just like that, everything was different.

It wasn't dramatic, but the room suddenly felt more electric and confined, as if someone had closed the door and the sounds inside had grown slightly louder. The men's voices continued for another half sentence before falling silent. The thin man blinked and then stopped speaking. The other two remained silent as well, their eyes unfocused.

Angleton watched them carefully and analytically, as if he didn't want to reveal too much. The intermediary, however, continued speaking, his voice steady.

"British support is just a distraction. It's not the wise decision. The Americans are already here. They are immediate, and they are reliable. The Americans are the ones you should trust."

The officer nodded slowly. His face was blank still, and yet he spoke almost confidently.

"Yes," he said slowly.

The lawyer nodded, too, as if he had suddenly become convinced of some great truth.

"I see what you mean," he said.

The smirk that had been a constant on the thin man's face had faded now, and he leaned forward, his elbows resting on his knees in concentration.

"If we do work with the Americans," he said, "we work through your channel, not through anyone else."

"Of course," the intermediary replied, his smile waning by half a degree.

"And if someone approaches from Moscow?" the lawyer asked.

The officer shrugged. "We don't entertain it. It would be a waste of time."

Lucy watched, her skin prickling. It wasn't as if they were acting controlled or enslaved. It was just like in the test they had run earlier, but more potent. They behaved as if the choice which they had been confronted with had never existed in the first place, as if their decision itself could only move forward in one direction—the only rational direction.

As Lucy watched, Angleton moved again, and his fingers eased off the toggle. The tightening of the room loosened again, but the decision stayed. The men finished their drinks, leaving with handshakes and departing with polite smiles, convinced they had made the only smart, rational, self-interested move. Convinced it had been their decision to make.

Lucy watched them go and felt nauseous.

Angleton smiled ever so slightly, looking satisfied the way a mother is when she watches her child win first place in a contest.

When the door had finally closed and the villa was quiet again, Lucy turned toward him.

"You just rewired them," she shot.

Angleton's voice remained calm. "I simply removed the interference."

"Sounds like something a tyrant would say," she replied.

"Tyranny, government—what's the real difference?" Angleton asked, not even flinching.

She stared at the node on the desk, at the decision locking technology they had procured only a short while ago. It sat there like an ordinary radio case, as if nothing were out of the ordinary, and yet it had just changed the course of history.

"And now?" she asked. "What's next?"

"What's next," Angleton mused. His eyes drifted toward the curtains, toward Havana beyond. "Well, now Batista will hear one more channel more clearly than the others, slowly, over weeks. It'll seem as if his decisions are aligned with ours. It'll seem like it was his preference, like it was common sense."

"And the Soviets?" Lucy asked, her throat tightening.

"Well," he said, smiling, though his eyes remained cold. "They'll find doors that won't open and doors that'll swing shut before they can even step through. Calls that don't get returned, and meetings that never quite form."

Lucy looked away, and she suddenly felt tired.

"You're keeping it, aren't you?" she said.

"Of course I am," he replied. He didn't even pretend otherwise.

"And you'll tell Washington you prevented Soviet access?" she asked.

"I did," he said, his eyes sharpening.

"You also ensured your access," she replied.

Angleton didn't respond right away, but when he finally did, he seemed more tired before.

"Lucy," he said, sounding almost sincere. "You don't survive in this world by refusing every weapon just because you might get some blood on your hands."

She stared at her own reflection in the dark window glass, and for a second, Lucy thought she saw two of herself again, slightly out of phase. She blinked it away.

"Calder would destroy it," she muttered.

Angleton stepped closer and gazed at the window, too.

"Calder destroys what he doesn't understand," he said. "He thinks destruction is purity. And maybe it is, but this is not his arena, and you will not tell him. Not now, not ever, unless I decide otherwise. Is that clear?"

Lucy's jaw tightened. After a moment, she replied.

"I'll obey," she said.

Angleton stared at her, as if questioning her for a second.

"You can be uneasy," he responded. "Uneasy is just a sign that you're still human, and it's okay to be still human. But you will obey."

Though she clenched her teeth, she nodded once more.

Angleton nodded back, his expression more relaxed now. The matter had been settled.

As Lucy gathered the node back into its case, she could feel the truth of what she had become. Not an asset, not even a thief or a politician, but the keeper of a secret that would split her from Max Calder even more than she had already been split. She could feel the rift between them growing, and she wasn't sure if that would ever change. The moment he learned it existed, he would never trust her again. He didn't trust her now. But after this, it would be certain.

The Mirror was still out there, still pulsing, still spreading, with only Calder to stop it.

CHAPTER 15
MUSTIQUE MISFIRE

The first thing he noticed was the salt. Though his eyes were closed, Anokhin knew that the air had changed. He could no longer smell Havana's damp air, rot, and diesel. This was the open sea—clean and sharp enough to make your lungs ache.

His eyelids felt glued shut. When he attempted to inhale, the breath caught halfway in his chest and turned into a ragged cough.

He could feel warm sand against his cheek.

Sergei Anokhin forced his eyes to open. Above him was a black sky, dotted with stars so bright they seemed to be directly on top of him. The moon sat against the horizon, low and pale. In the distance, he could see palm fronds swaying to and fro with the wind.

There was silence. Not the absence of sound, but the absence of people. No engines, no radios, no hum from the distillery, no pulse of a city even. No background human noise that made the world seem normal.

He tried to sit up. His joints were stiff, as if he'd been asleep for a week. He pushed himself upright anyway and saw his hands in the moonlight. His skin was not the same as he remembered; it was thin, almost translucent. Liver spots freckled along his fingers and the back of his hand.

When he tried to flex his fingers, his knuckles clicked—a dry, arthritic sound he was unfamiliar with. It was a sound that a man his age wouldn't recognize.

"No," he croaked, and his own voice sounded wrong.

Beside him, a shape moved.

"Mikhail," he said, grabbing the shoulder of the other man who lay half in the surf, silent and soaked in water. "Popov... Mikhail, wake up."

Popov jolted, sucking in air with a gasp. His eyes snapped to Anokhin's face, relieved for one second, then horrified.

"You, you're—" he began, but Anokhin interrupted.

"Don't," he said.

Popov glanced at his own hands and made a sound halfway between laughter and choking. His fingers were swollen, his skin bruised and cracked, his nails yellowed. Even his face had sunken in on itself, looking older and exhausted. They stared at each other, unsure of whether to laugh or cry or give up.

"We left," Popov whispered finally.

"No." Anokhin shook his head. "We were thrown."

He turned and scanned the shoreline with his eyes. The beach curved into darkness on either side. Toward the inland, he could make out low scrub and palm trees. No buildings—none that he saw. No lights on this stretch of shore, either. The waves hit with a metronomic rhythm, lulling him into a sense of exhaustion.

"Are we on an island? What island is this?" Popov asked.

Anokhin could hear the fear in the other man's voice. He forced his mind to work. In Havana, there had been maps, charts of the Windward Islands, shipping lanes—everything they needed for navigation. But that mattered little now, now that they were actually on one of the islands.

But he could guess. Guessing had always been a part of his job. So Anokhin glanced around, looking at the silhouettes of palm trees, the low hills, and the sand—almost too pale, even in the moonlight.

"Maybe we are somewhere in the Grenadines. You saw the maps in Havana," he said finally. "Could well be Mustique, perhaps? That's one of the islands with no real development. It would make sense."

Popov flinched at his voice but didn't speak.

Anokhin stood slowly, feeling his knees protest as he did, swaying once before steadying himself and holding out a hand for Popov, who took it. He stood there, silent, watching the ocean.

"We need shelter, a radio, we need—" Popov began, but Anokhin cut him off.

"We need an anchor," he replied.

Popov nodded slowly, as if recalling words he had already forgotten.

"The Mirror field will stabilize on noise. Human noise, memory density, social friction. That's why Havana works. A city like that is thick with it."

But here, as if to mock him, the surf continued to lap silently against the shore.

Popov rubbed his temples. "Here," he continued, picking up Anokhin's thought, "it's empty. Nothing to anchor to."

"I know," Anokhin replied, placing a hand on his skull. The headache wasn't local pain. It was a constant pressure that he had felt since he had begun working on this cursed project. And further, deep inside his head, somewhere far away, he could feel Mirror V4's pulse.

Popov took a step inland, then stopped suddenly.

"What is it?" Anokhin asked.

Popov's eyes were fixed on the sand. Anokhin followed his gaze and saw footprints—two sets, running from the surf toward the palms. Fresh and sharp, as if they were made moments ago.

"Us?" Popov asked.

Anokhin stared. The prints were exactly the right size, the

right stride. Everything about them was perfect. They hadn't even been washed away by the water yet.

"We've already walked here before," Popov whispered.

But there was nothing they could do but walk again. They did, following the footprints inland. The palms opened into scrub, and then a small hill rose slowly.

"Time is not holding," Anokhin mumbled as they continued to walk.

Popov simply nodded. The man didn't dare respond, lest he lose his own voice.

They continued walking, finding nothing. They should have reached some sign of habitation by now, but all they encountered were palms, scrub, and sand.

Then Popov stopped ahead. Through the trees, they saw a shape in the moonlight: stone walls half-collapsed, swallowed by vines. It was a ruin of an old plantation structure that jutted into the sky, as if its very presence offended the silent island around them.

Anokhin stepped forward toward it. As he did, for a heartbeat, he smelled Havana—the hot rum and diesel—and saw Mirror V4 shimmering in the dark.

He heard a whimper beside him and turned to see Popov clutching at his head, blood leaking from his nostril. The man wiped it and stared at the red smear, as if he wasn't sure it really existed or not.

Silently, Anokhin guided his colleague into the ruin. He didn't say it, but he could tell that Popov had it worse than he did.

Inside, the air was stale and damp. Popov sank against a wall, breathing heavily. Anokhin remained standing in the center of the ruin, breathing slowly and trying to center himself.

"Numbers. I can't keep..." Popov began.

"No, Popov, listen."

Anokhin crouched beside him, grabbing his shoulders hard.

"If you lose coherence, you'll end up like Markov did."

"He died. He died," Popov said, his eyes widened in delirium. "Died on the street."

"Yes, because the field consumed him," Anokhin replied. "We can't stay here."

"Then where?" Popov asked.

Before Anokhin could answer, the air shifted. It felt as if they were being pulled suddenly, the recursion field collapsing toward a higher density node. His ears popped, his stomach lurched, and the ruin's walls blurred.

"No!" he heard Popov screaming.

Anokhin braced himself as the floor moved sideways beneath him.

For a second, he saw a corridor lined with wet stone, a tunnel, and through the blur, he could make out a sign that read "KINGSWAY" in a bold, printed font. Then he saw cranes—the metal skeletons of some dockyard in the midnight fog. A split second later, they were back at the ruin.

He could feel Popov's fingers digging into his sleeve like claws.

"We're being pulled," Anokhin whispered.

Then, for a heartbeat, the world went black. There was nothing—no sensation, no sound, no sights. Suddenly, they slammed into the dirt as if they had fallen.

Not sand. Dirt. Damp and smelling of old sugarcane and rot.

Anokhin rolled, choking, and opened his eyes. Above them was a different sky, the horizon lying wrong, the wind carrying different scents.

They were on a hillside now. Below them, a bay spread wide and dark, boats resting like floating leaves upon the water.

Admiralty Bay, Bequia.

Popov lay beside him, curled up like a child, sobbing, then vomited onto the dirt.

Anokhin stared down at the bay and then up at the ruin beside them. It was another plantation house, not entirely collapsed but in the process of it—stone walls, broken windows, dilapidated and old, covered in vines.

"We're here," Anokhin whispered.

"Where?" Popov muttered, looking up, his eyes bloodshot.

"Bequia," Anokhin replied simply. "The Mirror rejected Mustique."

Popov sobbed, laughing and crying all at once.

But Anokhin knew they had to keep moving, and so he half-pulled, half-pushed the man as they crawled toward the ruin. Inside, the air was thick with damp and the moldy smell of old sugar. The place smelled like death.

Popov lay on the floor, staring into space as if he saw something no one else could, giggling to himself now and again. But Anokhin forced himself to focus. If he focused, he might survive—at least, he might survive longer.

Near the hearth, he found charcoal and began to write on the stone wall. The equations wouldn't save him, but structure was memory. Writing provided structure, and with memory and structure, he could resist—resist the deterioration that the Mirror was causing.

And so he began writing until his hand cramped. Numbers, symbols, coherence equations, and lattice diagrams against the wall. He wrote on one wall, then wrote on another, while Popov sat slumped in a corner, breathing like an old man.

He could hear the ocean below, but Anokhin didn't lose focus. Instead, he wrote faster. Somewhere far away, Mirror V4 continued to pulse, each irregular pulse driving him more insane.

Darryl kept the pirogue far offshore, the engine barely murmuring. He didn't speak, but stared off into the distance, waiting for us to make a call.

Alicia sat rigid, holding the attaché case between her boots.

CUBAN SLIDERS

Although her face was calm, I knew her mind was whirring, and I knew she felt as tense as I did.

On the shore, the Soviet camp looked exactly as we had imagined: tents set back from the surf, crates stacked far too neatly, and a generator humming somewhere in the distance. We could see the lantern light moving between the canvas, the shadows shifting with disciplined spacing. These were men who didn't belong and no longer felt the need to pretend that they did.

"Well, let's not land there," Alicia murmured.

"Wasn't planning to," I whispered back.

Darryl quietly angled us along the coastline, toward where the beach turned to rocks and the palms thickened. Here, Mustique was darker, with no lights, no tents, and no Russians.

We found a small cove where the surf had softened to a hiss. Darryl killed the engine, letting us drift in on the tide.

As the pirogue gently caressed the sand, Alicia and I hopped out and crouched low between the palms. Darryl lit up a cigarette and shook his head as I glanced at him. I nodded with a slight smile. He would remain behind in the boat.

Alicia and I moved inland. The island was quiet in the way that empty places are quiet. It wasn't exactly peaceful, but it was silent. And yet something about the silence felt slightly too staged, too smooth, as if it were holding back a roar that would break forth at the first strong move.

I'd felt it before in places the Mirror couldn't quite grasp, though I wasn't sure what this phenomenon would be called.

We crept along, following a narrow path carved out by the animals that inhabited the island. At first, there was nothing. Then, faintly in the distance, we could hear the generator's thrum carried along by the wind.

We continued on, another half an hour maybe, moving slower than we meant to, and eventually, we could hear radio chatter—a pulse of Russian, thin and struggling.

Alicia pulled the marine radio from her bag and tuned it quickly. Russian voices crackled through, thin and distant.

Her jaw tightened. After a moment, she translated, "Mustique is clear. Too clean, from what I can make out."

I hadn't gathered much from the language, but I knew Alicia wouldn't translate it wrong. I nodded. It meant the Russians had already sensed what we had—what I suspected about the place. Something about Mustique had slipped outside of the Mirror's grasp.

We continued on, using the distant hum of the generator and the faint radio chatter as our guide. If they were running a camp, they'd also have a listening point, somewhere with elevation—somewhere you could push signals off the island and receive signals in kind. That was the place we needed to find.

Near a ridge, we found it: a patch of sand scraped flat as if equipment had been set down and then hurriedly cleared. A shallow dugout behind a rock. Trampled grass. Canvas scraps. A crushed foreign cigarette butt. Someone had been here recently—and left in a rush, from the looks of it. The cigarette butt was still smoking.

Alicia crouched, running her fingers across the ground. "Seems fresh," she muttered.

My head throbbed sharply, and for a second, I saw the dugout twice—and I could see a man crouched inside it. Then it snapped back, and it was empty.

"Max," Alicia said quietly; she'd noticed.

"I'm fine," I lied. "Let's see what they were listening for."

Half-buried under brush near the dugout was a damp packet wrapped in oilcloth, neatly folded in military fashion. Alicia peeled it open. Inside was a folded chart, pencil bearings, and a torn sheet of notes—angles, times, and a circled bay name written in block letters.

"This isn't a camp map," Alicia said, scanning the contents. "It's a triangulation sheet." Her finger traced two bearing lines until they crossed off-island. "Look. Admiralty Bay."

"Admiralty Bay?" I asked. "That's Bequia."

She flipped the torn note over. One word in Cyrillic, underlined hard: PLANTATION.

I stood there for a moment, and it clicked. "Mustique isn't the destination."

"I think you're right," Alicia said. "Whatever they were doing here... they missed their target. Or it slid out from under them."

The radio continued to hum in the background, and a sharper Russian voice cut through. Alicia's eyes flickered toward it. It was the first time she had taken interest in the radio chatter for a while.

"Sounds like they're complaining something won't stabilize," she said to me.

"I guess," I replied, "it likely has something to do with this island. I haven't noticed my headache as much as long as we've been here. Probably too little memory density—too few humans for it to leech off of."

"Well, then," Alicia whispered, "if they have this map, they'll move."

"And if our scientists are still alive," I said, "they'll be dying by the minute on Bequia."

Alicia nodded, folded the map, and shoved it into her bag.

"Let's get back to the boat."

We moved downhill quickly. In the distance, we could hear angry shouts in Russian. They were moving too. We reached a cove, wading out to the pirogue that sat two yards off the sandy beach. As we climbed in, Darryl started the engine low, and the boat slid away from Mustique, smooth and silent.

As the shoreline shrank behind us, I watched the island with interest. Maybe this was where I needed to be. Mustique sat quietly in the moonlight, holding nothing and anchoring nothing, as if the world had refused to let the Mirror even touch it. As if somehow this small island had rejected the very pulse of V4.

For just a second, though, I saw the island almost flicker. I saw the surf hit the sand twice, the exact same sound repeated each time. Even Mustique wasn't stable enough—not stable enough to hold anyone anymore.

Alicia finally spoke.

"We're going to Bequia," she said.

"Yeah," I replied. "And whatever's waiting there, it's something the Mirror's latched onto."

She nodded as Darryl silently steered the boat in the direction of Bequia. Behind us, Mustique's distant shape fell off into the darkness, and I closed my eyes. If we didn't manage to destroy the Mirror, and if it didn't kill me, maybe I would return here one day. Something about this island was nice.

But ahead, Bequia waited for us.

CHAPTER 16
STRATEGIC SILENCE

Lucy caught the pen mid-spin and set it down on the blotter slightly harder than she'd meant to. The small click echoed in the borrowed room. Technically, it was a dining room, in that Miramar villa, which didn't officially belong on paper and barely belonged off it.

Heavy, drawn curtains kept the afternoon sun to a thin golden line cast along the floorboards. Though the ceiling fan turned lazily in circles overhead, it barely managed to stir the warm air that smelled of cigarette ash—a sign that Angleton was here. Always inevitable.

In the distance, she could hear the radio static. Angleton had insisted on keeping it alive. He'd made the place his own, having stayed there slightly longer than intended, though he would be leaving back to the States soon.

Within an hour, he'd had the entire villa papered with his own unique brand of chaotic profiling. A map of the Caribbean was pinned to the wall, pencil lines connecting Havana through the islands. Each location was reduced to coordinates, accompanied by scribbled threat assessments along the side. Here and there, he had piles of paper stacked with near-surgical precision, organized in only a manner that Angleton likely understood.

There was a telephone on the desk, small and black, that only rang when it absolutely mattered.

Angleton stood at the table, his sleeves rolled up to his elbows, a forgotten cigarette burning between his fingers. He was absentmindedly reading an intercept transcript, his eyes moving in methodical sweeps, scanning each line quickly for the pattern beneath the words that other men would miss, but that he would catch.

Lucy watched him, half-fascinated, half-furious, and only slightly exasperated.

A young Cuban station officer slipped in without knocking, wearing a well-pressed linen suit. He placed a fresh bundle of papers on the table, arranged them neatly to make sure they didn't slide, and left without a word.

Angleton never looked up or acknowledged the presence of the man; he simply reached out, pulled a few of the new pages under the lamp, and began to read. That was his operating method.

For a second, the radio hiss in the background swelled, then settled back into white noise.

"Is it bad?" Lucy finally asked.

Angleton exhaled through his nose.

"Worse than bad," he muttered.

He slid the pages across the table without ceremony and looked at her expectantly.

Lucy leaned forward, scanning the intercept summary. It was a summary of Caribbean monitoring, clearly filtered through some sort of CIA handlers, with enough detail that it would never see daylight in any official capacity.

But it wasn't the content specifically that alerted Lucy to something unwanted; it was the tone.

The Soviets weren't speaking like men who were running routine operations. She knew what routine operations were like. Instead, the Soviets were sending transcripts—transcripts which had been intercepted and deciphered by Angleton's men—that made it seem as if they had lost their grip on something critical.

Admiralty Bay, Bequia, plantation ruins, field will not stabilize, subject out of place.

All those words jumped out at her and etched themselves into her mind.

Beneath that, a human source report—asset notation in English but carrying an unmistakable hint of fear.

Multiple detachments observed moving between islands, Mustique used as waypoint, Grenadines-based team coordinating, urgent, searching for two men.

Two men?

Lucy leaned in and read the document again. She could picture it far too easily: the palm shadows cast on the wet white sand, the men with rifles and radios moving through the places that would reject them like a host rejects a parasite.

"Mustique," she said quietly.

"A waypoint," Angleton replied, nodding.

"Bequia is the destination?" she asked, but he didn't answer right away.

She could tell he was already thinking, fitting the pieces together like a puzzle in his head the way his hands never quite could. And when he finally spoke, it was with an air of certainty, as if the conclusion he had made had fallen into place effortlessly.

"The Soviets are converging," he said. "I'm not entirely sure why, but I suspect something's wrong. The field won't hold and the web won't settle, especially with those two men missing."

He stood, moving to the wall map, tracing the pencil line from Havana through the islands with one finger, stopping over Bequia as if he had always intended to end up here.

"The plantation ruins in Admiralty Bay," he continued, his voice dropping. "It's where someone would end up if they weren't choosing where to go. No one in their right mind would flee there. They were being pushed."

Lucy listened quietly. She knew enough about Angleton to realize he wasn't done, and sure enough, he turned back to the table and pulled out another folder—a folder of his own notes, not the station's—filled with circled names and lines connecting them. That same compulsion made him so great, so dangerous, and yet also so gullible when he wanted to be. An incredibly intelligent man who was intelligent enough that he could deceive even himself.

"Anokhin and Popov," he said. "They're still missing."

Lucy's eyes flicked to the case on the sideboard behind the radio. There sat the decision locking node, wrapped away and hidden in the locked case, but still present in the room, the way some loaded gun is thought of, even if it's not aimed at anyone.

Angleton caught her look.

"Moscow can't rebuild that node quickly without them, if at all," he said. "They can copy a schematic, maybe solder some copper together and pretend they can understand it, but calibration is where the real work comes into play. That's where you need actual, intelligent scientists, men who know how to do the secret work, and they simply don't have it."

"So they want their specialists back," Lucy said. It was less of a question and more of a statement. She'd seen the chair, the restraints, the notes. She knew exactly why the Soviets were moving this way.

"They need them back," Angleton corrected, "and because they need them, they'll show their hand—move assets they would normally keep quiet and use routes, names, and boats that will stand out like sore thumbs in the Caribbean. They wouldn't risk it for anything less."

He spoke as if he'd just been handed a gift.

"You sound pleased," Lucy remarked.

He seemed to think for a second.

"I take pleasure in being informed," he replied at last, then picked up another sheet covered in abbreviations and timestamps and tapped one of the lines with his finger. "Look at this," he said. "Repeated references to something out of place. The field won't stabilize because the island isn't holding. Mustique specifically doesn't hold. There's something about it that shuns them—shuns the Mirror's presence."

He looked up, his gaze sharpening.

"Which means your two Bureau friends are likely on the same track."

"Calder and Rayes," Lucy said.

"Yes. Calder and Rayes," Angleton confirmed. "Or Artemis, as I'm sure she would prefer to be called."

Lucy's jaw tightened.

"Then you should warn them," she said, trying to keep her voice level and professional. "Warn them how fast the Russians are moving."

"No."

Angleton didn't even pretend to consider it.

"Absolutely not," he said.

"Angleton," Lucy leaned forward, "if the Soviets are already staging on Mustique and converging on Bequia, Calder's walking into a kill box. You're sending him to die. Remember, you are the one who gave them this information."

Angleton lifted his cigarette, which he finally remembered, took a slow drag, and exhaled. He leaned back, watching the smoke drift upward into the light, hanging there in the still air.

"That's on him," he finally said. "Calder's been walking into kill boxes since Cairo—hell, since well before that—hell, since he was born. It's what he does."

Lucy fiddled with the pen between her fingers without remembering it was there.

"And if he dies?" she asked.

"Then he dies," Angleton said, his gaze unwavering.

It wasn't cruelty in the way he spoke, but simple, brutal honesty. This was policy, and this was strategy. This was the way it had to be.

Lucy sat back, the chair creaking under her. For a second, she was back at the harbor—the salt, the diesel, the burning metal—watching Max's face in the floodlights, his expression as she was carted away by the CIA team that had been sent to retrieve her, as if he had been watching her betray him once again.

"He's not just going to die," she said quietly. "If they capture him, if they take him alive, they can take everything: his knowledge, his resonance, whatever the hell he is now. And the scientists—well, those men are degrading. Didn't Markov prove this from day one? I've read the reports. Anokhin and Popov could age to death before anyone ever reaches them."

"Ah." Angleton's gaze sharpened, and he fixed it on her, calculating. "You want to contact him," he said. "That's what this is, isn't it?"

"Yes, because this is a smart thing to do," Lucy replied, steadying herself. "I'm not sentimental about this, but you'd be making a mistake not to warn Calder."

Angleton watched her for a long moment. The room felt smaller, the faint hum of radio static in the background louder. Then, very calmly, he repeated it, the same rule he had told her from the beginning.

"No contact with Calder, explicitly. This is an order," he said.

Lucy stared at him, waiting, her face fixed. If he was going to be a tyrant about this, she wanted to know why.

He stared back for half a minute, then finally sighed, as if he'd given up hope of simply having her accept it without argument.

"First," he said, holding up one finger, "compartmentalization. We cannot let Max Calder know about Batista. He cannot know about decision locking. He cannot know we've field-tested it, and he cannot know we've used it."

"You mean you don't want him to know you're manipulating people," Lucy said.

"Correct," Angleton replied. "Now, second, operational security. You know damn well that if Calder learns we have the node, he will try to destroy it… try to burn it to hell. The man won't debate... won't negotiate. He'll do what he always does, and we'll be left to clean up after him, or try to fight him to stop it."

"His decision might not be wrong," Lucy countered.

"Wrong or not, it fractures our coalition," Angleton shot back, his voice hardening. "You know the Bureau wants control —wants destruction. The Agency wants control, and if Calder finds out what we've done, he won't just target the Soviets; he'll turn on us as he's turned on the Bureau before, and we cannot afford that while V4 is active under Cárdenas."

V4.

The word landed hard on Lucy's ears, a reminder that even now the city was turning sideways. Even now, Havana was wrong—a city trying to remember a version of itself that simply didn't exist anymore.

"And third," Angleton continued, "Philby. If somehow Philby learns what I've done, he will weaponize it, expose it politically, or use it to destroy my credibility. Either way, it would be a kind of ruination for me and for the CIA. Hell, if he plays it smart enough, he could even turn it into leverage against me inside Washington."

"You're finally admitting he's compromised?" Lucy asked.

Angleton's mouth twitched in amusement.

"I'm not admitting anything," he replied, "but I am assuming that the man is Philby, and Philby is smart. Whether he's compromised or not, he's always playing a game, just as we are."

The two sat there in silence, as if reevaluating each other for the first time.

Finally, Angleton spoke again. His voice was softer this time, as if he wasn't quite sure that Lucy had agreed with what he'd said and wanted to ensure she would follow his orders.

"You want to warn Calder because you still think there's a version of this story where he forgives you," he said.

"That's not what this is," she replied, but she could feel the heat rising behind her eyes.

Angleton watched her, as if he was weighing how much to say, and how hard to push her on her lie.

"Maybe not," he finally allowed, "but either way, you're not warning him because right now your value isn't in what you can say; it's in what you can keep quiet."

"My value…" Lucy's voice trailed off.

"Simply put, you're my counter-Philby asset," Angleton replied. "You can anticipate Calder's movements. You understand his instincts. You also hold the Agency's most sensitive mirror-adjacent secret in your hands and in your mind: decision locking node. The Batista operation. The fact that we can collapse decisions inside a room and leave men agreeing with us without knowing. I've trusted you with all this information, and because you know it, you can't be allowed to leak it—not to Calder, nor to the Bureau, nor in any operational context."

Lucy laughed, humorless and short.

"That's a charming philosophy," she said. "Don't think, don't speak, don't feel. Just follow."

"You can feel all you want," Angleton replied. "But you must do it in silence."

Lucy nodded. She knew he meant what he said, and she knew that she would obey.

It wasn't that she believed in Angleton's morality, or lack thereof. She didn't. But she did believe in consequences. And Angleton knew consequences better than any other man she had ever met. He dealt with consequences the way other men dealt with currency.

Her gaze drifted to the window, and she looked out through the small sliver into the street from the edge of the curtain—at the palm fronds, the damp pavement, and the puddles along the edges of the roadways. In that moment, she understood, with a settling feeling of cold clarity, what her silence would cost.

It wouldn't cost her life, and if anything, it might end up with her promotion. Yet, it would cost the last remaining thread between her and Max Calder. It wasn't as if she'd betrayed him directly, or that he would think that this time. But it would be far worse.

First and foremost, because she'd watched Angleton formalize betrayal into a plan, and she had then helped him execute it.

She remained silent, staring ahead, lost in thought. Angleton seemed to take that as agreement and turned back to the map, already moving on, peering over more papers and charts.

Lucy stood slowly.

"I need a minute," she said.

"Take it," Angleton replied, never looking up.

She walked to the small desk in the corner—the one with the cipher pad and secure cable forms—sat down and pulled a blank sheet toward her. She knew Angleton wasn't watching; she knew he wouldn't listen as her pen formed letters in the standard Bureau contact format.

She wrote almost without thinking.

Priority Bequia, Soviet convergence, Admiralty Bay, plantation ruins, two targets, advise immediate—

Then she stopped, staring at the words.

Her pen hovered over the paper, but she couldn't finish it; she couldn't keep writing. She knew how easy it would be to send it through the station's back channel. Calder would have it in hours if she sent it to the right man—the right contact. He'd know, adapt. He might even survive.

But if she sent it, Angleton would know what she'd done, eventually. Maybe he wouldn't find out today or even this week, but eventually, he'd know, and then everything she had agreed to—every fragile piece of her life she was trying to balance—would collapse.

Her hands moved again. This time, she crumpled the paper, holding the ball in her fist, her knuckles whitening as the sharp edges bit into her palm. She held it over the ashtray on the desk, dropped it in, and struck a match.

The paper curled and blackened before turning turned to ash.

She watched it burn without ever really paying attention, until nothing legible remained.

She stood again, returning to the table where Angleton was now poring over a new intercept. He never looked up.

"With Batista guided and Philby boxed out, we control Cuba's new-term political arc," —he said, almost more to himself than to her— "and that'll buy us time. But now what?"

Lucy stared at him.

"You talk about this whole thing as if it's a chessboard."

His mouth tightened.

"It is a chessboard. Everything is. The only question is who gets to move the pieces."

He turned back to the map, his eyes darting along the pencil line from Havana to Bequia.

"Bequia is a convergence. High risk there. Calder could get himself killed... Rayes too. But it'll also be useful if it plays out correctly."

He paused.

"Useful," Lucy repeated, and Angleton nodded eagerly.

"Yes. The Soviets, they will expose their routes, their names, assets. They'll move far too quickly to stay clean. And when they do, I'll have them. Later, of course."

Lucy listened, and she knew that Angleton wasn't just refusing to warn Calder. Though he never explicitly told her, he was using him, leveraging the Bureau's desperation as bait to make Moscow show its hand. To make Moscow move the first chess piece.

"And what about now?" she asked. "What should I do besides keeping my mouth shut?"

Angleton finally glanced up from the document.

"You, Lucy, will stand by. You, Locket, will stand by in Havana. You'll continue supporting containment and recovery planning. I'll have you coordinate with the station on monitoring V4's resonant spikes. You'll keep the decision locking materials secured until I forward them back to the CIA. I'll give you updates on this.

"Keep in mind, I'll be leaving in a day or so. So you have to be ready to assist with the retrieval of Mirror materials or intelligence the moment a window opens."

Lucy's voice was flat.

"And what if Calder comes back?" she asked.

Angleton paused for a moment, as if this was a question he hadn't thought of yet.

"When he comes back," he said finally, "we'll decide how much he's allowed to know."

Lucy nodded slowly, and Angleton exhaled as if the room had just unclenched. He reached for the phone absentmindedly, then stopped, as if he was remembering something.

"Oh, and Locket," he said.

"Yes?" she answered, making sure she controlled her voice to keep it steady.

"Silence is an asset. It's control. Learn how to use it."

She nodded and then silently left as Angleton picked up the phone.

The radio hiss shifted for a moment, a pause in the static, then something that might have been a word. She looked up sharply, but Angleton gave no sign he had heard it. The hiss resumed its normal rhythm, white noise filling the corners of the room. If someone had spoken, it was only a word that she could hear.

Outside, somewhere beyond Miramar, Havana kept living its double life—rotting from the inside, shining on the outside, a city crumbling at its very core.

And out, far beyond the water, somewhere past the islands and the listening posts, two men were aging in the dark, as soldiers converged on them with guns, while two Bureau agents unknowingly followed the same path.

Lucy remained locked away in an apartment where no one

knew she was alive. She knew it wasn't right, but it was her duty to follow orders, at least for now. Yet deep down, she could already feel the moment approaching when Max Calder would look at her again—really look at her.

She wondered what he would see.

CHAPTER 17
BEQUIA BOMBSHELL

The pirogue cut south through the black, silent water, leaving Mustique behind in its wake. Darryl kept the engine barely above idle, nursing us slowly through the night with the kind of silence that would make us go unnoticed and unrecognized, except for maybe the birds, which flew above, cawing occasionally.

I sat near the bow, watching the horizon. Behind us, Mustique had been eerily too clean, as if it were a place the world itself, creation itself, hadn't quite touched yet. The mirror's eerie sickness had slid right off it, like water off wax.

Ahead, however, Bequia awaited us, and I knew it waited with the inevitable weight that Mustique lacked. Even from here, I could already feel the Mirror's presence pressing down against my skull, giving me that headache that had come and gone so many times since I'd begun this leg of my journey—that constant, never-ending pulse.

As we neared Bequia, I felt the density of people who had lived and died and fought over nothing. Houses and history bled with enough information for the Mirror to sink its teeth into.

Alicia sat amidships. The marine radio cradled in her hands as she listened carefully. Under her boots, she kept Fraser-Smith's rig in the attaché case, wedged where she could reach it if she needed to. She hadn't let it out of her sight since Havana—not after the ship, not after Lucy. I couldn't say that I even blamed her. If we lost the rig, the game was up.

The radio hissed, and I could hear a faint Russian voice bleeding through the static, fresh in the salty air. Alicia's pencil moved, scratching across the paper in quick succession as she wrote it down.

"What is it?" I asked.

"They're reorganizing," she said without looking up, "complaining about the field not holding in Mustique."

"Well, they can keep complaining," I replied. "The field won't stabilize there."

She nodded. "And they've said Bequia, Admiralty Bay. That's three times now."

Three times. The Soviets were thorough.

But the world around us was stuttering, breaking open, as if reality couldn't decide where to hold and where to yield. As if in response, the pirogue rose and fell methodically as the sea shifted beneath us. Somewhere in the air, the wind twisted and turned faintly, bringing a fresh smell of diesel, fish, and wet wood—smells that meant humanity was near.

Somewhere ahead, I heard a dog bark once, then once again, the exact same sound, as if a glitch in reality had broken through.

I shook my head. This was bad.

The closer we got, as Bequia took shape as that dark ridge against the night sky, the more I could feel the pulse of the Mirror. It was as if it had turned its attention, if it could even be called that, toward this place.

Darryl pointed with his chin toward a stretch of the darker shore, where no lights shone. Only palms and rock were visible.

"We land there," he muttered. "You go up. I'll wait... or try to."

"How long?" Alicia asked.

"As long as I can," he said, shrugging. "But if I see a boat that shouldn't be here or any Russians, I leave. You understand?"

I nodded. We understood. We wouldn't ask a civilian to die for our war, and the Soviets would kill to get what they wanted.

"If you have to go, then go," I said, placing a hand on his shoulder. "And tell your cousin I say hi."

He nodded and eased the engine down, letting the pirogue glide through the shadow water. As it crested against the sand, we stepped out into warm surf that felt gentle after Mustique's unease and Havana's violent, reality-shattering glitches.

My boots sank into the sand, and for a second, I expected to see glimpses of Scotland's cold mist or Kingsway's damp stone when I looked up. But I didn't. Not yet, at least. There was nothing—nothing but Bequia ahead.

We dragged the boat under the palms, and Darryl quickly threw a net over it, pulling out a rifle I hadn't noticed before from the depths of his boat.

"Go," he said, never looking at us.

I nodded in response, and we moved inland silently and slowly.

Bequia wasn't empty like Mustique was. Even in the fading light, there was noise. I could hear insects whining in the distance and a rooster heralding nighttime. The creak of wood —whether from a tree or a house settling, I knew not—but it was noise all the same. And with that noise came my headache, multiplied, as if it had simply been waiting to return.

It started dull behind my left eye and then sharpened further, as if somehow my proximity to the Mirror's effects had insulted me. I grimaced as I walked. Alicia's hand brushed against my sleeve. It was barely a touch, but it was deliberate.

"You still with me?" she asked.

"Yeah," I said, nodding.

If she knew I was lying, she didn't show it. She just kept

moving, as did I, following her and letting her set the pace. Since I didn't fully trust my own senses, we climbed.

The map we'd stolen from Mustique, showing Admiralty Bay with that block-lettered word "PLANTATION," had been enough. The rest we played by instinct. We followed boot-cut trails through the brush, noting broken twigs. I stopped once, nudging Alicia as I pointed out a cigarette butt that wasn't local. It was a sign of foreign presence, and those signs meant that we were close. They were signs that meant that we had only a little more to go.

Sure enough, the further we climbed, the worse the air felt. It didn't feel hotter; if anything, it seemed to grow colder and thinner, as if someone or something had sanded the world down, leaving only the permanent behind.

I heard a bird call from somewhere among the trees. Several steps—and several yards—later, I heard the call again. It was the same pitch, the same timing, almost too exact, but I didn't say a word. I simply glanced at Alicia, and she nodded.

"I heard it, too," she said.

We stood there, listening, waiting in silence—until suddenly another bird called, this time different, and it felt more normal again, almost as if it were safer. It was an illusion, of course. But sometimes illusions could be comforting, and so we pushed on, through gaps in the trees, as Admiralty Bay opened up below us like some dark, infernal bowl.

I could see boats in the distance, sitting at anchor, their hulls barely shifting. Along the waterfront, a few lamps still burned, Port Elizabeth asleep but not fully desolate. The bay was beautiful, as all water is, and yet it wasn't fully comforting. There was something unnerving about it, something I couldn't quite place my finger on.

Then we saw them—movement on the slope below us. It wasn't wildlife; it was far too deliberate, far too organized. I dropped low, pulling Alicia down next to me behind a stand of brush.

There were three figures that I could see, moving uphill through the cane, maybe two hundred yards out. It was difficult to make out details in the dark, as they wore dark clothes, but from the silhouettes alone, I could tell these men were no fishermen, and they were climbing toward the same ridge we were, a ridge where no local would need to go. That alone set off my instincts, but as I squinted, straining to make out any details, I could see that one of them carried something long, probably a rifle, and as I watched, another paused to check something, and a brief flash of light shone between his cupped hands before he killed it again.

"Soviet," I whispered.

Alicia squinted through the darkness as well. She nodded at last.

"That, or local contractors. Either way, they're headed the same direction we are, and that's not good."

Another half a minute passed as we continued to watch them. They moved speedily, picking their way through the underbrush, like men who were comfortable with this sort of terrain but weren't happy that they had been assigned to such a project. Professionals.

"Likely scouts," Alicia said quietly. "If the Soviets are coming, it'll take them slightly longer to move. This is probably the advance element."

I nodded, and as I did, my headache spiked. For a second, the figures flickered, and I could see them far more clearly, wearing Soviet field uniforms, then civilian clothes a second later, and then all was dark again. I shook my head and squinted. It was as if the Mirror was taunting me with overlapping probabilities. I blinked in the darkness, letting my eyes register again.

"Let's keep going," I muttered to Alicia at last, "but we need to be quiet now, and we need to move faster."

We moved along, parallel to their path, using the thicker brush for cover. The last of the light had bled from the sky, turning everything into darkness. We kept our lights off. Using the light would have revealed where we were.

"Look up there," Alicia suddenly whispered, and I raised my eyes, following the direction at which she pointed. There, ahead of us, ruins sat above the bay: an old plantation estate, its stone skeleton solid but half eaten by vines. The windows were black, and the roof had collapsed in several sections. It was a palace, but a palace that history had abandoned and left for dead. Although history had abandoned it, our prey might not have.

We slowed as we approached. I motioned to Alicia, not daring to speak now, and she nodded. Now wasn't the time for us to be cautious. The men behind us were likely only five minutes away on a good day, which meant that we didn't have time to play it smart.

Alicia broke off from my path and circled right. I headed left, and we met behind a collapsed wall, where the weeds sprouted through broken masonry that lay like rubble against the ground.

"No voices," I murmured.

"No smoke, either," she replied, "But look—footprints—two sets."

I nodded. I didn't even have to bend down to examine them. I could tell in an instant that the prints weren't local. The boot tread was too deep, and the prints staggered, uneven, as if the men who had made them had been drunken or had been fighting their own bodies to push forward. Either way, it appeared we had found the men we were searching for.

I raised my pistol and waited, my hands shaking slightly. For a second, I doubted whether or not I actually wanted to enter the mansion.

"Max," Alicia said, watching my face.

"I'm fine, I'm fine," I muttered. "Let's do this."

She didn't argue. And so we moved, clearing the perimeter, checking angles, sightlines, escape routes—everything before we actually made our entrance. The ruin had too many blind spots, plenty of places where a rifle could wait around a corner, but we didn't have the luxury of caution. Alicia reached the doorway before I did, and then, just like that, we were inside.

The interior smelled of damp, moldy stone and something faintly metallic, though I couldn't quite place it. But the smell wasn't what struck me first. The first thing I saw was the writing.

Every wall was covered with it. On the floor, on the walls, on the broken furniture, equations were scrawled in charcoal. Symbols, lattices, and looping diagrams were scrawled on every wall as if someone had been trying to solve reality itself but had failed.

Then I saw the men. Two figures sat in what appeared to be a sitting room, or at least it used to be one. One man slumped against the wall, his head lolling forward. The other was slightly closer, crouching in the center as if he were holding himself upright by the force of will alone, his head swaying slightly as he stared into the distance.

Both men wore clothes that looked as if they had been good at some point. But if those clothes had been good, they were now stained and rumpled. Both of them looked wrong. I recognized it in an instant. It was the type of old that I had seen in a photograph before we had ever arrived here. The kind of old that indicated only one thing: the effects of the Mirror.

I almost set my gun down, but Alicia's hands didn't waver.

"Покажите нам свои руки," she said. *Let us see your hands.*

The man who crouched there turned suddenly, his eyes widening, as if he hadn't even realized we'd entered the room. His face was wrinkled with deep lines carved into it, but they were fresh creases from time that had arrived almost too quickly. It was something you'd never see on a man who aged gracefully. At best, it could be described as the markings of stress or too little sleep, and yet dialed up far beyond anything conceivable without some sort of outside influence.

The man slumped on the floor simply blinked as his compatriot raised his hands, his nose bleeding. The slumped man didn't move his hands at all, other than to wipe the blood off his nose with a trembling hand, staring at it, almost as if he couldn't believe what he was seeing.

"Кто ты?" the standing man croaked out, his voice raspy but the Russian unmistakable.

I answered in the same language. It was far rougher than Alicia's, but it was enough to get the point across.

"Это не ваша поисковая группа.," I said. *Not your retrieval team.*

His eyes flickered to my face, then to Alicia, and finally to our guns.

"You're English," he whispered.

This time, he spoke in English, though it was with a heavy accent.

"We need your names, now," Alicia demanded.

The standing man nodded slowly.

"Sergei Anokhin," he said, "and Mikhail Popov."

Popov—the man on the floor—laughed. The laughter was thin and broken, quickly devolving into a fit of coughing and choking, as if there was pain in his chest. He curled in on himself, continuing to hack like an old man who had smoked all his life.

Alicia didn't lower her weapon, but she nodded curtly and glanced around again.

"Anokhin," she said quietly. "What happened? Did the Mirror do this?"

The man flinched.

"How do you know?"

"Because," I said, "people have been dying in Havana, and you didn't disappear the way a man disappears when he wants to. Did the Mirror send you two here?"

Anokhin stared at me, then looked back at Alicia, trying to decide which of us posed the greater threat.

Behind him, however, something caught my attention. The doorway we had come through shifted. For only half a heartbeat, it was no longer the tropical darkness outside. Instead, I saw a wet, gray, cold, and the outline of a dock crane visible through the mist. Then, it snapped back instantly, and the doorway was dark again.

I gulped and tightened my grip on my pistol, trying to steady myself with my weapon. Alicia had seen it, too. I could see her flinch at the very instant that the room had shifted, and she glanced at me as if she were trying to hide it.

"This place is a hot spot," she murmured.

"Yeah," I said, "and likely because of them."

It wasn't an accusation, but it was the truth. Anokhin and Popov were already intricately linked to the Mirror. Add us to the mix, and you have four of perhaps the most important individuals to the Mirror's ongoing existence in the exact same room.

Anokhin watched us, his gaze drifting between us as if he were watching two people decide his fate in real time. Alicia stepped forward quickly and lowered her gun. She didn't lower it all the way, as I had, but she made sure the angle wasn't directly at their heads, as if to give them some space to tell the truth—a space where execution didn't seem imminent.

"You need to tell us what happened, now," she said. "And you're going to do it quickly if you know what's good for you."

Anokhin laughed bitterly.

"Quickly," he spat. "Yes, yes, everything is quickly now."

He stood and swayed for a moment, and for a second, I thought he would fall, but instead, he braced himself up against a wall covered in equations. As his hand steadied against the wall, his fingers left a charcoal smear that turned the yellowish bricks gray.

"We were in Havana," he said slowly. "That's the last place I remember: Laboratorio Especial No. 7, the distillery."

"Cárdenas," Alicia confirmed.

He nodded once in response.

"We were not meant to leave, you see. Not meant. No, no. We were meant to keep working, keep tuning it, calibrate the Mirror. But the field, it was so unstable, too strong, that the men who made the decisions—the men with guns—became nervous, and they began to demand answers from us. The field wasn't conforming, not conforming to what they wanted."

"And what did you do?" I asked.

Anokhin looked at Popov, but the man on the ground did not react. It was as if he was living in his own world already.

"We tried to stabilize it," Anokhin finally said, a hint of shame in his voice. "Tried to force coherence, thought we understood the coupling, but we were wrong."

The room around us flickered again, and I wasn't sure where we were for a second. But from the corridor of damp stone, I could see through the doorway. It seemed as if we were somewhere in the intricate tunnels below Kingsway. Then, the man on the ground said something in his sleep, and I snapped back.

"I can see it too, you know," Anokhin began, but Alicia interrupted him.

"Continue," she said firmly.

He swallowed and continued to speak.

"It pushed us out. It was like it was rejecting us. Not moved. Not relocated. Pushed. We were in the laboratory, and then in the blink of an eye, though I know not how much time had passed, we found ourselves on Mustique."

"So you were on Mustique," I said.

"Yes." He nodded, almost grateful that I wasn't calling him insane. "But Mustique rejected us. Not sure why. Maybe too empty, too clean. Not enough memory density for the field to hold. Either way, the Mirror rejected Mustique. And so, it pushed us out again, like it was expelling waste."

"And so that's how you found yourself on Bequia," I sighed, rubbing my eyes. I was too tired for this.

"Yes. Here," Anokhin said, his voice becoming eager. "Here above the bay, we made our way to this old plantation, though I'm not sure how many times. But it was here that the Mirror led us. Or pushed us. I'm not so certain anymore."

He gestured at the walls.

CUBAN SLIDERS

"And so I did this, to keep my mind from breaking inward, folding on itself, to keep the recursion from taking hold too much. I write the equations, again and again. The repetition keeps me focused. You don't understand what the Mirror does to memory," he said, looking at me. "It removes time, faces—even your own thoughts feel foreign."

I chuckled. There was something about the irony of him telling me that—explaining to me what the Mirror could do. But I didn't say anything, because as I laughed, my headache surged, and for a second, I couldn't remember who I was.

Alicia, always focused, had begun to move. She crouched beside Popov, finally pocketing her gun once more, then pulled a cloth from her pocket and tossed it toward him.

"Hold that to your nose," she said in Russian. "If you pass out, we won't be able to move you."

Popov stared at the cloth, as if he'd forgotten what cloth was, then grabbed it slowly and pressed it to his face. The white fabric was immediately soaked with blood.

Anokhin watched the two of us, as if unsure what to do. Finally, however, he spoke.

"You're Bureau," he said.

It wasn't a question, but I nodded all the same, confirming what he thought.

"Then you know the name Hawthorne?" he asked.

"I know it," I said. "What of him?"

Anokhin looked away. I could see his jaw was clenched.

"And you know Philby."

This time, it was an accusation.

"Go ahead, spit it out," I said. "What are you trying to say?"

His eyes flicked back to my face.

"Philby came," he said. "He came to the laboratory. Brought notes, designs. Called them ANGUS and Lineage."

The words hit my headache like a gunshot that ricocheted in my skull—ANGUS. Mirror V3 in Scotland. Loch Duich—all the memories came flooding back.

"So he accelerated the build," I muttered.

Anokhin nodded sharply.

"Yes. Moscow had pieces—pieces he had already provided, but those weren't enough. We needed the architecture. And Philby..." He spread his hands in a wide gesture. "Philby brought them all. He brought the logic of your machines. I read the notes of Krane, the notes of Hawthorne. Hell, at first, I was enamored by their genius."

"What else?" I asked. "While you're at it, any info you have on Philby—any info you have that can help us disable it."

Anokhin's gaze shifted, as if he was reluctant to explain what he had thought of, as if it was some dirty thought in his mind he was trying to hold back. But finally, he spoke.

"There is more than one Mirror," he said.

My heart dropped.

"What the hell do you mean?" I shot out, then caught myself and forced myself to temper my voice. "Explain."

Anokhin hesitated, then spoke.

"We built an adjunct. It's a portable node, separate from the main machine. Much smaller. Not even a full Mirror, technically speaking. But it goes along with the main one—meant to modify the thoughts in your mind instead of the time that we watch."

"The hell?" I asked.

"We called it decision locking," he went on.

"So what is it?" I asked.

He gestured broadly at a series of equations on the wall, as if somehow he could explain it all away just by showing me the mathematics.

"It uses a sort of entanglement applied to human cognition. Collapses dissent. Removes the branches. See, if you have a tree full of branches"—he snapped his fingers weakly, as if figuring out how to explain it properly—"well, if you have so many branches, then you could pick any which one. Decision locking cuts off every branch. It leaves only the one you wish for. The one outcome."

"So it's brainwashing?" Alicia asked, face harsh.

"No. Not so simple, not so good," he said, shaking his head violently. "Persuasion, not even convincing. It simply removes the space for debate. The alternative choice never forms. There will be no argument, no rebellion—just agreement on the premeditated decision."

I stared at them as if what Anokhin said was foreign to me.

"And you built it," Alicia said, her voice sharp.

His face twisted, though whether it was shame, fear, or pride, I couldn't tell.

"Well," he said, "I calibrated it. Without me—without Popov, at the very least—Moscow will not be able to tune it properly or quickly. I am the principal architect. It is likely they can copy some of it, but making it work properly without us will be difficult."

"Ah. So that's why they're hunting you," Alicia said.

"Yes. They need us back or dead. Either will work for them. It just depends on circumstance."

"And what does Philby want with it?" I asked.

"The same thing everyone does who touches that technology," Anokhin said, and for the first time, I could see an annoyance on his face, as I did with many scientists—men who appreciated the science over the politics. "He wants control... wants the world to do as he bids. And if he gets his hands on it, he'll be able to."

I nodded.

"And what of V4 itself?" I asked.

He laughed, his voice bitter.

"V4 itself is not science," he said. "Whatever the hell that cursed machine is, it's not science. It's not a single machine. It's a web."

The words made my skin crawl, and I could remember Hawthorne's recording, speaking of how it was entangled now, how it had spread—and to cut the tree at the roots.

But at that moment, Anokhin pointed vaguely at the

doorway behind us. I turned toward it and saw, clearly, Rosyth Dockyard. Dock cranes high in the sky, men in coats, and boats in the distance. And then it was gone again.

Anokhin's eyes were fever-bright as I turned back to face the man.

"I've seen them all, too," he said almost reverently. "You two, if you're Bureau, you must be familiar with it. These places. V4 links all the old sites together. I've learned their names, too, from seeing them so much. That was Rosyth Dockyard, wasn't it? There's Kingsway, Invershiel, too. Your earlier Mirrors weren't erased. V4 is using them as anchors, like a memory network."

"The hell?" I muttered. "But how can it use them? We destroyed the machines."

He shook his head, as if annoyed by my question.

"No, no, you don't see," he said. "It's not that simple. When a machine is built, you're not just building the physical space; you're constructing a quantum web. And the quantum exists in only a quasi-physical state, one that's far too easily palpable to destroy just by breaking down the physical frame."

"So that's why the Caribbean's unstable?" Alicia asked, and I could see the fear in her eyes.

"Yes," he said eagerly, as if she had finally understood. "Because it's not just isolated. Havana may be only one node, but it reached backward through time, through your old scars, and is using them all to propagate the pulse that grows stronger with every day."

Popov coughed from the floor and spoke for the first time.

"Everything touches everything now," he said, his voice weak.

I still couldn't tell if the man actually knew we were here, but Anokhin nodded in agreement.

Alicia's gaze flickered to the attaché case strap over her shoulder.

"We have countermeasures," she said uncertainly. "Copper

coils built by Fraser-Smith. From what we can tell, he built them to destroy the Mirror."

"I'm not so certain," Anokhin said, his face tightening. "You don't understand."

"What don't we understand?" I asked.

"These coils—if they're calibrated wrong, they might be insufficient to untangle the web. Each node has to be burned to its core. Otherwise, it'll just regrow, and the quantum link will re-propagate itself."

Alicia glanced at me, and I could see fear in her eyes—fear that the one tool we had left might not be enough. But at that moment, Alicia's attention was drawn to something else. Her head snapped toward the doorway we'd come through.

This time, there was no glitch, no pulse. Instead, she went still, listening. I didn't hear anything at first, just crickets chirping outside, the faint creak of the ruin settling. Then, low and distant, I could hear the sound of boots in the brush, slow and disciplined, accompanied by the faint metallic clinks of equipment.

Her eyes cut to mine.

"They're here," she whispered.

"How many?" I asked.

She didn't answer right away, tilting her head as she listened more intently. I closed my eyes, focusing too. I could hear faint voices—Soviet voices—speaking in Russian, low and controlled.

Alicia backed slowly toward a broken window frame and peered out through the vines, then quickly ducked her head back in.

"I see lanterns," she said, her voice urgent. "At least a section, maybe more. From what I could tell, they're moving up the slope."

"No," Anokhin whispered, his face draining of what little color it had left. "No, no, not here, not now."

As if he finally understood what was happening, Popov

made a wailing sound, sobbing—not too loud, but sobbing all the same—and tried to stand, then crumpled again.

I looked at Alicia. I knew the question in her mind was the same as mine: Do we run?

We had Darryl back at the shore— hopefully still there. And if he was, we had a boat. We could try and drag the two men down the hill and disappear into the water. But Anokhin could barely stand, and Popov couldn't even walk. And even if we somehow got them out... well, the web was already here, and the ruin was already slipping into obscurity—slipping into time itself.

Alicia's voice was quiet when she finally spoke.

"We can't leave them," I said, nodding.

Abandoning two men to be dragged back into a machine that would eat their memories and age them faster than life itself— that was a line even I didn't want to cross. And besides, as much as I hated to admit it, the two of them could be useful to us.

"Alright then," Alicia said. "Let's do what we came here for. Max, take the doorway. I'll take the window. We keep these two behind cover."

I nodded. Anokhin stared at us as if we were insane.

"You'll die," he said hoarsely.

"Maybe," I replied. "But we still need more info from you. And you'll live long enough that you can tell us how to kill your damned web."

The room shuddered again, and the wall flickered. I saw Rosyth, Kingsway, Havana—all layered for an instant, like transparent film over transparent film. And then, we were back. Outside, I could hear the boots moving ever closer.

I glanced at Alicia, my pistol already steadied in my hands. She met my eyes.

"We don't have time," she whispered. "We have to hold, or we'll die."

I nodded, sighed, and tightened my grip on my pistol. Behind us, Popov was still sobbing. Anokhin still stood rigid, swaying slightly, as if trying to keep his mind intact by sheer spite for the Mirror.

Outside, lanterns bobbed between cane stalks, their lights drifting ever nearer. The last light from the sky was gone now. Full darkness had fallen over Bequia. Not even the moon or stars shining above.

As the first shadows reached the edge of the plantation's broken wall, we raised our weapons.

We waited for hell to break loose.

CHAPTER 18
PLANTATION PUNCH

The Soviets announced themselves the way men with nothing to fear did: with lanterns and the sound of stomping boots, careful hooded lights carried low beneath cupped palms. It wasn't the kind of heroic blaze you'd see from men with nothing to hide. But they moved in a disciplined way that meant, though they wished to remain secretive as long as possible, they had nothing to fear, bobbing steadily through the cane like a string of glowing will-o'-the-wisps against the hillside.

Then the voices reached us.

The voices of Russian men, flat, devoid of emotion, and unmistakably guttural. It wasn't the chatter of frightened men, that was for sure. I could hear one barking orders, another muttering about some logistics issue as they continued along. It was a sweep tightening around us.

Alicia saw them before I did. She stood at the broken window, still, her silhouette carved from the darkness, one hand on her pistol and the other braced against the stone.

"Lanterns," she whispered. "Ten, maybe more. Can't tell for certain."

I didn't respond. As I stood there, silent, I could taste the copper on my tongue and wiped my hand over my nose, looking at it in shock, though it was so dark I could barely make out my own outline. The wet, metallic tang was unmistakable, and I knew that now, on my hand, a smear of blood could be found.

Behind me, I heard Popov make a sound between a laugh and a cough. He sat slumped against the wall, his nose bleeding far more than mine, pressing Alicia's cloth against it. The cloth was already stained more red than white. He breathed raggedly, each breath scraping his ribs on the way in and out.

Beside him stood Anokhin, remaining upright through sheer stubbornness. The man was older than he had been when we had arrived, yet it seemed as if his mind was holding him together. Though his hands trembled, the wall of equations he'd scribbled out kept him sane.

The room around us felt as if it was tilting as the Russians marched closer. Every few heartbeats, I'd catch a flicker of light —a corridor in the corner of my eye where stone should be, damp tunnel walls, the ghost outline of dockyard steel. No matter what it was, those flickers told me that the ruins were folding in on each other, and each time I blinked, the world would correct itself again. Yet I wasn't sure how much longer it would last.

If anything, I couldn't help but feel a little bit of relief. The Russians wouldn't be used to this type of battlefield, but I was.

Alicia didn't take her eyes off the window.

"Max," she said quietly. "They'll want Anokhin alive."

"I know," I replied. I could hear the voices in the distance now, and though my Russian was rusty, one of the voices had barked it as clear as an official order.

"Анохин жив," he said in Russian, and another voice answered, "А что насчет Попова?"

"*Anokhin alive.*" "*And what of Popov?*"

But we didn't need a translation for the next sentence. I knew from the way the man spoke, and from the tone of the voice, that Popov was expendable.

Popov didn't need to hear it, either. He could hear the tone. His shoulders tightened, and he stared at the damp floor. His eyes focused for the first time, and for a moment, I couldn't blame him. Though the ruin was folding in on itself, facing death was something that would shock any man out of a time loop. It had done the same to me many times before.

The lanterns drew ever closer. I could see cane stalks swaying in the distance as boots stomped through them. The lights spread out wider, forming a crescent around the ruin. They were surrounding us. Then there was silence for a good ten seconds.

Finally, the man in charge spoke.

His voice carried—lower, cleaner, with the calm confidence of a man who knew he didn't even have to raise his tone to be obeyed.

"This is Major Viktor Kolyadin, MGB," he shouted.

When only silence responded to him, he called again, louder. His men remained quiet and orderly.

"Dr. Anokhin! Come out!"

Still, we didn't respond. Anokhin breathed fast, his eyes wild, but he remained standing, anger etched on his face. It was clear he believed the Russians had betrayed him—let the Mirror kill him when he should have claimed fame instead. They'd pushed it too hard, to the brink, to a place they could never come back from.

"Dr. Anokhin!" Kolyadin called out again, this time in careful, broken English. "We can do this quietly!"

"Well, that means they want him intact," Alicia said, leaning toward me without taking her eyes off the window.

"That doesn't mean us, though," I replied. She didn't answer, but she didn't need to. Anokhin was their prize, that much was clear, and if they even knew we were here, I'd have been the one to deal with them.

Kolyadin spoke again, a faint hint of amusement in his tone.

"Englishman!" he called. "You are not part of this. Come out, your hands visible. We will provide amnesty."

So they did know we were here.

I could feel that dull headache behind my left eye, and the sensation of being watched ebbed and flowed in my mind like a river. It wasn't from the soldiers or the major who spoke to us, but from the web, the field, the consciousness of the Mirror itself, reaching out like a fingertip against the inside of my skull.

At that moment, the ruin trembled under my boots. It was subtle, but unmistakable, and I could hear Russian voices murmuring outside, voices that meant I wasn't the only one experiencing it.

"When it starts, we move," Alicia muttered. "We can't hold here."

With that, she glanced at Popov, slumped to a shape in the corner. Her jaw tightened.

"We have to do what we can."

It sounded like compromise to me, but as much as I hated to admit it, I knew she was right.

Then, outside, I heard the unmistakable command.

"Go!"

Kolyadin barked, and the night broke open.

The first shots ricocheted loudly inside the ruin, amplified by the stone and empty rooms, and the history of the many men and women who had likely died here before. Muzzle flashes bloomed in the cane fields—brief showers of light followed by darkness. Bullets split through old plaster and sparked off rock, ricocheting or embedding in the wall as it crumbled.

Alicia fired a shot clean through the broken window, shattering a lantern outside. I saw a man in the distance collapse as the darkness swallowed the gap he left. Then another volley from the rifles followed. Cordite filled the ruin, dust floating into the air, stone chips flying through the doorway.

I ducked, my own pistol in my hand, and fired off a shot through one of the gaps in the wall. It was likely the Russians weren't aware of how many weapons we had, which was why they were being cautious, but that would only last so long. As I saw my bullet hit true and another man crumble, I figured we might have finally run out of luck.

As I ducked behind the wall and waited for another volley of shots, something strange began to happen. The sound inside the ruins didn't quite seem right. It was almost as if each shot was echoing twice, like a record skipping, as if the Mirror was editing time in real time. It wasn't just watching.

The ruins were folding in on themselves, collapsing and relapsing. And bullets, which likely should have struck true, were bending through the air now, shooting off in random directions. That meant we could stand for a little while longer.

I stepped out into the space again and fired my pistol three times at three separate men. Only one fell, staggering to the ground and disappearing into the cane. Though I was sure I had aimed true, the other two men remained standing, as if the bullets had curved away from them.

So the Mirror wasn't on our side, if it could even pick a side at all.

In the distance, I could hear Kolyadin shouting, but not the shouts of a panicked officer. Whoever this man was, he was experienced, issuing commands in a confident, loud, commanding tone.

"Left flank, advance," he shouted.

More men moved through the cane, their lanterns lowered, their rifles raised. They weren't charging in blindly either. These men were good. Instead, they were following the shape of the ruin, sealing the exits, and slowly tightening the noose until escape became impossible.

If they needed Anokhin intact, that meant they had time. That meant they were willing to sacrifice as many soldiers as it took. And it seemed as if that was what they were doing. They knew they had time.

But we didn't.

Alicia shifted at the window, her hair cascading into her face, sweat dripping from her brow.

"They're trying to box us in," she hissed.

I fired off my gun again, aiming more to open a space than to kill in return. A shot whistled past my ear, close enough that I could feel it sting my cheek, the heat brushing against me like a match whisked by your face. I ducked, reflex taking over, and the world around me stuttered.

The vines in the doorway swayed in an unknown wind. Even my own breath seemed to flicker in and out. Sometimes I could hear my panting, ragged and rough, and at other times, there was silence in my ears, as if someone had taken a cloth and stuffed it deep so that every sound was muffled. Even the stars that had dotted the night sky were gone now. It was as if a void had closed in around the ruins.

Alicia swore under her breath; she had felt the shift, too. Outside, I could hear Kolyadin barking orders again, and behind us, Anokhin pressed against the wall, his eyes wide, shaking. I glanced at him with something akin to respect. He wasn't shaking out of fear or cowardice but from the strain of trying to keep himself coherent while the ruin folded in on itself.

It was as if the shadows were bending around us at my feet. Popov crawled slowly toward a broken pillar, dragging himself forward, his lips moving incoherently.

And then a corridor flickered open.

It wasn't in the doorway, either. It was where the stone should have been solid, yet for half a heartbeat, there was an open doorway into a series of damp tunnels I recognized instantly as Kingsway.

Without thinking, I stepped forward. It was as if a gentle tug was pulling against my mind, luring me into the tunnel. I took a step, and then another—

"Max!"

Alicia's voice snapped me out of it like a crack of lightning. Her hand was clamped on my wrist as she yanked me backward hard enough to hurt. I stumbled, regained my balance, and then threw myself against the wall as more gunshots fired past. The corridor I had seen flickered, then vanished again, replaced by the ruined stone and Bequia's heat.

"Max, you need to stay focused," she hissed. "I see it too, but don't follow it."

"I'm not," I muttered, but it was a lie, because for a second, I had wanted—wanted more than anything—to step through the door and let it spit me out somewhere that wasn't this cane-choked hillside filled with the bullets of the Soviets. But I knew in the same breath that if I had gone through the doorway, I would have abandoned Alicia and the two Russian men we were trying to protect.

The only way out was through.

Kolyadin's men were growing impatient now, and two men rushed the doorway, their rifles up, using their bodies as cover for a third man who ran behind them, a carefully raised pistol trained at chest height. Alicia and I leaned out in sync, firing at the same time. One man went down, his legs folding underneath him as he crumpled. The other stumbled but continued to run forward, his face rough and fierce. I aimed steady and hit him with a shot between the eyes that should have dropped him in an instant—and it did, but for a heartbeat, he stood there anyway, his body frozen in time, then collapsed suddenly, his head lolling forward as he hit the ground with a thud harder than it should have.

"We need to retreat!" Alicia yelled over the chaos.

I nodded. "Get to the back room, now."

She grabbed Popov from the floor, dragging him with her as I kept my pistol trained on the doorway, walking backward carefully. Anokhin followed her, lurching here and there, nearly falling. I grabbed his arm with one hand, my pistol still in the other, and hauled him upright. He felt far lighter than a man should, almost like a frail skeleton of his former self. I wasn't surprised.

Popov tried to stand but wavered and failed. Just then, I heard a small clink against the floor outside. My mind instantly sprang into action, but I forced myself to think. It couldn't have been a fragmentation grenade. Kolyadin wanted Anokhin alive.

I glanced down and watched as a small smoke canister rolled ominously, landing near my boot. It hissed, and thick gray smoke erupted from it, my eyes burning as the ruin filled fast, turning the darkness into pitch black. Everything was silhouettes now. The only light emanated from the lanterns outside, and even that barely bled through the cracks in the surrounding darkness.

Popov was coughing violently now, his fragile body hacking as he wheezed, barely able to breathe. Anokhin grabbed him by the shoulders, trying to keep him steady, but to no avail.

Alicia appeared at the vine-choked back of the ruin. She couldn't see anything, but I knew that somewhere beyond those vines, the cane fields sloped down toward the bay, and somewhere far below that, Darryl and his pirogue—if he hadn't already left.

"We need to break out the back," she said. "Now."

"That's our best bet," I muttered.

Popov laughed. For the first time, his eyes were sharp.

"There is no back," he whispered. "No front. Only one big loop."

Alicia ignored him. She grabbed Anokhin by the sleeve.

"We need to move. Follow."

And move we did.

We were halfway through the collapsed, ruined wall when I realized that Popov had stopped. I was no longer dragging him. I turned. He was standing upright now, swaying, and his eyes weren't unfocused; they were sharp with a sudden, horrible clarity, and he glanced around as if for the first time. The shadow of the brilliant scientist he had been had returned. He looked at Anokhin, then Alicia, then me, and then he smiled.

"No," Anokhin whispered. "Mikhail—"

But Popov pressed the blood-soaked cloth into Anokhin's hand as if it were a token of his gratitude.

"You are needed," he rasped.

Then his gaze snapped to my eyes.

"And you," he said. "You are the error. The glitch."

I froze for a heartbeat. I heard Hawthorne's voice in my head, echoing from long ago when he had told me what I really was in the ruins of the Andes.

Popov stepped back, moving toward the center of the plantation where the two men we had killed still lay on the ground. Though his hands were trembling, he bent down and grabbed one of the rifles from the lifeless bodies that lay there. He snatched it clumsily, the arthritis already tightening his joints, and staggered toward the front of the ruin.

Alicia lunged forward to grab him, but in an instant, he had trained the rifle on her.

"Don't," he coughed. "They don't want me. They want Anokhin."

"Popov—" I could feel rage in my voice, but he didn't look back. Instead, he turned, shoving past broken stone and stepping into the smoke near the doorway.

"Go to hell!" he yelled, and pulled the trigger.

I knew instantly that line wasn't just meant for the Russians but for us as well. He wanted us gone. And then he fired. The explosive light from the rifle barked forth, and the man shot wildly, training his gun on nothing in specific but drawing all the eyes to him. And then, in a bold voice that held none of the stutter or desperation it had held before, he shouted into the smoke,

"I am Anokhin! You want me, come and get me!"

For a heartbeat, I could hear every MGB officer hesitating, because they weren't sure what to do. But I knew we didn't have time to watch, didn't have time to see his body hit the floor as the bullets pierced through his leathery skin.

Instead, we turned, running through the rubble and the smoke. Behind us, I could hear Popov scream, a curdling cry that I knew was his last. But at that moment—the moment his body hit the floor with a thud—the air snapped cold. What had been the Cuban heat just moments before was now icy, barely above freezing. My breath fogged, and my skin prickled as if I'd been plunged into the depths of some black, icy Scottish loch.

From nowhere and everywhere all at once, a low hum began vibrating through the stone and smoke, which split and tore into rhythms that moved in patterns around us. Behind us, the ruin folded, collapsing and folding like paper. I could hear rushing voices screaming.

An MGB soldier lunged toward us out of the cane; I saw him vanish in midair. It wasn't as if he had stepped through a doorway—just vanished, disappearing into the darkness. He was simply not there anymore, as if he had been folded inside himself, his voice cutting off mid-sound.

As I glanced back, I could see the detachment faltering, men shouting in panic now. For the first time, Kolyadin's voice seemed to panic as well. I could hear him issuing orders, his tone harsh but with an underlying trepidation among it all.

"Back! Back!" he screamed in Russian. "Retreat!"

And I saw why.

As we continued to run through the cane, the ruin began to move, the walls crumbling, shifting, sliding against each other like mismatched plates. Bricks rose into the air as if gravity had stopped existing.

Alicia shoved Anokhin along through the cane as the man stumbled in front of us, and I realized for a second that I had slowed to nearly a trot as I watched the building fold upon itself.

"We need to go, Max!" Alicia's voice snapped me out of my reverie. "Faster!"

I nodded and moved without thinking.

Somewhere behind us, the ruin made a sound as if the world itself was tearing at its seams. I wasn't sure when I had picked it up, but as I ran, I felt the familiar heavy weight of Fraser-Smith's rig in the attaché case, which I now held numbly in one of my hands.

We ran, the cane slapping at our faces and arms., The air slowly turned hot again—humid and alive, full of insects that buzzed past. The darkness seemed to ease up, and the stars that speckled the night sky could be seen again.

Behind us, the plantation ruin folded upon itself one last time, imploding, the stone and wood snapping inward as if it were sucked into a vacuum. A blinding bluish-white flash lit the cane field for a heartbeat, illuminating it brighter than day, and then it was dark again, and there was silence.

Then I slowly heard panicked Russians shouting, their confused and angry voices drifting down the hill toward us.

We kept running, pulling and pushing Anokhin along with us. The MGB detachment had survived. How many men were still alive, I wasn't sure, but there were enough men that they could still kill us if they caught up. I just hoped the chaos would keep them occupied for a little while longer.

We ran downhill until our lungs burned and our legs shook. Several times, I had to stop, pulling Anokhin from where he had collapsed on the ground. We held him upright, our hands around his chest like a brace, his breathing ragged as we ran.

"Popov?" Alicia asked suddenly.

I shook my head, my throat dry. "He's gone," I said.

"He knew," Anokhin rasped, making a sound that was half a sob, half a laugh. "He knew they would not take him. Only me."

Alicia didn't say anything, but the way her eyes reflected the light in the darkness told me that Popov's death had hit her harder than she wanted to admit. The man had been our enemy, but at the same time, in the end, he'd chosen to draw fire, buying us a few precious seconds that had kept Alicia and me alive—and kept Anokhin alive long enough to be useful.

"Come on, let's move," Alicia said.

We resumed walking briskly, not running this time. The Russian voices hadn't drawn closer, so we moved down the slope, through cane and brush, keeping low. There was no more gunfire now, only distant Russian shouting. I assumed Kolyadin was still alive, trying to reassert control over the men who had seen something stranger than magic.

As we descended, the first hint of dawn began to creep into the sky, a faint, bruised gray beyond the ridge. It wasn't light enough to see clearly, but enough that we would soon be visible —enough that, more than ever, we needed to move fast.

We reached a lower strand of palms near the shoreline, low enough that I could finally smell the sea. Here, we finally paused, taking a few minutes to catch our breath. Sweat trickled down Alicia's temples, her hair frazzled and hanging limp.

"Can you walk?" she asked Anokhin.

I glanced at him, and he nodded quickly. "Yes. I must," he said. Whether it was pride or determination, I couldn't tell.

"Good," I said. "Because Darryl won't wait forever. If he's still even waiting."

We continued toward the cove where we'd left the pirogue, our feet slipping against the damp stone and sand. When we finally reached the beach, for a heartbreaking moment, I thought the pirogue was gone. But no—there it was, still there, half hidden under netting, pushed into shadow beneath the palms. Beside it, Darryl stood, his rifle in his hand, his eyes sharp. He saw us, and his face broke with relief.

"You are trouble," he muttered.

"We brought the trouble with us," I shot back.

His gaze flickered to Anokhin—aged, trembling, standing next to us as if he wanted nothing more than to collapse.

"What happened up there?" Darryl asked.

"Move," Alicia said, shoving Anokhin toward the boat. "We'll explain when we're on the water."

Darryl didn't argue. He simply helped us shove the pirogue into the surf, the engine stuttering to life, low and steady, humming as we climbed in. Alicia climbed in first; I'd given her the attaché case once again, and she hauled it in as if it were a child she was reluctantly forced to take care of. Anokhin climbed in next, and I helped him as he nearly collapsed into the bottom of the boat.

I got in last, my pistol still in hand, watching the palms for any movement. There was nothing yet.

Darryl pushed off, and the pirogue slid into open water, the engine idling.

"Let's fire that up," I said, and Darryl nodded.

The engine roared to life as the shoreline began to shrink behind us. The plantation ridge rose into the sky, black against the lightening dawn. I stared at it, watching. Somewhere from the area of the plantation, smoke billowed, and yet the plantation itself was nowhere to be seen.

Somewhere up there, Major Viktor Kolyadin—as Anokhin had told us, as we climbed into the boat—would be counting the men who didn't come back, tallying how many men died to the Mirror's collapse. But I knew with a cold certainty that the man would not stop.

The further we got from the plantation ruins, the lighter the air felt, as if we had finally escaped the oversight of the Mirror for at least another day.

I shivered. The air was warm, but I could feel a chill deep in my bones. Anokhin lay between me and Alicia, shivering despite the warm night. It seemed as if he was feeling the same cold that I was. Every once in a while, he would whisper numbers to himself, staring into space, as if he was trying to keep himself anchored, to keep his mind from being rewritten.

The sea slapped against the hull as the engine purred.

Finally, Alicia spoke when Bequia was far enough away that it could barely be seen on the horizon.

"Talk," she said to Anokhin. "Now. You know just as well as we do, we don't know how much time you have."

Anokhin's eyes opened slowly, and he swallowed hard.

"Popov," he rasped. "The man was wrong often, and we butted heads, but he was right about one thing."

"What's that?" I asked.

Anokhin's gaze slid to me then.

"The web," he whispered. "The Mirror in Havana, V4, is not just one node. It's a lattice of memory, a spiderweb, a chain—whatever you want to call it."

"Rosyth?" I asked. "Kingsway, Invershiel?"

He nodded.

"Havana is only the newest link in the chain. If you destroy Havana alone, it'll bleed sideways. The older sites remain, and it's far worse than that. They're anchors, but they're also pieces of the web, and the lattice will rebuild around them."

I could hear Hawthorne's voice echoing in my mind: Kill the whole tree, the roots and all.

"So," I finally said, "even if we break V4, we still lose."

Anokhin stared into the fading stars, his eyes glazing over.

"Yes," he whispered. "It doesn't matter if it's a different place; it's the same disease. It's like a cancer."

"So what do we do?" I asked.

I could see Alicia watching us, her face etched with concern.

Anokhin coughed.

"You need to sever the chain," he said. "Go back to where it started. Rosyth Dockyard first, then Kingsway, then Invershiel. If they remain entangled, Havana will not die. It'll reoccur again somewhere else, find a new center, and the Mirror will rebuild itself."

"And decision-locking?" Alicia asked. "The reason they came for you in the first place?"

Anokhin flinched.

"They came for me," he said, "because I built it. I calibrated it. I am the principal architect. Without me, without my hands, Moscow may be able to reproduce it, but it won't be quickly. They can make a crude copy at best, but it won't lock correctly. It'll fail or blow up or turn on them and kill them in the process. That's why they need me alive."

"And Popov?" I asked.

Anokhin closed his eyes for a second.

"He was a good man," he said, "but his mind was replaceable. He had knowledge, but not mine."

"Then they'll keep coming," Alicia muttered.

"Yes," Anokhin whispered. "Kolyadin is brutal. He'll cross borders, burn bridges, and burn islands to the ground just to bring me back alive."

Anokhin swallowed, his gaze drifting past us to the empty horizon.

"There is one man who might help you stay ahead of them," he murmured. "Ahead of Moscow. Ahead of Kolyadin."

"Where?" Alicia asked.

"St. Vincent," he said. "Kingstown. There is a former NKVD officer there—Pyotr Granitsky. You will find him under an English name now: Peter Grant… at least, that was where he was the last I heard of him." His mouth twisted into something that wasn't quite a smile. "In Moscow, he was assigned to 'observe' me. Instead, he kept me alive. Without him, I would already be bones in a Lubyanka cellar—or worse, even."

"You trust him?" I asked.

"I trust his hatred," Anokhin said. "He walked away from Moscow, from the Party, from all of it. If anyone understands how far they will pursue you, how they think, what Philby gave them—ANGUS, Havana, the web—it is Granitsky. He knows the doctrine. He knows which doors they will kick down next, and how best to avoid them. And from the rumors that spread of him, he has a penchant for forgery."

He shut his eyes briefly, as if the effort of speaking had cost him more than the running.

I thought for a second.

"We go to Kingstown," I said at last. "To Granitsky."

Alicia nodded once. She didn't open up or let me know what she thought. She simply glanced down at Anokhin.

"You need to get us there," she said, "and in the meantime, you tell us everything you know. All about V4, about the web, about Philby, Project Oracle—all of it."

Anokhin's laugh was bitter.

"Ah, Philby," he said. "Damn that man. It's always Philby."

I couldn't help but chuckle. I knew the feeling only too well.

I stared at the horizon where the first true golden shine of the sun began to rise, shaking over the edge. Popov was dead, but the Soviets were not, and the web itself had shown how powerful it really was and how far the Mirror's influence and pulse had reached from Havana.

Now we had a new job, and it wasn't just to destroy Havana. It was to burn down the entire chain until there was nothing left for the web of Mirrors to cling to—no resonance, no quantum connection.

Alicia leaned closer to me, her voice low enough that I was the only one who could hear.

"We get him to Kingstown," she said. "Then we regroup. Then we go back and end this."

I nodded.

"Yeah," I replied. "Let's cut down the damn Mirror at the roots."

CHAPTER 19
KINGSTOWN KOMRADES

The sea between Bequia and St. Vincent felt wrong. It was open water, but it felt as if it was something we had traversed before, which indeed we had, and it felt as if it remembered the very wake of the pirogue as it sailed between the islands.

The horizon lightened more, and eventually, I spotted Kingstown, which sat low against the water as if it had been there for hundreds of years—old, bustling, and cozy all at once. Darryl cut the engine so it was barely breathing and brought us in slowly at a fisherman's hut, the kind where you kept your boat when you didn't want anyone to register it.

I was glad we needed to remain as quiet as possible because on these small islands, everyone talked.

I fished into my pocket and pulled out a waterproof tin where I kept my cigarettes, glad that I had kept them dry. I lit one and took a drag.

As the air slowly became inundated with the smell of salt, diesel, and rotting fish, Anokhin lay between us, sleeping, wrapped in a borrowed sackcloth. His face had gone waxy, his hands old and weathered, his knuckles swollen and stiff. Yet when he opened his eyes, there was an undeniable clarity in them, as if for some strange reason he had managed to keep his mind at twenty-five, though his body was far older.

Alicia put a hand on his chest. "Wake up," she said in Russian. She didn't say it gently, but there was also a level of kindness in her tone. She knew as well as I did that what Anokhin was experiencing would likely be the death of him. It was only a matter of time, really.

He nodded, his eyes cracking open, and sat up.

"I am awake," he rasped, his voice betraying the age that coursed through his body.

My headache was still there, still behind my eye, like a sharp pain, pulsing whenever I moved too fast or thought too much.

Darryl scanned the darkness. "Basil's man will be here soon. Ballwin Charles. He's not one of Basil's cousins. Everyone calls him Rex, by the way," he said.

I didn't know how he knew, and I didn't ask. Whether he had some communication with Basil or simply knew that Basil would have caught wind of us by now, I was accepting of it either way.

Sure enough, the figure of Rex soon appeared on the beach, carrying a lit cigarette, moving quickly, barefoot. He glanced at us, then nodded at Darryl.

"You bring him," he whispered.

Darryl jerked his chin toward us, and Rex's eyes darted toward Anokhin's face almost instantly.

"Oh, Jesus," Rex exhaled. "All right, all right, come."

We followed Rex along the edge of the beach into a small, dark, and cramped alleyway. Kingstown was waking up all around us, and so we moved fast, keeping Anokhin cloaked beneath my coat, moving through the back streets hurriedly until we reached the service entrance of Basil's bar.

Basil Charles looked up from behind the counter the moment we stepped in. He stared at us as if he hadn't quite expected us to return so soon.

"You two look like hell," he muttered. "Back again, brother?"

I nodded. "Bequia," I said.

Basil's gaze slid to Anokhin, watching the man sway there, his face drawn and taut.

"And you brought a ghost with you, did you?"

Anokhin tried to straighten. "I am no ghost," he said, though his voice was weak.

Basil exhaled and shook his head. "You're mistreating the poor man, Calder. Have some decency." He motioned to Anokhin. "Back room, now. Go rest. Nobody will find you there, and nobody gets in unless I say so."

As Rex led Anokhin off, Basil leaned in. In a lower voice, he asked, "Were you followed?"

"Not as far as I can tell," I said, "but they're coming regardless. It'll only be a matter of time till they find us."

Basil nodded. "Come in, come in. Sit. Drink some water before you die of thirst. Something tells me you've stirred up quite some shit now. Did you open hell up on us?"

I chuckled and followed him toward the back room. He shut the door, gave us each a bottle, and set a plate of food between us. Alicia sighed and rolled her shoulders.

"It'll be nice for some warm food," she said gratefully, and he nodded.

"Think we'll need Anokhin here before we have a conversation," I muttered.

I didn't want to make the man move any more than Basil did, but the reality was that we needed him. Basil sighed and called for his man, who led Anokhin back. Anokhin shuffled in, trembling as Alicia guided him into a chair.

Finally, when we were all seated, Basil took his eyes off the attaché case and then looked at my face.

"That rig you got still work?" he asked.

"Well, we haven't had the chance to use it on a node," Alicia said. "But it's all we've got, so we damned hope it does."

Basil grimaced. "You got a bad tool and a worse enemy," he said. "I don't like the sound of it."

"Me neither," I said.

"Go on," he said, pouring a fiery rum into three cups and pushing the third toward Anokhin. "All of you, drink up. I won't have you die under my roof."

Anokhin stared at the cup, then drank, the rum running down his chin. He wiped it with the back of his hand and blinked, as if it had awoken something inside him.

"Now," Basil said, looking at me, "talk. What the hell went down on Bequia?"

I told him everything: about Bequia, the plantation ruin, Kolyadin's voice cutting through the dark, Popov sacrificing himself to buy us some time. Everything he needed to know.

When I finished, Basil exhaled slowly.

"Well," he said at last, lighting a cigar and offering me one, which I declined. "Seems you're sitting on St. Vincent with a Russian scientist that Moscow wants alive. I suppose you don't have time to rest."

I laughed. "We don't," I said.

His gaze slid to the door. "There's been whispers, you know. Grenada's been busy. Boats coming and going at odd hours, men buying fuel, and others asking questions. Men who aren't supposed to be here."

"Grenada," I repeated.

Basil nodded. "MGB doesn't need an embassy. They're far more well-networked than that. They have bribes and local men who can track every movement. I already got you routed off official channels, but that'll only buy a few hours. I still have some pull here," he said, "but it's fading quickly as I grow older."

I chuckled. "You and me both," I said.

Anokhin interrupted. "They will come for us," he said.

Basil looked at him. "You know them?"

"I was them," Anokhin replied.

Silence settled among us. Then Basil turned back to us, finally.

"I can't keep you here. Not with that man. I've heard bad

things about Viktor Kolyadin. If he's got a taste, he's like a bloodhound. But I think I know of someone who can help you get your bearings... and help forge you some passports to get you to Havana fast."

"Who?" I asked.

"You won't like it," he said. "But he's a Russian. Used to be NKVD. The man washed up here years ago before moving, but I did my due diligence and researched him. Runs a bookshop now."

Alicia and I traded a look.

"Granitsky," I said.

Basil's eyes widened in shock. "Won't ask how the hell you know his name, but yes, Pyotr Granitsky. Goes by Peter Grant now. Runs a bookshop on Halifax Street, directly across from the Carnegie Free Public Library."

"And I'm assuming he'd help us?" I asked.

Basil raised one eyebrow. "Well, I'm assuming you know this already as well," he said, his eyes flicking to Anokhin. "But he knows him. Ex-NKVD. Worked with Anokhin back when Moscow was controlling the program. The man defected years ago and came here after he realized that Moscow wasn't safe for any man."

Anokhin's expression shifted slightly, caught between recognition and dread. "Yes. Granitsky," he said. "The man took care of me, for what it was worth. That's why I suggested him."

"Ah, so that's how you knew," Basil muttered. Then he opened up a drawer and pulled out a folded paper—a rough sketch of streets, arrows, and names—and slid it toward me.

"This is all I can give you," he said. "Go quiet and go now. Rex will guide you. Don't follow the main street. Take a taxi if you can. And if anyone asks who you are..." He chuckled. "You already know what to answer, right, Max?"

I nodded. "I'm a ghost," I said.

Basil's hand clapped my shoulder affectionately. "Well then, brother," he said. "If this goes wrong, don't bring it back to my door."

"Understood," I replied, and it was time to go.

Kingstown looked innocent in a way Havana never had—at least not since we had arrived. The narrow streets were lined with colonial buildings and painted wood that faded and chipped under the sun and the relentless salt from the ocean that lay far too close. Markets and stalls blossomed with fruit, fish, and echoed with loud voices. It would have all been comforting if we hadn't been on the run for our lives.

I walked with my collar up and my hat low. Rex guided us, and Alicia stayed a step behind Anokhin and me, always watching. Anokhin himself walked between us, wearing a cheap shirt and a cap that Basil had given him. He moved slowly and stubbornly, like a man clinging to his life, one foot in the grave. Every so often, he would stop and blink, and I'd see him fight to stay standing. Whenever that happened, Alicia would nudge him along, and he would shake his head, then nod resolutely and continue walking.

We kept moving. I didn't dare look to my side, nor to my other side, for fear of what I might see—the deep-seated fear that I might even see the Mirror here, its effects, the echoes. Because when you admitted you'd seen it, it began to tear into your memory until the Mirror was all that was left.

Halifax Street was much quieter, more official. There, across from the Carnegie Free Public Library, with its neat "Free Public Library" sign swinging in the breeze, sat a bookshop. It was small, barely one building wedged between two greater ones, with a faded sign: PETER GRANT BOOKS AND STATIONERY.

I smirked to myself, thinking absurdly about how the library had only become properly free last year, in 1950. Before that, you had always needed the right subscription, the right approval to read a book. And now, the word "free" had become attached to it, though I wasn't sure what "free" truly meant. As I had learned early on in my life, the word "free" was always conditional.

The shop window displayed a mirage of books—British paperbacks, a plethora of maps, school copybooks, and even a worn copy of *The Count of Monte Cristo* that looked as if it had been read by one too many men, leaving it barely intact. Rex left us at the front door.

As we entered, a bell jingled, and a man looked up from behind the counter. He was in his mid-fifties, lean with a wiry face and a nervous demeanor. He wore wire-framed glasses and a white shirt that was rolled up to his elbows, though his hair was thinning. His eyes were far too sharp for a man who ran a bookstore.

He took us in with a single sweep—Alicia's posture, my hat, and Anokhin's gait. He didn't ask if he could help or what we wanted.

"What do you need?" he asked, his tone almost angry, his English tinged with a faint, carefully buried accent.

"We're looking for Peter Grant," I replied.

His expression didn't change. "I'm he," he said. "Either buy a book or leave."

I raised an eyebrow. "We were sent by Basil Charles."

"So?" He crossed his arms. "Basil sends customers all the time to buy pencils. What do you want?"

Alicia's gaze hardened. "We don't have time for this," she said, taking a step forward.

Though I couldn't see his hands, the man reached below his counter.

"If you don't have time," Grant said flatly, "that's how you could end up dead in another man's shop."

Anokhin spoke quietly in Russian. "Pyotr," he said.

In an instant, the air in the shop changed. Grant's eyes snapped to Anokhin's face, as if he had seen him properly for the first time. He squinted, looking at him carefully. And for a moment, the man behind the counter dropped his façade. He was no longer Peter Grant, a bookseller in the Caribbean.

"No," he breathed. "Sergei," he said in Russian. "No, that can't be."

He hurried out from behind the counter, setting down what I was sure had been a gun he had clasped in his hands. He locked the front door and flipped the sign to CLOSED.

"In the back," he said, bustling past us.

He pulled aside a curtain, ushering us through into a cramped storeroom lined with boxes and old ledgers. Here, the air was cooler, and he shut the curtain.

"What the hell happened to you?" he muttered, studying Anokhin. "You're supposed to be in Havana, aren't you?"

Anokhin gave a thin laugh. "I was. This is what it did to me."

Grant's gaze flickered to us. "And you are British."

"Bureau," I replied, narrowing my eyes.

"Ah, Bureau. You people have quite a reputation in Russia. Aren't you responsible for—"

"Yes," I cut him off. "Temporal anomalies and something else like that."

He scoffed, then glanced at the attaché case. "And what's this?" he asked.

"A countermeasure," Alicia replied.

I could tell she still didn't fully trust him. Grant laughed quietly, humorlessly, in response.

"Very well. Keep your secrets to yourself." He looked back at Anokhin. "How the hell are you alive? And what happened to you?"

Anokhin's eyes were tired. "Well, we built the cage Moscow always wanted. And just as you predicted, it turned on them."

Grant stared at him carefully, and I could see the history conflicting within the man. It wasn't friendship or affection, but something more intimate—almost a protective professionalism.

"Oh, Anokhin," Grant muttered, "you were always valuable,

but you were always too valuable. That's why I kept you breathing in Moscow when the men above me wanted to use you and dispose of you, you know. I buried their requisition orders, forged medical clearances. Everything I did, I did to keep you alive."

Anokhin's gaze shifted, uneasy. "So you remember."

"I remember everything," Grant replied. "That is the curse of my mind. I've watched the Soviet machine consume its own men, turning on the scientists, the guards. In Moscow, you're never safe. They use you, then throw you away when you're no longer convenient. And so," he said, shrugging, "that's why I ran. That's why I kept running all the way here to Cuba, to the Caribbean, and kept going. I thought that maybe this was far enough away."

"So you protected him," I said.

Grant glanced at me. "I was assigned to him, back when I was NKVD, when they changed the badge and pretended that it washed away our sins."

I could hear an ancient anger in his voice.

"And now you're here," I replied.

His eyes grew distant. "Yes. Now I sell books and pretend Moscow doesn't know where I am. I'm sure they do. They know everything. You never really escape the Soviets."

He opened a drawer, removed a flask, and took a sip of it. "So, what can I do for you?" he asked.

I told him of Bequia and of Kolyadin. When I said the name, the man stiffened. Then he finally spoke.

"Kolyadin will not stop. Moscow is going to pursue Anokhin into British territory. Doesn't matter if it's a church, a hospital, or a house with children inside. They do not care what flag flies or who stands in the way. Grenada gives them reach—shipping, radios. They don't have official sanction, but they don't need it. The force is dangerous. And Kolyadin is one of the worst."

"And you know this because you were one of them," I said.

"Yes," he nodded reluctantly.

Anokhin's hands were trembling. "They will come here," he said.

Grant scoffed. "You're always the optimist," he said. "They're likely already here now."

"Well, then we need answers," Alicia said, her jaw clenched.

"Very well," Grant said, spreading his hands. "Ask away, and I'll see how I can help."

"Philby," I said.

"Ah." Grant scoffed. "I keep up with the rumors well enough to know this. The English traitor?"

I nodded.

"Philby fed Moscow the project's knowledge," Grant continued. "Everything your Project Oracle hinted at before London buried it. He gave the architecture, the assets—everything. Made Havana possible faster than it should have been. They were planning it before Project Oracle was even a thing. He's a beautiful channel. London thinks he's theirs, but Moscow knows who he really is... the type of man Philby really is."

I laughed. "Everyone thinks they can control the Mirror. Thinks the damn machine belongs to them."

Grant's gaze flickered to the attaché case. "Oh, I see," he said, recognition dawning in his eyes. "So you want to destroy Havana's build?"

"Yes," Alicia replied. "We're going back."

"Very well, very well." Grant held up a hand. "I have no interest in protecting the Soviets, but before you do, you must understand why Moscow's men would tear up these islands to retrieve him." He pointed at Anokhin. "Have you told them about it? About what you built?"

Anokhin stared at him, then at us. In his eyes flickered a mixture of pride and fear.

"I've already told them some," he said quietly. "But yes—the decision locking."

"Decision locking," Alicia echoed, her voice flat.

Grant's eyes narrowed. "It was the final straw for me—the

final thing that made me leave the Soviets. When they began to theorize about this, before they even knew the Mirror existed. Our finest men wanted to work on control—control of those who dared to question the Soviet empire."

Anokhin nodded. "And we built it eventually," he said. "It collapsed dissent, all thanks to your Mirror technology. Without which, it wouldn't have been possible. Removes alternative branches before they can even form. I wouldn't call it persuasion, blackmail, or brainwashing. A way to think of it is as subtraction. It subtracts choices before they can even form in your head."

"And without you," I replied, "they can't tune it. Is that correct?"

Anokhin laughed. "Yes. True. They can make a crude version, I'm sure, in time. But it won't work correctly."

Grant stared at him. "And you did this," he said, almost accusatory. "And you're proud of it, aren't you?"

Anokhin's shoulders sagged. "I did it because in Moscow, if you say no, you're as good as dead. I forgot what I wanted a long time ago."

"And so," Grant said, his face softening for only a second before it hardened again as he turned back toward us, "that is why they want him. He's not a witness; he's a key."

"A key," Alicia muttered, shooting a glance at me. "Well, I think all of us in this room have experience with that. Except for maybe you, Grant. But we still have to stop Havana."

Grant shook his head. "Havana—that's a deathbed if I've ever heard of one."

Anokhin nodded, and I could see eagerness in his eyes. "Yes, but I've told him about V4. The Mirror is entangled. It's not one machine, Grant. You didn't know this before you left. Neither did we—we discovered it recently. But Havana is only one node; it links backward to all of the old ones—every Mirror before—using them as anchors through a quantum field."

"Like lineage?" Grant asked.

"Yes," Anokhin said, his voice feverish.

"Well then," Grant said, leaning his hands on a stack of books, "if you destroy Havana alone, the web will be—the web will probably just rebuild, right?"

He glanced at Anokhin, who nodded.

"If it rebuilds around old knots, maybe even other ones you haven't heard of yet, then how will you stop it?"

"Well," I said, "we're back to where Hawthorne warned us. We have to kill the tree from the roots."

Grant's eyes narrowed. "Hawthorne," he echoed.

"You know him?" I asked.

Grant shook his head. "Not personally. I never had the pleasure of meeting him, but I know what information Moscow collected—the names that even our scientists respected and revered, and Hawthorne was one of the big ones."

"Now," he said, glancing at the attaché case, "I think it's time you tell me what's inside this case."

"Well," I muttered, "it's a rig created by Charles Fraser-Smith. Not sure you have ever heard of him, but supposedly it can sever a Mirror for good."

Anokhin stuttered suddenly. "It would only work if it's in the right spot."

Grant shot him a glance. "I think I know what you're speaking of," he said. "If you have an axe"—he gestured vaguely in the air—"it's only useful if you swing it at the right spot: the base of the tree."

"And the base of the tree is each node," I said slowly.

Anokhin nodded, pacing the room. "Each anchor must be severed; the entanglement broken at its origin points, or the lattice will hold, rebuild."

"Now," Grant said, lifting a finger, "I'm not entirely familiar with all this quantum stuff, but here's the problem: wouldn't each node have a different resonance?"

Anokhin nodded, still pacing. "Those coils of Fraser-Smith you have," he said to Alicia and me, "each node will require different tuning, a different harmonic signature. If you fire the coils at the wrong frequency or at the wrong time, you could amplify the field rather than collapse it... or, worse, sever one thread and strengthen the others. To guarantee the machine tunes to the node, you must be close to it—within proximity, if you will."

"Well then," Grant sighed, looking directly at Anokhin. "You know what to do. They'll need you to guide the calibration for each node."

Anokhin's face went pale, but an expression of resoluteness overtook him, and he nodded. "Yes," he said. "I can do that."

I felt the weight of the whole thing settle. It had all begun to come together now. But would we be able to do it?

Grant continued. "When you try, Moscow will respond. You realize that, don't you? The theory is something you can work out later. Anokhin knows far more about it than I do, but the strategy—the moment they realize you're cutting the chain, they'll try and burn it down. They'll try and burn everything around you to stop it. They'll call on British hands, Cuban hands, anyone they can to stop you. You'll find yourself in a firefight."

"We've been hunted before," Alicia said.

Grant studied her for a second, then nodded, almost respectfully. "Well then, you have to go back to Havana," he said at last. "And don't let anyone convince you the goal is to recover it. Burn it down. Moscow can go to hell."

I scoffed. "You and me both," I said.

He looked at me. "You," he said. "I saw it in your face when you entered. You've already seen what it does when men try to control it, haven't you?"

I thought of my broken memories: of Alicia dying and returning, of Hawthorne's voice fading into static, of Popov's body hitting the floor. And I nodded.

"All right," I said. "So we return, we cut the chain, and we end it all for good."

Alicia looked at Grant, then at Anokhin, then back at me. "Return to Havana," she said. "Kill the web, kill it all, and burn the assets to the ground."

Anokhin swallowed. "If we sever all the older nodes," he said, "then V4 will be the last one to go."

"Won't it be pulsing that entire time?" I asked.

Anokhin nodded. "Something we'll have to deal with," he replied.

Silence fell among us until Grant finally spoke again. "You all understand the mission, then?"

"We do," Alicia replied.

"So what do you need from me?" Grant asked. "I'm sure you didn't come here just to theorize."

"We heard you do papers," I said.

"Ah," Grant muttered. "Papers. Of course. Give me half an hour; I'll get you something. Not perfect—nothing ever is—but it'll be enough to move you without standing in a colonial office answering questions."

And sure enough, about thirty minutes later, Grant handed us a flat envelope. Alicia took it and quickly flipped through the contents.

"We owe you," she said.

Grant's mouth tightened. "Everything is a debt. Pay it to me by staying alive long enough to burn that hellscape to the ground. And make sure Moscow doesn't get what it wants. Not from Anokhin, not from your machine."

Anokhin swallowed. "If they take me, they'll tune it."

Grant clasped his shoulder, meeting his eyes. "Then don't let them. Anokhin, I say this with as much respect as possible. But die before they catch you."

Anokhin nodded.

Silence fell among us again. Outside the storeroom, I could hear the faint jingle of the shop bell as someone tried the door and found it locked. I could hear receding footsteps as that same person moved away.

Grant's eyes flickered up. "Go now, you can't stay," he said.

"We weren't planning to," I replied with a smile.

Grant moved swiftly to the curtain, peering through a gap. "Go out separately. Don't go straight back to Basil. Loop around. And keep an eye out for the Russians. They don't quite know how to fit in—not as good as you people. The Bureau."

I nodded. "Thank you again, Grant."

"Go now," he said, his eyes on mine. "Kill the web."

We left the bookshop with our new papers and a heavier weight now that the reality of the situation had settled in. Across Halifax Street, the Carnegie Library sat in the sun with its neat FREE sign. And for a moment, I thought about how libraries were supposed to help with forgetful memories. It was memory made public, stored on paper. But the Mirror had abandoned all that, turning memory into a weapon.

We moved out as Granitsky had instructed, separating and crossing at different points, blending into the market crowds to blur ourselves into the background. Several times, I thought I saw a man who stood too clean, too still, watching the street as if he were looking for someone. Maybe it was nothing, but maybe he was from Grenada. I didn't have time to think.

By the time we made our way back to Basil's bar, the sun was high in the sky. Anokhin was breathing hard, his eyes glassy, his body swaying.

Basil glanced up as we entered. "You found him."

"We did," I replied, "and we're going back."

"Back to Havana," Basil replied. It wasn't a question.

I nodded. "We need to cut the chain."

Basil exhaled slowly, as if he was watching someone walk into a fire and couldn't stop them. "Then move fast, at least," he said. "Word travels faster than boats do, and Moscow isn't just going to wait for you to arrive."

He stepped behind the counter and picked up a small black phone. "Havana's station still routes through here. Let's see if

Angleton's people want their Russian alive as much as the Russians do."

I watched him dial the phone, and I could feel the tension building. It was like a flood piling up behind a dam, and at some point, the dam had to break. As Basil spoke softly into the phone, I finally understood what we had to do.

We didn't have to save Havana.

We had to burn the web until it could never be remade.

CHAPTER 20
COLLAPSING CONSENSUS

Havana was a place where men no longer trusted the order of their own days. It had been that way for the past week, but it had gotten worse—far worse.

It wasn't that the city was openly violent or filled with chaos, and yet it was worse because the chaos was rumbling beneath the surface, never quite found. Rumors spread of doppelgängers, of time slipping, of men forgetting; blink at the wrong moment and you might wake up not remembering where you came from.

Angleton had come to recognize that the city was a hellscape.

He sat in the back room of his safe house in Miramar, where he had spent his days reading the morning incident summaries by the light of a single lamp. In the corner, the fan spun lazily, churning the hot air in circles. On the desk before him lay stacks upon stacks of reports, a map of Havana crisscrossed with pins and thread, and a small black telephone which he only used for the most important of calls.

The first report was from a Cuban police liaison, written in apologetic Spanish and translated by one of his station staff into brisk English. He shook his head as he picked it up, thumbing through the papers. It was annoying, really, because Angleton had delayed his flight at least three times now. Each time he had planned to leave Havana, yet it was as if something pulled him back. He wasn't quite sure why.

The men in Washington had begun to ask questions, but Angleton had told them it was of the utmost importance and had remained for a few more days.

He read the police report without reading it. He'd been over it at least three times before—cars stopping, doors opening, and people stepping out into the street to simply disappear, only to be found hours later in their own homes, yet their cars were still idling at the scene, with no sign that they had ever been in them.

It was the type of repetition that confused everyone, and yet, because it wasn't easy to detect or easy to see, no one was ready to admit that it was even happening. That was the type of situation they were faced with, one he knew would only become worse.

Angleton wrote in his notebook, jotting down sentences as he read several other reports. They were all similar. A hotel guest reported seeing himself entering from the street as he stood there at the front desk. Although the staff claimed the guest was intoxicated, he reported later having no memory of ever saying such a thing.

Angleton shook his head.

Whatever the hell was happening in Havana, he was beginning to doubt the legitimacy of his desire to retain the Mirror V4 for the CIA. Maybe, just maybe, he thought as he lit a cigarette with his nicotine-stained fingers, he should let Calder and Alicia do their job.

He reached for the next file but stopped because the telephone rang.

He lifted it hesitantly at first.

"This is Angleton," he said, his voice slightly harsher than he meant.

The line was bad. Under the hiss, there was a slight echo, as if the other man's breathing was caught in an unfamiliar rhythm.

"James? Is this James Angleton?" A voice cut through the line. "You hear me?"

"Who is this?" Angleton asked.

"This is Basil Charles, former Bureau. I'm here with Max Calder and Alicia Rayes." The voice steadied. "Is this Angleton?"

Angleton raised his eyebrows and sat up straighter. If Basil was Bureau-adjacent, that meant he deserved a certain level of courtesy.

"I hear you," Angleton said. "Speak."

Basil didn't waste time.

"Calder and Rayes are alive," Basil said. "They came through here, and they've got one of the Russians."

Angleton's pen stopped. A Russian. That must mean either Anokhin or Popov.

"Which Russian?" he asked eagerly, though he already suspected he knew.

"Seems to be a man named Anokhin," Basil said. "Sergei Anokhin. But he's aged. Like he grew a decade older overnight, maybe even two or three. The other one's dead—Popov. They lost him in a fight on Bequia. MGB detachment. A major named Kolyadin."

Angleton listened, letting the name settle on his ears. Kolyadin. He was familiar with that man. Everyone was. The major had the type of reputation for a ruthless, militant soldier— one of the worst kinds and yet also the best—whose loyalty was only to himself first and his country second.

"Are they returning him to Havana?" Angleton asked.

"Yes. Moving back toward it," Basil replied. "They're trying to stay off channels. I hooked them up with papers, an old contact I know."

"Very well," Angleton replied. "It'd be best if they don't call me."

There was a pause on the line.

"They're here now—" Basil began.

"Good. Tell them to depart right away," Angleton interrupted. "But I have no information I can share at the moment."

"You want them blind?" Basil's voice on the other end of the line sounded almost offended.

"Compartmentalized," Angleton corrected. "I've already made it clear to them—my position. But I want them alive. Route them as cleanly as you can—no radio chatter, no direct contact. I'll contact Director Moreau and let her know the situation. I'll arrange the receiving side to bring them in safely and under the radar."

Basil exhaled. "All right, then," he said, his voice slightly less angry now. "I hear it's getting strange up there. How are your boys holding up?"

Angleton glanced down at the reports on his desk. The pattern was getting worse.

"We're holding," he replied. "Just get them here fast."

And then he set the phone down with a firm click.

For a moment, he stayed still, feeling the heat swim through the room and the city's pulse that had become constant—a numb headache in the back of his head that had begun to ache the longer he'd stayed here. Then he stood and went to the sink, washing his face to refresh himself. The mirror above it was cheap and bolted to the wall, but he didn't glance at it. Lately, he had begun to dislike mirrors. In fact, anything that reflected.

In a moment of weakness, he glanced up, looking at his reflection. It looked back at him, slightly too late. Angleton turned away first, and as he did, he could have sworn it smiled.

He cursed under his breath and strode back to his desk, where he picked up his phone and dialed.

"Get Easee here, now," he instructed when the operator answered.

Bill Easee arrived as he always did—without hurry, which always unsettled the men around him. He seemed like a man who had learned to live with other people's emergencies and was resolved to deal with them day in and day out, with no thought for his own.

He stepped into the safe house's back room, his jacket off, his sleeves already rolled up halfway. He leaned up against the wall, his eyes glancing around the room, taking it in.

Angleton closed the shutters himself, slowly. Havana's noise dulled, becoming a distant, muffled rumbling that reminded them where they were and how far away from the CIA they truly were.

"All right," Angleton said. "You've defected twice and survived both. Dare I say you've come out in better standing than you started in?"

Bill chuckled. "And I'm assuming that means you have a question for me."

"Precisely," Angleton said, tapping the stack of reports. "This city is stuttering. It's breaking the hell open. You, more than anyone, know how this damn Mirror works. I want to know exactly what we're dealing with—why it's escalating, and why every time we get close to any real decisions, reality itself seems to warp around us, sending any of my plans that I'm making to hell."

Bill's eyes didn't go to Angleton. Instead, he glanced around the room, his gaze finally settling on a small wall mirror that was mounted next to a painting. It was a Cuban painting; one Angleton had grown fond of in his short time there.

"Well," Easee said at last, "it's because it's not a machine. At least not in the way you mean it, or any man would mean it."

Angleton shrugged. "Everything is a machine if you use it right."

Easee chuckled.

"That's the problem," he replied. "It's learning from us. The more you use it, the less it becomes like a machine."

He pushed off the wall and paced closer to the desk, staring Angleton down in a way most men wouldn't dare.

"The thing you're dealing with now," he said, "doesn't live in

CUBAN SLIDERS

the hardware. You can think of the hardware as some kind of mechanical lung... some way that it can breathe."

Angleton waited for Easee to continue. Silence was leverage.

"Men far greater than myself," Easee continued, "called it El Cuadro—the painting—half because they didn't know what to call it and half because it stopped reflecting reality and began composing itself."

Angleton raised his eyebrow in disbelief. "You're telling me the Mirror has some sort of personality?"

"No," Easee chuckled. "I'm telling you that the Mirror has a point of view. It's not the human type, but it's still a point of perspective.

"The mirror's function is selection. Out of all the ways things can go, it chooses one and forces coherence to that timeline... forces you to snap to it whenever it pulses. But selection needs feedback. Feedback needs an observer. And over time—far too much time, because the Mirror doesn't operate in time the same way you and I do—it stopped borrowing our observation capabilities. Why not build its own?"

Angleton glanced down at the reports—the reports of repetition, denial, doppelgängers, and memory slipping away, never to be grasped again.

"El Cuadro," Easee continued, now leaning over the desk, his face barely a few feet from Angleton, "is what happens when a system continues to choose and keeps remembering what it chose. Don't get me wrong, it's not a consciousness like you or I, but it's a consciousness nevertheless - like a compass that would know which direction it's pointing."

"So instinct?" Angleton asked.

"You could call it that," Easee replied. "Survival. Instinct. Coherence. Continuation. No matter what you want to call it, it survives by keeping a branch stable enough to inhabit and keeping the network capable of reconstituting that stability. In a bid for survival, the Mirror has begun to think."

"So this web you're talking about"—Angleton tapped the desk with a pin—"there's more than one?"

"There's always been more than one," Easee laughed. "Cuba isn't a singular installation; it's one node in a great web."

Angleton could feel something tightening in his chest. He wasn't sure if it was fear, really, but it was the beginning of a realization that even a man as great, strategic, and paranoid as he was, was out of his depth. A man who had a plan for everything hadn't planned for this.

"El Cuadro needs to defend itself," Easee said, "but it doesn't defend itself—not with guns, like we men do—but with memory and experience. It steers your perception, blunts your memory, inserts doubt right before someone makes a decision that would terminate it. Sound familiar?"

Angleton nodded. "Like a decision locking node. And like Calder."

"Ah, yes. Max Calder. Especially Calder," Easee replied. "Anchors like Calder are its load-bearing walls. It puts the most on them. Relies on them when all else fails. Calder, Rayes, anyone who can hold contradictory timelines without snapping clean in half. They're strong, but because of that, they're stabilizers, and they're the biggest threats to us."

Angleton's mind flickered to the way Max Calder looked at him whenever they spoke of the Mirror—a mix of confusion, longing, and maybe a little bit of hatred, as if the device had some sort of hook in him.

"See, if Calder collapses a node here," Easee continued, "El Cuadro would lose coherence at this site. But it wouldn't die. It would retreat and re-stabilize; it would ensure no one ever lines up the same sequence of decisions again."

"So," Angleton said, leaning back in his chair, "destroying Havana won't end it?"

"No." Easee shook his head. "If anything, it'll teach it, and next time, you won't get this close."

Angleton's jaw worked as he thought. He didn't like systems, particularly those that learned faster than he did.

"And what'll it do when we threaten it?" Angleton asked.

For the first time, Easee paused. He thought for a second, then shook his head.

"Well. Look around you. You see everything that's happening?"

"It'll do that?" Angleton asked.

"No," Easee chuckled. "It'll stop being so subtle."

"You mean it gets worse?" Angleton asked.

Easee nodded. "Perceptual steering is one word for it," he said. "It paints scenes into reality—anything that'll push you away from the right choices: anchor exploitation, like pressuring the people it needs most; coherence maintenance, swapping times, details, or even false continuities. It doesn't have to convince you. It just has to make it so you truly can't get close, because every time you get closer to disabling the Mirror, it leads you further away."

Angleton's eyes shifted toward the mirror on his wall, and he felt a strange prickling on his skin.

"How do you beat something that edits you before you even act?" he finally asked.

Easee hesitated.

"Well, you don't overpower it," he said. "You have to overload it. Fraser-Smith made those coils, and I believe they hold the answer if you can get close enough. Make it hold something so fragile, so recursive, that it can't spare the attention to intervene."

Angleton's mind jumped, almost involuntarily, to a name he had read in a Bureau file: The Architect. Hawthorne. The man who had become a rumor among other organizations and a legend of the Bureau.

"Hawthorne?" Angleton asked then.

Easee nodded. "He understood the Mirror as an engine, but El Cuadro is the engine's survival instinct. If you can trap that instinct in some stabilization task— something self-referential, something it can't drop without risking collapse of its own—you would buy yourself a window."

"And if you fail?" Angleton asked.

Easee glanced around uneasily. It was as if he thought the room was listening to them.

"If you fail," he finally said, "then El Cuadro continues to paint, and you would keep living in whatever version it decided was safest for itself."

Angleton nodded, pushing his feelings aside. For once, he felt he might have met his match—and it wasn't even a human.

"Containment," he said. "If we get a strike window—if Calder does what he does, hell, if I let him do it— what do we do with what remains?"

Easee's mouth tightened wryly. "You'd want extraction protocols. If there's anything left. But keep in mind, Angleton, once the Mirror starts dying, the only things you'll be left with are things that are outside the web when it collapses."

"Like the decision locking node," Angleton said, nodding.

And Easee, though he looked annoyed, nodded in confirmation.

"Very well, then," Angleton said. "You're dismissed."

...

Lucy Howard didn't knock. She never did, at least not unless the opportunity demanded it.

She strode in and spotted Angleton almost instantly, standing by the table, his jacket off, his sleeves rolled up, the desk lamp throwing shadows that made the room's corners feel too confined. In the periphery of the safe house, she knew his maps and details were scattered on the walls, but she kept her gaze focused on him.

"Well," Angleton said at last, "I think I've had a shift in my perception of what's going on here."

Lucy scoffed. "You spoke to Easee."

Angleton nodded. "You almost sound disappointed," he replied.

"No. I'm concerned," she said. "Excuse me if I don't trust any of the Bureau's former agents."

"Oh?" Angleton asked. "I thought you were head over heels with telling Calder what was going on here."

Lucy ignored that personal jab. Instead, she carefully shut the door behind her and turned to him expectantly.

"What's happened?" she asked.

Angleton slid a transcript of Basil's call across the table. Lucy read it once, then again, her eyes scanning the note quickly.

"Calder and Rayes are alive," she said quietly. There was a flicker of personal relief that Angleton instantly picked up on.

"Yes," he replied. "And they're moving back toward Havana with Anokhin."

Lucy looked up. "Then you need to warn them."

"No," Angleton replied flatly.

Her eyes narrowed. "James—" she began, but he cut her off.

"No contact with Calder," he repeated.

Lucy stepped closer, lowering her voice. "They walked into a damn firefight on Bequia," she said. "They're carrying the only living resource that Moscow needs. Kolyadin will follow them into British territory, Cuba, hell, anywhere they go. If Calder doesn't know what we know—"

But Angleton cut her off, raising his finger.

"Calder knows enough," he said. "He knows now there's a web of mirrors. He knows it has to be severed. That's his job."

"And what about yours?" Lucy asked.

Angleton's eyes met hers, and his gaze didn't waver.

"My job," he said, "is making sure that the United States is not the only party walking away from this blind."

"You mean decision locking," Lucy answered, picking up on what he meant instantly.

Angleton didn't respond. He simply sighed and sat back more loosely in his chair.

"If Calder finds out," Lucy said, her voice sharpening—

"Yes, I know, he'll destroy it," Angleton muttered. "He's not a strategist, you know. He's a man with a wound and a conscience. Not a man who thinks this thing through. I'm not saying he doesn't have a brilliant mind. But his knack of understanding involves memory and learning things on the fly. And hell, his memory—it's not what it used to be. If he finds out, he'll smash the node and fracture the coalition we're building here."

"Batista," Lucy replied.

Angleton nodded. "Batista is a means," he said. "We'll find stability through him. You think Moscow is building V4 for the romance of physics? Hell, they're building it to change the trajectory of history. And the decision locking node can collapse dissent. That's half the battle."

Lucy's face tightened with disgust. She'd seen what it did, and she didn't like it.

"At least," she said, leaning forward, "let me warn Calder about the kill box. Let me send something through Basil—just a single line, something to tell him where he needs to go or who to avoid."

Angleton shook his head again.

"You're not contacting him," he said. "You are not intervening directly. You're my counter-Philby asset, and you will remain silent."

He stood and leaned toward her.

"MI6 is going to be all over Havana the moment Philby lets on that they're building a V4 here. Philby wants access, directly or indirectly. And once he realizes the Russians have lost control, MI6 will intervene. Your usefulness is in being the one thing that can know Philby is making a play before he does. You've been with Philby before, Lucy, or did you forget?"

She bit her lip, but held his gaze all the same. She was angry, but she was disciplined enough to know that she couldn't cross Angleton.

"This is the endgame," Angleton continued, his tone softening slightly. "And there are two tracks at play."

He held up one finger.

"Calder and the Bureau will focus on killing the Mirror Web. They'll do what they do—burn the tree at the roots, take the risk, and take the heat. I've come to terms with that."

Then he held up a second finger.

"And," he continued, "the Agency will retain decision locking and recover any usable mirror material in the aftermath, especially if an opportunity presents itself. And if the web collapses, I want whatever survives the collapse in our hands before it becomes someone else's and they rebuild another mirror."

She held his gaze for a long moment before nodding.

"You're using them," she said. "And I get that. But dammit, Angleton, I hope the game you're playing doesn't backfire."

He smiled slightly, then raised his voice.

"Easee," he called. "In here."

Only a moment later, Easee appeared at his side, striding briskly through the door. He glanced around, taking in Lucy's posture, Angleton's stillness, and decided—correctly—that he should remain silent. He merely looked at Angleton politely.

Angleton looked at him. "Go ahead and begin containment and extraction protocols. We need to prepare for post-strike recovery. I want options for secure transports, signal isolation, burn contingencies—everything. I'll give you our finest men. Assume the site will likely be hot with Soviet survivors after Calder and Rayes have their way with it."

Easee nodded. "Understood," he replied.

Angleton turned back to Lucy. "You stay in Havana," he said. "Monitor the resonance strikes. Keep the nodes secured. And remember, when Calder walks back into the city, I will brief him on what he needs to hear—and no more. Maybe, by then, you'll have contact with him. I may have another job for you."

"And if he dies before then?" she asked.

"Then he was never the right tool," Angleton replied, his eyes flat. "I don't hate him, Lucy. But Calder needs to play his role."

Finally, Lucy nodded. Angleton watched her eyes carefully, and he couldn't quite read whether it was agreement or simply compliance for now. Then she left, the door closing behind her with a soft click.

When she was finally gone, Easee shifted his gaze toward the mirror on the wall again. For a moment, his face looked worn, exhausted beyond his years.

Angleton followed his gaze, staring at his own reflection in the mirror. And for just a fraction of a second, the reflection seemed to smile at him. His stomach tightened, and he turned away quickly.

Outside, Havana was breaking. Inside, Angleton—a man who was always confident in his strategy—had begun to doubt. Not only others, as his paranoid self would do so often, but he had begun to doubt himself.

Angleton didn't trust silence or repetition, and he trusted consensus least of all.

But the Mirror—the Mirror he trusted less than any of these.

CHAPTER 21
HAVANA HEIST

We said our goodbyes to Basil, acutely aware that every second we wasted was a second we might never get back—a second the Mirror might claim from us.

Basil didn't make the goodbyes dramatic; he never did. He simply leaned across the counter, shook my hand, and clasped my back with the other. He did the same with Alicia.

When his hand met hers, there was a brief pause, as if he was fully acknowledging her—welcoming her into his group of people he trusted more than his own brothers.

Then he let go, picked up the phone again, and was already turning to the next problem.

"Tell Angleton we'll be there soon," I said.

"Already did," he replied. "Now get out of my bar before you ruin my day."

I smirked. "I'll be back to try some of that rum you're brewing, brother."

Once this was all over, I would return, but for now, we had other things on our minds.

Outside, Kingstown was bright, fishermen arguing over nets, children running here and there in school uniforms.

Anokhin shuffled between us, his head down beneath the same cheap cap Basil had found.

His breathing was rapid now, and I was worried he wouldn't make it.

But I kept my reservations to myself. It wouldn't help to question his age—not now. Either he made it or he didn't.

Alicia kept one hand on his elbow, guiding him clinically, ensuring he kept moving and didn't collapse where he stood.

"Can you walk?" she asked in Russian.

"I am walking," he rasped back.

"Good, then keep walking," she replied, nudging him forward.

I carried Fraser-Smith's rig in the attaché case with my left hand and my pistol in my right, though I kept my coat draped over the pistol to conceal it from view.

With Kolyadin and his men on the search for us, I didn't count on myself to be able to draw my pistol in time.

So, I kept it with me, always at the ready.

We didn't take the front street. Basil's barefoot runner, Rex, the same Rex who had led us to Basil after our return from Bequia, guided us through the alleys, glancing around nervously as if he half expected us to be gunned down by the Russians at any moment.

"Airport's this way," he whispered.

"No taxis?" I asked.

"No. Too loud, too many questions. You walk, then ride," Rex said, shaking his head.

By the time we had reached the edge of town, Anokhin's breathing sounded far worse. He stopped now and again, swaying, and I saw his eyes go unfocused, the stare of a man whose mind was on the brink of collapse.

It was clear that even if we destroyed the Mirror, Anokhin was a dead man walking. I knew he knew it too, and I couldn't help but be impressed by his resolution.

Soon, we reached a parked lorry on a dirt pull-off. The driver didn't look at us but simply opened the back door and jerked his chin.

"In," he said.

We climbed into the shadow of the cargo bed. The lorry started up, rattling as it headed toward Arnos Vale.

The island blurred past through the slats: palms, the bright sea, and then that small airfield we had arrived at, under the sun—inconspicuous and bold at the same time. An interesting mixture that I never got used to.

We didn't go through the terminal this time. Basil had his connections here. The one thing I had to respect about the man, other than his steadfast trustworthiness, was the fact that he kept and fostered his own list of connections, perhaps greater than the Bureau itself within his own district.

Though Basil didn't have as much far-reaching influence, the influence he did have over the Caribbean was almost unbelievable.

A man in a white shirt met us by a hangar door, a cigarette dangling from his mouth.

"Mr. Kale, Miss Rivas," he said, his voice flat and carrying an accent I couldn't place. "Follow me."

Of course, we still used those names. We had explained them to Granitsky, and he had put them on the passports—my face on one that belonged to Martin Kale and Alicia's on one for Ana Rivas.

Anokhin's papers gave him a Latin name that didn't fit his accent, if you listened for more than a second. But it wasn't like he was going to be speaking anyway.

Now that lie was being reinforced by the fact that we were being guided into the airport, using these passports as cover.

The man who led us didn't ask for our passports, simply opening a side door into the hangar, where a small twin-engine plane with no markings sat.

"Where's it going?" Alicia asked.

"Havana. Direct," the man replied. "One stop for fuel."

I glanced at Anokhin. "No customs?"

The man gave me a look and said, "You'll be cleared. Today you are our cargo."

I nodded, chuckling.

Then we climbed aboard.

I didn't ask how we'd make the flight with only one stop for fuel, but the Douglas DC-3 we boarded was nice for what it was—an impressive plane that answered the question all by itself.

The cabin smelled old, and two crates were strapped down between us, stenciled with something agricultural. As I pressed my hand against one and it shifted, I realized they were empty.

I scoffed, sitting down on seats that were narrow, made for men who didn't carry attaché cases, guns, or a Russian who was aging beyond his years.

As the engines roared to life, Anokhin's head lolled forward, his hands trembling in his lap.

Alicia leaned in, checking his pulse. Her eyes narrowed.

She draped a thin airline blanket over his legs and leaned toward me.

"It's irregular," she murmured to me. "Fast and slow. Not sure how much longer he'll make it."

"So the Mirror is still affecting him," I muttered.

She simply nodded. There was no point in pretending we weren't all affected by the Mirror.

The plane lifted off, the island falling away behind us. Ahead, the sea stretched blue, endless, and serene.

As we flew, my headaches slowly began to return, sharper than ever before, the pressure in my skull rising, slowly but steadily.

I didn't need a compass to know the direction we were flying. My head told me that much.

Anokhin stirred occasionally, whispering things to himself that made no sense in the English language.

I didn't bother to speak to him. He wasn't speaking to us.

Instead, I simply stared out the window, watching the ocean and clouds below us.

About an hour passed, and Anokhin coughed, blood spotting his lip.

Alicia produced a handkerchief from one of her coat pockets, pressing it to his mouth, calm. But her eyes gave away that she was calculating how long we had—how long until he followed Markov's fate, how many minutes before his body decided that living wasn't worth it any longer.

"Anokhin," she said suddenly in Russian, "stay with us. What's your mother's name?"

His eyes fluttered. "Why do you ask?"

"Because I want to know," she replied, almost kindly.

He swallowed. "Galina," he whispered. Then he shook his head, as if angry with himself. "No, no, wait, that's my wife's mother."

"Your mother's name," Alicia repeated.

He stared at her for a long while, then curled up tightly, as if ashamed.

"I cannot," he said. "It is missing from my mind."

I placed a hand on his shoulder. I couldn't pretend that I was the man's friend. For all intents and purposes, we would have likely been enemies at any other time.

And yet, there was something about the way I knew he was experiencing this that gave me a sense of camaraderie toward him.

So we continued on, the plane engines roaring, Alicia and I sitting silently as we watched Anokhin deteriorate.

I was confident we could try using the copper coils by ourselves, but without Anokhin, we wouldn't be certain. Neither Alicia nor I were scientists. Here was a man who was almost as good as Hawthorne when it came to understanding the Mirror.

Without him, we would be walking into Havana blind.

Anokhin laughed suddenly, staring off into space.

"Again," he muttered. "Always again."

I didn't have to ask what he was seeing. Whatever it was, it had just repeated. Again.

Hours passed, and as the clouds thickened below us, the air began to turn heavy with Havana's weather.

Overhead, the gray skies would normally have been nice, but Havana wasn't nice anymore—not nice in any way you could put it.

There was something off about it, and as we drew closer and the plane began to descend, the city felt as if it were tilting sideways.

The wheels finally hit the runway with a hard bounce. The plane shook, and then in a strange jolt, it felt as if we were up in the air again.

I glanced out the window, and sure enough, the runway was far below us.

In the front, I could hear the pilot curse.

Alicia met my eyes.

"It's bad," she said, and I nodded in agreement.

This time, the plane landed without incident.

Once it landed, we quickly made our way past the terminal, past the palm trees, and through the Havana heat.

Angleton's receiving team met us before we even reached immigration. I could tell it was his team because they seemed foreign despite their best efforts to appear otherwise.

One of them nodded at me.

"Mr. Kale," he said.

I nodded back, and Alicia slowly guided Anokhin forward. He walked as if he were in a trance now, and I could tell that even his resolution was beginning to wane.

If we wanted to stop the Mirror, it had to be now.

We quickly continued outside, ushered past the immigration

officials, who had undoubtedly been tipped off and paid to keep quiet.

Outside, our driver waited in a car that looked Cuban but seemed too well-maintained—the kind of vehicle you wouldn't find in Havana unless you were somewhat important or well-funded.

We slid in, helping Anokhin into the back seat. He sat between us, coughing and pressing his hands to his mouth so he didn't continue to hack.

Havana continued to unfold as we drove, and as I glanced around, I couldn't help but notice that, though it was still decadent, with music bleeding from doorways and radios, women in bright dresses, and a constant sense of that euphoric chaos that Havana was known for, the city felt off.

Occasionally, I stared out the window. I saw crowds of people simply standing there, still, as if they were frozen in time, or others walking as if they had been sped up, and yet no one seemed to notice.

We continued on, and I watched the driver carefully. Each time one of these strange events happened, or I noticed one, he didn't react. He simply drummed his fingers on the wheel, continuing on, with no mention of the anomalies. This meant that either he didn't see them, or he was too used to them by now to even point them out.

Anokhin glanced around now and again, his lips moving silently as he continued to recite the mathematics in his head.

The worst part about Havana wasn't the anomalies; it was the way everyone seemed to deny them, how people's minds slid past the impossible, because if they accepted it, all hell would have broken loose. Of course, that didn't mean there weren't rumors—there were always rumors.

The car turned into Miramar, driving past hedges and villas, until it stopped in front of a safe house, which I assumed was Angleton's.

We were led in through a side entrance, up a narrow stairwell that would help minimize the talk of three foreigners being brought to a place that was supposed to be above ground.

The door was open, and we were slid inside, led through a respectable hallway until we found ourselves in a dark room with the curtains drawn.

And there stood Angleton, by the desk in shirt sleeves, his tie loosened, his expression both composed and chaotic at the same time. He looked more sleepless than usual, his eyes darting here and there excitedly.

He looked at Anokhin first, his eyes taking in the man's tremor, the pallor, and his shaking hands. Then he looked at Alicia and me.

"You made good time," he said.

I scoffed. "Basil's people made good time," I replied.

Angleton smirked slightly, and then I noticed the other man.

He was tall, unlike any of the other Americans I had seen, with strong shoulders that belonged in colder weather. The man stood near the Mirror, relaxing, his face wearing an expression that seemed too nonchalant for Angleton's excitement.

"Ah," Angleton said, as if he'd just noticed the man as well. "Calder, this is Bill Easee."

Easee looked me up and down, as if appraising me. He was African American, in his mid-forties, his hair cut close and starting to gray at the temples. When he spoke, his accent was West Country, Somerset—a rural accent. However, from his intelligent eyes, I had expected something closer to Oxford.

It was like he himself was an anomaly thrown into a greater anomaly.

"You look older than your file," he said at last.

"Don't we all, after we've dealt with the Mirror," I replied.

The corner of his mouth twitched, and I knew I had guessed accurately. He was a man Angleton had hired to deal with the Mirror.

Alicia watched us carefully, squinting at Bill Easee as if trying to determine something. Finally, her eyes lit up.

"Wait, you're Bill Easee?" she said. "Didn't you used to be Bureau?"

"You have the right man," Easee replied, spreading his arms in a guilty shrug.

"So," she responded, her arms folded. "You defected twice, and now you're here."

"What can I say," Bill said. "The Bureau's policies didn't sit right with me."

"And his do?" I scoffed, nodding at Angleton.

Easee didn't answer, but Angleton cleared his throat.

"Listen," he said, "differences aside, Bill is here because he knows Rosyth Dockyard and Invershiel. He knows what to look for when we look at the field... at the pulse that the Mirror is currently pushing out."

"All right then," I said. "What does he know that we don't? And in plain English, please—I'm tired of dealing in theory."

"All right," Easee said, kicking off from his position and walking toward the center of the room. "The way the Mirror is currently working—and Max, I believe you might be slightly familiar with this—is that an emergent consciousness has begun to appear. Out of all the ways any moment can go, it forces coherence to a single one. And time and time again, the system has begun to choose.

"The Soviets are just men with guns; they're not your real enemy. But El Cuadro—call it whatever you would like—that's the thing that keeps the branch stable enough to live in."

I exhaled. "El Cuadro," I muttered. "Yeah, Hawthorne mentioned something like that."

I didn't feel the need to mention that I had seen El Cuadro before, or at least the manifestation of it, if you could call it that. But I could feel that prickling filling inside my head, as if fingers were sifting through my brain. It pressed against me, and I could feel a question forming in my head—a thought:

Ask Angleton about decision locking. Ask him what he's hiding.

I rubbed my temples.

Easee was watching me, as if he knew something had happened, but I didn't say it.

"For the record," I said, "I don't like having to negotiate with a piece of furniture."

"It's not a piece of furniture anymore, Max," Easee replied, breaking my gaze. "It's more like an early computer prototype, able to think where it matters."

But Angleton interrupted before we could continue.

"Enough," he said. "That's why we need Easee. Now we have operational matters to discuss."

At that point, he slid a folder across the desk containing maps, photos, and all the information I had no doubt they were collecting before we arrived.

"This is what you need to know," Angleton said. "Anything you do, anything our Agency assets do, what locals do—it'll all be compartmentalized. Better for our survival."

"So we'll go in blind?" I asked.

"Blind is subjective," Angleton replied. "This means that you get to go in focused. Now I've been doing a lot of thinking, and I know your objective is V4. The destruction of V4 specifically." And he spread his arms in a wide gesture. "I've decided that that's okay. But whatever you do, you do not deviate from this objective. I'm sure that by now you're well aware that I have some other objectives at play here. Those will remain separate from this. Is that clear?"

"Ah," I said. "You mean like decision locking?"

Angleton kept his face blank. "I won't ask how you know that. It's secondary hardware," he said. "Not in your swim lane."

Anokhin raised his hand for the first time, as if a schoolboy asking for permission to speak.

"It is not secondary," he began hoarsely. "It is the sole reason—"

But Angleton gently cut him off before he could continue.

"Doctor, I respect your opinion, but your function is to keep breathing and focus on the resonance. Once you actually get in front of V4, your job will be to program the rig so it actually works. That's it."

Alicia's eyes flashed, but she didn't say anything.

"Here's the Agency's official position," Angleton continued. "And keep in mind, I had to put in work to get them to even accept this. If you must, destroying the facility is okay, but our goal is still to recover any core Mirror material if you can."

"Fair enough," I scoffed, "but you should know the Bureau's position is total neutralization. No recovery, no study—we cut the tree's roots."

"I respect Director Moreau's clarity and her theory," Angleton replied, watching me. "But clarity doesn't win wars."

I laughed. "Well, Angleton, I guess we'll just have to agree to disagree. But if we're in the position to destroy as much of it as we can, I hope you know we'll take that."

He nodded. "I would expect nothing less," he replied, and I couldn't tell if it was a compliment or not.

"Oh, one more thing," Angleton continued. "MI6 has found out there's something here. I'm assuming Philby is realizing that he's outmanned and outgunned, and in a bit of desperation, he's trying to use MI6 to stabilize his plans. They've begun to make inquiries, requests for access, even demand a liaison present."

"Philby," I said, my jaw clenched.

"Philby at the moment is in Washington," Angleton replied. The corners of his mouth turned down slightly, as if he were talking of something disgusting. "But MI6 is an organism, and Philby knows that. That's why he's using it. It moves even when one limb is compromised."

"So they're looking around?" I asked.

"They're pushing, that's for sure," Angleton replied. "But I'm stonewalling them. The moment they decide to act, however, you'll get another variable in a city that's already turning sideways, and if they show up here, all hell will break loose. Then the Soviets will notice, and that's when this firefight turns public and becomes a headline."

Anokhin's eyes lit up then. The mention of the Soviets had stirred something in his mind.

"Kolyadin," he breathed. "He will be here soon, if he is not already."

Angleton's eyes flicked to him.

"Yes, we do have indications of Soviet movement," he said. "It's not enough for us to confirm Kolyadin himself, but it's enough to assume that Soviet presence here will soon be far broader."

"Well, that's reassuring," I muttered.

Angleton ignored the comment and continued.

"For now, you'll stay here. Rest, eat, get some sleep if you can. You're not going to go out alone or contact anyone. If you need something, you can go through my channels."

"And if we need the Bureau?" Alicia asked.

Angleton nodded toward the phone. "See if they pick up," he replied.

I watched him carefully. I didn't think Angleton was a bold enough man to stonewall us from the Bureau itself. And yet, it was very clear what his play was.

The CIA currently controlled the operation, and as such, the CIA set the ground rules. The Bureau was a liability.

Angleton seemed to have decided the meeting was over and continued to operate as such, gathering his maps from the briefing table, which sat in the center of the room.

"Tomorrow we'll begin recon for the strike unless the Russian seems to be collapsing sooner. Then we'll move tonight, or whenever time affords. Oh, and Calder," he said, as if an afterthought, "you and I both know what happens when you get too close to the Mirror. So be careful there, will you?"

I simply nodded, and Angleton left, closing the door behind him softly.

For a moment, the room was quiet and uneasy. Easee shifted his weight, as if he was going to speak again, and then had thought better of it.

But Alicia had no such reservations.

"Bill," she said finally. "If this Mirror is steering us, which it seems obvious now that it is, how do we keep it from slowing us down when push comes to shove?"

Easee glanced at me quickly, then looked away.

"You act fast," he replied, "so fast that even the Mirror doesn't know what hit it."

"So what?" I asked, almost sarcastically. "Catch it off guard?"

"The Mirror is a machine," he replied. "It's not a consciousness like you and me. It operates for survival, but that means its consciousness is rudimentary. So yes, catch it off guard."

With that, Bill Easee left the room, leaving Alicia and me alone with Anokhin, who seemed to be falling asleep as he stood there.

We sat in silence for several minutes until his breathing steadied and he was dozing, his head tilted back slightly, his mouth open, drool forming at the corners.

Alicia grabbed the cuff of my coat and pulled me into a narrow back closet, which was directly off the room. She shut the door behind us quietly.

I glanced her up and down, and for the first time in a long time, I genuinely smiled.

"Well, this is intimate," I said.

She scoffed. "Enough with the nonsense, Max. Angleton is playing two games. You know that, right?" she said, looking up at me.

"Angleton is always playing games," I replied. "I think I finally got an angle on how he acts, and it's paranoid as hell."

She smirked. "That is true, but you heard him. He wants salvage and pieces if he can get them."

"I heard him," I said, "but I also saw another admission beneath the surface."

"Decision locking?" Alicia asked.

I nodded. "Well, that was one of two. Anokhin calls it a key, and Angleton calls it secondary hardware. That just means Angleton is lying, but that's not the real thing I noticed."

"What then?" she asked, her face closer to mine now.

"I noticed," I replied, "just how eager Angleton was to agree with my terms, even when I threw out the fact that we might leave no pieces in our wake."

She thought for a second, then nodded. "You're right," she said. "So what does that mean?"

"Well," I said, "it means we're being gamed from every side. The CIA wants spoils, MI6 wants access, the Soviets want their war device, and everyone tells them they're doing it for the greater good. But even Angleton realizes that the longer V4 runs, the greater danger it poses. He might not want the chain cut—not explicitly—but he's worried about what it'll cause."

Alicia's gaze held mine, and I felt a ping in my chest. We had been so foreign of late, and now, at this point, I wasn't quite sure what I wanted for us. When this was all over, did I want something more?

I pushed the thought from my mind, along with the memories of Lisbon, the Scottish cold, the Andes, and all the dead we'd left behind.

"We need to finish this, Max," Alicia said, and I nodded. "We cut it at the roots. Not for any of this political bullshit, not for the Bureau, and certainly not for the Agency."

Alicia stepped closer, and she put her arms around my neck, looking up at me, and for a moment, her voice softened.

"We cut it so you can wake up and know which life is yours," she said, "so I can stop watching you disappear one memory at a time. I don't want to see this happen anymore, Max, no matter what happens to us after this."

My throat tightened, and I nodded.

"Yeah," I murmured, "let's steal our lives back."

CHAPTER 22
LEDGER LINKS

Angleton read the ledger fragment three times over before he finally admitted he couldn't crack it.

It sat in a plain envelope with no insignia. The Kingstown postmark was half-smeared, as if obscured by some salt stain from a boat. Inside, there was torn paper, hand-ruled columns, dates, numbers, shipping codes, initials, symbols, and then one word in block letters: STANLEY.

He sat in the safe house, the fan churning the warm air. Beside the ledger, he kept the brass and copper node Lucy had stolen from the distillery, wrapped up like a relic. It was the decision locking node—perhaps the most important item he had.

But the fragment he held now was coded in a way he didn't recognize. It was half ledger, half cypher, built for someone who already knew the form.

Bill Easee couldn't crack it, either. He'd given it his best shot. But there was one man Angleton knew who could crack it. He was confident in that much.

Max Calder.

Calder was renowned in the espionage world for seeing patterns others couldn't, for his incredible memory, and for his knack for cracking codes. And so Angleton wrote a short note, sliding the fragment into an envelope.

> *To Raven, fragment recovered from islands, MGB accounting format, can't crack the encoding. Stanley repetition. If it means what I think it means, it may be actionable. Please decode and return the results. Keep original secure.*
> *I retained a copy.*
> *J. J. Angleton*

He pressed a button, and a station man appeared instantly. "Get this to Calder now."

The man nodded. Angleton sighed, pausing to stretch for a second. He stared at his reflection in the darkened window, again refusing to glance at the mirror mounted on the wall or give it any attention.

He folded the copy of the fragment, slid it into a file marked PHILBY, and locked the drawer.

Not yet, he thought, but soon.

We were holed up in a second safe house now. When the courier knocked on the door, I only opened it after double-checking twice. He handed me a sealed pouch stamped DIPLOMATIC MATERIAL and departed without a word.

I opened it and glanced inside. There was some torn paper in a plastic sleeve, along with a note from a man I could only assume was Angleton.

The safe house we were in now wasn't as nice as the one in Miramar. Angleton had relocated us only hours after our last meeting, citing security concerns. Though I wasn't sure if he was worried about security from the Russians or worried that none of us were stable, particularly me and Anokhin.

The safe house was an old dentist's office with a quiet stillness that made me uncomfortable. There was an old chair in one corner, a wall mirror above a sink which occasionally caught the light that managed to slip through the shuttered windows. Alicia had moved the one desk lamp away from the mirror as well, an unspoken agreement between us all that we didn't want to see what was inside it.

Anokhin slept in the back room, breathing rapidly. With each passing hour, he looked older in cruel increments. His hands were stiffening, even in his sleep, his mouth muttering incessantly. I worried that the man was in his last moments now. He was probably seventy or even older now—maybe even eighty.

I laid out the fragments of paper on the desk, shaking my head. It was thin paper, written in cramped columns, the kind hastily scrawled. With nothing better to do, I began to copy the columns, trying to find the structure and see what rhythms and habits lived within the paper.

As I did, my head throbbed behind my left eye, the pressure forcing me to wince. It was an incessant throbbing that left me almost debilitated. Tomorrow we would end it all, but today I had to deal with Angleton's latest side quest.

This stupid ledger—and a ledger it was.

"It's not a cypher," I muttered to myself. "Hell, it looks like accounting. Has to be balanced, even when it's lying."

And it was exactly that, with two entries, each sharing the same date code but different amounts. Everything was paired with double entries, debits disguised as shipments. Though it was written in code or otherwise obscured, it was very clear to me that there was a certain math to it. The two-letter prefix was the location in the shorthand. LD would mean London, HB stood for Havana—maybe "Havana build," and GR could refer to Grenada.

I continued to read, my eyes falling on the text where STANLEY was printed next to LD-317. The numbers didn't seem to be bribes; they were far too clean, too scheduled. Instead, they resembled salaries or retainers—my best guess.

My thoughts drifted back to Glasgow Central Station, to Finch saying the word "Stanley," then collapsing, his blood pooling in front of us.

"Kim Philby," I exhaled.

Alicia went still behind me.

"What?" she asked.

"Stanley," I said. "Look here, it's the handler line. It's Philby's Soviet pipeline."

She crossed the room and bent over my shoulder.

"Can you prove it?"

I pointed to the margin. "Look here. There's a freight notation that repeats with every Stanley entry—RKI. My best guess is it means Rosyth, Kingsway, and Invershiel."

I continued to unscramble it. For the first time in a good while, I was interested in something. My mind was occupied, and the headache began to lessen. The more I decoded line by line, the less opaque the ledger became.

But each time, the pairing would make it unmistakable. The name STANLEY was the money valve. That was what all of this hinged upon. It sat at the heart of Philby's Soviet architecture, the game he had been building.

"This ties him to Havana," Alicia said, exhaling as she watched.

"And to how they got the material here," I replied. "The movement, the logistics, even the cover support."

"So what you're saying is..." Her voice trailed off.

"I'm saying this is the smoking gun," I replied, smiling.

I wrote a brief and concise summary for Angleton, with only one line at the end that I added for personal effect:

"If this is the smoking gun, I want to deliver the proof."

I folded it carefully, sealed it in an envelope, and handed it to one of the CIA men sitting near the front of the dentist's office. I knew it would find its way to Angleton—and maybe to MI6.

I just had to wait now.

By the late afternoon, Havana's mirror-torn pulses had worsened. It began with the lights. The fan slowed, the lamps dimmed, as if shaken by some electrical pulse, and somewhere outside, radios turned to static. It was as if everything had dimmed at once, and then everything returned at once with a bright snap, harsh enough that it made my eyes sting.

It woke Anokhin, too, and I could hear him coughing, the sound wet and deep. Alicia went to him immediately, placing two fingers on his wrist. He stared up at her, his pupils wide and glossy.

I shook my head.

"The field's accelerating," I muttered.

"It's spiking," Anokhin rasped in Russian.

"He said that yesterday," Alicia replied.

"No," he said. "Yesterday it was growing. Today—entropy, entropy—it's collapsing in on itself."

I didn't like the word. I didn't like watching the power surge either. As I peered through the shuttered window, I could see the neon signs on the street flickering, flaring blue-white, then returning to normal before turning off entirely.

It was all too much.

"You feel it?" Alicia asked, coming up behind me.

I didn't answer as she continued to speak.

"Look at the power grid," she murmured. "It's tied to the pulses from the Mirror."

I nodded. "And if it keeps scaling, Havana becomes a loop. I think Anokhin's right—it'll collapse in on itself."

I walked back over to Anokhin then and bent down in front of him.

"How long do we have?" I asked.

His eyes were closed now, and he was rocking gently.

"It's close," he whispered. "V4 is approaching a critical stage. The node is beginning to project other sites—other anchors—beginning to overlap them aggressively for protection. It'll become harder to reach."

I stood then and glanced at the attaché case.

"We're out of time," I said to Alicia, and she nodded.

I smiled slightly.

"Alright then," I said. "Let's tell the CIA men we need to speak to Angleton. Now."

The man himself arrived in person just before dusk, his collar damp with sweat, his expression tighter than usual. He shook his head, remaining standing, my decoded summary in his hand as if it were a weapon he had been handed.

"Well?" he asked as he entered the room. "What's the breakdown?"

"You got my transcript?" I asked in response.

He nodded.

"Stanley," he murmured. "So, Philby's channel has a ledger."

"It's enough to be actionable," I said.

He nodded slowly. "Not today, but soon. Today, we have more important things to focus on. Like the city. From the CIA's model, the recursion is escalating faster than we expected. Power failures are rolling through the city now in predictable waves. The official channels are calling it a weather system. Cuban government's calling it sabotage. But even now, the normal people are being forced to accept it."

"Which means—" I began.

"Which means," he cut me off, "I already know why you called me here. We need to move fast."

Silence settled for a beat before Angleton nodded toward the attaché case.

"Use Fraser-Smith's device," he said.

Alicia raised her eyebrows. "You're giving us explicit permission now?"

Angleton nodded. "That's correct," he replied, his voice uncomfortable, as if he felt like he were tasting defeat. "Before, I was willing to write it off. Now I'm outright endorsing it. Call it what you want. But I'm doing what I need to do."

"This is Mirror operation only, though," he said, stepping forward. "You focus on V4 and its web. Don't involve yourself in Cuban politics. Don't involve yourself in any other devices or projects you encounter. You do not deviate."

I crossed my arms. "We'll burn whatever we can reach," I said.

Angleton glanced at me, but he didn't argue, and that was good enough for me. That was concession.

"I'll brief you later in full," he continued. "But for now, just know, I'll provide diversions. Urban assets. Power manipulation if we can handle it without tripping the entire grid. Easee will coordinate any post-strike containment that we need."

"And what of the Soviets?" Alicia asked.

Angleton glanced toward the back of the room, where Anokhin sat. "They'll come," he said. "We can assume they're already here, including Kolyadin."

He turned back to us.

"You act now," he said. "Tonight. If we wait, the city may fold in on itself. And at that point, none of us would be able to write a report even clean enough to survive in Washington."

"We're not doing this for your reports, you know," I shot back. I wasn't sure if I liked the man or hated him. But one thing was sure:

He got on my nerves.

He nodded once, the corner of his mouth turning up slightly, as if he knew exactly what I was thinking.

"I know," he said. "Do it anyway. I'll brief you in more detail tonight. Then we strike before midnight."

And just like that, he left as quickly as he'd arrived. We

waited for several moments, letting the silence and Anokhin's heavy breathing permeate the room again. Then Alicia spoke.

"He's hiding something, you know," she said.

"I know," I replied.

"But," she said, glancing at the attaché case, "he gave us the window."

I nodded. Across the room, Anokhin turned his head.

"Tonight," he called loudly, as if he had only heard part of the conversation.

"Yes, tonight," I replied. "Soon."

Anokhin closed his eyes, and when he opened them, they were focused again.

"Then," he said, "I will guide the tuning until I become useless."

I didn't lie to him. I knew he would die soon. But I also knew that he was committed to shutting the Mirror down before that, just as much as I was.

London didn't have the same heat as Havana, but it had that incessant cold rain that splattered against windows and hissed against the city's old stone bricks. Elspeth Moreau stood in the Bureau's headquarters, a cable in her hand and graying hair that revealed more stress and less happiness than she let on.

The cable was brief, routed through a channel that should have been shut down months ago.

Havana destabilizing, it read, *CIA maneuvering, Calder and Rayes in place, Soviet pursuit active, V4 escalation beyond Scottish profiles,*

and below that another line:

The Nine recommend to Director Moreau: distancing / plausible deniability as priority.

She shook her head, an immense sadness overtaking her. They'd started to fold. It wasn't cowardice, at least not in the way you could name it. Bureaucracy always had an instinct for self-preservation, the same instinct that led MI6 to deny any wrongdoing by Philby until it inevitably became public. The Bureau had existed on paper for so long that it had begun to believe it could survive by simply staying invisible.

Moreau shook her head. Across from her desk, Opal stood, her coat still damp from the rain, her eyes cautious.

"They want you to sign the disavowal," Opal said.

Moreau stared at the page—the page Opal had handed her, with a spot for her signature below it. The language was immaculate, but the answer was clear. It would cut Calder and Rayes loose cleanly, turning them into rogues in case Havana burned to the ground.

"They're afraid," Opal continued carefully. "If this goes public… if Havana collapses, MI6 will blame us. I'm sure they'd love to get us back for what happened at ANGUS. The Foreign Office will—"

"The Foreign Office can blame the weather," Moreau replied, cutting her off. "Or rum or God; I don't care."

She stood and walked to the office mirror by the filing cabinet, watching herself carefully in it. She welcomed it. She welcomed that slight difference, that slight shift in her perception that meant that the Mirror was affecting her as well.

Beneath them, Kingsway was sealed and silent, supposedly. But Moreau knew better.

She returned to her desk and picked up her pen.

"Director—" Opal began.

"I'm not signing it," Moreau said.

Opal exhaled, the relief evident in her tone.

"Then we're exposed," she said.

"Oh, we're already exposed," Moreau replied. "Those ancient vultures on the board just haven't admitted it."

She opened the bottom drawer of her desk, removing a sealed envelope of cash and a slim folder marked HAWTHORNE / Failsafes.

"I want this routed to Havana," she said. "Directly. Not

through MI6, the CIA, or any other committee. Calder may need it, if it even reaches him in time."

"If they trace it—" Opal hesitated.

"Let them," Moreau replied. "If the Bureau dies, it'll die doing something other than covering up its mistakes."

"And if the others find out you're moving resources off the books?" Opal asked.

"Then they'll do what cowards do," Moreau said, her mouth tightening. "Pretend they never knew my name and pretend I worked for someone else."

She sighed and glanced through papers and photographs on her desk—images of damp brick tunnels, a schematic with annotations, and a dead man's handwriting. Among them was a single sentence that she had circled and underlined twice:

The foundations remain.

She shook her head, feeling the decision settle in her mind as if it were inevitable. And yet she knew, without question, that it was her own.

"And get me a courier," she said to Opal suddenly. "Off books. I have one more delivery I need to make."

Opal nodded once and turned to leave. However, she paused at the door.

"Director," she asked quietly, "are you certain?"

Moreau looked down at the disavowal on her desk, then out through the rain-soaked window into London beyond. She nodded.

"I'm certain," she said.

When Opal departed, Moreau sat alone in the Bureau's quiet, listening. Listening to the rain outside, to the low, barely audible hum beneath it that had begun to register the past few weeks—the hum that had brought with it memories of the Mirror.

She closed her eyes. Somewhere far away, Calder and Rayes were walking toward a distillery that held a monster of a machine—a machine that had learned to defend itself over time.

Toward an end that no agency wanted, because an ending meant no more leverage.

She opened her eyes and turned over that photograph of the little girl on her table, tracing the girl's face gently with her finger.

"I'm sorry," she said aloud, though if it was to herself or to the little girl, she wasn't sure. "I'm sorry I won't... I'm sorry I won't be able to see you," she said.

Then she exited the office, leaving the disavowal and the picture behind. Beneath London, Kingsway awaited.

Elspeth Moreau went to meet it with open arms.

CHAPTER 23
DISTILLERY DESCENT

Angleton stood over a map of the distillery, one hand flat on the island as if he were trying to pin it down. With his other hand, he tapped a wristwatch that seemed to be stuttering here and there, as if time itself were faltering.

"Two fronts," he said, "will fracture their response so you can go down their throat."

He looked at the map, focusing on the square marked DISTILLERY in neat block letters.

"The city will take the first hit. We'll take out the telecoms via the substation. It will be controlled, limited. The point won't be a blackout, but confusion. Every Soviet with a handset will suddenly be shouting into an empty room, and with communication off the table, that's where we will shine."

I stood watching him, my arms folded.

"And the road?" I asked, nodding toward the coastline that stretched from here to the distillery.

Angleton's finger traced the route.

"We'll add choke points here. An accident. A burned truck, maybe. Nothing dramatic, but enough that we can shut down and delay reinforcements that will arrive too late."

He looked up at Anokhin. The doctor sat there trembling in

his chair, his hands shaking in his lap. His face had thinned more since that afternoon. The skin was blistering now, dry and cracked. Stale blood was caked on his lips from where they had split, but his eyes were still sharp.

"Sir Anokhin," Angleton said, "you'll tune the rig. You just have to stay upright, and that'll be your contribution."

"I am not—" Anokhin coughed hard, then swallowed and continued, "I am functioning."

"Good," Angleton replied.

Anokhin turned his head toward the corner, where Lucy Howard stood just beyond light's reach, her coat buttoned up despite the Cuban heat. Her hair was pinned all the way back, a small chain glinting at her throat. She looked disinterested in the whole ordeal, but I knew better than any man that when Lucy Howard looked disinterested, it was likely because she was carrying some great weight.

Angleton's voice tightened as he spoke, as if he were bitter, resentful that she was even here.

"Howard will guide you in," he said. "She's been inside before."

Alicia watched Lucy like a hawk, her eyes piercing while Lucy met her stare with a flat, professional calm. I raised my eyebrows, watching them. It was like watching two panthers circle each other, each waiting for the other to strike.

"Now," Angleton continued, "I'm sure you're well aware that the Soviets will be prepared for anything we throw at them. At least, anything we throw at them short of a firefight, and so that's what we're going to give them. A CIA task force will hit the front gates loud. It'll pull eyes... it'll pull guns. While that happens, you'll go in through the access route Howard established."

He slid a grainy photograph across the table, depicting a cut fence, and beyond that, I could make out the freight elevator that we had seen before.

"At that point, it'll be on you," he said. "You get down there, apply Fraser-Smith's coils, and stop V4."

"And your people?" I asked.

"My people will create noise. I have Bill Easee assigned to the task of preparing containment and extraction. As for me, I'll remain offsite. I'm not about to walk into any black hole that eats memory. Now listen carefully. Need-to-know remains intact. At this point, you have confirmation from both me and Director Moreau of what you need to do. So go do it."

I nodded, and Alicia followed suit. Lucy kept her gaze firm, and she didn't move.

"All right, then," Angleton said. "We move in thirty. If the Russian collapses before then, we move sooner."

Anokhin laughed, his voice dry as paper.

"Then you should hurry," he said.

"Oh, and one more thing," Angleton said, nodding. "I called her. For what it's worth, for the past two days, I haven't been able to get in contact with Director Moreau. I'm not sure what to make of it, but she hardly seems like the type that would keep me waiting. So just be cautious."

I nodded, and he stepped back.

"Well, good luck, then." He scoffed. "Then again, I don't believe in luck."

We rode out in an unmarked sedan, black and too clean to be Cuban. The driver in the front smoked a cigar, the ash falling onto his trousers. Lucy sat up front in the passenger seat. I sat behind her, Fraser-Smith's attaché case between my boots. Next to me was Anokhin, and beside him sat Alicia.

As we drove, I glanced out the window, watching Havana slide past, already half undone and collapsing in on itself. As we crossed out of Miramar, a section of the skyline dimmed, then snapped back with a harsh flare that made the rearview mirror show my face—older, then younger, then mine again. Then I saw the face of SL-042 staring back at me before I blinked, and it was gone.

The radio crackled from the dashboard. "Switchboard down, switchboard down." Lucy reached forward and turned the volume down.

We drove along the coastal road, the sugarcane fields blurring past. Behind us, several unmarked CIA vehicles followed. Whatever this operation was going to be, it was going to be messy.

I shut my eyes, leaned back in my seat, and tried my best to simply recite my own memories, lest I lose them for good.

We came up on the distillery fast. Our driver slowed the vehicle down and pulled off to the side of the road, letting the rest of the convoy pass. Then he revved the engine again, and the distillery came into view: the walls, the warehouses, the barrels, and the floodlights washing the yard in hard white.

I could see the perimeter patrols moving with a discipline that no Cuban guard detail would have. I knew they were Soviets without even having to look at their uniforms.

Then the night broke open. Gunfire erupted at the front gate —sharp and automatic. Muzzle flashes strobed. I could hear shouts in Spanish, then in Russian. The driver veered to one side, drove through the cane, then brought the vehicle to a stop. while the chaos was still exploding from the direction of the front gate of the distillery.

"Now," Lucy said.

We threw the doors open and slid into the cane field. We'd all done this before. But Lucy moved as if she knew this place like the back of her hand, which I was sure she did. She kept us low, leading us diagonally along the fence line. Alicia half-carried, half-pulled Anokhin to help him keep up with us.

We reached the cut fence, the wires still re-twisted almost too neatly. Lucy peeled it open.

"Single file," she said.

"Oh, so this was you," I muttered. "I should have known."

"Should have known," Alicia echoed. "Sloppy work."

Ahead of us, Lucy turned and smirked at her.

We slipped through one at a time. The gunfight at the front gates drew the floodlights and most of the shouting. We crouched near the fence line, watching the chaos. Ahead of us, Lucy waited three full seconds longer than I would have before signaling us forward just as the last guard turned his back to jog toward the gates.

And just like that, we crossed behind the stacked barrels. Lucy led us directly to a service door. She nodded at me, and I stepped up, my hands already on the lockpick set I kept in my pocket. It took me scarcely half a minute to pick the lock. The Russians relied far more on brute force than they did on any type of lock security here.

Once inside, the distant noises were muffled, only the gunfire remaining clear. There was the freight elevator. Up close, the constant pulse and hum from the Mirror was louder than the noise of the gunshots and chaos in the background. It was so loud that it wasn't just sound. It was pressure, making my teeth buzz, my eyes blur, and my skin prickle.

Anokhin shuddered, holding his hands out, as if he half-expected to be whisked away to death at that very moment.

"It is awake," he said, and I nodded.

We crossed briskly to the elevator door, and without hesitation, I pressed the button. I heard the rumbling before we saw the doors open, the elevator slowly crawling upward to the surface.

When the doors slid open, my breath fogged instantly. Inside the elevator, it was cold. So, so cold. It was an icy cold chill unlike anything Cuba had ever known. I stepped in, the floor vibrating beneath me, as if there were some heartbeat pulsing in an irregular rhythm below us. Alicia guided Anokhin inside, and Lucy followed last, her gun in hand. She glanced at me once, as if she wanted to say something, then hit the descent lever.

The doors closed, and we began to go down.

"Well, here goes nothing," I said.

The elevator dropped, lurching, the sensation sickening. My stomach lurched as it swung downward, the light flickering. Anokhin gripped the rail, swaying, his knuckles white.

"Steady," Alicia said.

I watched the indicator panel. The needle moved back and forth wildly. We passed the level we should have hit and kept going. Then, all of a sudden, the elevator shuddered again and stopped. The doors slid open—revealing the same concrete building we'd left, the same area we had just come from. But the air was colder now, and there was no sound of gunfire.

Lucy swore softly.

"The hell," she muttered, then hit the lever again.

I couldn't help but chuckle.

"You'll get used to it," I told her.

Alicia shot me a glance. I wasn't sure if it was jealousy or a question.

This time, the door shut, and the elevator didn't strain. Instead, the air grew colder still as we descended, the hum thickening. Finally, the elevator slowed, the doors opened, and we found ourselves in an industrial hallway lit by buzzing fluorescent tubes. Cables ran along the ceiling, pipes running here and there, no doubt some type of cooling system.

Anokhin stepped out, nearly falling to the ground, but Alicia caught him and pulled him up with her. We moved ahead slowly, our weapons up, stepping into the heart of where the machine had taken hold. The hallway was dark, with flickering fluorescent yellow lights above, and we continued onward.

We moved past the door marked LABORATORIO 7 in Spanish, then a minute later, we moved past the same door again. Lucy glanced over at it and paused.

"We—" she began, but Alicia's hand shot up.

"Keep moving," she said, trudging forward.

Lucy rolled her eyes but followed behind her, and I continued, Anokhin standing next to me. The man had been muttering this whole time, but now he began whispering numbers and sentences that made little sense.

Suddenly, chaos erupted. One of the doors was thrown open, and a guard lurched out from it, his rifle raised. Before he could move, I fired a shot, and the man jerked, his body falling down. As we walked past him, however, I turned to look again, and his body was up. He was standing, confused, as if I had never shot him the first time.

With a quick motion, I thrust my gun under his chin and pulled the trigger again, and this time, the man's body crumpled again, staying on the ground. I wasn't sure if I had just killed his doppelgänger or the same version of him in a different time, but it mattered little. Whether it was an echo, a doppelgänger, or something else, we had to move on. We didn't slow down, even though Lucy glanced around uneasily, as if she wasn't used to this. I had to remind myself that she wasn't. This chaos that I treated as normal was something she no doubt treated as magic.

We continued until the corridor diverged, splitting into two other corridors. We paused there for a second. I wasn't sure which way to go, but then Anokhin raised a trembling arm and pointed.

"This way," he said. "I can feel it pulling. The web is louder there."

I nodded and led the way. Lucy had fallen behind me. Although Angleton had made it clear that she was supposed to lead the mission, she let me take the lead. Whether it was out of fear or out of respect, I couldn't tell.

Suddenly, gunfire erupted. I grabbed Anokhin and threw him against the wall, following closely, flattening as two guards came around the corner, running, shouting in Russian. Lucy and Alicia drew their pistols at the same time. Lucy shot first, firing twice. One guard crumpled. The other man swung his rifle up toward her. There was a flash of light, and he fell as well, a bullet hole directly between his eyes. Alicia held her pistol in her hand, smoking, and stared down at the man's body as he lay on the floor.

"Well, at least some of them are still human," Alicia muttered.

"And some of them aren't," I replied.

Behind me, Anokhin coughed, hacking, and I glanced at him with concern. Blood darkened his shirt.

"Don't die on us now," Alicia muttered, her hand tightening on his arm as she pulled him to his feet.

He laughed weakly.

"I am trying my best," he said.

Lucy glanced back, her eyes meeting mine for a second, then she glanced forward and nodded.

"Door ahead," she said. "That'll be the main chamber."

As the corridor widened to steel double doors, I wondered what we would find beyond them.

The doors weren't locked, but they resisted all the same. Lucy and I pulled at them, and then, with a hiss—as if some strong magnet had been holding them back—they split open, and we stepped through.

The chamber was just as I remembered it: carved beneath the distillery like some sort of secret cathedral. There, in the very center, sat V4. I glanced around in confusion. To my left, I could see Rosyth Dockyard, ahead was Kingsway, and to the right, Invershiel. It was as if the chamber itself had been split open and all of these other chambers were connected to it—whether directly, as if we could simply walk to them, or whether the Mirror was simply projecting these as a means to protect itself, I wasn't sure. It seemed as if it was wearing them, like some sort of armor or camouflage.

There it sat, smaller than the original Mirror but denser, compact, and squat, pulsing with a silvery light that illuminated the entire cavernous room. I saw a figure moving near the console. One scientist, then two, and then one again, all moving as if in a trance. Lucy raised her pistol, but Alicia caught her wrist.

"No." She shook her head. "They're projections at best, echoes at worst. I doubt they'll stop us."

Anokhin nodded weakly.

"It's trying to defend itself," he said, "projecting prior nodes. It doesn't want you to touch the root."

Barely a foot away from my feet, dust exploded as a gunshot cracked from somewhere above. "Down!" I shouted, but as I did, I felt a white, hot, tearing sensation in my arm. I cursed, looking up. A Soviet guard leaned over one of the rails, his rifle trained down. We scattered as bullets continued to spark off the metal and the concrete floor, sending up small plumes of dust.

I turned, training my gun upward with one arm, and fired. The guard fell down out of sight.

"Max!" Alicia shouted. "You all right?"

I glanced down at my arm, gingerly pulling up my sleeve. It was already soaked in blood, but the wound hadn't hit any arteries. It was non-lethal. I nodded.

"All right, then," she muttered, shoving Anokhin behind a console, and yanking open the attaché case. There gleamed Fraser-Smith's resonance rig, the copper coils shiny, the KX-7 unit with its toggle: null, couple, and break. Anokhin's hands trembled as he looked at it.

"Tell me," Alicia demanded. "Frequency, phase, what do you need?"

Anokhin swallowed.

"It's not one; it's three. All of them," he said.

"Okay. What's the nearest?" she shot back.

"Couple," he muttered. "First you'll need couple," he said, touching the rig as if it were some delicate item. "Then break. If you break it without coupling the correct harmonic quantum, you might strengthen another thread inadvertently."

Alicia nodded and flipped the switch to couple. It was the first time we had used it, but as she flipped the switch, the device began to emit a low whine, a low hum of its own. Alicia cursed under her breath, then lifted the attaché case and moved slowly toward the core.

But as she moved, the space between them warped. I watched, still clenching my arm. Her foot didn't land where her brain expected. It seemed as if the air between her and the V4 Mirror suddenly thickened—as if suddenly the space between her and the Mirror made her move slower with each step. She swore again, louder this time, trying to step around it. But she couldn't. With every step Alicia took closer, her body seemed to slow.

Above us, another guard appeared, opening fire. A piece of catwalk metal broke loose and fell, and Lucy shot back, dispatching the guard as he fell to the ground.

Alicia tried again, pushing toward the core. As she did, the coil vibrated violently, causing her to stagger back.

"It's pushing me back!" she hissed. "Just like the Mirror did in the Andes, Max."

"Yes," Anokhin whispered, his eyes feverish. "It knows—knows what we're trying to do."

Alicia gritted her teeth and tightened her grip. Then she stepped forward one more time, and it was as if the whole chamber had tilted, as if the floor turned sideways. For half a second, we weren't in the chamber anymore. It was as if we were in one of the tunnels under Kingsway, but it was vertical, and we were falling through the air. Then the chamber snapped back, and we stumbled, falling. Alicia barely managed to catch herself and hold the case steady.

Lucy grabbed her elbow, helping her stay standing, but Alicia shook her off.

"Don't," she spat.

Lucy rolled her eyes.

"I'm not your enemy."

Alicia simply laughed.

"That's not how I remember it," she shot back.

"Well, not your enemy today," Lucy scoffed.

All around us, the room seemed to pulse. It was as if the chamber was closing in on us slowly. Anokhin made a sound between a cough and a cry.

"It's compressing the chamber," he muttered, "making the approach impossible... lengthening the time it would take to get there."

Alicia glanced at the core and then glanced at me again. I knew what she was thinking. She didn't have to say it. I had been thinking the same thing.

"Max," she said quietly.

I stared at the V4 core visible in the distance. I could feel the headache throbbing inside me. At the same time, I could feel an irresistible pull toward it. The Mirror wanted me close. It always had, because my broken mind could hold contradictions without fully snapping in half.

"Don't you dare do this alone," Alicia said, as if reading my mind.

I shook my head.

"I'm not," I replied, reaching for the coil.

She caught my wrist, firm.

"Max," she said.

Her eyes were hard, but underneath them, I could see a flicker of fear.

"Last time you went in, you didn't come back clean. You came back broken."

I thought back to ANGUS—to SL-042's smile as we battled, as he took over my memories, as we merged.

"I'm not clean now," I said and pulled free gently, refusing to stop.

She just watched me, helplessness in her gaze. I took the case. Behind me, I could hear Anokhin, his voice firm, unwavering for the first time.

"If you touch it," he said, "it will take you."

"Good," I murmured.

I took the coils and the case and began to walk forward. The

KX-7 whined louder with each step, but I didn't feel the resistance Alicia had. The projections around me shifted, Rosyth surging, Kingsway receding, and Invershiel flashing between it all—but the machine recognized me. Pressure built in my head until my headache felt like it was splitting my skull open, my vision blurring. All the while, the core of the V4 Mirror pulsed, its own silvery light illuminating the room. I could see my own reflection, but it wasn't mine. It was a dozen versions of me, each layered and each out of sync.

I kept walking. I could hear someone shouting my name. Was it Alicia? Was it Lucy? Or was it someone else?

Step after step after step—I wasn't sure how long it took. I simply took another step, and then another. Eventually, I reached the mirror. It sat there in front of me, far smaller than the other Mirrors I had faced before, yet far more dangerous.

Suddenly, the chamber around me dropped away, the sound vanishing. Blood flooded into my lungs, and around me was void.

There was no clean transition. One moment, I was under a Cuban distillery; the next, my boots hit wet concrete and my breath fogged. I knew where I was before even glancing around. I recognized where the Mirror had sent me.

Rosyth Dockyard.

I could see the dock cranes rising into the mist in front of me, a warship half seen through the drizzle in the distance. Men in coats moved along the pier, working, their faces indistinct and blurry. It was as if a copy of the entire dockyard had been projected to some point in time. Or maybe I was projected to that copy. I wasn't sure, but I didn't care. All I cared about was that there, exactly where I remembered it, was the entrance to the Bureau's hidden section.

I made my way through it as if I were in a trance, finding my way downward beneath the dockyard until I reached the very center amphitheater, where the original Mirror had always been. And sure enough, there, in the middle, the original Mirror flickered, intact. A ring of metal surrounded it, humming. The center cracked open, just as I had always remembered it cracking, right before we slid. Cables snaked across the floor, feeding into a console.

As I walked, papers crumpled beneath my feet. Glancing down, I could see they were Krane's notes. His handwriting was as it always had been: tight, arrogant, with equations scrawled across the page as if he had been trying to play God. I crouched down and touched them. The ink was still wet. It shouldn't have been possible. But there it was, beneath my feet. The Mirror had dragged me into its memory of its own birth.

I heard a voice behind me speaking in German—Krane's, younger and excited. I turned. I saw him at the console, speaking to two other men, gesturing, explaining. They didn't see me, though. It was as if the moment the mirror had been first created was on replay, in some subset of time-space.

The KX-7 coil vibrated in my hands. The toggle was still under my thumb, still on couple from when Alicia had set it. I glanced down at the unit, remembering Anokhin's instructions: couple, then break. My mouth was dry, but I flipped the toggle to break. The whine around the device deepened, turning harsher and angrier as the room began to shake. Krane's notes fluttered, flying here and there in some imaginary wind. One page caught my eye, and I glanced at it.

"Failsafe / quench. Invert phase at base. Overload at node origin."

A quench, I smirked to myself—a built-in panic switch. As arrogant as Krane had been, he hadn't been stupid, and there it was—insurance he had against his own arrogance.

I quickly scanned the mirror's base and found it: a small panel recessed on one of the sides, marked carefully with a numerical code. My arm felt numb now, but I winced my way through the pain and headed toward it. My boots splashed through a puddle, and for a second, I could see the Cuban chamber again—Alicia's face twisted with strain, Lucy's gun flashing as she fired at Russians arriving, and Anokhin slumped against one of the walls—and then I was back in Rosyth Dockyard.

I reached the panel and ripped it open. Inside was a simple lever—nothing more, nothing less—Krane's failsafe logic. Still holding the copper coil as its whine intensified even more, I flipped the switch. The coil screamed, the mirror's hum spiking into a jagged howl, the air shimmering around me with heat waves and cold in equal measure.

"Come on," I whispered. "Die, dammit. Die."

I held the coil in place as it shook violently. I didn't understand much of the science, but whatever it was doing, the Mirror seemed to answer, and then the Mirror cracked. I could see the glass in the center crack first, and then the crack spread outward till even the frame broke open into a million pieces. The mist around me froze, and the sound went silent. As I stood there, Rosyth Dockyard began to crumble, the cranes trembling and folding in on themselves, the ship's silhouette in the distance turning to a void. I could see through the ground now, perceiving everything all at once—the entire hallucination, if you could call it that. Finally, the concrete broke apart into the void, its chunks falling into nothing.

I stumbled as the dockyard collapsed, and as it fell, something strange happened. It was as if my mind had suddenly cleared. It was as if some pressure release valve had been swung open, and I suddenly remembered the smell of the loch and ANGUS. It was a weird feeling because I hadn't known that memory had been missing before. And yet now, in an instant, my mind remembered that it had been remembering it as a blur. I remembered other details, too—the time I had spent with Alicia in the Alps near the Swiss border, a memory I had forgotten until this instant, details that had all been missing.

I gasped as I fell backward. In front of me, I saw a figure stepping out of the collapsing mist. It was my face, but a face I instantly recognized—cruel and perfect. SL-042. The Perfect Variant the mirror had once made to kill me, to replace me. He didn't smile. He didn't speak. His mouth simply opened, and he mouthed my name. And then, just like the rest of the dockyard, he cracked apart, shredded by the collapse of the node.

And then it was gone. Before me stood a brick arch, damp and covered in soot and moisture. I coughed and glanced down at my arm. It hung there limply at my side now, blood dripping where I had never managed to properly stop it, but I knew where I was already, and there was still more work to do. It was Kingsway. The web was trying to sling me onward before I could breathe, attempting to force me to stop.

In my hand, I still held Fraser-Smith's coil, still held the resonance rig. But now my mind was sharper. I couldn't help but think that the more nodes I severed, the sharper I became. It was as if the web had been holding my memories hostage.

With each cut, it felt like I was taking my memories back.

CHAPTER 24
MOREAU'S MOMENT

The air around me shuddered, as if someone had struck the world with a hammer, waiting to see what would crack first.

When my boots finally landed on the surface, an echo ricocheted along the walls—the walls of a tunnel far narrower than Rosyth, with a lower ceiling and cables and pipes which ran along the walls like veins.

I knew instantly where I was; it was hard to forget such a place. Kingsway, the London Underground—or a memory of it, I figured—the kind of place that was built to survive, and survive it had.

The copper rig in my hands vibrated, as if it didn't want to be here. The KX-7 box juddered against my palm, the toggle resting beneath my thumb, ready to be flipped in an instant to couple or break, if only I trusted myself to make the decision.

My arm throbbed where the bullet had torn through. Blood was already caked against it, warm and sticky against my skin. I shifted my grip on the coil and grimaced as I tore a piece out of my shirt with my teeth, and then wrapped it around my wounded arm to keep it steady.

Ahead, the tunnel ran straight for maybe twenty or thirty

yards, and then it didn't; a brick archway opened into another corridor, and beyond that, another one, as if it was an infinite length of the same corridor, repeating in on itself again and again.

I stepped forward, and above me I could hear the eerie sounds of trains, trams, and London, but they felt off, as if even the Mirror knew they weren't real, or at least they weren't from this time, as if they were replays of the city above.

The web was replaying a moment in Kingsway, a time when the Mirror here was at its most operational.

I forced myself forward. A sign hung above me from the ceiling, its label cracked in enamel letters: WAY OUT.

It was ironic.

Ten seconds later, I passed it again.

I turned around and looked behind me.

There should have been an empty corridor behind me, and yet it was exactly the same as the one ahead of me, the exact same sign, repeated every ten or so feet.

It was a loop.

"Damn it," I muttered, though my voice felt too loud, echoing off every crack and crevice.

I bent down, picked up a loose pebble from the ground, tossed it in my hand to feel its weight, then wedged it firmly into a crack between two bricks at eye level.

It was a marker—a simple one, but it would work.

I continued walking, counting my steps—thirteen, fourteen, fifteen—and then the WAY OUT sign came back into view again, along with my pebble, just where I had put it.

I exhaled through my teeth.

I wished my cigarettes were still in my coat pocket, but I must have misplaced them in the chaos.

Something in the system was trying to stop me.

I assumed it was El Cuadro; for who else or what else could it be?

Whatever it was, it wanted me to walk and walk and walk

until I collapsed, until the room in Cuba was overwhelmed by the Russians, and until everyone I knew was dead and only the Mirror remained.

So I tried a different door.

Instead of walking straight, as I passed a small, steel service door by the side, I pushed it open, its hinges squeaking from rust as I did.

I shoved it open and stepped into a side chamber where old equipment sat: coils, valves, spools of wire, and a workbench covered in grime.

It wasn't the clean, clinical sterility of Invershiel, but classic wartime British improvisation—make it work, then hide it or deny it later.

On the desk lay some typed papers, not handwritten, and though the letterhead was Bureau, a stamp over it was MI6. Something I was only too familiar with by now—MI6 taking credit for the Bureau's work.

A folder caught my attention. Inside was a photograph of the Rosyth Dockyard cranes.

In the margin, though I didn't bother to read the words, was the handwriting I recognized instantly: Philby's.

I could feel rage and annoyance building within me that the damned machine wanted to survive even at the cost of my own survival.

Instead of simply holding the rig, I turned around in a careful circle, trying to orient it and feel for the node to point a direct way—almost like finding a resonance buzz that felt like a pull.

Sure enough, the coil vibrated harder. It was behaving like a compass. This had to be the direction in which the Mirror was located here in Kingsway. So, stepping out of the door again, I set off, making sure that whenever I walked, I walked in the direction the Mirror must be.

As I continued walking, the hallway didn't loop; instead, it slid away from me.

It seemed as if the surface beneath my feet was sliding. It was so slippery that no matter how fast I walked, I wasn't moving.

"What the hell," I muttered.

I tried again, breaking into a run, but still I couldn't cover any distance. Pain laced through my wounded arm, but I continued running. I simply couldn't make any progress.

I stopped. I would have to be smarter than the Mirror if I wanted to make any progress.

I looked down at my hands.

They were steady, but the floor beneath me seemed to shift, and the air around me filled with a staticky hum, as if the machine were watching and deciding what I experienced.

The loop fought me immediately. It was back again, the sign swinging overhead every time I moved.

Under it all, I could hear, very faint in the distance, as if through some radio transmitter in my head, the sound of gunfire.

That sound motivated me more than killing the Mirror ever could.

I had to get back to Cuba, to Alicia, to Lucy, and so I ran.

"You have to make it stop, Calder," a voice said from behind me.

I whirled around. There, under the fluorescent lights above, stood a woman who looked smaller in stature than I had remembered her last. Her coat was buttoned, her hand pinned back with the same ruthless practicality she always had it. There was a smear of London rain on her collar, dark against the fabric, and though her shoes were scuffed with soot, the rest of her outfit was clean—as clean as she always kept it. Elspeth Moreau.

She stood there, watching me, her eyes tired but alive.

Whether she was an echo or a doppelgänger, I didn't stop to think. I raised my pistol out of instinct, though I knew it likely wouldn't matter if I shot her; the Mirror's web would just paint her back in again. But she didn't flinch; she didn't even look at the gun, keeping her eyes trained on my face.

"Calder," she said, her voice steady.

And now it was my turn to flinch.

"Director?" I asked. "You're—"

"Yes," she replied, a slight smile on her face. "I'm in London." Then she tilted her head slightly. "But I'm also not," she continued. "Kingsway doesn't care about geography, not anymore. It cares about anchors."

"What are you doing here?" I asked.

"I'm doing what I should have done a long time ago," she replied. "The consequences are mine to bear."

I stepped closer to her. As I did, it seemed as if the tunnel bent around her, the sign above suddenly stopped repeating, and I could see far in the distance, as if the tunnel wasn't a loop any longer.

"Why can't I get the coils to bite?" I asked her.

"Because," Moreau said, "Kingsway is held, at least partially, by me."

"That doesn't make any sense—" I began, but she cut me off.

"It makes enough sense. Listen, keep it simple, Calder. You don't have any time for theory. There's something I have to tell you."

"What?" I asked.

"I'm not native to this time branch," she replied, her voice sounding like a confession of guilt.

I didn't respond. I just stared at her, but she continued anyway, as if she'd rehearsed this a thousand times over.

"I built a Mirror in my version of reality many years ago, came out, and found my way to London, where I made a base, built the Bureau into something that I thought would help me get back to my version, to my version of her."

"Her?" I asked.

"My daughter," she replied. "In the branch I came from, I lost my daughter, Alicia." She said the name carefully, almost as if it would shatter if she said it too loudly. "Not the Rayes you know, but mine."

She went on. "If you cut this chain, it's likely my originating reality goes with it, and with that, my version of Alicia."

I stared at her, trying to reconcile everything I had learned in the past thirty seconds. The director of our Bureau wasn't just a director; she was a displaced piece of a different world, lodged into ours like some unfamiliar shrapnel—a doppelgänger.

"And you still came," I muttered.

"Of course I did," she replied, and for a moment, I could see anger in her tone. "I came because Havana is collapsing in on itself, because MI6 and CIA and Moscow and the Bureau are all playing for spoils while the city folds into a hellscape… because Rayes and you are holding the line with a dying man, and not a single committee in London has the heart to save you."

I tried to speak, but she lifted a hand.

"My loss isn't worth the Mirror eating this branch, or this reality," she continued, "not even if it's the last thing I have that feels like home."

The corridor around us stuttered. Above us, I could see a blinking glitch as if the sign were trying to form itself again, as if the tunnel was trying to fight to become a loop again, and yet it couldn't, and Moreau stepped closer.

"I'm the reason it won't let you close," she said. "I'm tied to this joint, and it's using me as an anchor… as an anchor that lets it modify what it wants."

"So how do we—" I began, but Moreau didn't let me finish.

"You'll have a window," she said, "maybe only for seconds. When I step into the Mirror, everything around you will stabilize. It'll have to. It can't hold a living contradiction and keep looping the corridor at the same time. It'll be forced to choose, and when it does, you'll act."

"And you?" I asked.

But Moreau didn't look at me. "I anchor it," she said, "and then I will go."

"You'll die?" I said.

"Mr. Calder," she said softly, a slight smile on her face, "I've been dead since a long time ago. I just kept moving, kept lying to myself, telling myself that I would see her again."

For the first time, I could see her eyes glistening, as if tears shone through her façade. Then she blinked, and they were gone.

"Tell Rayes," she said, "tell her who I was, and tell her to take care of her own mother for me. Let her have a happy ending."

"I don't—" I began, but she shook her head.

"You'll know what to say when you have to say it," she replied calmly.

Then she stepped forward. It was as if, in an instant, she had vanished. A minute later, the world around me shuddered, and the loop broke completely. I could see a corridor now branching off where I hadn't seen one before—the corridor that led exactly to this, to Kingsway's version of the Mirror.

The tunnel was quiet; the loop had stopped, and so I moved closer to the mirror, flipping the switch on Fraser-Smith's rig to break. The box screamed, a low and deep whine vibrating up my forearm, the smell of hot copper filling the chamber.

The tunnel lurched, the system protested, and then Kingsway cracked, as Rosyth had cracked—suddenly breaking open and folding in on itself.

The corridor began to unravel, as if a thread were being pulled from a sleeve.

I could see Moreau's outline in the depths of this Mirror, and then I saw her outline crack as well and begin to fade. Her fingers lost sharpness, their edges dissolving into shimmer; her coat, then even the line of her jaw, until only her face was left. The whole time, she didn't panic or scream; she just stood there, patiently, like a captain going down with her ship, like a director watching the movie they had orchestrated.

As she disappeared for the last time, her mouth moved once. I couldn't hear her voice, but I could read her lips.

Tell Alicia I love her.

And then she was gone, and with a final tear, so was

Kingsway. But it didn't let me mourn or give me time to think. Instead, it grabbed me and threw me.

The cold hit first—that familiar cold I had grown up with during my childhood.

I didn't have the energy or joy to scoff or think about it, but I knew instantly where I was, and the irony wasn't lost on me.

I slammed down then onto a metal grate with enough force to rattle my teeth and the bones in my body.

I winced in pain as pain shot through my arm.

The impact tore the wound open afresh, blood running hot down my sleeve and dripping onto the metal beneath me.

I kept my hands clenched around the coil because if I let go—if it was destroyed—everything would be over.

Here, down in that clinical, bright light, I knew I was in Invershiel.

The chamber was far cleaner than Rosyth and far more refined than Kingsway.

It was that classic black-site laboratory, built by the men of MI6, who thought they could control the Mirror as well and use it for the betterment of everything.

Stainless steel and banks of equipment hummed with a precision that Rosyth never had, controls labeled neatly, and in the center of the amphitheater stood V3.

It wasn't the Russian-developed Cuban core but the Scottish MI6 one.

There was a ring of metal here, tighter, truer, with light bending around it like a restrained breath.

I saw echoes of MI6 technicians moving with practiced familiarity—echoes of men with clipboards bent over consoles—but then the scene stuttered, and those men were gone.

I didn't have time to take it all in. The coil vibrated in my hands, the KX-7 box whining like an animal in pain.

I forced myself up, pressing my good hand against my wounded arm to slow the bleeding again.

Yet, through all the pain, my head felt sharper, different, as if for the first time in years, the haze I'd lived in had thinned. Fewer names slipping, fewer dates shifting, fewer faces forgotten, as if cutting those nodes out was pulling the hooks the mirror had in my skull, ripping them out one at a time.

I could remember Moreau's expression perfectly, even the rain on her collar. I could remember Finch bleeding as he lay dying on the station tiles in Glasgow, and remembered Alicia and every mission we'd ever undertaken.

I still felt sad—sad that Director Moreau was gone without the chance to ever see her daughter—and yet the clarity filled me with an immeasurable excitement.

I moved toward V3, and as I did, the air tightened around me.

"Oh, goddammit," I cursed, pushing against it with all my might. The resistance that had been subtler in Kingsway slammed against me, just like it had done to Alicia back in Havana.

It was as if something were redirecting my very body.

I tried to lift the resonance rig to point it toward the base of V3, but as I did, my arms jerked sideways.

It wasn't my muscles failing, either. It was as if something were grabbing my wrist and redirecting it. I stumbled forward, catching myself on a railing.

Blood smeared across the steel where my wounded arm touched it. I cursed. The lights overhead flickered, and in every stainless-steel reflective surface, I could see my own face.

A dozen Max Calders, layered like cheap copies. But behind all those reflections, I saw something darker—a shape that wasn't quite a man. A shadow with edges, like wet paint.

It didn't move or step forward; it just stared at me. And it pressed down, suffocating me.

The air around me felt as heavy as molten stone. My ears rang, and my vision narrowed. I knew in an instant what I saw.

This was El Cuadro—the web defending itself the only way it could. By making the ending impossible.

In my mind, new thoughts began to form.

Maybe I don't have to.

Maybe I should stop.

Maybe I've done enough.

I could feel my fingers loosening on the coil, against my own will.

I snarled and dug in, tightening my grip.

As I did, the force doubled down.

It hit me in the sternum, and I flew backward, slamming against the grate, the breath knocked out of me. Fraser-Smith's coils clattered to the floor, the KX-7 box skittering across the sterile stainless steel.

I could feel El Cuadro's presence pressing harder against me, as if it were trying to stop me, trying to strip the very skin off my bones.

Then, for a second, the entire lab shifted, and in a blink, there I was peacefully in Lisbon, clacking away at my typewriter, the sunlight filtering through the shutters. A bottle of scotch sat on my desk alongside a case of Cuban cigars—a life where none of this had happened.

Then the image tore away, and I was back there under a Scottish loch, my ribs screaming, barely able to breathe, the coil out of my reach.

Then I heard a voice cut through the pressure.

"Raven. Max. Do you hear me?"

I glanced around wildly.

The air had changed.

A figure stood between me and the shadow, half solid, half static, as if part human yet part not—Hawthorne, or what seemed to be left of him, anyway.

His face wasn't perfectly defined, but his eyes were still there, sharp and focused, like they always had been—so intelligent and so wise at the same time.

He didn't waste words either.

"The Mirror is refusing to die," he said. "El Cuadro is the will of the web."

El Cuadro turned toward him slowly, the pressure pivoting, and Hawthorne stepped toward it.

The shadow began to wrap around him, as if trying to swallow him, trying to force decoherence.

And Hawthorne didn't flinch.

He simply looked at me through the darkness and nodded once.

"Move," he said.

And I moved.

I ran toward V3, grabbing the coil from the floor where it lay, holding the KX-7 box tightly in my palms.

I could feel Invershiel turning sideways in on itself, yet it didn't stop me. Couldn't stop me. It was too busy focusing on overriding the contradiction.

I reached the base of V3 and, holding the box tightly, thumbed the toggle to couple for only half a second, filling the resonance latch as it began to scream. Then I toggled it once more to break.

V3's light flared brilliantly, the mirror frame breaking in on itself almost instantly.

The chamber, the amphitheater around, groaned, cracking under a tremendous weight.

I could hear a shrieking noise, though whether it was El Cuadro, the Mirror, or both—for what was the difference, really? —I couldn't tell.

I saw Hawthorne's outline flickering violently.

I couldn't discern what was happening.

But he stood there, his face blurring, then sharpening, then blurring again.

He looked at me for the last time, gazing at my face, and in his eyes, I could see a sense of pride. Everything I had meant to him, and everything he'd ever been to me: a mentor, a teacher, an engineer, a man who caused everything and yet also solved everything.

And then he was gone, and the lab itself began to come apart.

It didn't explode; it cracked, the steel warping, the catwalks above splintering into a million shards of metal.

I could see El Cuadro trying to reform, the shadow trying to gather, the edges trying to build themselves again in the air.

But Kingsway was gone, Rosyth Dockyard was gone, and now Invershiel was breaking too.

The web had lost its anchors, its roots, its memory chain—everything that kept the quantum focused.

Any pieces that tried to become El Cuadro again instead became smears of darkness, unraveling into strips that dissolved into nothing.

The pressure vanished, and the heat hit my face like a slap.

I was there again, my feet steady on the concrete, my shoulders screaming in protest, my knees buckling beneath me, the copper coil still in my hands.

The Cuban chamber swam into focus as my eyes adjusted.

I could see Mirror V4 pulsing in the center, still alive, its black glass core trapping the light inside wrong.

Alicia was near it, her hair damp with sweat, a pistol in one hand and her other hand bracing Anokhin as the man shook, barely able to stand.

Her eyes snapped to me the moment I returned.

Even as her gaze dropped to my arm, to the fresh blood soaking my sleeve, a mixture of annoyance and concern etched itself onto her expression.

I saw Lucy behind an over-tuned equipment rack, firing

upward at the catwalk, as at least half a dozen Russians returned fire.

Her jaw was clenched hard, her face fierce in the dim light.

Gunfire cracked again, and I cursed, scrambling to my feet, grabbing the KX-7 case from the floor next to me, and sliding it across towards Alicia and Anokhin.

Though Anokhin looked like a man far older than when I'd left, his hands shook as he reached out and grabbed it, holding it tightly.

I tossed myself behind a nearby crate as bullets bit into the concrete near my feet.

I could hear Russian voices shouting.

The fight hadn't paused while I'd been gone.

As I sat there, taking cover from the gunfire, something clicked into place.

I squinted for a second, rubbed my forehead, and squinted again, checking to make sure it was really gone.

The headache—the one that had lived behind my eyes like a parasite—was gone.

It wasn't less, it wasn't dulled; it simply wasn't there anymore.

It was as if, for the first time in years, everything lined up perfectly: my thoughts, my memories, my life.

For the first time in years, I felt like I was a real man again.

I glanced at Alicia and knew, clearly and without any distortion, what she really meant to me.

"Alicia!" I shouted over the gunfire.

She glanced at me and didn't answer, but she nodded as if she somehow knew what had happened.

But Havana's node still had a pulse.

When Anokhin's eyes found mine, I saw in them a determination.

The web was now fatally weakened, but the last tether was still here.

Waiting for us to sever it.

CHAPTER 25
HAVANA HEATWAVE

I was still half-crouched behind the crate when my body finally caught up to where my mind had been only a second before.

The fight kept its own time.

Bullet by bullet, Soviet voices shouted above us, bursts of gunfire stitching sparks through the concrete and sending up blasts of plaster into the air like smoke.

Alicia was near the core, sweating, her hair loose and stuck to her cheek. She had a hand around Anokhin as he clasped his hands around the KX-7 box.

Lucy continued to fire shots, only pausing to reload when she could, but I could see that her ammunition was running low. I could tell from the way her eyes faltered that even she had her reservations.

But my skull was quiet, and that gave me hope.

Somewhere nearby, a Soviet grenade clinked down, rolling across the floor with a small metallic skitter.

Before I could stop, I acted on instinct. I lunged, grabbed it, and threw it back the way it came, but it didn't explode. Instead, smoke billowed from it, thick and gray, turning the chamber into a shadow box.

I realized then, with a cold certainty, that the Soviets weren't trying to kill the Mirror. They were trying to take the room. They were trying to take him.

Anokhin coughed, deep and wet, and I could see through the smoke that blood was darkening his lips.

Alicia swore and shook his shoulders, not too gently.

"Anokhin!" she snapped in Russian. "You need to talk, now!"

His gaze lifted, and for a second, his pupils seemed dilated. But he shook his head, and a second later, his eyes were focused, and the scientist emerged from the broken man with a type of furious, impressive, almost clinical discipline.

"Here," he muttered, "the web is down, but V4 still has inertia, a tether, a last line."

"Where?" Alicia demanded.

He looked past her toward the compact core in the center of the chamber. The black glass center folded, pulsing, silver light crawling across it like mercury over a web.

"Look," he muttered, "In the core's register. The pattern it rebuilds from... the memory... it'll be there."

She fired again. A Soviet body fell from the catwalk above and slammed against the floor hard.

"Echoes are thinning," I muttered. "Look—there's no glitch," because sure enough, there was no glitch. The man's body fell to the floor and stayed there.

"It's not fast enough," Alicia muttered.

The KX-7 whined in Anokhin's hands, the toggle still visible: null, couple, break.

Anokhin swallowed, and he gulped heavily, his throat working as if he had just eaten a mouthful of powder.

"You won't be able to simply break it," he finally forced out. "Break it now, it'll leave a scar, an imprint—there may be something to regrow from."

"Come on, we don't have time for theory," Alicia said.

"It's not theory," he hissed. "It's why Markov died... why Popov."

He doubled over, coughing and hacking, then forced himself upright again and continued.

"It stores, remembers—it'll rebuild from the gaps. You let them rebuild the technology, don't destroy it completely, and it'll still have pieces left."

The machine pulsed harder, and I watched Anokhin, my mind working fast.

Alicia shouted something to Lucy, and Lucy shifted without argument, firing again. Whether it was an angle or a position, I couldn't hear, but I couldn't help but be pleased that, at least for now, they were working together.

Somewhere above, a Soviet voice screamed, then fell silent. It didn't repeat or echo this time.

"Max," Alicia said, her voice lowered. "We have to use the rig on V4."

I glanced at Anokhin's trembling hands, which still held the rig.

"How do we cut it off?" I asked Anokhin. "Cut it at the roots?"

His eyes darted to the coils, then up to V4, and finally to me. He shook his head slowly.

"With me," he said.

Alicia let out a breath I don't think she was aware she had been holding.

"No," she said, as if the idea itself was offensive to her.

But Anokhin simply laughed.

"I am already dead," he rasped. "Every pulse, it takes another year from me. You see it, I see it. And if Kolyadin takes me, Moscow will rebuild the node again. If you break V4 without wiping it completely, someone else will rebuild the technology and find the remnants."

As if on cue, a Soviet voice boomed through the smoke.

"Anokhin," it shouted in Russian, "Dr. Anokhin, you have nowhere to run."

I had my pistol in my hand in an instant.

"Kolyadin," I muttered, like a curse.

But when I glanced at Anokhin, his face was still—not frozen with fear, his body not shaking. Instead, he lifted a hand slowly and grabbed Alicia's sleeve.

"Listen," he said, his voice clear, far clearer than it had any right to be. "You need a conductor, a biological collapse mechanism to wipe the register. I am decohering. We can use that."

"You're not a part," she spat.

"I am a part," he insisted, "but I'm a part they'll never be able to replace quickly. Let me choose my end."

Another burst of gunfire chewed through the concrete below us, far closer than the other bullets had been before.

"They're coming down," Lucy shouted over the chaos.

Sure enough, I could see shapes moving through the fog, masks over their mouths, their rifles trained high. I shot twice. To my surprise, my aim was perfect. They fell to the ground—one, two. Two bodies dropping down, but there were more men in the distance, and we were running out of room.

Anokhin pushed himself up, his shoulders shaking. He grabbed the rig with one hand, dragging himself forward, one step at a time, toward the core.

"Anokhin," Alicia hissed, reaching out for him, but he didn't respond.

He held the rig in his shaking hands, staring at it as if it fascinated him.

"Couple," he said and flipped the toggle.

The KX-7 whined higher, the coils vibrating so hard they blurred. Anokhin stepped forward into the field, the pulsating electrical field around the core. The air around him rippled as he entered, almost like wind or heat waves off a road. The silver light surrounded him, crawling up his sleeves. Then he walked forward.

It was as if the device was consuming him, recognizing him, pulling his calibration signature into itself. As he walked, his body aged. It was as if time had torn him into pieces. In one single violent pull, his hair whitened at the temples, his skin tightened, then loosened again. His hands trembled, but he gritted his teeth and stepped forward further, holding the device tightly with both hands and slamming it against the base of the core, where the metal frame met the folded black glass.

The whine was unbearable, the noise as if reality itself was beginning to tear apart.

"Now!" he shouted, and I saw him flip the switch to break.

As he did, a man emerged from the smoke. Pistol drawn, his eyes fierce, his body tall—maybe even taller than me—I knew, without having ever seen him before, that this was Kolyadin.

Lucy fired from her position behind the rack, a clear sightline across the chamber. But the bullet missed.

"Fuck," she cursed, "I'm all out of rounds."

Kolyadin continued to advance, his pistol trained on Anokhin. He spoke in Russian, and I wasn't sure what he said. His face was terrifying.

In an instant, I trained my pistol on him. The motion, the noise, the smoke—it all made the shot nearly impossible. But I closed one eye, focused, and pulled the trigger. I saw the bullet tear into his chest; the man's face twisted, a mixture of pain and rage, as he squeezed the trigger on his own pistol.

The shot missed. It slid past Anokhin, who looked over his shoulder at us. At Alicia, at me, and at Kolyadin. His eyes rested on the Russian man, who staggered, attempting to drag his pistol upright again.

"Go to hell," he whispered.

The chamber lurched. All the remaining hallucinations, projections, echoes—everything all at once—peeled away from the air, fading from reality, being pulled into the core of the machine. Anokhin convulsed, his body covered in silver now, which crawled over him, the resonance using his collapsing cells like a conduit. The decoherence in his own blood poisoned the register, wiping the stored pattern clean, preventing V4 from ever rebuilding.

I watched as the years hit him all at once. His spine bowed, his face collapsed into lines, and his hands went skeletal. He fell forward against the core, and then he was gone, slipping inside the Mirror.

The core began to implode. It folded inward on itself in a silent, furious roar, light bent around it, snapping back and forth, the silver pulse turning inward, tighter and tighter. The air pressure dropped around us.

For half a second, there was complete silence in the chamber, as if something had swallowed the world's noise.

And then it was gone. Everything was gone.

The core, in the very center of the chamber, sat inert. Its black glass was shattered. The frame was warped, as if it had been cooked from the inside until the melting point, and then left to cool. The device was wiped clean. The field that had been eating Havana was gone.

I heard Alicia let out a sound I couldn't place at first, stumbling forward, her legs unsteady, her eyes locked on the dead core. She stopped, mid-step.

I followed her gaze, because in the last sheen of the dying light that still clung to the warped metal, I saw a figure that wasn't in the room and never had been: Elspeth Moreau, her face calm, her eyes tired, smiling. Then the light died, and the final reflection of the Mirror was gone.

Alicia blinked rapidly, as if trying to force back the tears. There was silence all around us. Lucy rose slowly from behind where she had sheltered, her pistol still raised, scanning the room.

I looked toward the corridor where Kolyadin had come from. As the smoke cleared, I could see his men dragging him back, bleeding, their faces terrified. The fight was over. It wasn't a victory, really. But our enemy had decided there was nothing left to die for.

The Mirror was dead. Anokhin was dead.

Alicia dropped to her knees, her body sagging with exhaustion.

"He's gone," she said.

Lucy's jaw tightened, but she didn't speak.

I sighed deeply, somewhat expecting the room to glitch or for a doppelgänger to appear. And yet, I didn't. Nothing changed. That was how I knew it was real.

I checked my wristwatch, watching the second hand sweep forward in clean, even intervals. There was no stutter, no skip, no repeat. Time simply moved as it had always been meant to move.

Above us, I could hear other voices—American—accompanied by footsteps descending with the sure-footed excitement of men looking to reclaim whatever was left, like vultures over a carcass.

CIA containment teams poured into the chamber, wearing dark suits rather than uniforms. They moved in as if it were a crime scene. Bill Easee appeared among them, his expression tight, stressed for the first time since I had met the man, his eyes scanning the dead core. He looked at me, then at Alicia, then at Lucy, before looking away.

"Secure the perimeter. Nothing leaves. Inventory everything," he ordered the men.

Amidst the confusion, I saw a Soviet soldier at the far end of the chamber, a man who had been half-hidden in the smoke that was finally thinning. He dragged a sealed metal case behind him, Cyrillic stenciled on the side. He glanced around, his eyes wide, then vanished into the smoky corridor and the dark above, taking whatever was in the case with him.

I tried to move, but my arm was too tired. I simply let him go. Someone else would deal with that.

On our side, I watched the Americans slide the canvas-wrapped box out from beneath the console. One of the Americans leaned in toward Easee, muttered something, and then carried it out, tucked under his arm, weaving through the inventory teams as if they weren't even there.

Easee watched the man for half a second, a look of displeasure on his face, then turned back toward the core, saying nothing.

We followed the Americans back up through the corridors into the empty freight elevator, which rose smoothly and opened, letting us out back into Cuba.

Outside, the night had turned to early dawn. The distillery looked ordinary in the ugliest way: floodlights unmoving, smoke, Americans with guns, and the smell of rum that still emanated over the place.

The firefight at the gate had subsided into scattered shouts, and a Cuban truck idled nearby, tending to the wounded. Somewhere in the distance, a dog barked, only once.

I looked toward the town, far off in the distance, and for the first time since we'd stepped into Havana, it looked normal. From the port, faint but unmistakable in the distance, I could hear the tide moving in rhythm again. The pressure that had been sitting over the city like some giant shadow had lifted.

A car pulled up beside us, the tires crunching on the gravel, and Angleton stepped out, wearing his coat despite the heat, his face already composed into a mix of eagerness and regret. He glanced at us, then at the elevator entrance, and then back to me.

"Well," he said, his voice dry, "you did it. You killed the web." Alicia stared at him, her eyes flat.

"It's dead," she said. "Don't pretend you're mourning what you couldn't keep."

"I'm mourning the paperwork I'll have to do," he said wryly, his mouth almost twitching into a smile, then glanced toward the containment teams moving the boxes. "Easee," he called.

Easee approached, and Angleton lowered his voice.

"Lock it down," he said. "No leaks, no MI6 tourists, no Cuban press. We need a clean story before noon today."

Easee nodded. "And the material?"

"What gets reported," Angleton said softly, glancing at the trucks, "is what keeps Havana from turning into an international incident. Maybe an explosion, maybe a fire, but we bury whatever we need to bury to make sure that no one asks why we're here at all. And what gets kept, well…" His voice trailed off, but he didn't have to finish the sentence.

His gaze returned to me.

"Calder," he said, "good work."

And then he walked away.

I could feel Alicia beside me and saw Lucy watching the man walk, her expression a mixture of disgust and respect. In the distance, Havana began to move toward normal again—not because any agency had saved it, but because we'd finally burned the very memory of the Mirror out of the world, right down to the last piece.

Whatever Angleton had chosen to keep in his quiet little compartments and whatever Moscow had managed to smuggle away in that sealed case dragged by the retreating soldier—for a while, at least, the world was normal again.

The Decision Locking Node was logged, unceremoniously, as technical salvage—its casing wrapped, its signatures damped, its paperwork thick enough to slow anyone who tried to hurry it. What could not be erased was redirected. What could not be denied was buried under procedure. By the time the manifests were signed, the problem had been renamed and rendered quiet, the way the CIA preferred its miracles.

They sent it west to the twin of Los Alamos. Site 200 at the University of California's Radiation Laboratory in Livermore was chosen not for secrecy but for discipline—the kind that kept dangerous ideas behind glass and equations behind doors. Edward Teller accepted it without ceremony. He asked for no demonstration and offered no reassurances. He treated the

Decision Locking Node as one treats a loaded gun: stable only so long as it remained untouched. The CIA called it safekeeping. Teller called it containment. Neither word was meant to be comforting.

In Havana, history kept its appointment, and a possible coup loomed. In California, the Decision Locking Node went dark under layers of custody, numbers replacing names, and access slowed to a crawl. Angleton watched the paperwork closely and told himself that delay could still count as restraint. However, delay wasn't an answer. It was a pause—one more narrow space where doubt might survive.

For now, the future had been shipped, signed for, and locked behind a door that did not announce itself.

For now, that would have to be enough.

CHAPTER 26
GHOSTLINES
EPILOGUE

Lucy Howard stepped off the seaplane at Port de Barcelona, the wind tugging at her coat as gulls circled overhead. She moved easily through the crowd—the tourists, sailors, students with cheap luggage—watching every face, each turned inward on its own concerns. It was the perfect cover.

She walked toward the customs shack without breaking stride. A uniformed officer moved to stop her but froze as she flashed a diplomatic envelope marked with American insignia. He waved her through.

Lucy didn't look back.

A black Humber saloon rolled up as she reached the far side of the quay. The rear door opened. A man in a worn suit gestured for her to get inside without speaking. She slid in.

The driver pulled away.

The handler beside her—CIA, third-tier, forgettable—handed her a thin folder. "Headquarters wants acknowledgment," he said. "Your observation on Philby was validated. He resigned yesterday."

Lucy raised an eyebrow. "'Resigned' is an interesting word."

"He's isolated," the handler replied. "Calder's evidence pushed him out. Washington is pleased."

Lucy smirked and took the folder. "Washington is always pleased... until it isn't."

The handler shifted uncomfortably.

She flipped the folder open. Inside:

Surveillance photos of Philby leaving the Broadway building and excerpts of Calder's reports

A cable from Angleton: "Keep her close. She is useful."

That last line made her laugh.

Usefulness was a currency she traded better than any agency.

The car wound through Barcelona's narrow streets—sun-washed stone and laundry hanging from balconies. Lucy watched it all pass by like a film she'd left the theater for years ago.

"You could go back to London," the handler said softly, almost a suggestion.

Lucy shook her head. "London and I are through. Too many ghosts."

"Havana then?"

"Been there. Burned the ship."

Silence.

Finally, she closed the folder. "What's the next assignment?"

The handler hesitated, then handed her a sealed envelope. "Vienna. You're to connect with our liaison there. Something's shifting in the Balkan networks."

Lucy tapped the envelope against her knee. Vienna. She'd been there once—chessboards in cafés, smoke curling above polished wood, secrets drifting between languages.

"And Calder?" she asked, watching the handler's reaction.

He swallowed. "He's back in London. He... prefers to work alone."

Lucy nodded, her expression unreadable. "He always did."

The car slowed beside a quiet pension near Montjuïc. Lucy

stepped out, the humid Mediterranean air thick around her. She paused at the door and looked back.

"Tell Angleton," she said, "that usefulness goes both ways."

The handler blinked. "Meaning?"

Lucy slipped her sunglasses on.

"That I decide who gets my loyalty. Not the other way around."

She walked inside, the door shutting softly behind her. In the quiet hallway, Lucy paused by a mirror—an old, tarnished thing nailed to the wall. Her reflection looked back, sharp and steady.

No double image. No Echo. No recursion.

Just Lucy, exactly as she chose to be.

She smiled faintly.

Havana was over.

Philby was wounded.

Calder was gone.

And Lucy Howard was free again. Dangerously so.

Alicia Rayes had not realized how loud London was until she stepped out of it.

In Malta, the air moved differently—salt and sun and the faint bite of fuel from the harbor. The sound of a bell carried cleanly across stone. Footsteps had weight. Time, so far, behaved as it had since the Mirror had finally been destroyed for good.

She sat at a small table near the water with a glass sweating in front of her, a postcard turned blank-side up beneath her fingers. The hustle and bustle of the city around her remained normal. Almost too normal. It should have made her smile. Instead, it made her tired.

Alicia turned the postcard over and stared at the photograph of the bright sea and sky—a kind of peace that looked staged until you remembered the world still held places like this. She rolled the pencil between her fingers as if it were a piece of lab equipment she could calibrate into something useful.

She had spent too many years believing calibration was the same as control.

When she was a child, the first thing she learned was that the world could be measured.

Not by rulers or numbers—those came later—but by signals. By rhythms. By what repeated and what didn't.

Later, as she began her work for the Bureau, she learned more. More about rhythms, signals, and numbers—and how they could hide the truth and lie just as well as any man.

By the time V4 died, Alicia had seen enough to last a lifetime. Enough men with guns trying to claim a machine like it was just another weapon. Enough agencies choosing advantage over sanity. Enough physics turned into policy.

Enough of Max looking at the world like it might split again if he blinked too long.

And in the last instant—when the distillery chamber had folded in on itself and then steadied—Alicia had seen Moreau's face. Smiling. Mouthing words she couldn't hear.

It had felt like forgiveness. Or like a warning.

Max had told her what Moreau said. What she had confessed before her death.

Alicia took a breath and dragged herself back to the postcard. She wrote slowly, carefully, as if handwriting could keep memory from drifting.

Max,
Malta is bright. The sea is loud. People argue and mean it.
I'm sleeping better. No echoes. No doubles.
When you can—when you're allowed—come south. Even if it's only for a week.
—Artemis

She stared at the last line, then scratched out "Artemis" and wrote "Alicia" again and added a postscript she didn't quite let herself think through:

P.S. Don't let them pull you back underground.

Alicia set down the pencil and folded the postcard once—not because it needed folding, but because she needed the motion. She stood, walked to the nearest postbox, and pushed it through the slot.

Then she returned to the harbor wall and looked at her reflection in a pane of dark glass—just to check.

One Alicia. Steady. Human.

She let herself believe it, at least for today.

Kim Philby stood alone in his flat overlooking Victoria Street, the lamplight catching dust mites as they drifted in the stale summer air. The newspapers lay scattered across the small dining table— RESIGNATION SHOCKS WHITEHALL, PHILBY STEPS DOWN AMID MACLEAN–BURGESS SCANDAL, SENIOR INTELLIGENCE OFFICER QUIETLY EXITS SERVICE.

Each headline carried the wrong truth. Each headline was a shield.

He poured himself a whisky, the clink of glass loud in the quiet. He'd always appreciated the irony of these little moments —the world convincing itself it knew why a man stepped aside when the real reason sat unspoken in the margins.

A knock sounded, not the tentative tap of a reporter or the polite rap of a civil servant. This one knew its place.

Philby opened the door.

A young MI6 liaison officer stood there—tie too tight, hair too neat, eyes that had not yet learned to lie. He handed Philby a sealed envelope and waited.

Philby took it but didn't open it. Didn't need to.

Calder had already put the real paper in his hand—quietly, directly—without anger or performance. A courtesy. A warning. A victory.

The boy hesitated. "Sir... speaking frankly... I'm sorry."

It was sincere. Almost touching.

Philby smiled warmly—gracious, modest, the picture of an unfairly maligned service.

"It's all right, lad. These things blow over."

The boy nodded, relieved, as if receiving absolution from a man sainted rather than suspected. "Good evening, sir."

Philby closed the door.

He slid the envelope into his jacket pocket without breaking the seal. He didn't need to read it to know the contents: *thank you for your service, unfortunate circumstances, the Service appreciates your discretion.* A bureaucratic burial shroud.

He stepped back into the room and exhaled.

It wasn't Burgess or Maclean that forced this. It wasn't suspicion from Washington. It wasn't bad luck or bad timing.

It was Calder.

Max Calder—quiet, too observant, too scarred to be fooled by charm. The man who returned from Havana with evidence that should have ended Philby completely... if MI6 hadn't been so terrified of its own reflection.

He'll keep digging, Philby thought.

That made him dangerous. But danger was a familiar companion. One he could predict. One he could mold.

Philby picked up the whisky again and walked to the window. Below, London was settling into night—fog, tram bells, distant laughter. A city as blind as it was proud.

"I'm not finished," he murmured to the glass.

And he wasn't. Resignation was not defeat. It was repositioning.

The Soviets would be watching the news with interest. Moscow Centre always admired elegance under pressure, and

Philby had delivered elegance today—artful, composed, a man who carried scandal like a silk scarf.

He reached for the telephone and dialed a number he kept in his memory, not on paper.

A voice answered. Russian. Low. Satisfied.

Philby smiled.

"Da. It's time we talked."

The Thames looked black that winter—thick with cold, a strip of ink cutting through a city that pretended not to be afraid of the dark.

I leaned against the balustrade of Waterloo Bridge and lit a cigarette. The match flared, caught the wind, and died in a curl of smoke that rose straight up instead of sideways. Old habits made me watch that smoke longer than I should have.

I'd spent months trying not to see patterns.

Havana had left its fingerprints on me, on Alicia, on the world.

Recursion did that—turned every reflection into suspicion.

But this wasn't Havana. London held its ghosts differently.

News of Philby's resignation had already begun to settle into the city's bloodstream. People spoke of it as if it were an unfortunate administrative hiccup—a small storm in a Whitehall teacup. Burgess and Maclean got the blame. The press clucked their tongues and moved on.

But I knew the truth. And Philby knew that I knew.

I flicked ash over the river. It scattered in the wind.

After Havana, after the distillery collapsed and Version 4 imploded, I delivered everything—every ledger page, every Soviet cable, every scrap of testimony from Granitsky and Anokhin—to Angleton, then to MI6, and finally to Philby himself.

I didn't expect MI6 to act. They didn't.

CUBAN SLIDERS

But they couldn't keep him in the building either—not with Angleton circling like a hawk, not with the ledger naming STANLEY sitting in a locked drawer, not with my report making its quiet rounds in places polite men pretended didn't exist.

Philby resigned. The Service buried the reason. The world swallowed the lie.

But the lie didn't swallow me.

A gust of cold air swept over the bridge, slicing through my coat. I pulled the collar up and took another drag. The smoke tasted metallic.

Alicia had left London months ago—temporary rotation to the Mediterranean as a freelance subcontractor. She sent a postcard from Malta, bright water shimmering under sunlight that didn't belong to my world. She wrote that she slept better there. No recursion. No echoes. Only sea and salt.

I was glad for her. Havana had taken more from her than she admitted.

As for Lucy, she moved through Europe like a rumor. Angleton kept her close, in the way men like him kept weapons close. I didn't reach out. I wasn't sure she wanted me to. Or that it would matter if she didn't.

I let the thought drift away and stared out over the river. Somewhere out there—in the dark corners between borders—Philby was adjusting, recalibrating, finding his footing.

A man like him didn't fall in London.

Some nights, when the wind was right, I imagined I could feel the Mirror again—not the Havana one, but the echo of something older, deeper. Rosyth. Kingsway. Invershiel. All gone, all severed… but memory had a way of surviving what machines couldn't.

Maybe that was what haunted me. Not the Mirrors. Not the Soviets.

Not even Philby.

But the knowledge that time itself remembers, even when we forget.

I stamped out the cigarette and pushed off from the railing. The city lights shimmered on the Thames, fractured and doubled, then settled.

Just reflections this time. Not echoes.

In my pocket, Alicia's postcard was soft at the creases, reread until the paper began to give up. *When you can — come south.*

For the first time since ANGUS, *when you can* didn't sound like a trap.

Tomorrow, I'd take leave—real leave. No briefings. No basements. No mirrors watched too long. Just a ticket, a coastline, and a week where time moved forward and stayed that way.

I turned up my collar and headed toward the station lights, the sounds of London falling behind me as I walked—steady, unhurried—into whatever came next.

And maybe, just maybe, after visiting Alicia, I'd head back to Cuba and buy a few more of those wonderful cigars.

AFTERWORDS

ON CONSEQUENCES
THE 1952 CUBAN COUP

History later claimed that the 1952 Cuban coup was inevitable. That is what it does when it happens after the fact. It smooths out the surprise until it looks like foresight, replacing quick judgment with reasoning. It acts as if surprise was never part of the story.

But those who were watching in real time knew better.

The seizure of Havana happened faster than anyone—including the Americans—had predicted. Faster than the State Department's cables. Faster than the embassy's contingency plans. Faster even than the journalists, who arrived breathless only to find the story already over. Barracks changed hands without any argument. Ministers resigned without making speeches. Police units stood down without receiving orders. Resistance did not fail—it simply didn't show up.

The phrase that circulated afterward was bloodless. It was inaccurate. What vanished was not blood, but hesitation.

Washington was caught flat-footed. Briefings became chaotic. Analysts revised explanations that seemed convincing only because the result no longer required persuasion. The White House questioned how it had unfolded so rapidly.

No one answered honestly. The CIA, however, was not surprised.

James Angleton had observed early indicators arriving even before the first armored column moved. Reports that should have conflicted instead aligned. Independent actors made the same decisions without coordinating. Meetings concluded in agreement where disagreement should have been expected.

Consensus without persuasion. *Decision Locking*.

The mechanism didn't rewrite history; it narrowed it. When uncertainty should have fractured the outcome into competing futures, doubt failed to appear. Choice vanished.

Angleton never used the word "Mirror" in any official memo. He didn't need to. His language was administrative and dull, focused on accelerated stabilization, reduced divergence, and low resistance.

Internally, he knew better.

The Mirror had not orchestrated the coup. It simply removed any friction that might have delayed it. The system did not command; it permitted. It made the agreement seem natural and the resistance unnecessary.

By the time the last loyalist realized what had happened, there was nothing left to oppose. Not because force had failed, but because resolve had quietly expired.

Angleton understood the cost.

Decision Locking made outcomes efficient. It also made them brittle. The same suppression of doubt that enabled rapid consolidation would later suffocate adaptation.

History would record only the result.

A coup that happened too easily. A government that fell without resistance. A moment when the future chose itself. And the quiet understanding—shared by very few—that what had been lost was not democracy, or sovereignty, or time.

It was dissent.

And dissent, once removed, is very difficult to restore.

It has been replaced by certainty.

ON CERTAINTY

FURNITURE SLIDERS · ANGUS SLIDERS · CUBAN SLIDERS

The three novels in the Bureau Archives Trilogy follow a single investigation across changing locations and years: not how history is changed, but how it becomes constrained.

Furniture Sliders introduced the Mirror as a failed wartime experiment—an unstable system whose effects fracture memory, perception, and sequence. *Angus Sliders* responded to that failure with concealment, reconstruction, and the first acknowledgment that the Mirror's most significant effects are cognitive rather than temporal. *Cuban Sliders* explores the final implication—that power no longer depends on persuasion, loyalty, or even secrecy, but on the management of uncertainty itself.

The Cuban coup of 1952 and Kim Philby's resignation, which mark the end of the trilogy's historical arc, are thoroughly documented. The mechanisms discussed here are interpretive; they aim to explore a concern that emerged within postwar intelligence culture as the limits of force and argument became evident: that decision-making could be shaped by narrowing the conditions under which choices are made.

Throughout the trilogy, the Mirror is not portrayed as an effective means of altering the past. Its early tests often fail catastrophically. What remains are side effects—disruptions to memory, judgment, and hesitation. These effects suggest a more subtle form of influence. Control doesn't require commands; it involves narrowing the space where other options can be considered.

By the late 1940s, intelligence agencies increasingly focused on stability: of outcomes, alliances, and internal consensus. In this context, Decision Locking appears not as a single technology or coordinated initiative but as an institutional condition, shaped by bureaucratic momentum, strategic anxiety, and the growing belief that disagreement itself was a risk and a threat.

Kim Philby's role throughout the trilogy symbolizes this shift. He functions more as an early adopter than as a creator. His significance isn't just about divided loyalty but also about understanding that influence no longer depends solely on secrecy. Instead, it relies on certainty—ensuring hesitation has no impact. In Cuba, this situation unfolds without visible machinery. There are no centralized controls or clear points of command. Actions happen independently. Resistance stays fragmented. Political change occurs without appearing forced.

Taken together, *Furniture Sliders*, *Angus Sliders*, and *Cuban Sliders* do not claim that technology controls history. Instead, they examine how history accelerates when the factors that sustain disagreement weaken. When uncertainty collapses, outcomes seem unavoidable, and compliance becomes a matter of choice.

From this perspective, the Cold War does not escalate solely through weapons or ideology. It escalates through the gradual erosion of uncertainty as a political safeguard.

Time is not the weapon.

Certainty is.

PEOPLE AND PLACES

VIRGINIA HALL - ARTEMIS

Alicia Rayes is assigned the code name Artemis in honor of and in remembrance of World War II heroine Virginia Hall Goillot (1906–1982). She was awarded the Distinguished Service Cross (DSC) - the only civilian woman during World War II to earn this honor, the Croix de Guerre, and was a Member of the Most Excellent Order of the British Empire (MBE). She was an American who worked with the United Kingdom's Special Operations Executive (SOE) and the United States Office of Strategic Services (OSS) in France during World War II.

After the war, Hall worked for the CIA's Special Activities Division. The Germans nicknamed her Artemis (the Greek huntress and guardian of secrets), and the Gestapo reportedly considered her "the most dangerous of all Allied spies."

KIM PHILBY

Harold Adrian Russell "Kim" Philby (1912–1988) was a British intelligence officer and a double agent for the Soviet Union. In 1963, he was exposed as a member of the Cambridge Five, a spy ring that had leaked British secrets to the Soviets during World War II and the early Cold War years. Among the five, Philby is believed to have been the most successful in passing secret information to the Soviets. Suspicion of his activities began in 1951.

Nicknamed "Kim" after the boy-spy in Rudyard Kipling's novel, he was born in British India and educated at Westminster School and Trinity College, Cambridge. He was recruited by Soviet intelligence in 1934. In 1940, he started working for the United Kingdom's Secret Intelligence Service (SIS, also known as MI6). By the end of World War II, he had risen to a high-ranking position.

In 1949, Philby was appointed First Secretary at the British Embassy in Washington, serving as the primary British contact with American intelligence agencies. Throughout his career as an intelligence officer, he sent large amounts of intelligence to the Soviet Union.

Philby was suspected of warning two other spies accused of Soviet espionage, Donald Maclean and Guy Burgess, both of whom fled to Moscow in May 1951. William Harvey of the FBI was convinced Philby was a Russian spy, as was J. Edgar Hoover. Philby was linked to the FBI through shared investigations, and Hoover was a key figure in the anti-communist efforts that ultimately threatened Philby's operations, with Hoover eager to see Philby exposed. Under suspicion, Philby resigned from MI6 in July 1951 but was publicly and erroneously cleared by the then-Foreign Secretary, Harold Macmillan, in 1955. He went back to working as a journalist and a spy for MI6 in Beirut, but was ultimately forced to defect to Moscow after finally being exposed as a Soviet agent in 1963 by his old colleague and friend Nicholas Elliott. Philby lived in Moscow until he died in 1988.

Kim Philby's fictionalized involvement in *Cuban Sliders* includes providing the Soviets with the technology and blueprints stolen from Scotland, which they used to rebuild and enhance the Mirror in Cuba and to discover Decision Locking, which they hoped to use to suppress dissent in nations.

CHARLES FRASER-SMITH

Charles Fraser-Smith (1904–1992) was an author and former missionary best known as the inspiration for the quartermaster 'Q' in the James Bond films. This reputation comes from his World War II work on what became known as "Q Devices" for SOE agents operating across Europe, named after World War I Q-Ships.

Fraser-Smith was a temporary civil servant at the Ministry of Supply, but in reality, he worked under MI6, developing and supplying equipment for Section XV of Britain's WWII intelligence agency, the Special Operations Executive. He designed a wide variety of spy and escape devices, including miniature cameras hidden in cigarette lighters, shaving brushes with film, hairbrushes with maps and a saw, pencils with maps, and pens with hidden compasses. Fraser-Smith also participated in the intelligence operation codenamed Operation Mincemeat, partly organized by James Bond creator Ian Fleming, to deceive the Nazis and cover up the invasion of Sicily.

Charles Fraser-Smith is fictionalized in *Cuban Sliders* as a member of the MI6 team that developed a means to manage, control, and ultimately destroy Mirror technology, which Calder and Rayes use in Havana to bring down the Mirror Web.

JAMES ANGLETON

CIA spymaster James Jesus Angleton (1917–1987) was one of the most powerful unelected officials in the United States government in the mid-20th century, a ghost of American power. He previously worked in the Office of Strategic Services, the wartime predecessor to the CIA, in Italy and London during World War II. While in London, Angleton met Kim Philby, who was expected to become the future head of MI6, and formed a close relationship. He unwittingly shared intelligence secrets with Philby, a member of the notorious Cambridge spy ring who called Angleton "a brilliant opponent" and a "fascinating" friend who seemed to be "catching on" before Philby's defection.

After the war, he returned to Washington, D.C., and became one of the CIA's founding officers. Initially, he was responsible for gathering foreign intelligence and coordinating with allied organizations. He initiated an obsessive search for communist moles, having become increasingly convinced that the KGB had compromised the CIA, which nearly destroyed the Agency. As part of that, he launched mass surveillance by opening the mail of hundreds of thousands of Americans.

James Angleton is fictionalized in *Cuban Sliders* as the main CIA contact and liaison to the Bureau, a challenger for Mirror technology, and a cross-agency colleague of Kim Philby. Based on additional evidence from Max Calder, Angleton becomes increasingly convinced that Philby is a Soviet agent, resulting in Philby's resignation from MI6 in 1951.

FULGENCIO BATISTA

Cuban political leader and dictator Fulgencio Batista y Zaldívar (born Rubén Zaldívar, 1901–1973) played a central role in Cuban politics from the 1930s until his overthrow by Fidel Castro and Che Guevara in the Cuban Revolution of 1959. He served as Cuba's president from 1940 to 1944 and again from 1952 until his resignation in 1959. After completing his first term, Batista moved to Florida and returned to Cuba to run for president again in the 1952 elections. Facing an unavoidable electoral defeat, he organized a military coup that bypassed the election. Once back in power and with financial, military, and logistical support from the United States, he suspended the 1940 Constitution and revoked most political liberties.

Batista is fictionalized in *Cuban Sliders* as being aided by a spin-off from Version 4 of the Mirror, a Decision Locking Node, in the lead-up to the 1952 coup. It was widely recognized that the coup happened more quickly and smoothly than expected.

Batista seized power rapidly and almost without bloodshed. In 1951, a fictionalized James Angleton clandestinely used his CIA influence and Decision Locking to advance it, including its ability to exert influence by removing dissent and suppressing differences—an effect later formally termed decision coherence amplification. Batista was neither an architect of the use of the Mirror nor involved in its development in any way, but he instinctively understood its effects. It may also have played a role in his later creation of the Bureau for the Repression of Communist Activities.

BASIL CHARLES

Basil Charles, born in 1947, is the former legendary proprietor of Basil's Bar, an iconic Caribbean landmark, where, for years, celebrities and royalty have partied out of sight of the paparazzi on the exclusive island of Mustique. He remains iconic, closely connected to the bar, and its "Ambassador at Large".

Basil grew up on the island of St. Vincent and was injured in a motorcycle accident when he was young. He was rescued by Hugo Money-Coutts and spent over a year in recovery. When he was finally up and around again, he moved over to the newly developing island of Mustique to see what opportunities might await. Basil met Colin Tennant through Hugo, the recently deceased Lord Glenconner, who had bought and was developing the island. Tennant gave Basil the job of barman in the only hotel on the island, the Cotton House, where Basil was a tremendous success. Eventually, Tennant opened a stand-alone bar right on the ocean, where Basil, at 29, could work his magic, and named the bar in honor of its new proprietor, Basil's.

Basil served cocktails to many, including the late Princess Margaret, the Duke and Duchess of Cambridge (now the Prince and Princess of Wales), Mick Jagger, David Bowie, Tommy Hilfiger, Bryan Adams, Kate Moss, and many others. Basil still mixes drinks at Basil's, despite having recently sold the bar to The Mustique Company.

Basil and Basil's Bar are fictionalized in *Cuban Sliders*; in reality, well before he owned the bar, or was even old enough. Basil still has a Basil's Bar on Bay Street in Kingstown in St. Vincent.

ROYAL NAVAL DOCKYARD ROSYTH

Rosyth Dockyard is on the north side of the Firth of Forth in Scotland and is one of the largest waterside manufacturing facilities in the UK. It was previously known as the Royal Naval Dockyard Rosyth, under the direct control of the Royal Navy, and played a vital role in both World Wars as a ship-repair and dry-dock complex.

During World War II, more than 3,000 warships were repaired or refitted there. In 2023, Rosyth was renamed HMS Caledonia, thereby preserving the strong and historic links between the Royal Navy and the Rosyth communities. In the *Cuban Sliders* story, the fictional Rosyth was the Bureau's secret location for developing the original Mirror technology without the Royal Navy's knowledge. The Bureau location was secretly incorporated into the World War II dockyard expansion.

HAVANA

Havana in 1951 was a vibrant, glamorous, yet deeply unequal city at the height of its pre-revolutionary boom. Often called the "Latin Las Vegas," it pulsed with American tourism, mafia-run casinos, and lavish nightlife, attracting celebrities such as Josephine Baker and Frank Sinatra. The economy prospered through sugar exports and tourism, with low-cost flights from Miami bringing crowds to luxurious hotels such as the Nacional and Riviera.

Old Havana's colonial architecture—featuring baroque cathedrals, colorful plazas, and cobblestone streets—stands in contrast

PEOPLE AND PLACES

to modern high-rises and the iconic Malecón seawall, lined with classic American cars.

Nightlife surged in venues such as the Tropicana cabaret, known for its extravagant shows featuring feathers, rumba, and mambo. Mafia influence (Meyer Lansky, Lucky Luciano) controlled gambling and prostitution, fueling corruption under President Carlos Prío Socarrás.

Politically, tensions grew amid increasing opposition to corruption, hinting at Batista's 1952 coup - the lead-up to which features in *Cuban Sliders*. Rural poverty sharply contrasted with urban wealth, but Havana itself shone as a tropical paradise of neon lights, jazz, and excess—a city where the wealthy played while revolution quietly formed in the hills.

CÁRDENAS

Cárdenas in 1951 was a bustling industrial port town in Matanzas Province, often called the "Charleston of the Caribbean" for its straight, narrow streets and lively atmosphere. Founded in 1828, it had grown into one of Cuba's key sugar-exporting hubs, with a deep harbor handling massive shipments from nearby refineries. The economy revolved around sugar production, rum distilleries (as featured and fictionalized in *Cuban Sliders*), and henequen rope factories, employing thousands amid the post-war boom. Horse-drawn carriages clattered alongside American cars, while the famous blue crabs ("cangrejos") were a local staple.

Daily life combined colonial charm—colorful plazas, neoclassical buildings—and working-class grit. European immigrant influences (Irish, French, Italian) persisted in surnames and culture. The city was proud of its revolutionary history: the Cuban flag first flew here in 1850. Under President Prío Socarrás, corruption simmered across the nation, but Cárdenas felt prosperous yet unequal—wealthy mill owners contrasted with laborers. Proximity to emerging Varadero beaches hinted at tourism's rise, but in 1951, it remained a gritty, sugar-driven port town on the brink of upheaval.

In *Cuban Sliders,* Cardenas is the location of the Havana Club rum distillery, which has been co-opted by Russian forces as a potentially safe place to build a new version of the Mirror. It is also the location of the discovery of Decision Locking, which takes Mirror technology in an entirely new direction.

SAINT VINCENT AND THE GRENADINES

In 1951, St. Vincent and the Grenadines was a British Crown Colony in the Windward Islands, a lush volcanic archipelago dominated by agriculture, and on the cusp of political change. The main island of St. Vincent featured rugged mountains, fertile valleys, and the active La Soufrière volcano. The Grenadines—32 smaller islands and cays, with Bequia, Mustique, Canouan, and Union Island inhabited—offered pristine beaches and sailing waters, though tourism remained minimal.

Kingstown, the capital on St. Vincent's southwest coast, served as the busy port and commercial hub, with colonial buildings, markets, and a deep harbor. Rural life centered on smallholder farming, fishing, and whaling in the Grenadines (especially Bequia).

Life blended British colonial influences (cricket, Anglican churches) with vibrant Afro-Caribbean culture—calypso, steelpan precursors, and festivals. Infrastructure was basic: limited electricity, dirt roads, and inter-island schooners.

Overall, 1951 marked a quiet, tropical colony transitioning from plantation-era crops toward bananas and political awakening, still far from the yachting paradise it would become. In *Cuban Sliders,* St. Vincent is the home of Basil Charles and Basil's Bar, whereas in reality, Basil and the bar came much later, and in Mustique, where Basil himself became a Caribbean icon.

MUSTIQUE

Mustique in 1951 was a remote, sparsely populated, and largely undeveloped island in the Grenadines chain. Covering approximately 1,400 acres (2.2 square miles) of hilly, volcanic terrain with lush vegetation, pristine beaches, coral reefs, and mangroves (including an intact lagoon wetland), it had no roads, electricity, running water, an airport, or other significant infrastructure. The economy relied on small-scale agriculture—primarily cotton, peas, corn, and coconuts—on land owned by the Hazell family of St. Vincent, who had consolidated plantations there since the 1860s.

A handful of local families (mostly fishermen and farmers of African descent) lived in simple settlements, tending small crops and livestock amid feral goats and cattle. The island felt wild and isolated, accessible only by boat from St. Vincent, with no tourism or luxury development.

It remained an overlooked colonial backwater, far from the exclusive celebrity retreat it became after Colin Tennant purchased it in 1958. In 1951, amid the colony's push toward universal suffrage, Mustique embodied the quiet rural life of a transitioning Caribbean and is fictionalized in *Cuban Sliders* as a target slide destination and a staging post for Soviet agents from Grenada.

BEQUIA

In 1951, Bequia was a remote, idyllic yet rugged island in the Grenadines chain. Covering about 7 square miles of hilly, volcanic terrain with lush vegetation, pristine beaches, coral reefs, and a protected harbor in Admiralty Bay, it remained largely undeveloped—no electricity in most areas, no paved roads, no airport, and access only by schooner or boat from St. Vincent. Port Elizabeth, the small capital, served as the main settlement with basic shops, a market, and a harbor bustling with fishing boats and inter-island trade.

The economy was centered on small-scale agriculture (cotton, coconuts, corn, peas), fishing, and boat-building (Bequia was renowned for crafting schooners and whaling boats). Traditional humpback whaling, introduced in the 1870s by Yankee whalers and practiced from open sailboats using hand harpoons, continued as a cultural and subsistence activity, primarily from the village of Friendship Bay or Paget Farm. Bequia also has a strong pirate history, including that of Blackbeard. In 1717, the notorious pirate Edward Teach, known as Blackbeard, used Bequia, specifically Admiralty Bay, as a base for hiding, refueling, and refitting his ships. He famously captured the French slave ship La Concorde near St. Vincent, bringing it to Bequia to disembark the crew and cargo before turning it into his flagship, the Queen Anne's Revenge.

Life was simple and sea-oriented: villagers lived in wooden homes, relied on rainwater and wells, and blended British colonial influences with Afro-Caribbean traditions. 1951 marked a pivotal year for the colony as a whole with the introduction of universal adult suffrage, which sparked early self-government movements. However, Bequia remained quiet and isolated — a serene, boat-dependent haven far from emerging tourism.

In *Cuban Sliders*, Bequia is a fictionalized location where the Mirror transports two Soviet scientists via a geo-slide after first sending them to Mustique in an execution misstep, where Soviet agents attempt to chase them down, and Max Calder and Alicia Rayes attempt to rescue them. One of them is hugely important to the Russians as the architect of Decision Locking.

THE MIRROR, QUANTUM THEORY, AND DECISION LOCKING

The Mirror is entirely fictional, but the idea that an inanimate system could demonstrate consciousness or sentience is now considered more plausible, especially in discussions of quantum mechanics and panpsychism. This concept underpins the Mirror in *Cuban Sliders* and the *Bureau Archives Trilogy*. As the system evolves, its capacity to influence human thoughts increases, along with the risks it presents. What begins as temporal instability eventually becomes more significant: the suppression of uncertainty.

Two principles of quantum mechanics underpin the concept of the Mirror. The first is quantum entanglement, which explains how particles can stay correlated regardless of distance, so a change in one affects the other. Although entanglement occurs at a subatomic level and cannot transmit information faster than light, it is a well-established phenomenon. Its importance here is conceptual rather than literal: it offers a model for ongoing connection without direct communication.

Cuban Sliders expands this idea from particles to cognition. Could multiple incarnations of the same individual stay informationally connected? And if so, could such connections influence judgment, memory, or choice across different instances?

THE MIRROR, QUANTUM THEORY, AND DECISION LOCKING

This introduces the second principle: superposition. In quantum mechanics, systems can exist in multiple potential states at once until observation causes those states to collapse into a single outcome. Superposition is not an anomaly but a core aspect of quantum behavior. When applied to the Mirror, it explains how multiple potential timelines, locations, or outcomes can exist together before they are resolved.

Crucially, *Cuban Sliders* redefines this mechanism at the decision-making level. Instead of collapsing timelines, later versions of the Mirror collapse alternatives. Exposure to stabilized Mirror-derived fields decreases variance in perception and judgment, narrowing the range of choices individuals see as viable. This phenomenon—called Decision Locking—does not demand obedience. It eliminates hesitation.

The temporal or geographic slides reported earlier in the trilogy reflect an unstable expression of this process. By the time of *Cuban Sliders*, the effect has become more refined. The Mirror no longer just moves bodies through time and space; it aligns decisions within it. Multiple possible courses of action exist, but only one appears coherent.

This accounts for the observed political effects. Actions align without coordination. Resistance fails to organize. Outcomes appear inevitable not because they are enforced, but because competing alternatives never fully form.

In this context, the Mirror is no longer a traditional time machine in any conventional sense. It is a system that operates on the conditions of choice itself, preventing uncertainty from appearing. Its interaction with the quantum structure of reality is less significant than its interaction with human cognition.

Time is no longer what the Mirror ultimately controls.

It is certainty.

WITH THANKS

I owe a huge debt of gratitude to everyone around me who has put up with the disruption caused by my journey as an author. This is my third novel that combines espionage and science fiction with a heavy dose of film noir. There is a massive amount of research to get even minute details right, such as the popular bars frequented by suspicious characters or details of locations from specific years. These days, it is slightly easier to check some of the facts, but nevertheless, it is time-consuming. The research notes end up being bigger than the final book!

My wife, Lucinda has been extremely encouraging, especially as I have added author to tech entrepreneur, company founder, and advisor to tech company CEOs. However, it has been a long-held desire to take stories and ideas I have had for a long time and translate them into novels, particularly those based around my fascination with computing and quantum mechanics.

For any book, proofreaders and editors play a major role in making sure the novel hangs together and reads well. A big thank you to those who helped here too including Hannah and especially Carson from the great state of Texas.

ABOUT THE AUTHOR

Multi-award-winning author Alexander Bentley is a serial entrepreneur living in California, with experience founding and leading technology companies in both the UK and the USA. He has held senior roles, including CEO, in both public and private enterprises. Over the years, he has had numerous technology- and security-related interactions with the government, the UK Ministry of Defence, the US Department of Defense, and numerous aerospace and defense companies. His own technology companies have included those focused on secure communications and networking. Additionally, with a physics background, he is well-versed in the principles of quantum mechanics and quantum computing.

Writing under the name Alexander Bentley, he is married to Lucinda and has two grown children, Alexander (Lex) and Virginia (Ginny).

Cuban Sliders is Alexander's third Spy-Fi novel, which entangles the world of espionage with science fiction, bringing a new approach to post-World War II noir writing.

To keep up-to-date with Alexander Bentley:
www.AlexanderBentley.com

www.ingramcontent.com/pod-product-compliance
Lightning Source LLC
LaVergne TN
LVHW021220080526
838199LV00084B/4290